I0823647

Myths, Gods & Immortals

Medusa

New & Ancient Greek Tales

This is a FLAME TREE Book

FLAME TREE PUBLISHING
6 Melbray Mews, Fulham,
London SW6 3NS, United Kingdom
www.flametreepublishing.com

First published 2024

24 26 28 29 27 25
1 3 5 7 9 10 8 6 4 2

ISBN: 978-1-80417-933-8

Publisher's Note: The stories within this book are works of fiction. Names, characters, places, and incidents are a product of the authors' imaginations. Locales and public names are sometimes used for atmospheric purposes. Any resemblance to actual people, living or dead, or to businesses, companies, events, institutions, or locales is completely coincidental.

Content Note: The stories in this book may contain descriptions of, or references to, difficult subjects such as violence, death and rape, but always contextualized within the setting of mythic narrative, archetype and metaphor. Similarly, language can sometimes be strong but is at the artistic discretion of the authors.

Cover art by Flame Tree Studio based on elements from Shutterstock.com: MaksimVector, Tiny Art, Golden Shrimp, SvetlanaDesign06685, Zdenka Darula.

A copy of the CIP data for this book is available from the British Library.

Printed and bound in China

Myths, Gods & Immortals
Medusa
New & Ancient Greek Tales
FLAME TREE
PUBLISHING

Contents

FOREWORD

Miriam Robbins Dexter 6

ANCIENT & MODERN: INTRODUCING MEDUSA

by Liv Albert 10

1. Medusa, Divine & Monstrous: Her Origins 11

2. Slithering Through Medusa's Rocky History 37

3. Beyond Oceanos: Medusa's Ancient Evolution 56

4. Mythical Maiden, Modern Monster 84

MODERN SHORT STORIES OF MEDUSA

The Wise Look for All of the Stories

Alicia K. Anderson 113

How to Tame a Head of Snakes

Mel Attica 128

In the Temple of Athena

Casey Banks 142

Pegasus

Danai Christopoulou 152

The Toll of the Snake

Grace P. Fong 157

What Actually Happened

Rhys Hughes 176

A Heart of Stone
Tom Johnstone 194
Medusa with the Heads of Men
Amanda Cecelia Lang.. 208
The Haunting of Athena
Megan Mahoney... 237
In the Blood
Tracie McBride 248
Athena's Favorite
Zenobia Neil 257
The Medusa Rondanini
Gabriella Ramalho.. 271
The Balm Yard
Oneness Sankara.. 288
Snakes and Stones, We'll Break Their Bones
Zach Shephard 301
Woman Embracing Woman, on Loan From Private Collection
Liv Strom... 318
Unbound
Theresa Tyree.. 324
Freely Given
Leah Warren 344

BIOGRAPHIES... 361

MYTHS, GODS & IMMORTALS.. 367

FLAME TREE FICTION.. 368

Foreword

Miriam Robbins Dexter

The Gorgon Medusa has fascinated people for at least 2 ¾ millennia, since her first mention in Homer's *Iliad*: in the Underworld, Athena wore on her aegis:

'the Gorgon head of the terrible monster, terrible and fearful, a portent of aegis-holding Zeus.'

The Medusa head was fearsome, meant to frighten the enemy.

Not too long after Homer, the poet Hesiod named Medusa as the only mortal sister of the three Gorgons. According to Hesiod, with Medusa:

'lay the dark-blue-haired one (Poseidon) in a soft meadow.'

Far from being ugly, she was attractive enough for Poseidon to chase her. In antiquity, Medusa was viewed with multiple lenses: in the poet Ovid, she was punished by Athena, who turned her beautiful hair into ugly snakes (Medusa's hair is snaky in Classical art hundreds of years before Ovid); she was treated as a scapegoat. She could be fearsome: she turned into stone those men and women who gazed into her face. She was beneficial and apotropaic: figures of her head were modeled on antefixes affixed to temple walls and to roofs; her head guarded doors of ovens and kilns, the shields of soldiers. In addition to snaky hair, Medusa sometimes has wings (the winged Medusa gave birth to the horse Pegasus, who thereafter was depicted with wings; we see this, for example, in the Winged Medusa and Perseus from the island of Melos, displayed in the British Museum), as well as other attributes. The avian and viperine iconography goes back to prehistoric female figurines frequently depicted as bird-women, snake-women, or bird-snakes, excavated throughout Europe and elsewhere: that is, Medusa was the descendant of the Neolithic Divine Feminine.

Medusa in Greek means the 'ruling woman'. (Medusa is the present participle of the Greek verb *μέδω* (medō), 'I rule'. Medusa, or Medousa, is spelled with a short -e- in Greek, as opposed to the long ē found in Mēdea.) This may give us a clue to how she was viewed before the advent of patriarchy in Western Europe.

In modern culture, there have been positive re-tellings of (patriarchal) Classical stories which have scapegoated women. One of the earliest authors of such re-tellings is Charlene Spretnak, who wrote *Lost Goddesses of Early Greece: A Collection of Pre-Hellenic Myths* (1978; she tells the stories of several Greek goddesses, but Medusa is not included). There have been several books honoring Medusa since then. Medusa is viewed with fascination in art, in novels, in poetry. *The Medusa Reader*, edited by Marjorie Garber and Nancy J. Vickers (2003), contains articles on Medusa by twentieth-century feminists and earlier not-so-feminist psychologists such as Freud. In the twenty-first century, Girl God books (published and edited by Trista Hendren) published two books honoring Medusa. The first, written especially for children, and again in a very positive manner regarding Medusa, is *My Name is Medusa*. The artwork in the book is gorgeous. The second book on Medusa is an anthology of articles, poetry, and art, *Re-visioning Medusa: From Monster to Divine Wisdom*. In my article in this anthology, I decided to translate most of the Greek and Roman texts which mention her, in chronological order, so that the reader might understand Medusa's many facets, and how views of her changed through time: from the Greek *Iliad* of Homer, through the Roman Ovid, through the later Greek Lucian (who wrote of the beauty of the Gorgons), and the Greek traveler and geographer Pausanias, who tells of the burial of Medusa's head in the sacred precinct of the Argives, the *agora*, for protection of the land and its people.

Thus Medusa, even in the Classical era, was believed to give protection. In fact, her blood is twofold: in Euripides' play *Ion*, Queen Creusa tells an old servant about Medusa's blood, which Athena gave to Erichthonius, the ancestor of the Athenian line:

'Two drops of blood from the Gorgon … One [is] deadly; the other brings healing of diseases.'

Medusa has been portrayed in art for over two millennia. My favorite ancient image of Medusa is the bent-knee Medusa on the western pediment of the Doric Artemis temple in Corfu (in the Archaeological Museum of Corfu, which dates to the sixth century BCE). Her face is beautiful. She is nine feet tall; her waist is cinched with serpents, and there are only a couple of discrete snakes in her hair. She has wings on her lower legs. She is the prehistoric bird-snake!

Some modern artists have used the concept of Medusa as a means to access their pain and anger, and some have given a decidedly feminist slant to her depiction. The Italian scholar and artist, Cristina Biaggi, who now works in the United States, incorporated her studies of prehistory and ancient history and myth into a powerful fiberglass sculpture, *Raging Medusa* (2000). The sculpture is 5.5 feet in diameter and it weighs 98 pounds. One piece of modern art turns the tables on Medusa and Perseus, as depicted in text in the Classical era and in sculptures of the Renaissance: a sculpture of Medusa holding a sword and the head of Perseus, created by Luciano Garbati in 2008. This sculpture incorporates a role reversal of the Greek myth of Perseus cutting off the head of Medusa (with the help of a mirror, so he is not turned to stone by her gaze), and an image reversal of a bronze sculpture made by Benvenuto Cellini in the period 1545–54 (it stands in the Loggia dei Lanzi in the Piazza della Signoria in Florence, Italy).

This new anthology, *Myths, Gods & Immortals: Medusa*, is the latest to contain pieces which re-story Medusa. Thus the honoring continues.

Miriam Robbins Dexter
(the above translations from the Greek are by the author)

Ancient & Modern: Introducing Medusa

by Liv Albert

1.
Medusa, Divine & Monstrous: Her Origins

Its horror and its beauty are divine.
Upon its lips and eyelids seems to lie
Loveliness like a shadow, from which shrine,
Fiery and lurid, struggling underneath,
The agonies of anguish and of death.
– Percy Bysshe Shelley, from 'On the Medusa of Leonardo Da Vinci in the Florentine Gallery' (1824)

MY MEDUSA

he word *enigma* comes from the ancient Greek for 'speaking in riddles', and though Medusa wasn't known for riddles like her fellow monstrous woman the Sphinx, in the twenty-first century she's become more riddle than myth. My own journey to obsess over the Gorgon and her story came about in a similar way. Like most in the English-speaking world, I was more than familiar with her as a character. I knew her myth, or I thought I did, from both the ancient world and the many, many appearances she makes throughout Western popular culture. From books to movies, TV shows to video games,

Medusa is one of the most prolific characters from Greek myth. But, unlike many other famous mythological figures, Medusa's mythological origins have been altered over the many millennia that have passed since her story was first told.

Years ago I sat down to tell her story. I thought it would be simple enough, since she's so famous and so well known. I imagined that Medusa's popularized story is seemingly so set in stone (you can look forward to more petrifying puns) that certainly the original sources that tell it were equally straightforward. Nothing could be further from the truth. Instead, the Medusae (a plural form for the word nerds out there) that we see today rarely resemble the character from the ancient sources, both textually and visually. I found myself in the depths of the enigma that is Medusa, the riddles contained in the sources that share her story and in the changes that have been made to it since that time. I've been utterly consumed by her mysteries ever since. Writing this, too, has only made me more convinced that she is unique among the rest of Greek mythology's many, many characters. Medusa stands apart as a monster, maiden, victim and survivor all formed into one multi-faceted and enigmatic creature. Because of this, too, she is wide open to all forms of interpretation. Personally, I come to Medusa as a staunch feminist. To me she is a symbol as much as she is a character; she is an icon of the power of women, a version formed by women navigating male fear of that power and how it manifests around them.

To me, Medusa is also a symbol of the ways that other women participate as agents of the patriarchy and how that affects the equally feminine victims of it. I preface with this because my understanding of her character influences how I speak of her and how I read her story and the evidence surrounding it. It's impossible for me to separate myself from these notions, nor do I want to, as I believe they give me exactly the types of insights that I am most interested in. My reading of Medusa is not universal, but it is informed by the ancient sources and the world in which they were written (in addition to my modern notions of feminism and mythology). I will be sharing those ancient sources with you in great detail, so whether or not you agree with how I read them, and her, you'll have the evidence to make up your own mind.

Monster, Maiden, Victim, Survivor

The many forms of Medusa most easily available to us today often stand in contrast to one another. She is a monster, born terrible and terrifying, a creature of nightmares who stalks the lands and turns unlucky men to stone. She is a symbol of male fear, a representation of their inability to resist the seductive force of a woman and their own ruin at the hands of her terrifying (gasp!) *sexuality*. She is an existential threat, a representation of the otherworldly, a natural force that promises destruction and chaos. She is a maiden, a virgin ripe for plucking and ruined not by the man who raped her but by the goddess who took issue with it. She is a victim, broken by the violence of a man only to be rescued by a kind goddess seeking to save her from the horrors of women's realities. She is a survivor, a symbol of strength and an emblem of resistance and revolt. She is a hideous hag, wrinkled and horrible and ready to inflict the same on the virile young men unlucky enough to stumble upon her lair. She is a Gorgon, a divine creature born monstrous but not ugly, mortal but not helpless, innocent but not virginal, killed not because she posed a threat but because she was, simply, killable. She is a disembodied head, a weapon and a shield, terror and protection, and – finally, in death – immortal.

Medusa's story is simultaneously minimal and fragmentary, complex and varied. Even now, any attempt to learn her story will find the student lost in an ocean of contradictions and confusing ideas about true myths and *real* Medusae. Unless someone with a casual interest, or even a burgeoning obsession like my own, finds Medusa's most ancient of sources, they're unlikely to come away with knowledge of her character as it was understood in the ancient Greek world. And even that, really, is impossible. Medusa has been transforming and changing from the very moments of her existence. The ancient Greeks didn't know what to make of the monster they created, and the ancient Romans who came after them muddied the waters even further. The nearly 2,000 years that followed saw still more metamorphosing of Medusa.

Now her story is something else entirely. She is at times a horrible monster whose terrorizing of humanity necessitated her demise, while at others she is a beautiful woman cursed by a goddess. But at her most ancient, Medusa is somewhere in between: a sympathetic creature whose fate was determined by others.

There Is No 'Real' Medusa

Like much of Greek myth, there is no 'real' Medusa, by which I mean there is no 'true story' or even 'original myth'. She is open to interpretation within the ancient sources that survive, and for those who choose to speculate, she is whatever we want her to be. Here I intend to share as much of her as possible, from her most ancient of origins, down through the changes and distortions made over the centuries and, later, millennia. We'll look at her appearances in ancient Greek sources and imagery, then into the Romans, and through to the world we live in now, where Medusa is simultaneously a symbol of misogyny and feminism. It's important, though, to understand that ultimately there is no right answer to the question of 'Who is Medusa?' or, really, even 'What is her story?' Instead I seek to share what survives from the ancient world and my own interpretations of her many facets. Mythology broadly, and Medusa very specifically, is subjective; it is by its very nature meant to be interpreted by those who consume it. The Medusae I share with you here are based in ancient and modern sources, but they are being interpreted by me. My love of Medusa lies in her ancient origins and my fascination with her lies in the ways that she has been altered and adulterated through time.

While modern versions and understanding of Medusa hold value, the Medusa of ancient Greek mythology, found in the sources from the ancient world that survive, is a much more complex character than even the broad swath of modern interpretations can encapsulate. The Medusa of ancient Greek myth is simultaneously both monstrous and beautiful, terrifying and sympathetic, and distinctly *in*human. In its most ancient forms, Medusa's story is brief. She is a passing reference, a sad footnote in the story of someone else, and even in that form, she is an enigma whose tale is ripe for interpretation.

The Missing Medusa

Before we talk about the Medusa that survives, I want to mention the one that is missing. The sources that survive from ancient Greece are, almost exclusively, those written by men. That isn't to say that others didn't have a hand in her cultural creation or that their voices aren't found in her surviving form, it means that we simply... don't know. We don't know what form Medusa took when women gathered together to share their stories, their feelings, their traumas. We don't know how they saw and understood her, how they connected with her story or in what way. There is a missing piece to the puzzle of Medusa, and it's at the heart of her. This is true of the rest of Greek myth too; we just... don't know.

But she – and Greek myth broadly – has also been separated from her modern sisters. As an English-speaking person from North America I am not fit to speak about how Medusa lives on in modern Greek culture and its women, but I can say with certainty that she does. Though I can't tell that story, it's important to remember that ancient Greece is not some lost place or long-gone culture; it lives on in the people of Greece today. The people of Greece may have a very different way of understanding her than I – as a person who is looking at her ancient sources only as they're interpreted by the English world – am capable of understanding in any meaningful way.

I do hope, though, that my interpretation of ancient Medusa and how I present her to you might have made the women of ancient Greece smile, and that maybe, even, they might feel I've made her proud.

MEDUSA'S FATE, SIMPLIFIED

There's nothing simple about Greek myth.

Any book or work that presents Greek myth as simple, canonical stories with a beginning, middle and end is no doubt taking a lot of liberties with what we actually know of ancient Greek myth and the sources that survive. This doesn't apply to all the stories we have today, but the vast majority of them. Many of the most famous stories from the ancient Greek world are fragmentary or brief, a few lines of verse that have been re-interpreted into longer narratives for modern consumption. We'll look closer at why and how this is, but it's important to understand because the sources that give us Medusa's story are brief and lack detail, even if they are not necessarily as fragmentary as others.

Most importantly, there is no one true version of anything in ancient Greek myth, no 'original myth', no canonical version, nor even a coherent chronological structure across the stories. There are lots of reasons for this, which we'll get into, but until then.... Here is the oversimplified, contextually lacking but narratively complete (while still, explicitly, ancient Greek) story of Medusa, because we have to start somewhere.

Living at the Edge of Night

The Gorgons were three sisters born to the gods Phorcys and Ceto. Phorcys was a sea god, sometimes considered the god of the dangers within the sea, and Ceto was the goddess of sea monsters and lent her name to all of the monsters of the deep (think, *cetacean* – etymology is fun!). Though the Gorgons' parents were sea deities, they were themselves land-dwelling along with three other deities born to the two gods, the Graiae. The Gorgons were said to be monstrous; their descriptions vary, but imagining snakes for hair and large teeth, even tusks, is a safe bet. (If you're already internally screaming that I've missed out any number of important plot points that you're familiar with, don't worry – we'll get there.) For reasons never provided in the sources, two of the Gorgons were immortal while the third was mortal. Their names were Stheno, Euryale and Medusa. It was Medusa who was unlucky enough to be mortal: *killable*. During her life, Medusa was said to have had a sexual encounter with the god Poseidon (we will revisit this; I have so much to say).

Finally, the three Gorgon sisters lived in the furthest west of the mythologically known world, at the so-called edge of night, not far from their sisters the Graiae and the nymphs of the sunset, the Hesperides. There they lived in relative obscurity.

A 'Hero's' Journey

While the Gorgons were living at the edge of night with their sisters, there was a young man living on the Cycladic Greek island of Serifos. His name was Perseus, and he was a child of Zeus and a mortal woman named Danaë. He has a detailed story himself, in which the Gorgons were only a small piece, but they're the only piece we're interested in for this simplification of a serpentine tale. Besides, without Medusa, Perseus would have died before he had the chance to be much of a hero.

On Serifos, Perseus made an enemy of the king, Polydectes, who wanted to marry Danaë against the desires of her son (and Danaë herself, but that wasn't of concern to Polydectes). In an attempt to, at worst, distract Perseus long enough that Polydectes and Danaë could marry or, at best, see Perseus killed for his efforts, Polydectes requested a very unique gift from the young man: the head of the Gorgon Medusa. As the only mortal of the three sisters, Medusa's was the only head anyone could hope to retrieve, and Polydectes imagined that the quest would be deadly. It would've been deadly, surely, had Perseus not had divine help. As it turned out, the goddess Athena and god Hermes were determined to aid him on his quest. Athena instructed him on how to find the Gorgons: Perseus was to visit first the Graiae, three sisters who knew the location of the nymphs of the sunset, the Hesperides, who had gifts to help him further in his quest. The Graiae, famously, were known to share only one eye and one tooth. Perseus used this against them, stealing both and leaving the three women without sight or speech, threatening to return them only if the Graiae shared the location of the Hesperides. The nymphs gave to Perseus the divine gifts Athena had promised: Hermes' flying sandals, Hades' helmet of invisibility (sometimes called a cap, but helmet sure sounds more intimidating), and a bag with which to transport the Gorgon's severed head. Medusa's head was, famously, her most deadly feature: one look would turn a man to stone, so the bag was a necessity.

Life After Death

Armed with these invaluable gifts, off Perseus went in search of the Gorgon sisters at the edge of night. He snuck into the home of the trio while they were sleeping and before any could stop him, he cut the head off Medusa and stored it away in the divine bag. And then he fled. Medusa's sisters pursued him, screaming in grief and fury, but Perseus escaped and went on to use her severed head as a weapon. With it he rid himself of any enemy he came across (including, unsurprisingly, Polydectes).

Medusa left a legacy – and not just a cultural memory lasting enough for an entire book. Once Medusa's head was severed from her body, two children were born from the gore: Pegasus, the most famous of flying horses (this is his name, not the name of a race of flying horses, and Perseus never rode him), and Chrysaor, a young man who would later become father to Geryon, a monstrous man-giant killed by Heracles (better known as Hercules, who, contrary to popular culture, also did not ride Pegasus). Pegasus and Chrysaor were fathered by Poseidon, conceived during their sexual encounter earlier in Medusa's life. Both were born fully grown from their mother's corpse.

Eventually Medusa's weaponized head was placed in Athena's armour, where it became known as the Gorgoneion and was a vital piece of her iconography. So, Medusa's memory lived forever, if as a wartime accessory to the goddess who facilitated her death.

A STORY SPANNING CENTURIES

Medusa's story varies greatly across the sources. That's why it was necessary for me to share my own simplified version first, to give you a grounding in her story if you're unfamiliar with it, without overwhelming the narrative with the variations and details we'll explore later. But before we dive any deeper into what this simplified version of her story is lacking both in detail and context, and what her *unsimplified* story looks like, we have to understand the world Medusa existed in (in whatever way one can say that mythological figures 'existed').

It's impossible to fully comprehend the complexity of Medusa's story without a basic understanding of the world from which she comes. Medusa as a character and a story is a product of the world of ancient Greece and its mythological tradition. In the English-speaking world of today it has surpassed its mythological roots, but a comprehensive appreciation of her requires us to look at this tradition. What we think of as 'Greek myth' is often a sanitized, condensed version of many sources and stories, both detailed and fragmentary, spanning hundreds of years of cultural evolution and the broad range of ancient Greek regions and subcultures. And that's only the pieces that survive for us today: countless works are lost entirely or yet to be found. Because of this, as I've said, there is no such thing as an 'original myth' or even one that is right or wrong (though there is, absolutely, such a thing as 'this contradicts the ancient sources egregiously', and we'll look at those examples too).

Myth is fluid and perpetually transforming; it is cultural history as much as it is stories of gods, heroes and monsters. The sources that survive from the ancient Greek world are only that: those that *survive*. The stories we have access to today are not the only ones that existed in the ancient world; they're only what was deemed appropriate for preservation by any number of groups and people (more often than not, such decisions were made by not the Greeks themselves but, among others, later cultures who saw fit to copy texts onto longer-lasting materials). The very idea of an 'original myth' is contradictory to myth's purpose and our understanding of their transmission.

There Was No 'Greece'

Setting aside the fact that, *technically*, the word 'Greece' has its roots in Latin (it's 'Hellas', in transliterated Greek!), in the ancient world there was no unified country of Greece or even a unified Greek people or culture. Depending upon the time period, the ancient Greek world was instead made up of many small city-states and regions that shared only a language (though it had many, many varying dialects) and a broad understanding of a shared cultural identity. Not only that, but when we talk about 'ancient Greece' or even 'Greek mythology', we are talking about a culture that spanned well over a thousand years of history and a large and ever-changing region. Bronze Age Greece (*c.* 3000 BCE–1100 BCE, give or take a few centuries) was a very different place from the Iron Age Greece that followed, which was a very different place from Archaic Greece, and so on, through the Classical and Hellenistic periods, which lasted until the second century BCE when much of the Greek world was conquered by Rome. And even after Rome conquered Greece, it remained distinctly *Greek* and continued to expand its cultural and mythological traditions under the Roman Empire.

So, when we're looking at surviving sources, it's important to put them into chronological context. A source that survives from the eighth century BCE will have very different cultural connotations from one that survives from the first or second century CE. Both will be valid, but if we're looking to understand the cultural implications of a story like Medusa, the two will say very different things about two very different time periods and their cultures. Shakespeare's interpretation of English culture is very different from Harry Styles', but the number of centuries between the two pales in comparison to those between two of the most relevant sources for Medusa's story: Hesiod (*c.* eighth century BCE) and Ovid or Pseudo-Apollodorus (first and second centuries CE, respectively). Things can change considerably over that many centuries. Just ask Genghis Khan, who lived closer in time to us today than Ovid did to Hesiod.

Oral Storytelling of Ancient Greece

Ancient Greek myth began kind of like the game of telephone. That might be a dated reference now, but it's the idea that multiple people attempting to retell the same story based on the interpretation of the person before them will almost always result in a very different story by the end. Ancient Greek myth is like this, except it's taking place across multiple cultures and people, languages and dialects, over hundreds and hundreds of years.

The timeline for the most ancient of Greek sources is uncertain. This is because the culture had a long-standing tradition of oral storytelling: travelling bards, singers and storytellers who would share stories across the ancient Greek world. Through these songs, many of the mythological stories that we know so well came to exist. The most famous (and complete!) of the surviving epic songs from this tradition are Homer's *Iliad* and *Odyssey*, two epic poems which would have been originally sung and were shared via live performances by many ancient poets across the Greek world. At some point, probably the Archaic Period, these songs were recorded in a way that allowed them to be preserved and, eventually, reach us today. This is true for another important source for all of Greek mythology: Hesiod.

Both of these 'men' may or may not have existed as real people, but more likely (in my opinion; I won't pretend the experts have ever come to a consensus!) were names attributed to stories that were being told for decades, if not centuries, before they were ever written down. This means that, like the old game of telephone, the stories would have been altered or changed over time. If stories are only ever being told via performance and recitation, it's impossible that they could remain unchanged. One poet might emphasize one character's plight, while another might have a soft spot for a particular god. The stories would have been influenced by countless different voices, opinions and preferences, and only one version, selected by a very small and specific group of people, is what survives for us today. (Technically, there's more than one version of even the *Iliad*, but I'm trying to keep this simple!)

Ultimately, the reason for this context (in addition to being a pet obsession of mine) is to point out that the versions we have today are not necessarily the only versions that ever existed, and nor do they provide any kind of concrete insight into what was believed across the whole of the ancient Greek world. Instead, they are simply the sources *that we have*, and the more we understand the context surrounding them, the easier it is to understand the complexities that exist when retelling Medusa's story. A story which first appears in none other than Hesiod.

There Is No Canon

Because of how we, today, write and appreciate storytelling, modern audiences have a tendency to want Greek myths to have concrete – accurate, narratively complete, chronologically sensical – versions. This is particularly true of Medusa's story, from my experience. A brief internet search today suggests one version of Medusa is the 'true story' while another is 'wrong'. There are countless instances of this and not one can seem to agree on what version is 'true', let alone why that would be. Certainly, it's possible to find modern versions of myths that are entirely invented by their modern retellers and which have no basis in the ancient sources, but so long as a myth is coming from an ancient mythological source, there is no right or wrong version. Instead, there are versions which are older, more or less fragmentary, are Greek or Roman or otherwise, and which were or were not written for specific purposes. This is true for almost all Greek myths, but Medusa's many varied versions are some of the most frequently manipulated by the modern world, and often have come to lose all resemblance to versions of her that are found in the ancient sources.

You might find I harp on about this, perhaps excessively, but it's not only vitally important to a full understanding of how Greek myth functioned in the ancient world, it's also implicitly related to how Medusa is seen today. In writing this I have come upon countless, *countless* mentions of a so-called 'true story' of Medusa, and these 'true stories' always try to use their version to denigrate or deny another. But provided the version does indeed appear in an ancient Greek or adjacent source, there's really no reason to argue over what is right or wrong. They are, simply, *different*.

The Homeric Tradition, a Greek Playwright and a Roman Poet Walk Into a Bar

Another important detail when it comes to understanding how the ancient sources function is the purpose for which they were written. The sources that originate out of a tradition of oral storytelling – names like Hesiod and Homer – weren't written but *composed* over time and through many voices, understood to be a kind of cultural history of an earlier generation of people. They were also poems sung as songs, so certain asides or similes in the works might have been intended to keep an audience entertained, help the performer recall certain moments or details, or remind the audience of stories they might find relatable. Ultimately, though, they were a kind of mythical history rather than intended to convey concise or cohesive narratives.

Later, the Greek tragedians take up the mantle of storytelling and begin approaching these stories from very different perspectives. Ancient Greek plays like *Oedipus the King* or

Medea, while they relate stories based in myth, history, or combinations of the two, were written very intentionally by individuals set on not only entertaining and engaging with an audience, but also winning a contest and appeasing their polis (Athens, as all that survive are Athenian plays). They could be political, both overtly or by examining an ancient myth that they might use to convey a point about current events. Or they might be developed purely out of a desire to tell a particular story in that tragedian's own words. Comparatively to the oral tradition, the most important detail that differentiates the work of these playwrights is that the plays were written *intentionally*. The plays, no matter how famous they are now for their mythological storytelling, were themselves retellings of something more ancient. In many cases, that something more ancient is lost to us today and all we have are the plays. (For example, no detailed version of Oedipus' story exists outside of plays!)

Finally, there are Roman poets writing their Latinized versions of, often, originally Greek stories. In the case of Medusa, namely the Roman poet Ovid, whose version of her story has taken hold of the modern imagination. It's vital that, when looking at Ovid's very distinct version of Medusa's story, we remember not only why it was written, but that it was done so intentionally. We'll talk more about Ovid later, but his work the *Metamorphoses* primarily features characters whose origins are Greek, but who are now being reimagined by a Roman poet, and was ostensibly written to reimagine stories of transformation. Thus, Medusa is given a transformation arc. We can't say why, exactly, Ovid wrote his version of Medusa or whether he was working from a version of her lost to us today, but we can without a doubt label it as a Roman interpretation of her story. It is by nature infused not only with Ovid's intentional manipulations to fit his goal of 'metamorphoses', but also with Roman societal norms, their views on the gods, and their cultural traditions. And, most importantly, it was also written somewhere in the realm of 700 or 800 years after the earliest surviving version of her story. It's best to think of it like a reimagining of a classic, like Baz Luhrmann's simultaneously twentieth-century and Elizabethan take on *Romeo and Juliet* (*Romeo + Juliet*, 1996), or even Disney's *The Lion King* (1994), a full-blown reinterpretation of *Hamlet*. These pieces of reception are still adaptations of the Shakespearean originals even though they've been dramatically altered. Ovid's Medusa is just that: one man's reimagining of a centuries-old story that originated in a different culture from his own.

How and Why Sources Survive

This is an oversimplification for the sake of clarity. When we think of the ancient sources, it's easy to imagine some vast collection of papyri scrolls or something equally exciting. In truth, though, unless papyri are preserved in some way (typically, accidentally!), they deteriorate pretty fast in the grand scheme of ancient materials. Instead, much of what survives from the ancient world does so not through materials actually *from* the ancient world, but through those copied by the people of later periods, including by scribes of the Byzantine period for preservation and later into Arabic versions. Both groups had a great interest and appreciation of ancient Greek works and helped maintain them for later consumption and translation (they also ruled over lands that were once Greek colonies and thus had a lot of access to these materials). Still, the works preserved tend to be those that held particular importance in both the ancient and late antique periods, works that were considered worthy of study in schools and elsewhere.

There are some instances, though, where works survived not because they were deemed important enough for intentional preservation, but instead through random acts of nature and humanity (like a number of plays by Euripides, which were preserved because one volume of a random Byzantine collector's alphabetical set happened to survive!). In addition to the preservation of full works like this, fragments often survived through their inclusion in other works. Later authors might quote a selection from Hesiod in order to make a point, or refer back, and because of that we have a small quotation of a work that is otherwise lost. We'll see some examples of this as we dive into the surviving versions of Medusa's many, many ancient forms.

The Curse of the Patriarchy

Greek mythology did not exist in a vacuum. It was heavily, if not entirely, influenced by the culture in which it was recorded. I specify *recorded* because we have no way of knowing what changes might have been made to works based in the oral tradition when they were finally recorded for preservation. It's very possible, if not likely, that the people who handled such preservation made changes based on cultural norms of their time. This problem is bigger even than it seems due to the fact that so much of what survives for us today comes from Athens, which was, especially during the Archaic and Classical periods, particularly patriarchal. The fates of women were determined by men, and this is evidenced in the mythology. In many cases there is little indication of women's agency or consideration as to how they felt or behaved in any given situation. To go into detail about these issues would be a life's work, so instead I just want to draw your attention to a few particular issues that are widespread across the ancient sources and which have then bled into the modern realm of myth retellings and interpretations.

Unless you read Ancient Greek, you're probably accessing ancient sources via English translations, which means that issues with word choice can sometimes be a problem of translators, but also an issue in the sources themselves. Very often we see terms like 'seduce', 'lay with', 'ravish', 'carry off', 'rapt away', or even 'rape' (but used in its archaic form in place of 'kidnap' or 'abduct', rather than explicit sexual assault). Whether it's the ancient source or the translator, in my opinion, many if not most of these instances might be interpreted with a little more nuance. Not that it's particularly fun to believe these to be assault, just that we might maintain a level of credulity as to the experiences of women as they're relayed by men. The use of some of these terms is often defended with excuses like 'that's just how things were back then' or 'gods can't assault mortals', or, simply, 'well, it doesn't say it was nonconsensual so it was obviously not assault'. It's not that these excuses are wrong (they are gross, though) so much as they perpetuate the same problem: the issue isn't whether or not we can read the woman consenting to the god or hero, it's that the source wasn't concerned with her as a party who could consent. I don't mean to suggest that they hated women, merely that many of the cultures considered women to be the property of their fathers or husbands and thus decisions weren't up to them. They were often written as passive beings just along for the ride.

As modern readers, though, with complex views on consent and sexual violence, we can read between the lines and make our own assumptions about how the woman might have felt about, for example, having sex with a swan, eagle, bull, horse, etc. (Zeus, Zeus, Zeus, Poseidon, respectively). We might also consider the inherent power imbalance between the king of the gods 'seducing' a mortal woman and what that might mean for her experience. It's not that reading them as assault is more appealing (it is distinctly *not*), just that, at least as I see it, it's kinder to the experience of the real women living alongside these myths to imagine how they might have internalized these instances. Though this applies to the whole of Greek myth, it's particularly relevant to Medusa, as we'll come to see.

MEDUSA THE GORGON

The ancient sources agree on one thing: Medusa was one of three Gorgons. What that meant about her, though, isn't nearly as straightforward. They are monsters, yes, but that does not mean they were hated or even inherently feared and dangerous, just that they were divine and inhuman, with qualities (snake hair, wings, etc.) that constitute 'monstrosity'. But what is a Gorgon, really, and what does it mean for Medusa's character? Though their narrative stories are singular and revolve entirely around the death of Medusa, the Gorgons as creatures and concept were widespread across the ancient Mediterranean, with hundreds, if not thousands, of depictions surviving today in text and visual representations. But who, and what, were they?

The Monstrously Divine Family

Across the breadth of sources, we know with relative certainty that the three monstrous Gorgon sisters – Stheno, Euryale and Medusa – were daughters of the two sea deities Phorcys and Ceto. Both Phorcys and Ceto were children of Gaia, the primordial Mother Earth goddess who birthed – and was – the world and many of its earliest deities.

Phorcys was a god of the sea, more specifically its more dangerous aspects, and Ceto a goddess of the same, though she focused on its dangerous creatures and is better known as a sea-*monster* goddess. Together they were the progenitors of many monstrous creatures. The most important of these children (for us, at least) are the Gorgons and the Graiae. It's a fairly common occurrence, with divine creatures like these, that they are grouped together in threes. We shouldn't believe them to be triplets so much as divine groups who share both lineage and physical features.

Sharing Is Caring

The Graiae, the Grey Ones, were the three sisters of the three Gorgons (depending on the ancient source; Hesiod, for instance, names only two) who were born grey-haired, and sometimes described as swan-like in their form (no, I have never been able to sort out what this might look like). They, very notably, were famous for sharing one eye and one tooth between them, passing each back and forth when needed. The Graiae, like the Gorgons, are interesting as they only appear in this one story, acting as a stop on Perseus's quest for Medusa's head.

The Earth-Encircling River

While they had many monster siblings, the Gorgons were most closely associated with the Graiae. But while the six were siblings, the explicit notion of a sibling bond was limited to the individual trios of the Gorgons and Graiae. The two sets of three sisters lived near each other, in the farthest western reaches of the mythological world.

According to the early mythology (I emphasize mythology, because we shouldn't assume that the ancient Greek people necessarily believed this about the physical world!), the 'earth' was a kind of disk surrounded by a freshwater river called Oceanus (yes, quite an ironic term by modern English standards). Only a select few deities lived *beyond* Oceanus, and the Gorgons and Graiae were some of them. They were said to live in caves, bordered by either Oceanus or the sea, far away from humanity and mortals in general. Sometimes the region where they lived is given the name Sarpedon, or they're given a real-world location in the western reaches of North Africa.

What Defines a Gorgon?

Like the rest of Medusa's story, the nature of the Gorgons isn't straightforward. But what, exactly, this implied about them both in terms of character and physicality isn't entirely clear. This is common across many characters from Greek myth, primarily because of the nature of the stories. For the most part, Greek myths weren't developed to answer the questions that we have as a modern audience. The sources weren't necessarily concerned with what, exactly, it meant to be a Gorgon. This could be because the cultural idea of Gorgons was widespread enough that it was assumed everyone understood what or who they were, or simply because it wasn't considered necessary information for the story that was being told. As I said earlier, however, we know that they were *monstrous* (monstrosity, though, does not inherently mean they were violent).

In terms of textual physical descriptions, the Gorgons often leave us with more questions than answers. We know they are divine in some way, certainly; this is clear from both their divine parentage and in the explicit immortality of Stheno and Euryale. They are typically described as having snakes in place of hair, sometimes winged, and they are known for the power of their scream. And, of course, their petrifying gaze. The Gorgons are understood to be fierce and terrible (the word *gorgos*, the likely origin of Gorgon, meant 'terrible'), but beyond that there is little physical description. Visually, on the other hand, we have much more to work with.

The Gorgons appear in visual representation in a whole host of different ways. Medusa herself is depicted on a number of pieces of pottery, both before and after her beheading by Perseus. Sometimes she appears distinctly human, save for a few snakes in her hair and a set of wings sprouting from her back. She is often shown sleeping, unaware of Perseus sneaking up behind her. Other times she's depicted having just had her head sheared from her body, with the newly born Pegasus flying from her neck. In those cases, typically, we also see her sisters. Stheno and Euryale are, often, shown in their grief and rage as they grasp for Perseus who is just out of reach. These depictions of her before and during her death are distinctly sympathetic. Generally, she is not shown to be scary, or even threatening; she is only a woman with divine qualities who is either sleeping and about to be killed, or a newly lifeless corpse surrounded by her surviving siblings and children. Many depictions show the pain and sadness not only in her sisters as they attempt to avenge her, but in Medusa herself, whether she's living or dead.

Alternatively, there are (almost certainly) *thousands* of depictions of Medusa's head after Perseus has killed her and stolen it. Typically these are better described as 'the Head of a Gorgon' or the 'Gorgoneion'. This Gorgon (often assumed to be Medusa) appears *everywhere* (pottery, statuary, architecture, mosaics, you name it). She is a very commonly depicted figure, both because her story became so famous in the ancient world, and because of what her head came to represent once it was placed on Athena's shield (narratively, that is; culturally it's likely the head came first). We'll revisit Medusa as a part of Athena's shield, her aegis, but the Gorgon's head as it's shown in that way is often distinctly different from the depictions of Medusa's *story*. Though not exclusively, when she is shown alive and/or only just murdered, she is sometimes given a full and often human-like form. Rather, when it's just her head, she is indeed *monstrous*.

There is something to be said about the way this humanizing figure with a deadly gaze became known as *seductive*, but I choose to read these depictions as sympathetic rather than some kind of manifestation of male desire.

Depictions of the Gorgon head are fairly unified: it is wide-eyed and open-mouthed. She has fangs, or sometimes tusks, and her tongue is lolled out of her mouth in a kind of scream or cackle. She has snakes for hair, but also often a small set of wings nestled among them. These versions of her – and the Gorgon broadly – are inhuman, terrible and fearful. But they also, very specifically, were a symbol of protection and not violence. They were meant to be fearful, certainly, but the horrifying nature of her image was meant to scare away threats to whoever possessed her. She protected Athena once her head was placed in the goddess' shield, and thus we can imagine that she protected those who possessed her image.

2.
Slithering Through Medusa's Rocky History

And near [the Graiae] are their three winged sisters, the snake-haired Gorgons, loathed of mankind, whom no one of mortal kind shall look upon and still draw breath.
– Aeschylus, from *Prometheus Bound*
(Weir Smyth translation, 1930)

THE JOYS (AND FRUSTRATIONS) OF ANCIENT SOURCES

inally, we've reached the point where I can share the more complicated versions of Medusa's story as it survives in ancient texts. She, like many figures from Greek myth, exists in many forms across many sources. In the case of her ancient Greek sources, they tend to be not contradictory so much as varying in detail. But those details greatly affect how her story is told and what we as readers interpret from it. Medusa's story isn't simple; she is complex and layered and open to interpretation. And remember: there is no one true version of Medusa's story; there is no 'original myth'; there is only the sources that survive and what they tell us about her.

THE OLDEST (SURVIVING) MEDUSA

The oldest extant version of Medusa's story is found in an epic poem called the *Theogony*, variously dated to the eighth or seventh centuries BCE. It's attributed to a man named Hesiod who was said to have lived in the Greek region of Boeotia in the eighth century, but was originally from Cyme, a town in what is now Turkey. As I mentioned, the existence of a real man by that name is debated. It's possible (and likely, if you ask me!) that the *Theogony* and the other works associated with him were actually longstanding epic poems, part of the far-reaching tradition of oral storytelling, which were eventually recorded for preservation and attributed to one man by that name. It's generally accepted, though, that this poem would have been composed or developed after the Homeric epics the *Iliad* and the *Odyssey* (that will be important later).

The *Theogony* tells the story of the origins of the Greek mythological world, from the primordial mother Gaia, down through the generations until the line of heroes and some of their exploits. The *Theogony* is where we find the most ancient genealogical lines and the establishment of the Olympian gods as rulers of the Greek mythological world. More importantly, it's also where we find the most ancient version of Medusa's story.

Hesiod's story of Medusa is both brief and contextually vital. Here it is in its entirety, as translated by H.G. Evelyn-White (1914), with small language adjustments by me, for clarity.

Hesiod's Medusa

Ceto bore to Phorcys the fair-cheeked Graiae, sisters grey from their birth: and both deathless gods and men who walk on earth call them Graiae, Pemphredo well-clad, and saffron-robed Enyo, and the Gorgons who dwell beyond glorious Ocean in the frontier land towards Night where are the clear-voiced Hesperides, Stheno, and Euryale, and Medusa who suffered a woeful fate: she was mortal, but the two were undying and grew not old. With her lay [Poseidon,] the Dark-haired One in a soft meadow amid spring flowers. And when Perseus cut off her head, there sprang forth great Chrysaor and the horse Pegasus who is so called because he was born near the springs of Ocean; and that other, because he held a golden blade in his hands.

Before Her Gaze Was Stony

There are some very notable details missing from this earliest surviving version of Medusa's story. There is no mention of her most famous feature, that her gaze would turn any who looked upon her to stone, nor is there any reason given for Perseus's killing of her or what happened after he'd cut off her head. I don't mean to suggest that these details weren't known as far back as Hesiod (we can't be certain either way), but it is notable that these details that are now so vital to her story are missing from the most ancient sources. Here, instead of a story of a monster righteously defeated by a hero, we have the story of a woman – a Gorgon, certainly, but still a woman – with a 'woeful fate'.

This earliest Medusa is not terrifying (beyond the etymology – *gorgos*, terrible – of Gorgon). She is not dangerous or even monstrous in any explicit way. This earliest Medusa is sympathetic, mysterious and, distinctly and inarguably, a victim. That she is the child of two dangerous sea deities is notable and would have suggested something to the people of ancient Greece, that perhaps she is at least to be cautiously feared, but this is the extent of her explicit monstrosity.

Hesiod's deeply sympathetic version of her story is the perfect introduction to her most ancient forms because, as we'll see time and time again, there is no ancient Greek evidence of violence committed by a living Medusa or her Gorgon sisters.

The Gorgon 'Before' Medusa

Hesiod's story of Medusa might be the earliest surviving version of *her* story, but it isn't the earliest reference to a Gorgon. For that we can look to Homer's *Iliad* and *Odyssey*. There are many stark differences between the details of the *Iliad* and the *Odyssey*, which suggests (among other reasons) that it was not composed by a single person or even a unified group of composers. There are contradictory mythological details: which gods are or are not married to one another, and others with different parental origins across the two works, among others. The details of this and the argument that Homer was never one person but a name attributed to the long and storied history of oral storytelling in Iron Age Greece would be another book entirely, but I mention it because of one notable character who does appear to remain consistent between the two poems: the Gorgon.

Both the *Iliad* and the *Odyssey* make reference to an unnamed Gorgon – even, rather, the Gorgon as a monstrous concept separate from any particular character or story. We'll look at this in more detail a bit later, but it's important to note here that the concept of a Gorgon existed prior to Hesiod's *Theogony*, but the character of Medusa, a named Gorgon with a family and story, first appears in the *Theogony*.

THE MOST DETAILED NARRATIVE (WHILE STILL, TECHNICALLY, GREEK) MEDUSA

The source that's often used as a more detailed account of Medusa's story is attributed to a man named Apollodorus. Today the author is more accurately referred to as *Pseudo*-Apollodorus. This is common enough when it comes to ancient sources: they are at times attributed to people who we later determine could not have written the text for a host of reasons. That change doesn't make the source any less valuable; it just implies that we don't know the author's actual name and instead add the caveat of *Pseudo-*. In the case of Pseudo-Apollodorus, it also changed how we date the text, shifting it by about 300 years from the second century BCE, when the real Apollodorus lived, to the second century CE, when it's believed this text would have to have been written.

In this case, as compared to sources like Hesiod and Homer, we can generally assume that Pseudo-Apollodorus was, indeed, an individual who wrote the text we call the *Library of Greek Mythology*. I once saw someone refer to this text as the 'TL;DR of Greek myth': Too Long; Didn't Read, i.e., a synopsized version of something much longer, and it's a very apt way of describing the work.

Essentially, Pseudo-Apollodorus retells many of the most famous and lasting Greek myths, but in considerable brevity compared to other sources. It's quick and to the point in the case of many, but when it comes to Medusa it's actually the only detailed version of her story from an explicitly Greek source. Even still, chronologically speaking, Pseudo-Apollodorus comes many, many hundreds of years after Medusa first appears in Hesiod. As I mentioned, the text is now generally understood to date from the first or second century CE, when Greece was part of the Roman Empire, at least 800–900 years after Hesiod's *Theogony* was likely composed. This is important because it means that this text does not necessarily describe a story that was understood by all the ancient Greeks who preceded the Roman period. Still, it's an important source and provides details we don't get elsewhere (which doesn't mean they're more or less accurate than other sources, just *different*).

One Part of a Long Story

This is how Medusa's story – as well as the story of Perseus that precedes her – is told in Pseudo-Apollodorus's *Library of Greek Mythology*. I've adjusted and rewritten it from the J.G. Frazer translation (1921) for clarity and general readability. Because Medusa's story is, tragically, just a small part of Perseus's longer narrative, this telling includes his origins. Some details have been removed, if they're contradictory or confusing and not relevant to Medusa (this work is known for including many alternate ideas, but I've only removed those speculating on unrelated aspects of Perseus's story, since we don't care that much about him). You might also be surprised to see a reference to Ethiopia, but this isn't necessarily what we know as modern Ethiopia. It's obviously where we get the English name, but the Greeks sometimes used it to refer to a broad swath of what they knew of Africa. (Imagine somewhere along the coast of North Africa.) Finally, full disclosure, my amendments do make it seem like the writer was a little more interested in writing Perseus's mother as a human being as compared to the men (because Danaë deserves better). Despite desperately wanting to, I have not added any of my own commentary. But you might imagine someone screaming obscenities when you reach Perseus's conception.

Pseudo-Apollodorus's Medusa

Acrisius was king of Argos and had a daughter, Danaë. Because he had no heir, he sought guidance from the Oracle as to what he should do. The god's prophecy told him that his daughter would give birth to a son who would kill him. Fearing this, Acrisius built a bronze chamber underground where he imprisoned his daughter to ensure this couldn't come to pass. However, Zeus had intercourse with her in the shape of a stream of gold which poured through the roof into Danaë's lap. When Acrisius later learned that she had given birth to a child, Perseus, he refused to believe that she had been seduced by Zeus. Instead, furious, he imprisoned her, with her child, in a chest, which he cast into the sea. Eventually, the chest washed ashore on the island of Serifos, where a fisherman named Dictys found and rescued Danaë and her son. He took them in and helped to raise Perseus.

Dictys' brother, Polydectes, was king of Serifos and sought to marry Danaë. He couldn't get access to her, because Perseus was old enough to protect her both physically and legally. Instead, Polydectes called together his friends, including Perseus, under the pretext of collecting contributions towards a gift he hoped would help him marry another woman. Perseus declared that he would bring the king anything, even the head of a Gorgon. So, Polydectes asked the others to bring him horses as their contributions, but ordered Perseus instead to bring him the head.

With the guidance of Hermes and Athena, he made his way to the daughters of Phorcys, the Graiae, old women from their birth, named Enyo, [Pemphredo], and Dino. Phorcys and Ceto were their parents and they were sisters of the Gorgons. The three had but one eye and one tooth, and these they passed to each other in turn. Perseus stole from them the eye and the tooth, and when they asked for them back, he told them he would return the eye and tooth only if they would show him the way to the nymphs [of the Hesperides]. The nymphs, he learned, had winged sandals, a kibisis (a bag), and the cap of Hades. When the Graiae had shown him the way to the nymphs, he gave them back the tooth and the eye. Finding the Hesperides, Perseus slung the kibisis over his shoulder, fastened the sandals on his feet, and put the cap on his head, which made him invisible to others. Having already received from Hermes an adamantine sickle, Perseus flew to Oceanus and caught the Gorgons while they slept. They were Stheno, Euryale and Medusa. Medusa alone was mortal and for that reason it was her head that Perseus wanted. The Gorgons, though, had heads twined with the scales of dragons (snakes), great boar-like tusks, bronze hands, and golden wings.... And they turned to stone anyone who beheld them.

Perseus stood over them as they slept, and while Athena guided his hand he looked not directly at the Gorgons but through the shield's reflection. There he saw the image of the sleeping Gorgon, and he beheaded her. When her head was cut off, there sprang from the Gorgon the winged horse Pegasus and Chrysaor, the father of Geryon; these she conceived by Poseidon. Perseus put the head of Medusa in the kibisis. The two living Gorgons awoke and pursued him, but they couldn't see him because of the cap of invisibility.

Arriving in Ethiopia, where Cepheus was king, Perseus found the king's daughter Andromeda, who was imprisoned to be the prey of a sea monster. Cassiopeia, the wife of Cepheus and mother of Andromeda, boasted that she was more beautiful than the Nereids, nymphs of the sea. This angered them, and Poseidon, sharing their wrath, sent a flood and a monster to invade the land. One of their gods, Ammon, predicted that if Andromeda was exposed as prey to the monster, the kingdom would be saved. Cepheus was compelled by his people to do as the god ordered, and so he bound his daughter to a rock. When Perseus saw her, he loved her and promised Cepheus that he would kill the monster, provided he could marry Andromeda once she was rescued. The two agreed to these terms and so Perseus slew the monster and freed Andromeda. However, a brother of Cepheus, to whom Andromeda had been betrothed, plotted against him. Perseus discovered the plot and, by showing the Gorgon's head, turned him and his fellow conspirators to stone.

Returning to Serifos, he found that his mother and Dictys had taken refuge at the altars because of the violence of Polydectes, so he entered the palace where Polydectes had gathered his friends, and while averting his face Perseus showed them the Gorgon's head. All who beheld it were turned to stone, each in exactly the position and expression as when they looked at it. Having appointed Dictys king of Serifos, Perseus returned the sandals, the kibisis and the cap to Hermes, but he gave the Gorgon's head to Athena. Hermes returned the items to the nymphs and Athena placed the Gorgon's head in the middle of her shield.

It is alleged by some, however, that Medusa was beheaded because of Athena; they say that the Gorgon dared compare herself with the goddess even in beauty.

Details After Death

The differences between the versions featured in both Hesiod's *Theogony* (remember: *c.* eighth century BCE) and Pseudo-Apollodorus's *Library of Greek Mythology* (*c.* second century CE) perfectly encapsulate the frustration that comes with loving Greek myths as they exist in the sources. To love the ancient sources is to be simultaneously enthralled, confused, and aching for more detail.

In Hesiod's Iron Age/Archaic Period version of Medusa, we know only the basics: she was a Gorgon, Poseidon had sex with her, Perseus killed her. Meanwhile, nearly 1,000 years later, Pseudo-Apollodorus presents a long and storied tale of feats of heroism that surround the death of a woman while she slept. Neither is more or less accurate; they are simply products of their time. The *Theogony* was concerned with conveying a long tradition of mythic history and cosmogony, whereas Pseudo-

Apollodorus was concerned with syncretizing detailed stories that were, by his time, likely commonplace and broadly known across the culture. In fact, in another great example of the infuriating nature of fragmentary sources, we do know of one Archaic mythographer who detailed many of the same plot points as Pseudo-Apollodorus: a man named Pherekydes (sixth century BCE).

We know that the details *existed* in Pherekydes' extensive work covering large swaths of Greek myth, but we don't have them. Instead, we have references to his work by an unnamed person who had access to it and documented some details in his own work, which does survive. These details which are believed to have existed in Pherekydes' work involved Hermes' involvement in the story, the Graiae and Hesperides' various contributions, the means by which Medusa is killed, and her sisters' attempts to catch her killer. This means, at least, that those details almost certainly existed long before Pseudo-Apollodorus, perhaps even just shortly after Hesiod's surviving story was recorded. (In a truly poetic turn of events, I have only been able to read a modern author [Gantz, 1993] who has written about the scholiast who wrote about Pherekydes, and have been unable to find the actual fragments.)

It's impossible to say where these additional details originated, particularly in a story like that of Perseus, because even from the time of Homer and the oral tradition, his story was foundational to the mythical history of the Argolid Peninsula. He, certainly, existed, even if his detailed dealings with Medusa may not have. It's fascinating and frustrating that such a late source provides us with so many more aspects of Medusa's story and the characters that surround it, and leaves us wondering where certain details came from and how ancient or widespread they might have been.

Painting Between the Lines

Often we have to use visual representations to fill in the blanks left by the written sources. For instance, Pseudo-Apollodorus is our only detailed narrative source for certain details of Medusa's death: that Perseus came upon the Gorgons while they were sleeping and that her sisters pursued him in their heartbroken rage. But, while we may not have an earlier written source that clarifies these in the same detail, we do have paintings that show much the same plot points. Consider the pieces I mentioned earlier: pottery painted of Medusa that show her sleeping peacefully while Perseus sneaks in, beheads her, and flees from the pursuit of her horrified sisters. Through visual representations like these (particularly in Archaic and Classical pottery where we find a wealth of mythological content) we can be certain that these details were well known as far back as those periods (some 500–600 or more years before Pseudo-Apollodorus). This allows us to get at least a better understanding of what the story might have looked like to people of that time, even if we can't read it.

Those Who Dare to Feel Beautiful

There's a particular line in Pseudo-Apollodorus that we *have* to look at in detail. It's the final line in Medusa's story as I've included it, a kind of afterthought or post-script. We might imagine it a little more like this: 'Oh, by the way, some people say that actually Medusa was beheaded because Athena was pissed off that she dared say she was prettier.' It sounds like a catty jab, a tiny detail that threatens to overtake the entire story that's just been told. It's also, in my opinion, gross. It likens Medusa to so many other women in Greek myth who are punished by a goddess for daring to be beautiful or talented and reads more like a cautionary tale meant to keep women in their place than a distinct and culturally relevant mythological detail. Of course, similar plot points in other myths quite possibly were, at least in part, meant to do exactly that. The myths as they survive were recorded and interpreted by men, after all, and that is something I keep at the forefront of my mind as I interpret any and all ancient sources. As far as I've been able to determine, this is the only place where such a claim appears (and oh, have I scoured the sources and questioned many experts!). Personally, I don't believe it holds much cultural relevance beyond an insight into its misogyny.

THE LOST PLAY THAT HAUNTS MODERN DREAMS

That heading is a bit misleading; it may only be my dreams that are haunted by this lost play of Aeschylus. Aeschylus was the earliest of the three surviving Greek tragedians, writing his plays in the fifth century BCE (yes, only works from *three* tragedians survive today, despite there being a long history of playwrights and a longer list of works that are lost). He is most famous for being the tragedian behind the only surviving trilogy of plays, the *Oresteia*, but there is one lost work that may have held answers to all our burning questions about Medusa's fate.

Though we don't seem to have any distinct quotes from it, we do know that Aeschylus wrote a play called the *Phorkydes*, which means, essentially, 'children of Phorcys'. It's believed to have told the story of Perseus's search for the Gorgons and the death of Medusa, and heavily featured the Graiae. In Aeschylus's interpretation of the story, the Graiae were a kind of guardian to the Gorgons (Gantz, 1993). We know little else, but can only imagine what details of Medusa and the Gorgons it might have featured. When it comes to plays, though, we have to remember that, like movies adapting historical events, liberties will always be taken in order to tell a story in a way that not only suits a stage but entertains an audience. And, as Gantz points out, Aeschylus was limited by his stage and ancient stagecraft, so changes to setting would be necessary.

ALL SHE LEFT BEHIND

The beheading of Medusa – her murder by Perseus – is not the end of Medusa's story for countless reasons. There are the obvious things that follow: the rest of Perseus's story where he wields her severed head as a weapon and all that implies about her legacy; there are the children birthed from her murder and abandoned thereafter; and there are the many questions that modern readers are left to grapple with.

Children of Tragedy

No examination of Medusa's story is complete without looking at the children she left behind. In nearly every version of her story, and in many visual representations, Medusa's death results in the birth of her children, Pegasus and Chrysaor. They are born from her death, sprung from the severed stump of her neck. We don't hear of them interacting with either their mother's killer or the sisters she left behind, only that they are born from her demise. I won't pretend that this is the most unique birth story in all of Greek myth (poor Leda did 'give birth' to eggs when Zeus came for her as a swan), but it is one of the few so deeply tying birth with death. Based on how it's told, we can gather that it is only through her death that Medusa is able to give birth to children she has presumably been carrying for some time. Their births are always told as simple statements, as a kind of cause and effect, but the implications go much deeper than just children born of tragedy.

Medusa's children are born of explicit and deadly violence: their mother's head is sliced from her body in a disturbingly casual manner, while she sleeps soundly in the comfort of her home, and only then the children of her 'union' with Poseidon are able to be born. It's an inherently tragic moment; Medusa never gets to meet her children and they never get to meet their mother. They are born into the trauma of her death and, quite literally, from her bloodied corpse. We have no further details on their relation to her, nor do we get any insights into how they might have felt about her death, only that they were born. But born they were, and both went on to varying degrees of greatness. Pegasus was the most famous of all flying horses (and perhaps the only with a given name), notable for flying all the way to the heavens on Olympus; and Chrysaor became the father of a giant, Geryon, who is known for being part of Heracles' labours (this may not sound *that* impressive, but anything involving Heracles – also known as Hercules – was a pretty big deal). It isn't explicit, but their importance and lasting legacies reflect back on their mother and bring a certain lightness to her otherwise tragic story.

The Question of Consent

Many people who write about ancient Greek myth today choose not to discuss the question of consent in these stories of gods and mortals (and many, many nymphs), or to gloss over it as irrelevant because the active party is divine and thus capable of 'seduction' that renders consent moot. There are lots of arguments for this, but they typically hinge around the idea that because we don't have proof that the people of ancient Greece conceptualized consent in their myths in ways similar to our modern understanding, this means that it is irrelevant or even contradictory to the stories. In my opinion, this does a disservice to both the myths and the ancient people who created them. Whether or not there is an explicit notion of consent in the ancient sources, there are countless instances of moments we can easily interpret as being nonconsensual. Many encounters between gods and mortals, both men and women, begin with abduction and end with either death (or, in one case – Ganymede's – forced servitude) or a child. In my mind, this is more than enough to read the encounter as nonconsensual and I personally find it to be kinder to the mythological characters, if not also ancient victims and survivors of assault, to recognize the trauma this might have elicited in readers or audiences. It's not necessary, certainly, to appreciate the stories while also acknowledging these details, but I find that I cannot read the sources without examining those implications.

This is equally true when it comes to Medusa and the father of her children, Poseidon. There is a lot of debate to be had (and I will have it in a later section!) about whether or not the sexual encounter Medusa had with Poseidon was against her will. The simple argument is: if you're interested in considering how we might read consent in the sources, most of Poseidon's sexual encounters can (and, in my opinion, should) be read as nonconsensual. Poseidon is by nature a god of violence: the sea was and is a violent and dangerous place and the god of it has those same qualities.

Hesiod doesn't clarify consent, but it's clear he's not interested one way or the other. In Hesiod, it is a simple relation of events, but it is notable that he immediately precedes the mention of Poseidon 'laying with' Medusa with a note about her sad fate. Similarly, Poseidon is given the epithet 'Dark-haired One' in this scene and the encounter takes place among spring flowers. To me this screams of contrast, an implication that something violent happened, by a violent god, in a beautiful and otherwise happy place. Alternatively, Pseudo-Apollodorus mentions only the resulting children and makes no mention of how or when they were conceived. I would argue, too, that the way in which Pegasus and Chrysaor are born lends itself to the argument that their conception was not a pleasant experience for Medusa. Mythology, by its very nature, examines the humanity within stories of gods, mortals and monsters. That Medusa not only becomes mother to children by the most violent of the all-powerful Olympian gods, but that they are also unable to be born until she has died violently, seems to suggest something about their conception even if there is no (Greek) source that describes it explicitly as assault. Again, I don't mean to emphasize a further tragedy in her story, only to consider how it might have been viewed by people in the ancient world and how they may have connected with it through that.

A MONSTER WITHOUT TEETH

The most important detail to take from how the ancient sources treat Medusa's story is, in my opinion, the tragedy that is her fate. Even setting aside the Poseidon-of-it-all, she was a woman killed purely because she could be. We are given no indication that there was any reason for her death aside from the request made by Polydectes, one which can be easily read as an attempt on Perseus's life. He wanted Perseus killed in the process so that he could marry the hero's mother, not because he believed that Medusa was in any way deserving of death. This is emphasized in multiple ways: we are given no indication that she is dangerous; she does not fight back or even have the chance to attempt to defend herself. The target is on her, specifically, because she was mortal while her sisters were not. She was a monster, certainly, but she was not a dangerous one. She was born a Gorgon; her monstrosity was inherited, not earned. She *looked* monstrous but did not *behave* monstrously, and her death was sad and unnecessary. She was not a terrible seductress hiding away in a lair surrounded by stony figures, waiting for her next victim, like she is so often depicted today. In fact, for all I've scoured the ancient Greek sources available to us, there is not a single recognized instance of violence committed by Medusa while her head remained on her body.

Instead, much of how we view her monstrosity, that she struck fear into the hearts of men, that she seduced them to their deaths with her stony gaze, is much more reasonably read as post-antiquity male interpretation of a story that describes a powerful and deadly woman. She does no damage, so the fear of her is entirely based on her apparent monstrosity and the threat that she poses by simply continuing to exist, alive. She is feared purely because she is capable of hurting a man should he stumble into her 'lair' and, as these interpretations seem to suggest, be utterly incapable of resisting her.

The Medusa, and the Gorgon, as she survives from ancient Greece was, explicitly, a symbol of protection. There's little to no indication that ancient Greeks feared that a Gorgon might come upon them in the night, might strike and maim an unsuspecting victim. (There are a host of other monsters who serve this purpose and it may come as no surprise to hear that they are, also, all female). Instead, Medusa uses her monstrosity, her terror, to *protect*. She was meant to be scary, yes, but she was meant to be scary to the *aggressor*. Her petrifying gaze is a form of defence straight from the natural world and very well inspired by animals who have similar, if not literally *stony*, abilities. She is not meant to be feared unless you pose a threat to the person or place she is there to protect.

3.
Beyond Oceanos: Medusa's Ancient Evolution

Before the passage, horrid Hydra stands,
And Briareus with all his hundred hands;
Gorgons, Geryon with his triple frame;
And vain Chimaera vomits empty flame.
– Virgil, from the *Aeneid*, translated by John Dryden (1697)

THE UNNAMED GORGON

s I've mentioned, the concept of a Gorgon exists well beyond the named characters of Medusa, Stheno and Euryale. In addition to being the divine designation of the three sisters, the Gorgon is a creature that is at times equally separated from them. In other words, there can be a Gorgon without any Medusa, but there cannot be a Medusa without a Gorgon. This is somewhat unique among monstrous creatures. I can't personally recall any that exist so distinctly unnamed save maybe the Cyclopes or Gigantes (Giants). But neither come close to the level of ubiquity the Gorgons have across the

ancient Greek world and beyond. It's impossible to emphasize enough how widespread the imagery of Gorgons was in the broad world of ancient Greek art, architecture, and cult imagery. Representations of the unnamed Gorgon, often called Gorgoneia (plural of Gorgoneion), when they are just rendered as a bodiless head, have been found across nearly the whole of the ancient Mediterranean (and, as we'll see, she may have had origins even as far as the Mesopotamians in ancient Iraq). I don't want to suggest that these unnamed Gorgons weren't understood to be Medusa, only that they appear to exist with or without her individual name and its associated story.

A Face in the Aegis

The most famous and widespread place in which we find Medusa's face is in the goddess of warcraft and wisdom's shield. Athena's shield (which she inherited from Zeus, so it's sometimes referred back to him) is notorious for housing the original Gorgoneion. Sometimes it's not in a physical, handheld shield but in what's called her *aegis*, a kind of armour that is sometimes a breastplate or something that almost looks like a shawl, covering her shoulders and chest. Either way, this is where we often find the face of the Gorgon as a literal protective shield. Here her face serves as both a shield and a defensive weapon: she is terrible and frightening to anyone who sees her. And while in its place in the shield, Medusa no longer seems to have a *literally* petrifying gaze; she still remains arresting, instilling fear in the viewer, and so serves as a means of protecting the person who possesses her. This is true for all Gorgoneia, which we'll look at later. They are symbols of protection – apotropaic devices meant to protect the wearer or possessor and petrify the aggressor.

Homer's Gorgoneia

In the works of the Homeric tradition (the only surviving works that we know with near certainty preceded Hesiod's earliest named Medusa), the *Iliad* and the *Odyssey*, the notion of a Gorgon exists purely as a monstrous head that elicits utter terror in whoever sees it. This Gorgon appears on armour in the *Iliad*, most notably on Athena's aegis, where 'there was the head of the dread monster Gorgon, grim and awful to behold, portent of aegis-bearing [Zeus]' (Samuel Butler translation, 1898). In the *Odyssey*, rather than the Gorgon's face appearing on armour, it's suggested as a physical being in the Underworld that could be sent by its goddess, Persephone, to terrorize Odysseus. At the end of his experience with the ghosts of long-dead women and heroes, he describes the fear that gripped him: 'I was panic stricken lest [Persephone] should send up from the house of Hades the head of that awful monster Gorgon' (Butler translation, 1900).

The Phlegraean Gorgon

There is a Gorgon in Euripides' tragedy *Ion* (*c.* 413 BCE), which stands out as a particularly unique form of an otherwise ubiquitous monster. The Gorgon of this ancient Athenian playwright, at least as it appears in this play, wasn't a child of Phorcys and Ceto like the others, but was instead created of Gaia, Earth itself, during the divine war between the gods and the giants.

The Gigantomachy (basically 'War of the Giants') is a longstanding mythological tradition, depicted in countless visual representations but which doesn't survive in any detailed text form prior to Pseudo-Apollodorus. It was most commonly believed to have taken place on the Phlegraean Fields (now Campi Flegrei), a caldera outside modern Naples, Italy, where the volcanic nature of the land surrounding Vesuvius and the Campanian volcanic arc was believed to be a result of this divine war. The Gigantomachy is a great example of a myth we know was incredibly culturally important but which barely survives in text. In this war, it's the children of Gaia (the giants) against the Olympian gods and their allies.

Euripides, in *Ion*, presents the idea that during this war Gaia gave birth to a Gorgon to aid in battling the gods, who was then defeated by Athena and placed in her aegis. This Gorgon, we learn through dialogue between two characters in the play, had blood that was both poisonous and curative. The play's main character, Creusa (if you're familiar with Medea's story and find yourself confused, this is a different Creusa), possesses two drops of this Gorgon blood, one of which she says can poison (via the hair-snake's venom) and the other of which cures diseases and can even save a person's life.

Aside from how this blood plays into the plot of the tragedy, it presents a fascinating new version of the famed Gorgon. Though we don't have much in the way of other text sources for this Phlegraean Gorgon with its poisonous and curative blood, there's no reason to suggest it couldn't have existed in other traditions. Actually, Pseudo-Apollodorus presents a similar idea, but without the unique Gorgon. He notes that the god of healing, Asclepius, was given Gorgon blood and that of one side was deadly, and that of the other could raise the dead. And to return to Phlegraean Fields, Sicily and some of southern Italy have ancient Greek roots, having been Greek colonies for much of the ancient period, and are even now still heavily infused with Gorgon iconography.

That said, it's equally possible that Euripides invented this Phlegraean Gorgon as a plot device, since the poison is (unsurprisingly) a major plot point in the play. I don't think that's likely, personally, as there doesn't appear to be a reason why this Phlegraean Gorgon would be needed to fill in for Medusa. In fact, elsewhere Athena is given the epithet (kind of a nickname, in this case) 'slayer of Gorgo'. This could definitely be because she has Medusa's head in her shield, and helped Perseus, but it could also be more specifically referring to a different Gorgon, maybe the Phlegraean Gorgon, which she actually killed herself. Given that the Gigantomachy survives almost exclusively in detailed and widespread *visual* representations, just like the similarly commonplace unnamed or unspecified Gorgon, this lends itself to the idea there might have been two distinct ways of understanding Gorgons: one was a perhaps more primordial and all-powerful magical creature, with distinctly divine blood, and the other was the Medusa we know so well. This is the fun and fury of studying Greek myths: everything could also, possibly, be something else entirely, depending on the people telling the stories, the time period, the region in which they were told or popularized, or a whole host of other factors.

The Gorgon, Protector

The Gorgoneion, both as a protective device and more broadly, wasn't limited to Athena's aegis or depictions on armour. Across many centuries, and throughout the ancient Greek world and beyond, the Gorgoneion appeared on everything imaginable, from small seal stones and coinage; to a broad range of pottery painted in varying states of detail; to pieces, both painted or carved, which could have had countless possible origins and usages. The Gorgoneion is iconic; she is easily identifiable even as individual details can vary.

The Gorgoneion as she appears in most art, as I touched on at the beginning, has a wide, open mouth with her tongue lolling out; she has fangs or tusks, large teeth and wide eyes. She is sometimes bearded, other times bare-faced. She sometimes has wings among her hair of snakes, or hair that may or may not have easily identifiable serpents but somehow remains serpentine. The unnamed Gorgon, too, appears in many ancient finds as a full-body representation. She is unnamed, but she has a head, which could suggest she is meant to be one of the sisters, or Medusa before her death. That form, which has a similar head to the Gorgoneion and a body with wings spread, appeared on temple pediments and as ornamental statues on temples and other buildings. It's impossible to fully express just how ubiquitous a motif the Gorgon was, but she was almost certainly one of the most commonly depicted monsters.

The Gorgon Before Medusa

Though in surviving texts it's only the *Iliad* and the *Odyssey* that pre-date Hesiod's earliest named and sympathetic Medusa, it's still very possible that the Gorgon existed as something separate from Medusa and her sisters after Hesiod's naming of them. We always have to remember just how big and unconnected the ancient Greek world was; just because a source exists doesn't mean that it was known or acknowledged across the whole of the Greek world. We can say with almost certainty that an unnamed Gorgon, in at least the form of the Gorgoneion (that is, just the terrible head), existed prior to the concept of Medusa as an individual. What I think is most likely is that there are stories now lost to us which might have gone into even more detail about this Gorgon and its origins. And in that case, the story of Medusa as it appears in Hesiod, however brief, could have served as an explanation for previously existing Gorgoneia.

As we well know, the ancient Greeks loved to tell stories to explain the world they saw around them. This is true of the natural world, but also of buildings, ruins, or material objects that would have remained from earlier generations and which had by then lost whatever backstory they might have originally had. (Remember, there are just so many centuries of cultural evolution before the Greeks even had an alphabet with which to write anything down, let alone the centuries of cultural change that came after!)

If there existed a widespread tradition of a terrible being whose head was used as both a protective device and a method of instilling fear in the enemy, then it's not unlikely that later Greeks might wonder how, exactly, the monster's head came to be placed in Athena's aegis and elsewhere. It would also make sense, then, why the character of Medusa is mortal while her sisters are not. There is no explanation for this provided anywhere in the surviving Greek texts, but if someone is interested in inventing a backstory for the creatures, they would certainly be divine, and yet one of them must be able to be killed so that its head can, eventually, be placed in the aegis. What's even more interesting, though, at least in my opinion, is how sympathetic an origin story she was given. Why would they bestow one of the only sympathetic monster stories in all of Greek myth on a creature known exclusively to be petrifying? I think it suggests some kind of acknowledgment that she is petrifying explicitly as a defensive weapon, that while she was not dangerous while alive, as just a head she is something to be reckoned with.

MEDUSA THE BEAUTIFUL VICTIM

One of the most commonly told versions of Medusa's story features a transformation. In my experience, the most widespread versions in the zeitgeist (those that appear in online discussions and debates, storytelling and memes) typically fall into one of two categories: either she is a terrible creature who means certain death, or she was once a beautiful human woman. We'll return to the former, but first I want to talk about Medusa the beautiful victim.

This modern Medusa is found in nearly every discussion of her character; I've seen versions of it in endless Reddit threads and Tumblr memes, in fanfiction and personal anecdotes. She is so common that it's often difficult to find references to Medusa that don't mention this version of her, either defending that the beautiful human is the 'original' Medusa or denial of the same.

This beautiful Medusa's most prized attribute is her hair, and she is also often described as a priestess of Athena. This Medusa is raped by the god Poseidon while in Athena's temple. Athena witnesses the assault and chooses to punish her – Athena was famously a virgin goddess, a *parthenos* (really this means *childless* and *unmarried*, not the more comparatively modern concept of physical virginity), and so was said to be offended by the sexual display in her sacred space – transforming her beauty into a curse. Thus Medusa's hair was transformed into a mane of snakes, and her visage would from then on turn anyone who looked at her to stone. Sometimes there's an amendment to this Medusa, clarifying that *actually* it wasn't a punishment at all, but instead a means of preventing Medusa from ever being assaulted again.

There is, unsurprisingly, a lot to unpack in these versions of Medusa's story. Many of these details do, in fact, have basis in the ancient world, but they still represent a particularly unique version of the famed Gorgon's character, and one that is distinctly *not* ancient Greek.

Ovid's Lasting Influence

Many of the details of this modern Medusa are in fact Roman, rather than Greek. The version of Medusa's story where she is mortal and human (or at least appearing to be), assaulted by Poseidon in Athena's temple, and punished (or blessed, if that's your take) by the goddess, were likely invented by the Roman poet Ovid early in the first century CE, about 700–800 years after her Hesiodic storyline, the oldest that survives, which we looked at earlier.

Because Ovid's *Metamorphoses* is intended to tell stories of transformation, the wider story of Perseus's quest for Medusa is spread across multiple sections. I've included here a direct copy of the bit that's most relevant to Medusa. It begins as he speaks to the Ethiopians, having saved their princess Andromeda. This is the Brookes More translation (1922).

Ovid's Medusa, a Different Medusa

'There is,' continued Perseus of the house of Agenor, 'There is a spot beneath cold Atlas, where in bulwarks of enormous strength, to guard its rocky entrance, dwelt two sisters, born of Phorcys. These were wont to share in turn a single eye between them: this by craft I got possession of, when one essayed to hand it to the other. I put forth my hand and took it as it passed between: then, far, remote, through rocky pathless crags, over wild hills that bristled with great woods, I thence arrived to where the Gorgon dwelt. Along the way, in fields and by the roads, I saw on all sides men and animals – like statues – turned to flinty stone at sight of dread Medusa's visage. Nevertheless reflected on the brazen shield I bore upon my left, I saw her horrid face. When she was helpless in the power of sleep and even her serpent-hair was slumber-bound, I struck, and took her head sheer from the neck. – To winged Pegasus the blood gave birth, his brother also, twins of rapid wing.'

So did he speak, and truly told besides the perils of his journey, arduous and long – He told of seas and lands that far beneath him he had seen, and of the stars that he had touched while on his waving wings. And yet, before they were aware, the tale was ended; he was silent. Then rejoined a noble with enquiry why alone of those three sisters, snakes were interspersed in dread Medusa's locks. And he replied: – 'Because, O Stranger, it is your desire to learn what worthy is for me to tell, hear ye the cause: Beyond all others she was famed for beauty, and the envious hope of many suitors. Words would fail to tell the glory of her hair, most wonderful of all her charms – A friend declared to me he saw its lovely splendour. Fame declares the Sovereign of the Sea [note: Poseidon] attained her love in chaste Minerva's [Athena's] temple. While enraged she turned her head away and held her shield before her eyes. To punish that great crime Minerva changed the Gorgon's splendid hair to serpents horrible. And now to strike her foes with fear, she wears upon her breast those awful vipers – creatures of her rage.'

Metamorphosing Medusa

Because myth is amorphous, fluid and changing, we can't necessarily say this version is 'wrong', but we can accurately describe it as Not Greek. Ovid's story of Medusa's tragic fate is found in his *Metamorphoses*, a Latin epic poem that retells stories of transformation. Many of the characters and their origins have Greek roots, but Ovid expands upon a number of their stories and is often the only source that survives in any detail. The *Metamorphoses* is an incredible work from the ancient world and a fascinating source, but if we're to understand the contextual implications of his work and, specifically, Medusa's

Greek myth, we have to separate Ovid's alterations from their Greek origins. In the case of Medusa, Ovid makes a number of major changes to the story and characters that serve to sever it almost entirely from its Greek form. In Ovid, Medusa is not born a monster, and instead we presume her to appear human. She is beautiful, her hair is stunning, and she is sought after by suitors. In Ovid, Medusa is assaulted in Athena's temple, and the assault by Poseidon is explicit and violent. In Ovid, Medusa is punished, transformed by Athena for being raped in her temple.

Ovid's Medusa is interesting and deserving of analysis. It has provided countless new ways of understanding her character and has become a sort of survivor story, an emblem for people who have survived sexual assault. Today she is often used as a new kind of apotropaic, protective, device. She has value and I certainly don't seek to make her any less important or meaningful when I add: Ovid's Medusa, while powerful and valid, is not a Greek Medusa.

Because he is culturally and religiously Roman, Ovid's story is infused with the distinctly different culture in which he was writing. Though most of this isn't necessarily overt, it's obvious in his uses of the Roman names for their own Olympian gods: Poseidon becomes Neptune, Athena Minerva. (Often people will say that the Romans 'stole' their mythology from the Greeks in large part because of Ovid's work, but Ovid intentionally wrote stories with primarily Greek origins, and it's much more accurate to describe the Romans as having been inspired by the Greeks, along with many other ancient people of the region – something that is not at all unique to them.)

Ovid's changes to the story (that she was beautiful, assaulted in the temple, and punished with transformation) are interesting, certainly, but they also feel very removed from the versions we've looked at in the ancient Greek sources. Again, that doesn't make him wrong, but it does mean we need to put him into context. Not only is Ovid writing so much later than Medusa's most ancient versions, under the Roman Empire, but he is also writing in Rome during and soon after a time of enormous transition. Octavian Augustus had just taken control and changed Rome from a republic to an empire over which he ruled as Emperor (this is a huge simplification as I am happily not a Roman historian). He began introducing new laws and making major changes, including specifically things like morality laws. Augustus was very interested in what he saw as 'moral' and turned it into law. There's a lot of speculation as to how Ovid felt about Augustus. The *Metamorphoses* was ostensibly written in celebration of the emperor (the end literally tells the story of how Augustus became divinely ordained as their new leader), but it remains unclear whether he was writing Augustan propaganda seriously or satirically. On top of this, the work is explicitly written to tell stories of transformation, something that is not inherent in Medusa's Greek story. If she was going to be included, she needed to have a story of transformation, so Ovid invented one. Regardless of how Ovid felt about Augustus, this is where Medusa's story is being found and it does a disservice to her character to ignore the context surrounding the work. We can look to Minerva's reaction to the assault, too, as possibly relating to these morality laws.

Minerva, though she is often called plainly the 'Roman Athena', is ultimately another deity entirely. Where Athena was the Greek goddess of warcraft and wisdom, along with other crafts of more feminine association (weaving, for instance), the Roman Minerva was far less associated with war as compared to Athena. Even though Ovid was generally retelling stories with Greek origins, he is ultimately still writing the Roman Minerva, rather than the Greek Athena. I don't want to suggest that the Greek Athena was necessarily above such punishment, but it's still important (and interesting) to point out what it means that this work is Roman. It was, quite simply, an entirely different culture. Not only centuries removed from Hesiod's earliest Medusa, but also a different language, people and religion.

Again, this doesn't make Ovid's Medusa a 'wrong' Medusa; it just makes her a Roman or Ovidian Medusa. Ovid is re-interpreting something that he heard from a different culture from his own, and he's turning her into something new. It's a little more like fictional retellings today, just one from the ancient world.

Untethered from Ovid

There are a couple of details in the modern Medusa I mentioned earlier which are often said to be either her 'true story' or 'Ovid's version' but which, actually, don't appear in Ovid at all. Firstly, that she was originally a priestess of Athena. This is found in many, many versions of Medusa's story today, both culturally and in more formally published forms. I think it comes from her being assaulted in Athena's temple: people have taken that to imply that she was a priestess. It doesn't change much, really, to say that she was a priestess, but it's fascinating to me that it's become such a widespread idea even though it doesn't appear in Ovid.

The other major deviation is to suggest that Athena wasn't punishing Medusa but blessing her, saving her from a future of violence by making her the one with the capabilities for violence. Ovid, though, makes very clear that it is meant to be a punishment. Again, I don't share this to police modern understanding of her, only to point out what exists in the text and the ancient world. In the next section we'll look at what these modern ideas mean for her wider cultural identity today.

ANCIENT EVOLUTIONS: ATTEMPTS TO RATIONALIZE MEDUSA

A story like Medusa's naturally spawns attempts to explain her origins. This is true for both ancient and modern worlds. For as long as people have been questioning the background and origins of Greek myth, they've been questioning Medusa and the Gorgons. After all, there are lots of reasons to question the story as we know it. Flying horse and full-grown man birthed from a decapitation notwithstanding, the snakes-for-hair and petrifying gaze is ripe for interpretation.

It's easy to think of ancient Greece as a singular thing, a world of mythology and epics, playwrights and storytelling. A world where every person believed their mythology as divine truth. But, since the world of what we consider 'ancient Greece' spanned well over a thousand years, the knowledge and interests of the ancient Greek people varied across the centuries, let alone across the individual minds recording them. There wasn't a finite belief that the mythology developed over the centuries was true or even broadly known or accepted across the whole of the Greek world. Some people likely believed the stories to be based in some truth, and others sought to explain or understand how these fantastical stories came to be developed.

A number of ancient works survive that seek to rationalize myth broadly and Medusa specifically. They want to understand where the story came from, and how it may have fit into the real world. Not only are these interesting insights into ancient minds, but some of these attempts to rationalize her story are downright entertaining (there are pirates! warrior women! absurd levels of ancient misogyny! blood-born snakes!). Attempts to understand Medusa in the context of the real world survive from both Greek and later Roman authors, primarily during the later periods when people had developed a better understanding of the natural world and so were more likely to question the mythological histories of their ancestors.

Keep in mind, though, that while the ancient Greeks didn't conceptualize race and racism as we do today, there was still 'othering' of foreign cultures and people, particularly those they had limited contact with and thus had limited knowledge of. Both the word 'barbarian' and 'xenophobia' come from very relevant ancient Greek origins. Barbarian, essentially, referred to anyone who didn't speak Greek (it has onomatopoeic roots in the Greeks hearing indistinguishable words of non-Greek speakers!) and 'xenophobic' means, almost literally, 'fear of strangers'. As these are almost all stories of people foreign to the Greeks, it's important to remember that these are Greeks and Romans writing of cultures other than their own (the Romans also used the word 'barbarian' and there it tended to mean not Greek *or* Roman). But regardless of accuracy, these attempts to make Medusa into a real person who lived and died are a fascinating insight into how people attempted to understand stories from myth that were so removed from their later lived experiences and realities. Plus, like I said, warrior women and blood-born snakes.

Libya: The Land of Snakes

Many ancient Greek and Roman writers speak of the land of ancient Libya (what they called much of North Africa – don't worry about how that works with mythological/ancient Ethiopia; it's unnecessarily complicated) as home to many, *many* snakes. The deadliness of Libyan serpents is referenced in numerous works, along with the generally understood wildness of the region in the minds of the Greeks. (Again, I want to emphasize here, this is all the Greek and Roman imagination of a land and people they didn't know all that much about.)

Enter: Medusa. According to the Hellenistic epic poem by Apollonios, the *Argonautica* (third century BCE), and Ovid's *Metamorphoses* (early first century CE), the snakes that populated Libya were born of the blood that dripped from Medusa's severed head as Perseus flew with it over North Africa. Because of this, the famed snake-infested Libya (we can probably understand this as, simply, the ancient African continent had more, and certainly more deadly, snakes than the Greek world) was the perfect setting for attempts at real-world explanations of Medusa. Some later versions of her story situate her home with her Gorgon sisters as being in Libya itself (this might be because of the snakes but also fits into their more ancient and vague placement in the far west of the world, with the nymphs of the sunset).

Travels with Pausanias

Pausanias was a geographer – a travel writer – of Roman-period Greece (*c.* second century CE). He travelled the Greek world, spoke to locals, and recorded what he saw and heard. Not only is his work generally insightful into the real world in which he lived and travelled, but in many cases he is the only record we have for ancient structures that are long since lost. His work, creatively called *Descriptions of Greece*, details many instances of the Gorgoneia he saw on his travels. But there is one case where he blesses us with a note that he won't bother to retell the *myth*, but instead what he considers the *real* or *rational* story behind the beheading of Medusa.

Lady of the Lake

According to Pausanias, he places the real and human Medusa in Libya, as we will come to expect, and says that her father Phorcys reigned there around the lake called Tritonis. When Phorcys died, Medusa took her father's place as leader. Pausanias says that this Medusa not only reigned in place of her father, but that she hunted and even led her people into battle. It was during one of these battles that she fought Perseus, a man from the

Peloponnese, and was killed by him not during a battle but during the night as she slept.

This Perseus, we're told, was so in awe of Medusa's beauty that he removed her head and brought it back to show the Greeks at home.

(It was kind of a cool story until that end bit, wasn't it?)

Diodorus Siculus's Library of 'History'

Diodorus Siculus was a first-century-BCE Greek historian born in what is now Sicily (recall: it was historically an ancient Greek colony) and attempted to write what he considered to be a comprehensive history of humanity. He is also the author of what might be my favourite attempt at humanizing the Gorgons. We shouldn't consider the whole of his work to be any kind of true or confirmed history, but another insight into the minds of ancient people attempting to understand their own mythological history.

Gorgonian Amazons

In the case of the Gorgons, Diodorus speculates that the mythological characters are derived from a culture of ancient Libya, one populated with warrior women. He explains that Perseus waged a war with these warriors and that it was not only his greatest labour, but also that it was an example of the strength and skill of these warrior women (he also adds, so as not to suggest the women of his world attempt anything of the sort, that these Libyan warrior women are explicitly impressive *as compared* to women of his time). Diodorus connects them with the mythological Amazons, another 'race' of warrior women. He suggests the two groups were enemies, and both were eventually destroyed entirely by Heracles during his mythological labours in the region. Specifically, Diodorus explains that prior to their destruction, during the time Perseus waged war with these Gorgon warriors, they were led by a queen named Medusa. And, because misogynist associations with Medusa and the Gorgons are as timeless as the women themselves, Diodorus specifies that Heracles destroyed both the race of the Gorgons and the Amazons because, as the self-proclaimed hero of *man*kind, he couldn't permit any place in the world to be ruled by women (if you just rolled your eyes so hard it hurt, you're not alone).

This very slightly (the hope, it is so brief!) empowering attempt to rationalize and humanize the Gorgons, and Medusa specifically, is still hindered by the distinctly patriarchal and misogynist nature of the world in which these writers lived. This ancient writer could imagine the concept of women warriors, could *fathom* that they could be powerful and brave, but not without an addendum that they were killed off by ancient Greece's most important and all-powerful man, Heracles.

Palaephatus' Unbelievable Things

Like so many ancient sources, there's a work attributed to a person who maybe, probably, didn't actually write the work that's attributed to him. There are a whole host of issues when it comes to dating and confirming the text that we now call Palaephatus' *On Unbelievable Things*. The work, whoever wrote it at whatever time it was written (but certainly, it is ancient and Greek and thus worth looking at!), presents many famous moments and characters from Greek myth, explains why those moments and characters are too incredible to be true, and then gives the author's explanation for how the myth came into being.

The Gorgon: A Pirate's Tale

Palaephatus presents another story set in North Africa, by the ancient Pillars of Heracles (the strait of Gibraltar), where he places a king, named Phorcys, of an island called Kerne. These Kernaeans, he says, call Athena by the name 'Gorgo', and their king had a large gold statue made of the goddess. He died before the statue could be dedicated and his three unmarried daughters who survived him (unsurprisingly, Palaephatus names these Stheno, Euryale and Medusa) divided his possessions between them but were undecided on the statue, ultimately sharing it between their three treasuries. Phorcys left behind a companion whom the three daughters relied on for guidance and whom, as Palaephatus says, they called their 'Eye'.

According to Palaephatus, Perseus was a fugitive from the Greek city-state of Argos. He was a pirate who eventually captured the Eye. The Eye told Perseus about this gold Gorgo statue and its worth. Eventually the news gets back to the three sisters and they're told that if they give Perseus the Gorgo statue he'll free their Eye. Medusa opposed this, and for that he killed her but spared her sisters and returned the Eye. He took the Gorgo, cut it into pieces, and placed the head on the bow of his ship, which he renamed for the statue. Later, he came to the island of Serifos where he demanded money from the people there. They asked for a few days, and in that time found human-sized rocks which they placed in their city centre, then they fled. When Perseus returned for his money, he found only human-sized rocks, and so he used this as a means of instilling fear into people on other islands that he pirated, advising them not to behave like the people of Serifos, who saw the Gorgon's head and turned to stone.

Palaephatus' attempt to explain Medusa is an interesting one. While it seems to stretch the imagination and perhaps descend into a little minor absurdity, the idea of the Gorgons fighting against pirates in some way is thrilling!

More Unbelievable Things

There's another ancient work with the title *On Unbelievable Things*. This one is attributed to a man named Heracleitus (not the famous philosopher), but confirming the author's name or dating the work is, like Palaephatus, uncertain. Still, it is certainly ancient and it provides another bizarre insight into the tradition of rationalizing Medusa (plus it's weird and I think you should know it).

Cursed Courtesan

According to this attempt at understanding the bizarre story of a woman beheaded only to have a man and a flying horse spring from her neck (it's this author who chooses that detail of the myth to summarize before presenting his rationalization), this Medusa wasn't a monster, but instead a *hetaira*, a 'companion' (think 'escort' – these women were a high-end, wealthier form of ancient sex worker). She was said to be so beautiful that every man who saw her was so taken that they stopped to stare to such a degree that they were said to have turned to stone. She fell in love with a man named Perseus and, we're told, in doing so wasted her wealth and the best years of her life, growing old and lecherous. Women like this, the author notes, are sometimes called 'horses'. He then says that the story of Perseus taking her head was in fact him stealing her youth.

This attempt at rationalizing Medusa is gross for a great many reasons which I won't bother to explain, because, frankly, I hope it's obvious.

Lost Libyan Goddess?

Many stories and characters we know from Greek myth were, at least in some way, inspired by the mythos and traditions of people in the surrounding Mediterranean and beyond. Sometimes, too, there are hints to these origins in the stories themselves. Mythologically, the goddess Aphrodite was said to be born in the eastern Mediterranean off the coast of Cyprus. Historically, there's much to say about Aphrodite's at least partial origins in two more ancient eastern goddesses: Astarte, from the Phoenician people in the ancient Levant; and Ishtar (also called Inanna), from the Mesopotamian people in ancient Iraq. It's likely that her eastern origins came via Cyprus, and so that's where her mythological birthplace was located.

It's not impossible that something similar was happening with Medusa. That she is, at her most ancient, placed in the furthest west of the world, could be an indicator as to some kind of origin in that region. And later, when the ancient Greeks become more aware of those far reaches, that she is more specifically placed in Libya, North Africa, only seems to emphasize this possibility. In my research I've come across many claims of some kind of origin in a Libyan snake goddess, even that Medusa's snake hair could be linked with dreadlocks and so more explicitly symbolize some kind of connection with the people of some part of ancient North Africa. I haven't been able to find any explicit evidence of this, but I think it bears mentioning given the volume of attempts at rationalizing her as someone, divine or otherwise, who lived and ruled in North Africa. When we add in the many attempts to rationalize Medusa as not only a human woman from the region but one that is, in three instances, a ruling authority, and in two explicitly a formidable warrior woman, it suggests to me that there might be some truth to her Libyan origins. Or at least, that there were queens and warrior women of the region that Greeks encountered enough times, and were surprised enough to see there, that it influenced these rationalization attempts.

Inspired by the East

Medusa's story may place her in the west, but the Gorgoneion itself may have had origins in the east. Similarly to the idea of a lost Libyan goddess (though with more evidence that I can find), connections have been made between Gorgon iconography, specifically the disembodied head as I've already described it (but particularly the bearded versions), and the monstrous creature

Humbaba from the Mesopotamian mythology of ancient Iraq. Humbaba appears in the *Epic of Gilgamesh*, the oldest surviving epic poem (many versions exist in many forms, but it's generally from the very helpful and not at all broad period of 2100 BCE–1200 BCE). Having looked at representations of Humbaba, I can absolutely see where it might contain origins of Medusa and/or the Gorgoneion. There is also the possibility that the story of the heroes defeating the monster Humbaba equally inspired the story of Perseus and Medusa.

My bet is that the imagery of the Gorgon came from Humbaba and the story of Perseus and the named Medusa was added later, with inspiration from North Africa.

Travels Through Hell

Odysseus's near miss with a Gorgon in the Underworld in the *Odyssey* isn't the only instance of a Gorgon shade in the land of the dead. Likely inspired by the *Odyssey*, later authors continue to reference the idea that a kind of still-living Gorgon (in whatever way anything in the underworld 'lives'; perhaps 'animated' is a better word) resided in Hades' realm. The mythological Greek Underworld isn't a place easily conceptualized, so I'll only point out that it was ruled by Hades and Persephone (though the latter was a much more active ruler) and only a few select heroes made descents and later ascents from it (this is called a katabasis!). Likely the most famous Greek katabasis is achieved by Heracles when he travels to the Underworld to fetch Cerberus, the three-headed guard dog of Hades, as one of his labours. There, one of two figures who doesn't flee from Heracles is Medusa. He is said to have wielded his sword at her as though she were living, only to be told that she was merely a phantom.

Later, when the Roman poet Virgil wrote his *Aeneid* (late first century BCE), the Gorgons make another appearance in the Underworld. The *Aeneid* is intentionally very similar to the *Iliad* and the *Odyssey*. Unlike the Greek epics, the *Aeneid* was composed by one poet and meant to be read, rather than performed and originating from a culture of oral storytelling (and many argue it is explicit Augustan propaganda alongside Ovid's *Metamorphoses*). In the *Aeneid*, the Trojan hero Aeneas journeys from the remains of a now fallen Troy to the Italian mainland where he'll found a city that will lay the groundwork for Rome. Along the way, like Odysseus, he makes a stop in the Underworld and there he sees a great many monsters, the Gorgons among them.

Flash forwards 1,400 years and, once more, Medusa appears in the Underworld. In Dante Alighieri's fourteenth-century-CE work the *Inferno*, Virgil himself guides a fictionalized version of Dante through what is now distinctly the Catholic version of Hell. Though Christian, Dante's Hell is heavily inspired by the Classical world, specifically the *Aeneid* (if that isn't obvious from Virgil being the literal guide), and so there too we see not only the Gorgons but Medusa specifically. Or, rather, she is referenced as a threat rather than explicitly depicted. Instead, Dante and Virgil encounter the Erinyes, the Furies of Greek myth (another three divine women with a heavy emphasis on snakes), who threaten them with Medusa's stony gaze. This Stygian version of Medusa isn't ancient, but is so heavily inspired by the Classical versions that I couldn't resist including her.

THE CLOSEST WE CAN GET TO AN 'ORIGINAL MYTH'

Have I shared a few Too Many Medusae, I wonder? My personal obsession with her as a character is heavily rooted in the sheer volume of options we have. I am most interested in the wide range of interpretations, both in surviving texts and images, and whatever might have existed in between. I recognize, though, that for the casual reader or someone new to Medusa's story, this might be utterly overwhelming and you might find yourself with a desperate need for some kind of certainty. So, if we were to pick one Medusa to be the most 'accurate' in whatever way that is possible, let's look at who and what she would be and why.

As I've made annoyingly clear, there is no 'canonical' Medusa, no 'true story', but that doesn't mean we can't look through the versions and pull out what might be considered the most mythologically sound. Medusa is, by nature, a creature and being from Greek myth, so any singular version of her should be based in the Greek tradition. That means we'll politely push Ovid's Medusa to the side (but we will revisit what makes her special to many women of today, I promise) and focus on her Greek origins. In my opinion, a singular story for Medusa looks like a combination of Hesiod's Medusa and Pseudo-Apollodorus's (much like the simplified version I provided in the first section). Hesiod because it is the oldest and based on an oral tradition that defined much of the mythological works that followed it. And Pseudo-Apollodorus because while it is late, it intended not to reimagine myth but to syncretize what existed. There is no reason to believe that his attempt at her story was anything other than the cultural tradition of his time, one that would have been built on all that came between his time and Hesiod's.

A Medusa that combines these two works into one woman is, I believe, the closest we can possibly get to a 'true story' or 'original myth' of Medusa. That Medusa would have the long, plot-driven narrative of Pseudo-Apollodorus and the more complex and sympathetic origin of Hesiod. A singular Medusa, to me, is the Medusa I described at the very beginning of this piece. She is a Gorgon, a divine creature born monstrous but not ugly (what is ugly, anyway, but a subjective judgement of appearance); she is mortal but not helpless, innocent but not virginal; she is a creature, but a woman too, killed not because she posed a threat but because she was, simply, killable; she is a disembodied head, a defensive weapon and a shield, terrible and protective, she does not maim but defend; and she is – finally, in death – immortal.

4.
Mythical Maiden, Modern Monster

Become a [ ] and ever-shifting mirror
Of all the beauty and the terror there –
A woman's countenance, with serpent locks,
Gazing in death on heaven from those wet rocks.
– Percy Bysshe Shelley, from 'On the Medusa of Leonardo da Vinci in the Florentine Gallery'

2,000 YEARS OF TRANSFORMATION

nlike almost any other character derived from ancient Greek myth, the modern Medusa is today defined more by modern manipulations to her character than anything found in the surviving ancient Greek sources. A Google search for Medusa brings up images of a (in the Western imagination) stereotypically beautiful woman. Usually she has light skin and, of course, snakes for hair. These modern Medusae are at times haunting or terrifying, screaming in fury or crying out in agony. But she is almost always beautiful, seductive, and distinctly *human*. If she is not human in her modern forms then she is

something out of a horror movie (and a misogynist one, at that), shrieking and snarling in hysterical rage. Rarely, if ever, do these modern Medusae resemble the Gorgon of ancient Greece, a creature who is distinctly *inhuman*, a monster both terrible and sympathetic, while, explicitly and inarguably, protective rather than violent.

This entirely new Medusa exists only in small part because of the internet age, even if it may be easy to blame Reddit memes for the Gorgonian sins of humanity. There are over 2,000 years between Ovid's Medusa, reasonably defined as a sort of last 'ancient' Medusa and the Medusae of today.... And most of those 2,000 years have been defined by men, so very many men, and all their many opinions, fears and interests in the only mortal Gorgon. Fortunately, the last century has seen a resurgence in women's appreciation of her and many attempts to 'take back' Medusa's story and character. Here we're going to look at some of the ways Medusa has been defined over the last 2,000 years, and how many women now seek to claw her away from the tight grip of the patriarchy.

Medusa's Renaissance

Throughout the history of the Western world, Medusa has remained one of the most well known and recognizable characters. Maybe it's not so impressive that she is recognizable (she is unique), but that she has remained a beloved subject for artists for the last 3,000 or so years is quite the feat. During the Italian Renaissance, and into later periods of art history, a very human-like Medusa was a common motif and in most cases is one they seem to have had sympathy for. Even when she is sympathetic, though, she remains arresting, startling, just as she was in the world of ancient Greece. I could spend hours talking about the many forms of Medusa in art from the last 500-plus years, but I will share only two pieces with you now. To me, they are two of the most impactful representations of Medusa and they do this in two very different ways.

Caravaggio's painting *Medusa* (1597) is one of his most iconic uses of chiaroscuro: strong contrasts between darkness and light. For Caravaggio, Medusa is distinctly human save for her hair of snakes. Her head has only just been sliced from her body and blood drips from her neck. She is surprised, just as the viewer is meant to be, by the horror. Her face is etched with fear and disgust and anguish, an expression we're to assume will remain in death. The painting perfectly encapsulates the moment of utter terror and sadness, when her life is ended for no reason other than she, alone, was killable.

Bernini's *Medusa* (*c.* 1640), comparatively, is not newly killed but still very *alive*. His sculpted Medusa is just as human as Caravaggio's, but in an entirely different way. She is young and lively, not horrified or terrible at all, but content. Her snakes, too, are full of life and character; some nestle into her head, others nip at one another playfully. These snakes are not monstrous, but friendly and loving; they're just as much a part of her as anything else.

In both depictions Medusa is the subject, unlike so many other famous representations where she is only a head for Perseus to wield. In these, she is a real person who has either just experienced the worst possible fate, or is living in a lovely sort of ignorance of what's to come.

From Sympathetic to Loathsome

Somewhere in the long history of Medusa, she transformed. It wasn't a metamorphosis like the one detailed in Ovid, but a slow shifting of how we perceive not only her as a character, but her story. I wish I could trace how, exactly, this happened, or when, but her history is just as enigmatic now as it was then. Instead, we'll look at what it means that her story has been so thoroughly manipulated.

One of the most common refrains you'll find when speaking to people about Medusa, or when reading modern descriptions of her story, is that she was dangerous. This manifests in different ways. Some will say that she lived surrounded by the stone statues of her victims, or that she terrorized the lands where she lived, that she was an evil force whose death provided some kind of relief. Some descriptions of her so-called evil nature go even further. I once heard someone describe her death as a kind of necessary, balancing force for the universe. That her presence in the world was so negative and harmful that her death alleviated some existential weight. These kinds of arguments and interpretations often sound well researched and give an air of ancient spirituality, as though the ancient people saw her this way, that they saw the necessity in her demise, even that it helped them in some way. Unfortunately – or perhaps fortunately, for Medusa – these arguments have no basis in the ancient sources as they survive for us today.

In the ancient world Medusa was feared, certainly, but I don't believe there's any evidence to suggest she was feared in the same way she often is today. Today you find her and her Gorgon sisters described in very distinct ways. As I've dug through individual people's reactions and debates about her in YouTube comments, Reddit threads, podcasts and even my own Twitter replies, a very distinct version of Medusa appears. She is often seen as an 'abomination'; she is 'disgusting', 'hideous' and 'animalistic'; she 'terrorized the lands' and thus her death was 'necessary', maybe it even alleviated some 'weight' on the world.

Navigating Her Stony Victims

In the ancient Greek sources that survive, there are no confirmed victims of the living Medusa. There is no reference to her living surrounded by those unfortunate enough to have encountered her, who saw her face and turned to stone (Ovid is the first to suggest this). There are no references to violence or terror committed by her; there are no references, even, to anyone who might have feared her while she lived. She was not a monster meant to be killed for the greater good. She was not like the Hydra, the many-snake-headed beast who terrorized the lands of Lerna and who was defeated by Heracles; she was not like the Chimera, the lion-goat-snake hybrid that breathed fire over the plains of Anatolia; she was not like the Minotaur in the Labyrinth, feasting on young Athenians. Medusa, as her story survives in the ancient Greek sources, does not have a single victim that we know of. That is, until a man removed her head from her body and turned it into a weapon.

MISOGYNY'S BOGEYWOMAN

The modern idea that Medusa was inherently evil, villainous and violent, and so Perseus did the world a kindness by defeating her, persists to the point where it often overshadows her ancient origins. It's perpetuated by more reputable sources, too. Anthologies that purport to retell the ancient myths for modern audiences sometimes feature this disgusting, violent Medusa. A book simply titled *The Greek Myths* (Waterfield, 2011) describes the Gorgons as once-beautiful women, with all three punished by Athena for Medusa's 'coupling' (as this author calls it) with Poseidon in the goddess' temple. For this, Athena turns all three into monstrous Gorgons. There is a later suggestion, too, that the reason the Hesperides held gifts to aid Perseus was because Poseidon was afraid the Gorgons would terrorize the world and thus would require defeat by a hero. Even setting aside this gross conflation with Ovid's Medusa in a book purported to tell Greek myths (to utilize Ovid's exclusive storyline of Athena's punishment while denying the explicit rape contained within the same feels particularly nefarious), this includes inventions by the author which substantially change the story as it actually survives. These sorts of books are required to expand on the stories because they survive in such brief forms, but often then serve to invent or perpetuate notions that problematize an already fraught character. As I've laid out in the ancient sources surrounding her, and the iconography that existed, this idea of her posing a threat while alive is pretty plainly untrue for the ancient myth of Medusa.

That isn't to say we shouldn't read between the lines when it comes to how she might have been imagined in the ancient world, but readings like these threaten to, if not explicitly, cross a line where what we know as the ancient myth becomes lost in new details that are at best unfortunate manipulations to the story and at worst infuse modern misogyny into an ancient character. When Medusa becomes a dangerous creature who has left countless victims in her wake and thus requires killing, she no longer resembles what we know from the ancient world and instead becomes a stereotype for female rage and male response to it. It's an invented justification that makes Perseus the good guy and Medusa the villain, a woman who is wrathful and disgusting and whose death is a blessing.

We can and should understand Medusa and the Gorgons to have been terrifying figures in the ancient world, but not in this way. There's no reason to suggest that she was imagined to have been a danger while alive, or that she was considered a threat to humanity. Instead, she is terrifying as an idea, and explicitly terrifying after her death. Her nature was a threat, but it was a threat to those who threatened her; it was a defence mechanism straight out of the natural world. She petrified, but in defence of herself and, later, in death, those who possessed her image. To invent a villain arc that turns her and her defence mechanisms into a screeching, seductive female bent on killing heroic men with a simple look is pure misogyny. This form turns Perseus into a hero more righteous than he was, thereby also manipulating how the ancient Greeks saw their heroes (they were not meant to be flawless beacons of good, but complex characters who sometimes did terrible things). These forms untether both Medusa and Perseus from their ancient origins to create something entirely new and which is rooted in deeply anti-woman sentiments. These Medusae scream of fearing strong women who can defend themselves against the threat of men. They embody the patriarchal order and take a story of a woman defending herself against a man and turn her into a horrible monster who killed for the thrill of it.

Medusa was a monster in the ancient world, she was terrible and frightening, but what we actually know of her makes clear she was not a danger to innocents and instead protected them against aggressors. That isn't to say some of the ancient Medusa isn't also infused with misogyny, but the modern form is virulent; it suggests that a woman who is monstrous, unappealing to men, and who can defend herself against those who would hurt her, is a threat deserving of annihilation.

Psychoanalysing Snakes

When I see a snake, I immediately think of a penis, don't you? I'm lying, obviously, in an attempt to channel Sigmund Freud (before immediately realizing what a horrific idea that is). Before I continue, I must admit that I am not particularly interested in psychoanalysing anything from Greek myth. I do, however, have an interest in how men of the early twentieth century (let alone earlier) psychoanalysed Medusa, because of how it contributed to modern perceptions of both her and women broadly. Medusa may have been a monster, but at her heart she was a woman, and that womanhood is inextricably tied with her not only in the ancient world but also, much more explicitly, in the modern one.

To Freud, it seems, Medusa serves only to remind men of the terror they first felt at seeing a vagina. He wrote of Medusa in an essay called 'Medusa's Head' (1922). I am paraphrasing, and perhaps unfairly, but it seems that his idea about Medusa's true nature was that her decapitation symbolized the fear of castration, particularly as boys would fear it upon the sight of genitals that are lacking a penis. It appears to be a very blunt reading, suggesting that all forms of decapitation are inherently reminiscent of castration (I am not convinced this is a universal idea). Perhaps it is my own lack of a penis that prevents me from understanding why such a sight would immediately instil a fear of having one's own genitals removed, but alas, I am incapable. To Freud, also, the snakes of Medusa's hair must symbolize a woman's pubic hair while simultaneously acting as a kind of balm to the fear of castration by also representing replacement penises.

A friend of Freud's, neurologist Sándor Ferenczi, also wrote about Medusa and this seemingly universal fear of castration in a piece called 'On the Symbolism of the Head of Medusa' (1923). He mostly agrees with Freud's interpretation, confirming that in analysing dreams he has repeatedly found that the terrible Medusa is a symbol of women's genitals. Not to forget the more pressing fear, though, he is explicit in noting that the snakes of Medusa signify a lack of penis. Not to be outdone by his friend, Ferenczi adds that the fearsome image of Medusa itself is really the terrified expression that a child makes upon seeing a penisless genital (note, he does not clarify he means a male child, which frankly leaves me with even more questions). And finally, in case we weren't already overwhelmed by all the penises introduced by the pair, Ferenczi emphasizes himself by noting that there is of course yet another meaning to the fearsome, stony gaze of Medusa, and that is to represent erections.

One wonders if, just maybe, not everything in this world needs to be compared to male genitalia? Or, if that is too much of a stretch, maybe female genitalia does not need to explicitly be analysed for what it lacks compared to males'? As I have been perpetually reminded writing this section, though, I do not have a penis and, thus, like Medusa, I too represent the horrors of castration.

I don't mean to suggest that a phallic reading of Medusa's snakes is entirely out of the question, just that to tear down her story so that it represents nothing other than penises or a lack thereof is perhaps unfair to a character whose legacy spans 3,000 years and whose image (which, in its most Gorgoneion forms, has barely recognizable snakes, let alone anything particularly phallic) was one of the most widely represented forms of protection in the ancient Greek world. The ancient Greeks knew very well how to present phalloi, so we can't fault them for a lack of skill.

I don't include these sections purely to poke fun at the theories (though that was an added perk), but to emphasize the idea that so much of what we think we know of Medusa today, how we understand her character and her fate, is based almost entirely in male fear of powerful women. In my opinion, Medusa best represents the functions of the patriarchal order. She was a woman who could defend herself and that in itself represents the patriarchy's biggest threat. I say this with not only this work of extensive research into Medusa in the ancient world and in modern feminism and patriarchal structures, but another seven or so years of not only researching her but being faced with the wrath of modern men who so fear the power of a monstrous woman like Medusa that they've taken it upon themselves to tell me just how dangerous, how violent, how deadly Medusa was, how she terrorized the lands for so long, leaving so many victims in her wake, that surely Perseus's killing of her was a blessing for all humanity, a lightening of the world's evils, for that, really, is just how evil Medusa was. (Yes, these are all paraphrases of things that men have said to me over the years I've spent speaking about Medusa exactly how she appears in the ancient sources.)

He Said, She Said

It's not that Medusa isn't symbolic of male fear, just that I don't believe there's any real evidence to suggest that that fear had anything to do with genitals (but again, perhaps there is something I am lacking that keeps me from realizing what Freud believed was so obvious!). There are many monsters of Greek myth that can be reasonably read as representing, in some way, men's fear of women, but Medusa is almost certainly the most famous. She, like many monstrous and even divine women of Greek myth, can be seen not necessarily as representing something particularly specific that men feared in women (though that's possible too, at least for Medusa), but instead as the broader fear of the potential inherent in strong women. Like much of the Western world's ancient origins, the ancient Greek world (at least, post-Bronze Age, if not a bit earlier) was incredibly patriarchal in its structure. I need to generalize a little, across the millennia of Greek history that I'm referring to, but by and large women were not particularly enfranchised. Archaic and Classical Athens, where much of our legal and cultural text evidence comes from, was arguably the most strict. Higher rank women – that is, wives or daughters of citizen men – were considered property of their fathers until they were property of their husbands. They were, generally, expected to remain in their homes for much of their lives, raising children and tending to the household. This, like Medusa, is evidence of the ways in which men subjugated women in order to ensure they were as unthreatening to the patriarchal order as possible. There was a distinct fear of the reproductive power of the uterus; questions of paternity are in part why women were confined (lest they run off and be impregnated by the first man they meet!) and likely why so many myths feature divine impregnation. Athenian citizenship was incredibly strict and passed through only the male line, so ensuring your children were actually yours was a major concern.

Further back, in both the historical and the mythological record, we can see evidence of this slow subjugation taking place over time. The evidence from pre-Bronze Age cultures in ancient Greece is highly suggestive of primarily goddess worship (so many goddess figurines!), and even in the Bronze Age there are suggestions that goddesses were worshipped more widely than gods. By the time we have stories and texts that survive to tell us anything substantial about these goddesses, they've been brought to heel. The *Theogony* is, aside from being Medusa's oldest source, the earliest record we have for a historical hierarchy of the gods. In its cosmogony, leftover evidence of this slow devolution and subjugation of more powerful goddesses can be found. Gaia, earth, is literally covered on all sides by the husband she created to be her partner and he later traps her own children within her when he finds them to be a threat. Similar instances happen throughout the lineage of the gods, down the generations, with the goddesses becoming less and less powerful, until they are sufficiently lesser than their male counterparts.

It's not a stretch to see something similar happening in Medusa's story. She 'lays with' Poseidon (I promise, we're not finished with what this may mean) and then, narratively, is immediately killed by Perseus not because she was in any way violent, but purely because she was, firstly, able to be killed and, secondly, had the potential for violence if threatened. This is why he quite literally sneaks up on her while she is sleeping. She could have posed a threat to the gods, to the male power structure, and thus she couldn't live.

Her Hair Is Full of Secrets

There may be no 'true' story of Medusa, no 'original myth', but there are certainly modern versions we might fairly call *wrong* if only because they bear little to no resemblance to any source that survives (and often contain problematic inventions, whether they're intentional or not). I don't mean to suggest this is true of modern fictional adaptations, only versions that are presented as telling her story as it appeared in the ancient world. This is most rampant, as we might expect, in the wide realm of internet 'sources', but that doesn't stop them from muddying the waters for anyone seeking to learn of her.

It certainly doesn't need to be said that you shouldn't trust everything you read online, but there's something about Medusa's story and how it's been manipulated and corrupted through websites that purport to carry at least somewhat accurate versions of Greek myths that feels egregious. Because of how many places house misinformed retellings of her supposedly 'true myth', it's often difficult to find versions of her story that have grounding in the ancient sources as they survive, particularly if someone doesn't know what they're looking for.

For instance, places where one might hope to find an accurate (or close to it, at least) version of her story – that is, sites which purport to retell stories from Greek myth with accuracy – often contain not only the perpetuation of mythologically inaccurate details but other details which are invented and corrupt the story entirely. These can seem like small adjustments, the addition of descriptions here and there, but which ultimately hinge on misogynist and/or racist constructs. 'Versions' like these (really they are fictionalizations) often utilize common details from Ovid's Medusa as the basic plot (i.e. the notion that she was once beautiful and human and cursed by Athena) but add particularly descriptive details which nudge them from simply 'inaccurate according to the surviving sources' and into the territory of gross problematizing.

Adjusting Human Empathy

There are many places where you might find Medusa, when she was human, described as being a 'priestess of Athena' who was transformed and made 'ugly'. The original beautiful Medusa is often described as being 'light or fair-skinned' or having 'golden hair'. The transformed Medusa might be described as 'hideous', 'ugly', or a 'hag'. The details can seem minor, just additions to flesh out a plot and its characters, but they have much wider ramifications.

There's a 'documentary' clip that comes up as one of the first results of a Google search for Medusa. It's a little dated, certainly, but made by a major production company, aired on a network that (at least at one point) purported to air documentaries, features the talking heads of reputable names in ancient history, and yet it is not only inaccurate in its description of 'the myth' but also descends into not-so-thinly veiled misogyny in its depiction of her.

It begins by describing the story of Medusa, a being particularly insightful into the minds of ancient men who, we're to believe, are likely to be inherently fearful and threatened by the idea of a bewitching, seductive woman, of women who hold some kind of power over them, who devour and consume. It suggests that men being fearful of such a thing is a reasonable and justified fear and that because of this, the story of Medusa was considered one of the most terrifying stories for all ancient Greeks. The story proceeds much the same as Ovid's version (itself an issue given the rest of the video and experts are seeming to explicitly discuss the *Greek* myth) with some notable changes: here they repeat the commonly used detail that she was a priestess of Athena and that that was what led to her being assaulted by Poseidon. This is then inherently linked to the notion of purity that is then contaminated by both the assault and Athena's revenging curse. Once this Medusa is cursed (the 'documentary' includes very dramatic and special-effect filled re-enactments), she transforms from a beautiful, pure woman into a terrible monstrous hag. Once transformed by Athena, this Medusa not only has snakes for hair and a petrifying gaze, but she appears to age approximately 100 years. The story continues on much as Ovid's does, with Perseus eventually coming to kill her and remove her head for his own use.

It might be easy to dismiss something like this as simply telling Ovid's version of the story, but looking closer at both the story being told and the descriptions provided by the experts it becomes clear that there is far more at play, intentional or otherwise. Versions like this are often presented as being sympathetic to Medusa, and that's certainly the case for the documentary clip. These changes are quite common in modern versions of her story, and we've looked at them elsewhere already: she becomes a pure, virgin priestess of Athena and her transformation turns her from beautiful to ugly. The adjustments to the story might seem minor; they don't ultimately transform the narrative itself, but they do transform Medusa.

Priestess of Purity

By making Medusa both beautiful and seductive while also a priestess of Athena, Medusa is immediately made into a virgin due to the nature of Athena as a virgin goddess whose priestesses were meant to be the same. If Medusa is a seductive virgin who's then assaulted by Poseidon, then Athena's wrath can be aligned with the corruption of Medusa's purity rather than the assault itself (which Ovid made very clear is the issue; it isn't about purity). If the sexual assault by Poseidon is due in part to her alluring nature and the results of which are about a loss of virginity (something inherently tied to the structures of the patriarchy and ancient misogyny) rather than about a physical assault on a woman's mind and body, the impact of the crime is lessened. The more dangerous corruptions to Medusa's story, though, come when versions attempt to describe her as a beauty transformed. What is, mythologically, a monstrosity that comes naturally to her and is never suggested to be inherently *ugly*, becomes a trauma inflicted on her. The implication, then, is that when Medusa is 'good' she is beautiful and pure, and when she is 'evil' she is ugly and terrible.

WHAT MAKES A MONSTER?

A kind reading of these versions of Medusa as inherently evil, dangerous and deserving of death is based in her status as a 'monster'. There is an assumption based on that descriptor that monster must equal dangerous and danger must equal victims and victims must equal punishment for the monster. Medusa and the Gorgons were monsters, certainly, but what does it mean to be a monster in the ancient Greek world? Broadly, the notion of monstrosity means that she was not human and not anthropomorphic like the gods and nymphs. It implies that she was feared and that there was something about her inhumanity that inspired that fear. In the case of Medusa, I think we can safely determine her monstrosity to be her snake-like hair and that her gaze is petrifying, let alone the other features we see in Gorgon iconography. What is not inherent in this word 'monster' is actual violence – victims of the monstrosity. It also does not inherently mean there was anything wrong with her or the Gorgons; it does not imply 'ugliness' or a kind of opposite of beauty in whatever way we want to define either word.

Modern Monstrosity

Though a Google image search might seem to imply an undeniable humanity and femininity in modern Medusae, her on-screen and full-body representations of the last century tend towards a kind of monstrous snake-human hybrid. Made popular by movies like *Clash of the Titans* (1981 and 2010), a visualization of Medusa's body often depicts her with a human-like top-half and serpentine bottom. Almost as if she were a mermaid, but in place of a fish tail is a snake's. Even with this distinctly monstrous form, though, she still tends to have seductive and feminine qualities. This is less true for the original movie, though there she could certainly still be read as 'ugly'. Whereas in the remake, they introduce the story from Ovid and suggest Medusa was once a beautiful woman, punished by a goddess. Adding a sympathetic origin, though, does little when the transformed Medusa becomes a more overt reference to male fear of a beautiful, defensive woman. In so many ways, the terrifying or violent versions of Medusa today remain the same as they have been for centuries. When Medusa is seen as a threat to the hero, she is beautiful and seductive while simultaneously terrible and deadly, and it reads more like a glimpse into the psyche of someone who has felt wronged by a woman they found beautiful but who didn't want them back.

The Monstrously Ugly

Ovid's version of Medusa's story does explicitly mention that prior to her transformation by Athena, Medusa was beautiful and her hair was her most prized feature. He does not, however, claim that she is explicitly *human*, nor does he describe what her beauty looks like in any detail. He also, very notably, does not describe Medusa's transformed form as ugly or even unattractive. In fact he doesn't imply that any part of her transformed besides her hair becoming a collection of snakes. And yet, in countless places, Medusa's transformed form is described as 'ugly' and even 'hag-like' (the Waterfield book I mentioned earlier ostensibly describes her new form like the typical Gorgon, but manages to add that they were 'drooling' and had 'decaying skin').

I don't mean to suggest that the monstrous Medusa was what we might consider beautiful by today's standards, but instead that labelling her either beautiful or ugly is unnecessary and based in inherently misogynist ideas about who does or does not hold value. The term 'hag' possesses the same implications; it implies a decrepit old woman who no longer holds the same value as when she was beautiful. The word is also often used to describe both the Gorgon's Graiae sisters (who are, mythologically, just *grey*) and Medusa herself, and many visual representations of her can easily earn the adjective 'hag'. Even if they don't mean to, both ways of describing Medusa (and women, broadly!) suggest they are less worthy than their more beautiful counterparts, that they don't hold the same value. And that value is, of course, ultimately defined entirely by men even when it is women using these terms themselves. Setting the misogyny aside, the words 'beautiful' and 'ugly' are so inherently subjective as to become impossible adjectives with which to describe Medusa very specifically. Who, after all, could possibly make those judgements? To set eyes on her is to turn to stone, so it's objectively impossible to call her 'ugly' in any meaningful way.

The Monstrously Beautiful

We can't talk about ugliness as a patriarchal structure without doing the same for beauty. I don't describe Medusa as not 'ugly' in order to imply that she was 'beautiful'. Ugly might be the literal opposite of beautiful, but that doesn't mean if she isn't one then she must be the other. Beauty, too, is defined not by the viewed but by the viewer, and just as how we conceptualize ugliness today, it is also ultimately based in a misogynist structure of who is and is not attractive to men. I don't want to suggest that these are the only ways to define beauty or ugliness, just that our cultural ideas of both, in the Western world, are based in the patriarchal structure of that world. We can and should redefine both, but until the patriarchy no longer defines our lived experiences, we're stuck with these archaic ideas. Ovid defines Medusa as having been originally beautiful, and so often people today latch onto that idea with the intention of it being more sympathetic to her plight. I don't mean to offend those who've found comfort in this beauty, just to point out that I find it to be misguided. To say that she was once beautiful and turned ugly, or even simply monstrous, because of the actions of a man is no more kind to her story than to imagine her born a Gorgon, born monstrous. To be born monstrous is not to be born ugly, so adding former beauty does nothing but suggest that she was something that needed to be fixed or restored. Instead, if we view Medusa as a person who was simply born monstrous and with no concept of this being anything other than who she was, we empower both her as a character and women more broadly, women who seek not to be defined by the patriarchal structures of beauty and ugliness.

(Western) Empathy and Whiteness

Similarly to these inherently misogynist notions of Medusa's appearance after her transformation, the way she is portrayed before it has similarly problematic implications. When describing the Ovidian Medusa when she is understood to be 'beautiful', modern versions often want to provide specific details as to what that beauty looked like. In nearly all modern descriptions I've come across, Medusa's physicality is described as being fair- or light-skinned and/or that she has golden hair (in one instance I found her skin described as 'milky-white'!). Again, these little details might seem minor, but they not only dramatically alter the visual representations of Medusa but also have wider ramifications.

If and when Medusa is described as residing in any non-mythological lands, it's North Africa. As we saw across a number of sources, the ancient Greeks and Romans were in fairly broad agreement that if Medusa and the Gorgons ever lived on earth, they lived in Libya. Describing the explicitly sympathetic and 'beautiful' Medusa as being light-skinned with light hair implies that in order to be properly sympathetic and beautiful, she must have fallen into the stereotypically white ideas of beauty. From a translational standpoint, 'fair-skinned' appears often in English translations of ancient Greek texts, but the ancient Greek isn't meant to imply 'light' but rather 'nice' or 'appealing'. This screams of modern racism even if Medusa wasn't explicitly placed in Libya. There is a longstanding issue of placing modern notions of whiteness on the people and mythology of ancient Greece; it's a much wider issue than just Medusa. For her, specifically, not only does it erase her connection with the African continent, but by including those details so explicit in the version of her story where she was once a beautiful woman transformed into a monster, suggests that in order for Medusa to be both relatable and sympathetic, she must resemble the people we now describe as 'white'. That isn't to suggest these details always have racist intentions behind them; instead they are indicative of how much of the English-speaking world conceptualizes beauty and the type of woman who is deserving of sympathy.

MEDUSA THE FEMINIST

Today Medusa is both an icon of modern feminism and survivors of assault, and a bogeywoman for misogynists (the two are not unrelated). She has become a symbol of strength and resilience, of the power of women and the fear that power instils in men who see it as a threat to their dominance. Feminists use her as a symbol and so misogynists continue to perpetuate the idea of her as a dangerous creature who deserved her death (not unlike, I imagine, how many of them see feminism itself).

Years ago, shortly after the height of the #MeToo movement, a statue of Medusa holding Perseus's severed head made the news. Luciano Garbati's statue 'Medusa with the Head of Perseus' was sculpted in 2008, but in 2020 it had a major resurgence of popularity as a means to reclaiming the strength of Medusa. It isn't a favourite of mine, but its newfound popularity served to remind the broader world of Medusa's story in a meaningful way. It's not lost on me, though, that it took a man's statue of her to reignite broader interest in her 3,000-year-old story.

Medusa the Victim

Today, Ovid's version of Medusa is often described as being the 'true story' not because of anything about the dating of the source or its intentions, but because modern women have found a kind of connection with that version of her. She has become an emblem for women who have been victimized by men and found strength in Medusa's story. Using Ovid's Medusa in this way often comes along with the additional piece I mentioned earlier, the idea that actually Athena wasn't punishing her but protecting her, transforming her in order to ensure that she can no longer be a victim of dangerous men. This form is often viewed as a kind of origin, as though women of the ancient world told this version of the story and that's how it came to Ovid, or some similar idea. It's also sometimes accompanied by the 'fact' that Medusa's symbol was used as a symbol of protection specifically by assault survivors of the ancient world too (unfortunately there is no ancient evidence to back this). I want to be very clear that I don't intend to take this away from anyone who finds strength in this form of her, only to point out what lies beneath this idea and how we women and survivors might instead find the same, or more, strength in the more ancient Greek forms of Medusa.

As I have already detailed, there are inherent problems with the idea that Medusa was once 'beautiful' and had that 'beauty' taken from her as either a punishment or a curse. To me it screams of 'but what was she wearing?', whether intentional or otherwise. The implication that the nature of the Gorgons must be in contrast with 'beauty' suggests there was something wrong with them, rather than the simple fact that this is just... what they were. Similarly, the notion that Athena used a monstrous transformation to 'protect' Medusa from further assault implies (if unintentionally) that the only way to avoid sexual assault is to be unappealing to men, rather than to blame the assault on the man. Of course, goddesses are never capable of punishing gods for their crimes, but that doesn't take away from the implications it has for Medusa that monstrosity is the only way to 'keep her safe'. To me this reading is reminiscent of the longstanding issues of women learning how to avoid assault rather than men learning not to assault.

Still, I don't break down the issues I find in those readings without offering an alternative that I believe to be considerably more empowering to both Medusa and to modern feminists and survivors of assault.

Arguing Semantics of Assault

One of the most common themes of researching Medusa today is this debate over Ovid's version, how canonical it should be considered, and what, exactly, was outright invented by the Roman poet. It's a debate I've personally encountered in my own sometimes haunting Twitter replies, and one that rages on in more sub-Reddits than you can imagine. But what does it mean to argue over whether or not Medusa's story inherently involves sexual assault?

There's a line in Hesiod's version of Medusa that haunts me. Evelyn-White translates it as 'With her lay [Poseidon] the Dark-haired One in a soft meadow amid spring flowers.' This English verb 'lay with' is used often in translations of this particular line (Lattimore, 1959, also uses it, as does Kelk, 2021). The original Greek, though, is a little more complex. Reading consent or lack thereof into the ancient Greek sources is a complicated thing. Our understanding of it is modern, obviously, and so often, that's used as a reason to ignore all notions of consent in myth. Personally I find this to be both troubling and unfair to the ancient world. Just because we conceptualize consent differently today doesn't change the fact that sexual violence is a universal concept. Myth is fiction, certainly, so we aren't dealing with real people's experiences, but myth is also explicitly created to mirror and understand the real world and the people in it.

Greek mythology heavily features moments I believe should be read as sexual assault. These assaults are typically, but not always, committed against women. Sometimes this is explicit, but when we're looking at the most ancient of sources it's typically something that can be inferred by the story being told. Women – human, deity, or otherwise – are often abducted by a god and then have a child by them. The poem may not explicitly state this as sexual assault, but it's easy enough to connect the dots (forced abduction + an eventual child = sexual assault).

It's not usually controversial to come to these conclusions, but with Medusa there is often a backlash. People the world over have found in her story a kind of empowerment, or at least commiseration, due to her status as a survivor of assault, and this is why I personally find it to be beneficial to examine the evidence for that aspect of her story. For the same reasons, she is most often the character whose assault is often erased from the ancient sources. If a man can claim that assault was 'invented by Ovid' and not found in the earlier Greek, then the use of Medusa as a symbol of strength for survivors is equally denied. Because Ovid's version of her story makes this experience explicit, it's often described as having been invented by him. I argue, though, that this aspect of her character exists as far back as Medusa herself, in Hesiod's earliest surviving version of her story.

Medusa the Survivor

I believe that we can (and I certainly do!) read Medusa as a survivor of assault in the earliest of ancient Greek sources. I touched upon this a little earlier, but the god Poseidon is well acknowledged as one of the most violent gods of Greek myth. This is in large part due to what he represents, the sea, which would have been known as a dangerous and violent place (and undeniably still is). Because of this, Poseidon himself is dangerous. The encounter he has with Medusa in Hesiod's *Theogony* is not something that is explicitly clarified as assault, but that isn't enough to confirm that it wasn't understood as what we would now call sexual assault or rape. If the most violent god is coming upon a woman in a peaceful place like a meadow, and that him 'laying with' her is followed by a reference to her tragic fate, I believe there is an inherent reading of violence in that experience.

When I interpret Hesiod's earliest version of Medusa's story, I call her a survivor of Poseidon's sexual assault for all the reasons I just laid out. I believe she was a survivor of that assault, and that, combined with her ability to defend herself against further violence by men, meant she symbolized a threat to the patriarchal order. By killing her and transforming her defensive mechanism into an offensive weapon, she is effectively silenced and turned into a tool of that same patriarchy. To view her in this way today, I find, she becomes a considerably more empowering figure both as a mythological character worth examining in near-obsessive detail, and as a symbol of strength and empowerment for modern women, modern survivors.

A Symbol of Safety

Today, just like in the ancient world, Medusa has become a symbol of protection and safety. Tattoos of her are often used by survivors of assault as a means of commemorating their own strength and resilience, even signalling to others that there is a kind of shared experience being conveyed through Medusa's image. In the ancient world she was a broad symbol of protection, of the idea that her face alone could defend the bearer against any threat. Today, she often has this more specific usage by survivors, but her protective value and inherently comforting nature remains unchanged. She continues to symbolize strength and resilience in the face of outside threats, and particularly the strength and resilience of women living under the shadow of the patriarchal order. For every man who continues to call Medusa a terrible, ugly abomination whose heroic slaughter by Perseus was one of man's greatest feats, there is a woman there to defend her story as one of strength and resilience in the face of male-inflicted violence. Today the voices in her defence are often, finally, louder than those who seek to devalue her. Through art and fiction, creatives are taking back the strong Medusa of the ancient world, the monstrous but not evil or ugly Medusa, the dangerous but not violent Medusa, and the survivor Medusa. The themes that surround her in both her ancient and modern forms, are (tragically) timeless. For as long as the patriarchy reigns and seeks to tamp out the power of women, there will be versions of Medusa written to defend them, to defend her, against the violence of oppression.

Modern Short Stories of Medusa

The Wise Look for All of the Stories

Alicia K. Anderson

"Ever since the beginning of this new cycle, everyone seems to be absolutely losing their minds," Zeus complained. Athena had never seen her father look so defeated and miserable.

"It's an opportunity to change," she said reasonably. "We don't get those very often on Olympus. Heaven's apocalypse is giving all of us the opportunity to choose different stories, to become something new and different."

"Why does everyone want to be something new and different! It worked well the way it was before!" Zeus teetered into whining territory.

"For you," she said, her voice calm and quiet. "It worked well for *you*. Maybe Poseidon. Maybe Ares or Apollo. But it didn't always work well for everyone else." Athena wasn't sure where she, herself, fell on that scale. Had the old way worked for her? She was a successful goddess. But there was something missing. She refrained from telling her father that.

Zeus threw up his hands in exasperation. Athena pressed her lips together to suppress a smile. They gazed out the window together for a few silent moments, watching the snow fall. Demeter had opened up the bruised and purple skies in her rage at Kore's disappearance. Olympus would be buried under snow until the young woman was found. The fierce love of the girl's mother made Athena's heart ache. She had not had a mother, as far as she knew, in any of her stories.

Watching the flurries, she wondered.

* * *

"Will you take our picture?" A young woman held her mobile phone out and pointed at herself and her girlfriend as if Athena didn't understand her language. "With the statue?"

Athena pushed her glasses up her nose with one finger reflexively, and smiled at the woman, nodding. The gilded statue looming at the far end of the room looked nothing like her. While the alabaster skin and the wide blue eyes weren't entirely wrong, the face shape was strange. Too still. Too oval. Too remote. She captured the photographs with precision of the smiling women and the gigantic golden statue behind them.

If she left the Parthenon, Nashville would drift away from her like a dream. She could catch her breath in certain shops or restaurants, where her power was strong enough. But Nashville was not Athens. It was not her town to wander at will. Nashville was, of course, only a means to an end.

She sat on the bench in the cool of the building and watched the passersby stare up at her statue. She heard them whisper the words written on the placards encircling the room. Explanations of the Nike statuette, of the grimacing Gorgons on her breast plate and her shield. The explanations, like the statue itself, were neither wrong nor right. Athena could remember some – most – of her own stories. She knew that as the stories wrapped around time, they would change and evolve. As some of the stories were lost to the world, new ones would arise.

A woman sat beside Athena on the bench, propping a walking stick on her knee. Their eyes met, and the woman smiled at her, sadly, secretively. "There isn't a bay to carry her down to, to wash her in the sea," the woman said, after several moments of silence.

"There aren't any olive trees in this park," Athena replied.

The woman nodded. "Too cold here in the winter. They wouldn't survive. I don't like that they don't weave her new clothes every year."

Athena smiled softly in the dim light. "What else can you tell me about her?" she asked the woman.

"That you don't already know?"

Athena nodded.

"Her mother's name was Metis. Re-cast in Olympian stories as a Titaness of wisdom."

Light glinted off a few strands of silver hair at the woman's temples. The rest of her wavy hair was brown. It was impossible to tell how old she was. "Go on."

"Metis was swallowed by Zeus – I don't remember why." The woman fiddled with the cork handle of her walking stick. "And she lives still, in his belly, guiding him. Offering him her stolen wisdom in the form of intuition."

Athena was quiet beside the woman, who for her part was staring at the statue of a goddess at the other end of the room. "He gave birth to Athena, fully grown, wearing her armor, from his head. But everybody knows that." She said the words softly, for Athena's ears alone. Athena caught herself shoving her fake glasses up her nose again.

"There's a relief – in the British Museum – a relief of a goddess from Libya who gave birth to another goddess in full armor from her head. An ancient, primordial goddess of wisdom. No need for a father at all."

* * *

Athena stared at the carving before her, her mouth hanging open slightly. Her expression could have been due to the N95 mask on her face – a need to breathe, as opposed to dumbfounded shock. Her fingers itched to trace the raised image. For the first time in days, her head was clear. Though it was a small space – perhaps a meter or two – near the carving, she was standing in a place steeped with her own power. Abruptly upon nearing the carving, she didn't suffer the feeling of lucid dreaming that permeated the Olympians' trips to the human world. Here, the gods' stories crowded them and made it hard to navigate.

"That's Medusa," Athena finally said to the human woman beside her, her voice echoing in the wide chamber in spite of the mask muffling the sound. The frieze before her showed a story different from the ones she had known. The Gorgon was familiar to Athena, but this version of her story was not.

The woman nodded. Perhaps she had gone silent because she saw Athena in a place of her power. She had been chatting incessantly since they had departed Athens. Athena wondered, in a distant way, how she appeared to the human in this place.

They were in a museum in London. It was not where Athena had expected to travel in the search for her mother. And Medusa was *not* who she'd expected to find.

"In the Greek myth," the human said, clearing her throat, "Athena's mother was Metis – a Titaness of wisdom, skill, craft, and of time." The archeologist was glancing from the wall to Athena's face. Her gaze flickering back and forth.

"Yes, and Zeus ate her." Athena knew the story all too well.

The archeologist nodded. She continued, "And when their daughter was born, she sprang in full armor from his head."

Athena rubbed her palms on the thighs of her khaki trousers. The carving clearly showed that form of birth happening. A fully armored woman was springing from the head of another. It was ancient Libyan armor, as opposed to ancient Greek garb. But the idea was the same.

"And you think this carving predates that story," Athena said, pointing at the depiction of herself and a different sort of birth.

"I know it does. Archeologically, linguistically, this version predates the one with Zeus."

The carving showed her springing in full armor from the head of a Gorgon. A woman with serpents instead of hair. A woman with a grimace instead of a serene profile. The face and head Athena had borne on her breastplate or on her shield for a number of cycles.

"Tell me about the Gorgon," Athena said, still looking at Medusa's protruding tongue, shaped like a serpent.

"In Libya, she wasn't a monster at the time," the archeologist said. "The serpent is a symbol of rebirth, the cycle of life and death."

"Because it sheds its skin," Athena murmured.

"Among other things, yes." The archeologist was encouraged. "The serpent has long been a symbol of feminine wisdom – of goddesses of wisdom."

"So, in this myth, I – I mean, Athena – is a goddess of wisdom borne from the head of a goddess of deeper, older wisdom?"

"Yes," the archeologist pointed to some squiggles beyond Medusa. "She was a goddess of the sea, primordial and vast. Not wildly different from a Titaness, in other contexts. Too large to be approachable. She had a daughter," the woman swept her hand to show the springing action on the carving. "The daughter was a goddess of wisdom, as well, but more approachable for humans. The daughter was also armed, a defender of her people."

"A general," Athena whispered, looking at the Libyan blade on her ancient hip.

"Yes, a general. One that was wise enough to ensure the success of the polis, and to know how to pick her battles."

Athena stood back, trying to memorize the carving. She pulled a small notepad out of her pocket and began sketching it while the archeologist continued talking.

"Linguistically, 'Medusa' and 'Metis' aren't very different. They have different interpretations, and meanings, of course. But they aren't so distinct to rule out associations. Etymologically, they have the same Indo-European root word."

"You think this story," Athena glanced up from her sketch, "was changed."

"Sure. When Zeus came along, he needed to be the source and repository for wisdom. He ate the Titaness. And Athena changed stories, becoming her father's daughter."

What would it mean, to recapture her own story? Athena had known since the beginning of this cycle that there was more to the tales of her mother than her residence in her father's belly. She had known the stories she was stepping into were different, somehow.

She took a deep breath before asking her next question.

"In Greece, Athena wears Medusa's head on her breastplate, on her shield," she knew the overarching story about Poseidon's act, and her own vengeance wrought. It never sat well with her. "Why is that?"

"I think," the archeologist made a face like she was going out on an intellectual limb. "I think it's because they are aspects of one another. She is inextricably tied to the Gorgon, and when Medusa is no longer her mother, she has to become her enemy, and then her symbol. Athena as a goddess does have a destructive aspect. She's not all weaving and pottery and strategy. She can create chaos, death, and destruction. The Gorgon is that element within her."

There was an important statue of Athena in the Acropolis Museum at home where she was wearing a snakeskin cloak with a delicate lace edge made of serpents. She had never given it much thought.

"And the grimace?" Athena pointed at the face of the serpentine goddess on the wall. She sketched the protruding eyes and the wide mouth.

"Most experts believe the gorgoneion is a protective symbol, intended to frighten away enemies and evil spirits." The archeologist pointed at the tongue. "Some even suggest that the face mimics what happens to bodies and faces as they decompose after death. That it's a depiction of a corpse."

Athena nodded. She could see the resemblance. To all ancient peoples, the face of death was horrible and terrifying. She thought about her own connection to destruction – to death – as a general. The sound of her pencil scratching on the paper was the only thing they heard for a few beats.

"Thank you," she said, snapping the notebook shut. "This is exactly what I was looking for."

"You're welcome." The archeologist smiled at her, a hint of flirtation in the expression. "This is an area of some debate, you know."

"Debate?"

"Oh, yes. Archeologists, linguists, historians, everyone has a different take on the origins of Athena. This is my pet theory. There is much larger consensus tying Athena to the Egyptian goddess, Neith."

"Do we need to go to Egypt?" Athena asked, reluctant to leave the small space near the carving.

"Well," the archeologist grinned, "the Egyptian sections are upstairs and the floor above that." The archeologist gazed into the middle distance. "However, Neith does not have a mother in that mythology. She created herself. Parthenogenesis."

Athena had felt the segments of *her* Parthenon on the ground floor when they'd come into the building. She would be able to remain somewhat lucid for further exploration of the museum, at least. "Let's go," she said. "We're already here."

* * *

Athena trudged through knee-deep snow, listening to it squeak beneath her boots. She'd managed, in spite of Demeter's howling winter, to sail the choppy Olympian sea. The snow-laden gray sky turned the waves a dark pewter color.

She had disembarked on the rocky shore of an island in the western ocean, at the lip of the sunset. Her small skiff was still visible behind her, as she navigated the rocky cliffs of the island home of the Gorgons. On the horizon to the east, she could see the peak of Mount Olympus, where it rose above the surf. She was still in the world of the gods, still within her own story, though the place felt strange and raw around her.

"Halt!" Euryale leapt from a cliff to stop Athena's progress. Her boots sank into the snow. The serpents clung close to the Gorgon's head instead of splaying out the way it was usually depicted. It was as if they huddled against her scalp for warmth. Medusa's sister drew a short Greek blade, threatening Athena if she continued walking forward.

Athena decided not to draw her sword. She had not brought her shield – suspecting its presence and story would make this conversation more difficult. She held her hands palms forward, showing Euryale she was unarmed. "I intend peace," she shouted over the wind.

Euryale assessed her. She waded forward in the snow and looked at Athena's armor carefully. Athena was relieved she had not worn the breastplate with the symbol of the Gorgon in its center. Athena made no move to stop Euryale when she pulled the sword from its sheath at Athena's hip. "If you mean peace, then go unarmed." She flicked her head, as if Athena should precede her as a prisoner.

Squaring her shoulders, Athena continued down the path. As they rounded another bend and dropped deeper into a small canyon – blessedly out of the wind – the other sister, Stheno, appeared. Stheno stood, her arms crossed before her chest. She did not speak. But when Athena paused in front of the second Gorgon, the sisters exchanged glances over her shoulder.

"She says she intends peace," Euryale told Stheno. Stheno's gaze shifted from her sister back to Athena. Several of the serpents on her head hissed.

"We have a chance to choose new stories," Athena said, keeping her voice low and calm. The Gorgons (her… *aunts*?) stood in silent consultation with one another.

"What is your *peaceful* purpose for sailing to this isle?" Stheno asked.

Athena lifted her gaze to the Gorgon's, not entirely unafraid of turning to stone with the act. "I'm seeking Medusa, to discuss our stories," she replied. "We have the opportunity to choose new tales with the turn of the cycle, she and I."

Stheno scoffed. She rolled her eyes. "Poseidon already tried that," she said. "He still ended up trying—"

Athena shook her head. She knew what Poseidon would have tried to do. "Poseidon does not choose to change his story much this cycle. Though Demeter may inspire him to do otherwise. I am not worried about him, or his actions. This is between me and Medusa."

Stheno patted Athena's armor. She removed daggers from her belt and her boot. Further unarmed, Athena trudged through the snow toward the Gorgons' lair, followed closely by Medusa's immortal sisters.

The Gorgons' home was simple, tidy, and comfortable. Athena wasn't sure why she had been expecting a dank cave heaped with treasure, rather than a whistling tea kettle and soft chairs. Medusa's gaze was not like her sisters' immortal regards. She still could turn Athena herself to stone with a glance. Stheno drew a linen curtain across the seating area, allowing Athena and Medusa to speak through it without risking a glimpse of the arresting gaze.

Medusa entered the room from a small hallway, settling behind the curtain. Her silhouette flickered against the linen, backlit by a few gleaming lamps deeper in the chamber. The reptiles slithered on her head farther from her scalp than her sisters' had out in the cold weather. They writhed and danced, flickering tongues, and whispering quiet commentary.

"Athena," Medusa's voice was somber. "My sisters say you intend peace. They assure me that you are unarmed. What brings my old enemy to my door?"

Stheno hovered near, bristling with weaponry. Athena swallowed and tried to organize her words. Words she'd been practicing in the boat the entire way here.

"It's a new cycle. We have choices about which stories we step into – which stories are accurate for us in this new time." Athena's palms were sticky. "I went to the world below to learn more about the stories of my mother… to learn new stories for myself."

Medusa nodded in the shadow on the linen. It encouraged Athena to plunge on.

"I did not like the story of your creation or your destruction that was told. But honestly, I did not travel to the human realm with an intention to change or rectify that. For that I am sorry. I deeply apologize."

Stheno's shoulders dropped away from her ears by a fraction. She still crossed her arms over her chest, but she leaned back on a wall. She was no longer poised to pounce on Athena if she made the slightest wrong move. Athena took it as a good sign.

"Are you familiar with the frieze and the Libyan stories about… the two of us?" Athena asked the shadow behind the pale linen.

The figure stilled. The serpents on her head stilled. The little home rang momentarily with silence. "I am familiar," Medusa finally said.

Athena drew another unexpected connection in her mind in that very moment. "Oh, you were a primordial goddess of the sea! The reason Poseidon had to take—"

"My story is one of Zeus and Poseidon taking what is rightfully mine," Medusa nodded. "Why are you here to remind me of this injustice?"

Athena shook her head and gathered her thoughts. She wiped her sweating hands on her thighs. "I am not here to remind you of the injustice," she said, hoping she didn't sound frantic, "but to address what I saw on the frieze. That you are… my mother. In some stories."

The serpents on Stheno's head arched back and hissed. Athena's aunt's face showed surprise. There was another stunned silence. Athena resisted the anxious urge to fill it.

When the serpents in the shadow of Medusa's silhouette stilled and calmed, she turned her head, as if she might be lost in thought. "My daughter was another thing they took from me," she finally said. "She became her father's daughter, rather than a birth of my wisdom."

"I became—" Athena stammered. "I am your daughter. Or – or at least I want to be." She swallowed. Stheno nodded in encouragement, her eyes bright and dancing. "I would like to choose that story, this cycle. Not the revenge. Not the destruction. No sending heroes on errands with mirrors."

The figure behind the linen shifted in her seat. Athena imagined that even the snakes were striking so many thoughtful little poses in the lamplight. Stheno's face had split into a wide, delighted grin. Euryale had poked her head into the room from the kitchen with a curious, hopeful expression.

"Will you still wear the gorgoneion?" Medusa asked softly.

"Only if you so wish," Athena said. "I had lost a mother, but I held you close through all of those stories. I would love to wear your symbol with pride and honor. But that is your choice."

Medusa sighed audibly. She leaned back in her chair, the shadow behind the curtain distorting with the change in position.

"My gaze can only harm my enemies, Athena," she said, breaking the silence. "May I draw back the curtain and look at my daughter's face?"

Stheno did a little happy wiggle while she waited for Athena to respond, grinning at her. Athena smiled and nodded at her aunt, then found her voice to give consent. "Yes, please." Stheno drew the curtain, and Athena gazed upon the living face of the woman sitting in the chair opposite her for the first time in cycles. She had not seen Medusa, except in death, for thousands of years.

The black serpents that writhed like Medusa's hair hinted at Athena's dark curls. They had the same gray eyes. The same nose. The same strong, square jawline. Athena had always believed she resembled Zeus. But now, now she could see she was truly a blending of the parents she chose. Medusa smiled.

"What about Metis?" Euryale asked, bouncing into the room with a tea tray for everyone. Athena shifted as her aunts sat down to join them. Curious and excited, they were eager to explore this new choice of stories together.

"Metis and I have different stories, though we are also the same," Medusa said. "Poor thing still lives in Zeus's belly."

Athena nodded. "I can choose which of my own stories I keep and discard, but Metis has to choose her own story." She sipped the hot, pungent tea. "Or Zeus would have to choose—"

"Which he won't do," Medusa scoffed.

"Not unless forced to," Athena agreed. She nodded out toward the winter storm beyond their door. "But there may be things forcing him to change."

Medusa smiled a small smile as she sipped her tea. One of the snakes curled lovingly around her ear. "Do you really think this cycle will be so different?" Her voice was full of hope and wonder she did not dare to express.

Athena thought. She was a goddess of wisdom, as was Medusa before her. She wanted to give an honest answer. Finally, she said, "I think we have the opportunity to make it very different. But many of us have to make different choices."

"One good choice down!" Stheno clapped her hands. "Please say you'll stay for dinner, niece."

"I would love to."

How to Tame a Head of Snakes

Mel Attica

They pegged me as a man-hater, but they got that detail wrong. It's not that I had no reason to hate men, or gods, for that matter – the life they sentenced me to was a lonely one. There were long days and endless nights when I cursed them and railed against my fate. In the end, I had to let go of the anger and thirst for vengeance. It served no purpose and gave me a headache. The solitude, though, was a cage from which I couldn't escape, and that was what my jailers intended.

There I was, a prize bloom with no one to admire me. No suitors. No friends. No chance for a life with a lover, a partner, or a family. The gods made sure of that. Beauty does not go unpunished in this covetous world. They left me with nothing but murderous eyes and a head full of ornery snakes for company. What was a girl to do?

I admit, I got so desperate I looked in a mirror. Of course it didn't work. I don't know what made me think the gods would impart even the smallest kindness. Other options were out of the question. The sea was my nemesis – I wouldn't give Poseidon the satisfaction of watching me drown – and the thought of a violent end, falling from a cliff to the rocks below, repulsed me. What was left? If I wasn't going to die, I had to find a way to live.

I took to gardening early on. I had plenty of time and space to fill, so I turned my hand to the only form of creation available to me. I was utterly alone on the island of Sarpedon and wandering was a natural distraction. The climate was hospitable, home to a rainbow of flora.

The sharp scent of citrus wafted from orange and lemon trees, mingling with sweet plumeria, pungent rosemary, woody olive, and soft, herbal lavender. I strolled and plucked and collected samples. Soon I built my own private Olympus, lacking majestic peaks and columned porticos, but no less resplendent in fiery hibiscus, lush bougainvillea, and snowy, vanilla-scented oleander.

Hardscaping wasn't my forte. The best I could manage was a few rudimentary pathways composed of flat stones that were light enough to carry. Little did I know the fates would provide ample opportunity to round out my vibrant garden with lifelike statuary. It wasn't long before the first would-be vanquisher arrived on my doorstep, young and impetuous, if not very bright.

Truthfully, he caught me off guard. I wasn't expecting visitors and at the time, I had no idea of how notorious I'd become. I was pruning a batch of lavender gone wild, lulled by nature's orchestra. The rhythmic cooing of collared doves, the shuffle of hares in the underbrush, the timeless duet of sea and shoreline, and the ever-present rustling of snakeskin; these were the sounds that defined my small existence and lazed in the background of my conscious mind.

Focused as I was on stripping every last patch of withered lavender from the thriving bulk of the plant, the youth was nearly upon me before my mind grew alert to his creeping gait. He was too eager. I whirled, more in surprise than fear, my mane of snakes coiling and hissing displeasure. He was a mere two strides away, both hands gripping the sword lofted overhead as if preparing to smite a mighty chunk of firewood. The posture left his eyes exposed. Too eager, with so many lessons unlearned.

I caught just a glimpse of his handsome face, soft and unlined, cheeks pink with triumph, and a shadow of patchy stubble that would never grow to a full, manly beard. Then he was rendered in milky white marble, perfect and smooth, blank eyes unseeing, solid and still. It was as if he'd always loomed over my garden path, ready to strike.

The shock of the moment left me trembling, with the bitter tang of copper flooding my mouth. I stood for long moments, willing him to turn back to breathing, living flesh.

"Please, please, please," I whispered, and wept. I reached out to touch his face, still warm with the lingering essence of the boy, and recoiled as if scorched. I had done this. I was a murderer, however involuntary. I turned away, retching into a pile of dead lavender, while sympathetic snake heads stroked my forehead and cheeks.

It didn't matter that he was there to kill me, and if I hadn't turned, he would have completed his hateful mission. He was dead, along with a lifetime of potential, because of me. His parents would never know what befell their beloved child. The children he might have tucked in at night would never be born. All the good he might have done, the lives he could have touched, all swept away in an instant.

I didn't feel powerful or righteous. I was sick with shame. He'd been right to come for me. I was a monster, a blight. For days I steered clear of the lavender field. When I finally returned, I averted my eyes. I caught only a hint of his luminous outline, white as bone amid the vivid emerald, sage, blush, and periwinkle hues of my garden.

Over time I began to wonder about his life and what had brought him here. What was his name? Was there a family waiting? A girl who pined for him? Friends he'd left behind? Or was he alone, in search of fame that might bring him closer to dreams of fortune and esteem? Was he heroic? Was he malicious?

In the end, I decided he was simply a naive young man, misguided in his thinking and thrust into reckless action by others content to aim him at a target and let him loose. It eased my mind to believe he could have been any young fool, taken advantage of, cursed by the cruelty of men.

I felt closer to him, as though we were comrades in the same senseless war. Then I could look at his lovely remains with wistful regret instead of guilt. I belatedly anointed him with oil and, lacking cakes and libations, I wove him a crown of flowers. He served as my only friend for a time.

I dubbed him Sisyphus, burdened with a task he could never hope to complete. When loneliness descended like a lump of lead in my stomach, I sat at his feet and cried my troubles and frustrations into the dirt.

Time held no meaning on my little island, but visitors appeared with ever-greater frequency, sometimes only days apart. After my Sisyphus, I resolved not to kill again. I spoke from the shadows, asking for mercy, begging them to leave. I implored them to stay with me, to be my companion.

Some would speak with me, spilling their glorious intent: to kill the beast on Sarpedon Island. Some, cautious and confused, offered tidbits of news from the outside world, reminding me of the life I once had. This was knowledge I craved and reviled in equal measure. I yearned for that long-ago feeling of belonging but knew it was as unreachable as the pinnacle of Sisyphus's mountain.

In the end, my pleas went unheeded. I was forced to slay one man after another, populating the island with permanent reminders of my misdeeds. Stony attendants to greet the next visitor and fill him with fear. The boats they left on shore were no salvation to me. How could I return to the world of men, atrocity that I was? I stripped them of anything valuable and set them adrift, hollow ghosts.

Over time, the flood of determined heroes slowed as the young men who journeyed to Sarpedon, full of promise and spirit, failed to return. As their light in the world was snuffed out, my grim legend only grew.

Sometimes it felt like years passed before I added a new statue to my impressive collection. They never aged and neither did I. One day, after many seasons had passed and I wore my unwanted life more like a threadbare coat of fur than an itchy wool sweater, I spotted a ship across the water. I watched it crawl closer on the inbound current, biting down on the swell of excitement that accompanied the approach of that single, red-and-white-striped sail. I didn't dare hope anymore. It was death for him or for me.

As he jumped from his small boat to pull it from the water and onto the sand, I got a good look at him from behind a rocky shelter not far from the shore. His short tunic, clasped at one shoulder, left little to the imagination. Broad shoulders, bronzed skin, and magnificently sculpted legs told the story of a life in motion, while a battery of scars added rich dimension to his outer tapestry. He wasn't old, but neither was he new. This man had lived and fought. He had toiled and suffered, and emerged victorious more than once.

Unlike my Sisyphus, he had a lush beard to match his tempestuous head of sable curls, streaked with the barest hint of gray. His lips were full and shapely, his nose straight and strong. His eyes, fringed by inky lashes, were the silvery green of olive trees in autumn. A truly striking specimen. I knew he was here to end my life but I couldn't help it. I loved him instantly.

I watched closely as he pulled his short sword and shield from the boat and turned to survey the island. I knew every inch of terrain, so it was easy to remain hidden and follow along as he walked the coastline, no doubt strategizing the best way to flush me out. He was a hunter, a warrior. I hungered for him with an intensity that made me want to laugh and vomit and claw my own eyes out just to feel his arms around me and his breath on my lips. I wanted to be found.

But I had to be cautious. I had to play this right. How could I get him to lay down his sword and love a monster? How could I get him to trust me? As he wandered farther from his boat I turned back. When I was sure he was out of sight I darted from the shadows and pushed the boat out into the water, smiling in triumph as the waves caught it and cast it back to the uncaring sea, beyond reach. He was trapped. I had time.

I waited behind the same rocks where I'd first watched him come ashore. As day dwindled to darkness, he returned. He paced back and forth, unsure. I giggled at the thought of him wondering if this was indeed the spot or if he'd somehow misjudged. He knelt near the waterline where the boat had been, scrutinizing the deep cleft his hull had left in the sand. Did he see my footprints there or had the lapping waves obscured them? He hung his head, in defeat or contemplation, I knew not.

Elation mingled with uncertainty. Could my ploy possibly work? He stood and looked out at the sea for a time, at the sky turning to pink and purple as the sun disappeared below the horizon. The gods had granted me a beautiful prison, one that I now shared.

He trudged away from the water, climbing over rocks to reach the line of shrubs and trees. I held my breath and hugged the rock as he passed near, close enough to hear his soft tread. Although my snakes often quieted at night, the presence of a stranger caused them to twitch and flick their tongues restlessly. One let out a hiss and I grabbed for it, clamping its mouth shut. The man paused for a moment, then kept walking.

I'd pressed my luck enough for one night. As his footsteps faded, I crept away, back to the tiny hut at the center of my lovely, fearsome garden. Knowing the structure would be a sure target, I snatched up my woven blankets, a relic of my time at Athena's temple, and laid them out in a nearby grove of fragrant cedar. I fell asleep to the whisper of swaying boughs overhead and dreamed of a man I had yet to meet.

The next morning, munching an orange, I mulled over how to approach him. He was sure to be hungry – I'd sent all his supplies away with his boat. Over the years, I'd learned to forage and trap out of necessity. I didn't fish, though I was surrounded by water. Poseidon, I knew, was cruel and vengeful. He was the reason I was on this island, and I didn't want to stray too near his domain. A nearby rocky cavern served as cold storage for cured meats, dried fruits, and olive paste, ground in simple clay pots I had made myself.

I gathered fresh fruit and a small sampling of stored food in a gauzy length of cloth, then made my way to where I'd last seen the man. He'd emerged from the trees and seated himself on the sand, looking out over the water, perhaps hoping to see his boat bobbing back to him. I rolled out a small, woven mat I'd brought along, quietly laid my offering on a flat rock, and backed away.

Hiding in the tree line, I scooped up a handful of pebbles and threw them toward the rock, ducking down. Startled, the man whirled into a crouch, snatching up his sword. He spotted the small feast and approached with caution, his eyes scouring the rocks and trees, sliding past me.

He looked at the food, crouched to sniff it, poked it with a finger. Was it poison? Was he hungry enough to dare? He stood, eyes scanning the terrain and darting back to the meal before him. Then he sat and ate, fast and methodical. He gave no indication that he enjoyed it, apart from finishing every morsel and licking his fingers clean at the end.

"Why don't you come out?" he said, his voice smooth and sonorous. He didn't shout, but it surprised me all the same to hear another voice on my secluded island. I flinched and uttered an involuntary squeak. His eyes swiveled my way, but I was hidden far enough back that he couldn't pinpoint my exact location.

I prepared to bolt, but he didn't move. A true hunter, he wanted to snare me and he could be patient, I thought. He waited long moments, then spoke again.

"I think you know why I'm here," he said. Then his brow furrowed. "But I must admit, I'm confused. I expected to find a ruthless, cold-blooded monster. Instead, you sent my boat away. You kept me here not to murder me…but to feed me?" He paused, awaiting my reply. I stayed silent. It was a trap, I was sure.

"I suppose," he continued, "it must be lonely, living on this island, year after year, with your only company men who would murder you." He sighed. "Perhaps we can strike a truce. I think that perhaps you do not want to kill me. I don't particularly want to kill you, either, for reasons that are…complicated. If I'm to remain here, we're sure to meet eventually. Why not now?"

My heart was athunder with fear and hope. He wasn't wrong. The cloth I'd carried the food in was gripped in my hand. Smoothing it out, I draped it over my head, covering the snakes and shielding my eyes, and tied it in the back. The weave was loose and soft, allowing for cloudy vision, although I could see the ground clearly below the edge of the fabric. I took a deep breath for courage and rose, stepping forward and into the man's view.

He stayed still as I picked my way over the rocks. Within moments I stood before him. My boldness did not reach my tongue, dry and heavy as it was in my mouth. He looked me over, then looked to my face, unafraid.

"Hello," he said.

"Hello," I croaked back, my voice hoarse from lack of use. Not a great start.

"Would you like to sit?" He gestured across the rock table.

I shook my head no. I could still get out of this if I had to. I could step away, out of reach of his sword, and lift my veil.

"My name is Dimitrios."

"Medusa," I said, finding my voice. He smiled.

"Yes, I know. You're the reason I'm here."

"You came to kill me," I said.

"I came to kill the monster of legend. You don't seem to be a monster."

"Oh, but I am. I've taken the lives of many men. You walked the shoreline yesterday. There's more than one victim in plain view."

"I saw them," he said, picking his words carefully. "I couldn't help but notice that all of them were posed to attack. Not a single man cowering or cringing. Not even one shrinking in fear. To one familiar with battle, it looks more like you were defending yourself."

I stood silent. It was true. This man saw me like no other before. He spoke with compassion, with understanding. Could he be different? I wanted to believe it, but hope was a dangerous commodity.

"Perhaps I caught them off-guard," I said.

"Perhaps," he echoed, the corners of his lips twitching up in a smile. Against my better judgment, I smiled back and slowly sat down across from him. What was life without a little risk?

"So, Dimitrios, are you a farmer?" I asked. He barked a laugh.

"No, no, my parents were farmers. They named me to honor Demeter but I had greater ambition than tilling fields. They would have hidden me from the companies, but I ran out to join them when they came to collect. I've always been a fighter, in my heart and my head."

"And now?" I asked. He shrugged in a good-natured way.

"I tire of the bloodshed," he said. "My body aches and my mind grows weary of political intrigue. I long to be more than a pawn in another man's game of Zatrikion."

"So why are you here? Seeking glory like so many others?" I couldn't keep the sour edge of spite from my voice.

"In part," he admitted. "Mostly I just wanted to get away, to see what I could be, free from the yoke of the army."

"I'm sorry to tell you, there's nothing to do on this island but garden. It seems you may fulfill your parents' wish and become a farmer yet," I said. At this, he bellowed a hearty laugh, booming and rich. I laughed, too, at my cleverness, at how well this was going, so much better than I'd imagined.

We spent hours wandering along the beach, immersed in conversation. He told me tales of his youth on the farm, of the terror and excitement of joining the army. He talked of battles won and friends lost and cataloged his many scars.

I spoke of my own mortal youth and my service in the Temple of Athena. I glossed over how I'd ended up in my current state, but described all I'd learned since coming to Sarpedon and how I spent my days.

At last, I told him of my terror at killing that first boy, my Sisyphus, and the relentless loneliness I endured. That was my true prison. He took my hand in his and the comfort of that small gesture, so long denied to me, was too much to bear. Bitter sobs threatened to overwhelm me. I jerked my hand back, wanting suddenly to be far away from Dimitrios. Was he even real or was this some cruel jest, a mere whim of the gods to punish me further?

He grabbed my arm and pulled me close. His heat and vitality radiated against my body as he wrapped his arms around me, as I'd dreamed he would. I sagged into him, so desperate for the simple, human connection he offered. The snakes went wild, throwing off my veil and coiling to strike at his arms, chest, and face. They weren't venomous, but they could bite, and they did, over and over, painting bloody constellations across his flesh.

I squeezed my eyes shut and tried to push away but he held me firm until I stopped struggling. He began to hum a low, mournful tune, his chest vibrating. The snakes were lulled, settling back to their usual slow twining around my face and neck. His arms loosened then, one hand coming to rest on my cheek.

"How did you do that?" I asked.

"Magic," he said.

He lifted my face and kissed me, his lips firm and sure, his soft mustache and beard tickling pleasantly. I wished then only to gaze into his eyes and see myself reflected there. Instead, I lingered in the moment, gripping his sides and pressing myself fully to him, as if to make two bodies one. At that moment, I thought I could die happy, awash in the miracle of love and the promise of companionship.

I should have known better.

The water washed over our feet in the sand and pulled back, taking us with it. I tried to hold onto Dimitrios, but we were wrenched apart. I was tumbled and dragged along the sandy bottom, bumping and scraping patches of wickedly sharp coral reef as I strained to reach the surface, clawing vainly at the water. Time stretched out, every second too long as my lungs ached and my throat burned. Just as darkness began to blur my vision, I was pushed to the surface and thrown onto the sand.

Choking on seawater, gasping and retching, I struggled to crawl clear of the cursed tide. My snakes lay silent and limp. I clambered to my feet, searching the shore, desperate. There was no sign of Dimitrios. He'd been swallowed by the sea.

I knew he was gone, but I ran up and down the waterline, seeking any trace of his body floating atop the waves. I pleaded with Poseidon. I prayed for his ruin. How could he take so much from me and still want more? I screamed my wrath and fell to the sand, beating it with my bloody fists. No one answered. No one cared.

The snakes, my only remaining companions, never revived. They had drowned and I had not, another brutal reminder that nothing I had was truly my own. Not my body, not my life. There was nothing left for me. I returned to my nest among the cedars and tossed the blankets aside. I threw off my tunic and fell naked upon the cool, compact earth. There I would wait for death.

It was not quick in coming, but I lay there, still as stone, still as my statues, day after day, too tired to rise, too broken to care. Finally, on a bright, cool night when the moonlight filtered down through the cedars to illuminate my exposed flesh, I heard shuffling footsteps approaching. I turned my head to see a man moving carefully backward toward me, a curved sword in one hand. He used his gleaming bronze shield as a mirror, so as not to meet my gaze directly.

I felt no fear, no anger. It had all been washed away in the salt of sea and tears. I was dry as the dirt. I was cold as the stars of Haloa, the winter festival of Poseidon. If I felt anything at all, it was a twinge of relief, perhaps a trace of gratitude that my killer, my savior had arrived.

"I'm ready," I sighed.

I closed my eyes and let him claim his eternal glory.

In the Temple of Athena

Casey Banks

Look to the east and you'll see the sparkling metropolis of Athens. In this city built by kings stands the temple of Athena, a marble monument dedicated to her glory. Sunlight dazzles its halls, gleaming down on the crowds of devotees. Farmers and merchants, sailors and seamstresses, the barefoot and the sandaled, all push against one another as they wait their turn to kneel at the feet of the goddess's statues and press their brows against her golden altars.

Below the temple are vast rooms filled with treasure. Chests of gold, jeweled crowns, gifts from conquering heroes and tributes to their divine benefactress.

Further down still, beneath the cellars and down a shadowed hallway, is a door. Behind the door, in a nearly lightless chamber, is the aegis of Athena. A monstrous head melded to a shield of iron and bronze; a divine gift to serve as weapon and protection for the heroes of the goddess.

Resting on its barren altar of stone, in its dark room, the aegis of Athena waits.

It waits for the hero with the golden curls and flashing blade to return and finish what he started.

It waits for the goddess to grow bored and demand its destruction.

The part of the aegis that had been a person, the woman's head with lips that had tasted the sea salt in the wind, and eyes that had watched the waves tumble along the rocks, waits to be reunited with a heart and body long since rotted and turned to dust.

The years pile into decades. The devotees above continue to worship and pray at the stone feet of their goddess. The aegis can hear them when it bothers to listen, which is not often. The thick canvas sack, once a covering for the aegis and its horrifying visage, decays and falls to pieces, scattering amid the layers of dust.

The aegis waits in a darkness and silence broken only by the squeak and hiss of crawling things. And after a while, not even that.

It waits.

And then one day, there is a noise outside the door.

* * *

A heavy scraping pulls the aegis from a waking dream, dissolving the moonlit caverns and sea breeze, scattering the cliffside vista of churning clouds and blue-gray waves.

It watches with mild interest as the door opens and a human woman is shoved forward. Whoever had thrown her in, quickly closes and bolts the heavy iron door before the woman can escape. She is not blindfolded. Her eyes are not clouded over and sightless. The woman is young, her long legs and rounded face still marked with the plumpness of adolescence. The soft undyed tunic and skirt is twisting around her body as she throws herself at the door. Such a lovely thing, despite the terror etching lines into her face and making her eyes bulge with too much white. The man is probably a lesser priest of Athena's temple. The important ones wear ivory robes.

The woman frantically looks around the room, blinking as her eyes adjust. There are slight cracks in the walls, breaks between the stone seams that allow slivers of light. The woman takes in the stone floor, the marble columns, the empty oil lamps set in alcoves along the wall, and the unlit incense holders gray with dust. And then her gaze takes in the aegis atop the altar. Her eyes lock on the head that is without its neck, arms, and legs. The face that is watching her.

The woman trembles, a scream building behind her lips.

The aegis has not spoken for a long time. Not since the hero cleaved its neck in two. There had been other humans, but not for many years. Others had immediately cried out when they met its eyes. They had thrown their arms over their heads and cried for aid. This one has looked away, but she has not begged or attacked. For the first time in a long time, it has the urge to talk, to verbally acknowledge this woman who will soon die.

"Hello, little one. You must have angered someone very badly to have been placed in my chamber."

The woman flinches at the rasping sound, but she does not cover her ears. She still does not beat at the door or fall to her knees screaming for mercy. Instead, after a silent moment, she looks down at herself, touching her bare arms in wonder.

"I am not transformed. You haven't turned me to stone."

"No." It savors the vibrations on its tongue, shifting vocal timbres. It had almost forgotten what it felt like to form words and push them into the air. "What is your name, little slave?"

The woman's chin lifts slightly. "I am not a slave. I am Lydia, an acolyte of the wise and beautiful goddess Athena."

The aegis tries a chuckle, letting the rumble pulse down a throat it could somehow feel even though it was no longer there. "Lydia, acolyte of the wise and beautiful Athena. I take it you know what I am. You seem to have fallen from your goddess's favor. Come closer."

She will likely be dead within the hour. It will take weeks for the priests to find a servant willing to enter the room and retrieve her remains.

Lydia approaches slowly, sandaled feet marking a path through the unbroken dust. Either she does not realize her fate or she has forgotten it in her newfound resolve and awe.

"During harvest festival, storyweavers gather the children and recite your tale. Sometimes players act out the adventure with costumes and puppets. You really are just a head attached to a shield. You have no torso." She peers around the chamber, as if a body will be found slumped in a corner.

The aegis studies her face as she draws closer. She is younger than she appears. Probably no more than a season or two has passed since Lydia sat with the other children and watched men with wooden swords hack at monsters made of straw.

"Yes," agrees the aegis, "what you see is what remains of me. Long ago, I was slain by Perseus. He attached my head to this shield and gifted me to your mistress." The serpents at the crown of its head stir, rousing from dormancy. They might have woken from the jolt of feeling that had momentarily sparked in the aegis. A jolt of something that would have been anger if the aegis still had a heart to feel such things. It had not spoken the hero's name in a long time. His name should have been forgotten along with its own. The serpents uncurl and lift their heads, scenting the air with their tongues.

Lydia jerks back and screams. "You truly are as the stories say. Please don't kill me."

"You do not have to fear."

"They won't bite?"

"Of course they will, they are serpents, but you do not have to fear them or me. Have you ever heard tales from your storyweavers of me killing young women?"

"The shores of Aethiopia are littered with the petrified bodies of mariners and soldiers who came across your den. And everyone knows you've turned countless heroes into stone with your monstrous gaze."

The aegis falls silent, concentrating on the sleek muscles and smooth skin of the serpents as they slid along cheek and scalp, winding around each other in a dance. It lets the snakes' movement soothe away the tension. Faint footsteps several corridors away hurry through the subchambers of the temple. Lydia's priest must have heard her scream from seeing the serpents. He is coming back to find out why she isn't dead yet.

"Those heroes and soldiers you speak of, those men, with their questing hands and their questing swords, sought me out. When they found me, they looked into my eyes and saw the reflection of what they were, and they perished for it. I have met no man who has faced his true reflection in my gaze and survived."

"Perseus did not perish."

"Perseus did not look at me. Your mighty goddess made sure of that." It is good the priest is coming. The aegis is tired of this conversation and desires to return to its waiting. "The goddess's priests do not share in her wisdom. Every other decade or so, they seem to forget that I have never killed a woman, and lock some unfortunate in here with me."

Lydia freezes in place, no longer sidling away from the dancing snakes. "What happens to them?"

"They die. I am not the one who kills them. Usually, they try calling out to the man who put them in here, apologizing for offending him, promising to submit to his advances." Lydia twitches almost imperceptibly at that. It was not hard to guess. She is uncommonly pretty. "It never works. The man is angry at the noise and that his actions will be discovered, he comes back and stabs the woman or breaks her neck. The ones who do not make noise are left to starve, and eventually a blindfolded servant is forced inside to collect the body."

Lydia lets out a low moan and sinks to the floor.

The chamber has no windows, but cracks high in the wall along the ceiling are wide enough to show the day is fading. The light, already dim, is now barely a glow as the sun sinks to evening, deepening the shadows around the altar and throughout the room. As the aegis watches, Lydia seems to shrink with the dimming light, accepting the truth of the words without a fight. She does not weep or call out to Athena to save her. She wraps her arms around herself and stills. As if she is waiting for death.

The aegis sees that Lydia is clutching at her arms with calloused hands, roughened and knotted fingers that have clearly scrubbed floors and carried buckets. These are not the hands of an acolyte chosen to sit in prayer and interpret the divine messages of the goddess. Lydia is no earthly messenger of Olympus, like the priests and acolytes. She is likely a slave of the temple. There will be no divine intervention for one such as her. No rescue from the man's rage or blade. There is only the waiting.

The waiting and waiting.

The aegis rouses its snakes, silently asking them to reach out to their brethren who live in the walls of the temple. Obediently, they hiss out the request in an echoing sibilant chorus.

It is not long before shadows detach themselves from the walls, pushing out of cracks and dropping to the floor. Lydia notices the movement. She rears back, scrambling away from the walls. The snakes continue to come, slithering from beneath the altar, some arriving from underneath the door. They slide over one another, tangling and untangling as they move towards Lydia.

"What is happening?" She is on her feet, turning in alarm.

"I am going to release you from the waiting, before the priest returns and does it his way."

"You're killing me? You ordered the snakes to eat me?"

"The snakes are too small to eat you."

"They can still kill me." Her voice is rising in panic. She screams as more snakes fountain from the ceiling and trail down the columns. Underneath the silken movement of the snakes and Lydia's ragged breathing, the priest's footsteps grow louder.

"Your priest has returned. He will be here soon."

There is still a clear path to the door, although it is narrowing as the density of snakes turns the floor into a moving carpet. Lydia does not flee towards the door. Instead, she turns to face the aegis. "You said that men who seek you out and meet your gaze perish from their true reflection. What happens when women meet your gaze?"

"No woman has sought to meet my gaze."

The aegis watches as Lydia takes a step and then another, clearly straining to not look down at the serpents roiling under her feet. She keeps walking until she is directly in front of the aegis, face to face.

"I am meeting your gaze."

And she is. Her eyes no longer skirt around like a startled bird, darting in and away. Lydia's gaze holds firm and the aegis draws her in. Its eyes glow with an image of a small girl being handed over to the temple by thin and starving parents. The eyes of the aegis reflect a child's life of cleaning floors and washing linens, of listening to storyweavers from a distance behind a tree because temple slaves who try to join the village children for games and stories are beaten. It reflects days spent kneeling in prayer to the goddess, and the lingering glances of a priest as her girl's body grows into that of a woman. The gaze of the aegis rips through the comforting fog of denial and self-delusion, and finds that Lydia has already seen her true reflection. She saw it as she sought refuge from the priest at the feet of Athena's statue, and as she'd been dragged from that holy place of worship, and locked in a chamber with a weapon meant to destroy her.

The aegis reflects Lydia's life of devotion to a temple and a goddess indifferent to her existence; a short life of drudgery and degradation. Lydia does not turn from her reflection; she takes it in. As she does, she reaches out a hand to steady herself, touching the aegis's cheek. The touch is warm and gentle. The aegis can feel the pulse of Lydia's heartbeat in those fingers, a rhythm that it will never find within its own body ever again. It tries to close its eyes against the phantom of emotion, banish away the pain and return to the waiting. But it cannot look away, it cannot stop its own reflection from shining through.

Lydia inhales sharply, tears gathering in her eyes. "You were taken from your home too. They used you and now you think you're not a person. I'm so sorry. I'm sorry they locked you away from your home by the sea."

Lydia leans closer, pressing their foreheads together. And the emotions that should not have come, come. The grief and the anger, the rage and the loss, and the shouting inside. Softer, then louder, a scream from within, a single word over and over.

A name, her name.

There is movement above their heads. The snakes of the aegis writhe at the internal turmoil, confused and agitated. They settle their attention on Lydia, rearing back to strike. Lydia does not move away or lower her gaze. A look of wonder grows on her face as she reaches out a hand and touches the wetness that has appeared on the aegis's cheek. The snakes relax, some of them curl along Lydia's wrist, nuzzling against her fingers.

Lydia straightens, reaching around the aegis – no, not aegis, Medusa – and lifts it – her, Medusa – into the air. "You were the aegis of Athena and I thought I wanted to be her acolyte."

The world tilts as Lydia turns, tightening the shield straps to her arm. "I think it's time we both get out of here and become something different."

The snakes part as the young woman moves across the room and stands directly in front of the door. There is a heavy scraping as the door begins to open. No more waiting.

"Yes," Medusa says, and a smile curls along her lips for the first time in centuries.

Pegasus

Danai Christopoulou

I was safe inside my mother's ribs, breathing her every heartbeat.

There was no such thing as time. There was only warmth, and love, and the mighty muscle in her chest that pumped blood, putting me to sleep with its rhythmic workings.

Sometimes in the evenings – and I know it was in the evenings because my mother's heart beat slower – she would tell me stories. About how she and her Gorgon sisters would be called to bless the temples of old, to ensure the stonemasonry held. About how humans would carve my mother's likeness on those temples, her face both a warning and a benediction. About how the same humans forsook the Gorgons in time, trading their blessings for the new twelve gods, gods that looked more like them.

I didn't understand these stories, although I liked hearing my mother's voice. But she'd get sad and silent afterward, so I would stomp my hooves ever so gently, reminding her I was there. That I would never forsake her for anyone. Then my mother would laugh, and she would sing to me, and the cavern of her ribs would vibrate from the sound. I would unfurl my wings and flap them to the rhythm of the song, and then she'd laugh some more and tell me to settle in now, allow her to catch her breath.

Then I would sleep, happy, cradled in the echoes of her laughter.

* * *

One evening, my mother's heart picked up a new rhythm. Faster. Frantic.

I woke from my slumber to feel her springing into action. Adrenaline flooded her veins along with something else, something I'd never felt before. It was bitter, and rancid, and later in my life I would learn to call it 'fear'. My mother was struggling, fighting a moving obstacle I could not see. In that little space I occupied inside her, I stood up. Knees wobbly, but wings at the ready. If I flapped them hard enough, maybe I could lift us both up.

Away from whatever was pinning her down. Away from danger.

But I was small and weak and not fully shaped yet. I hadn't felt the wind currents caress my back; hadn't learned how to ride the sun's rays, or make the rivers change their routes on a whim. I didn't know, then, that so many things are made of air and water – and that I could bend those things to my will if I so chose. All I could do was hover a bit higher.

I reached my mother's throat. The forest of her vocal cords was burning.

My mother screamed.

I heard another voice then, alien and angry and so unlike the singing and the stories I was used to. The voice came from outside my mother, distorted by the barrier of flesh and bone that rose between us. It yelled something imperceptible. My mother fell silent on the outside, although her insides were still screaming, her heart a booming thunderstorm, her breathing a cyclone of chaos. There was a sound, like metal scraping on the stone walls of our cavern. I felt my mother's hands covering her heart. Protecting me.

Then I felt nothing as the world exploded.

* * *

The monster thought my mother was alone.

That he could harm her and have no one to bear witness to his crime.

But I was there. I saw. And as he turned his back to my mother's lifeless body, polishing his sword so certain of his victory, I erupted from her throat in all my newborn fury. I flapped my wings in the world for the very first time, causing a gust of wind so strong it toppled him over.

He turned around to face me then, my mother's killer.

He looked bizarre, misshapen, all pink exposed skin and barren limbs. He had no wings, no life in the hay-colored strands that covered his hideous head. His eyes bulged in their sockets, green murky things filled with dread. His pupils dilated in my presence, his mouth opened into a gaping hole. How dare he, such a clearly inferior being, take the life of one of the mighty Gorgons? Was he one of the humans my mother warned me about? Did the new gods put him up to this? Rage burst into my veins, searing everything.

I rose up on my two rear legs and stomped his chest with my hooves.

A crunch, like the shell of an egg being broken. A crater of white and crimson, of bone and sinew. I stepped aside, my sticky hooves coated with his bubbling blood. He was nothing, the man who caused my mother's heart to stop beating. Not even worth my reveling in my revenge. Maybe his gods will come and save him. Maybe not.

If I were them, I'd run.

I cast my first and final look at my mother's glorious shape. At the delicate body that had nurtured me with its essence, at the heavy head that carried so much wisdom even her hair pulsed with sentience. Perhaps she knew it would always come to this. That she would need to be cut in half, for me to fly free. I blinked away the tears that caused my mother's murdered form to blur, and turned my face toward the sun. I stood there, at our cave's opening, smelling of sunlight and carnage.

"The world is made of dirt and stone, of air and water," my mother used to say. I always knew she could control the first two, and that's the reason she and her sisters lived in caves. But up until that moment, when I spread my russet-colored wings preparing for my first flight and my hooves kicked the ground behind me, I had no idea how well I could control the other two.

I shot up like an arrow amid a sky I had no words for. The world of humans spread beneath me, a tapestry of greens and browns, of trees and roads. Further ahead, just at the corner of my eye, something flickered. I felt it call to me, as profound as my mother's past, as ever-flowing as her love.

Water.

My mother called me Pegasus; the one from whom water bursts forth. The one who can create streams, and springs, and rivers. She hoped that I would bring new life to this world.

She wasn't wrong. But for new life to bloom, the old first has to be extinguished. This became my mission, from that moment on. To find these puny gods, and the wretched humans who served them, and cut their life's thread just as that monster's sword cut off my mother's head. With no ambivalence. No mercy. No regrets.

I'll fly far and wide and I will land like a red rhomphaia, cutting the Earth with my wrath. And everywhere I stomp there will be blood, and water, and it will all flow for her.

For my mother.

Medusa.

The Toll of the Snake

Grace P. Fong

Suen Mei-Ko holds the gaze of the casting director in front of her. Minerva Kingsley is a spear clad in pinstriped rayon, sharp-edged from shoulder pads to blonde chignon. Mei-Ko feels Kingsley's gray eyes pan down every inch of her body, and she hurries to flatten a wrinkle in her shirtwaist. She hopes Kingsley won't notice its cream fabric used to be white, but it's the best dress Mei-Ko owns.

"Those're some doe-eyed peepers that America'll pay to see," Kingsley says with a knowing nod. "You know, you're the eighth screen test today alone! Didn't think this town even had that many. But none had eyes like yours. Too narrow, too slanted – that just won't do on film."

Kingsley reaches into a drawer of her mahogany desk and while her back is turned, Mei-Ko looks around. The airy space is filled with marble busts of the glitterati that Kingsley shaped into stars. One smiling ingenue – Mei-Ko recognizes Kingsley's star client, Patricia Hamlin – catches the afternoon sun and makes the room glow. Maybe Mei-Ko's just anxious, or maybe there really is something magic about Hollywood.

Her heart races all over again when Kingsley slides a contract in front of her. The pen she's handed is golden, too. It's real gold, isn't it? She's never touched real gold before. It feels amazing.

Kingsley frowns and taps her fingers on the desk. "You going to sign or what?"

Mei-Ko hurriedly scrawls her English name and initials on every line that asks for it.

Kingsley takes the papers and scrutinizes Mei-Ko's signatures before letting out a good-natured laugh. "Well, I won't even try to pronounce that."

She writes 'Suzy Moon' on the line next to Mei-Ko's name. "That's better. Pronounceable, memorable, and just a touch exotic. Everyone loves a bit of mystery."

"Suzy? But Suen's my last name."

"Oh, the audience won't know that." Kingsley shrugs. "May-Something might've worked, but no one will remember a rookie like you when there's already Mae West."

Unfortunate as it is, Mei-Ko has to agree. Still, she musters the courage to say, "If you don't mind my asking, Ms. Kingsley – why call for Chinese girls?"

Kingsley folds her manicured fingers together and smiles like she's the one on stage. "Because I believe in a brighter future, Miss Moon. Hollywood and all her stars are the shining beacons that lead everyday Americans. What with all our boys coming back from the Pacific, there'll be demand for faces like yours. Patriotic people want to support the poor, ravaged Chinese, and our best director, Porter Simpkin – he's one of them, a veritable visionary."

Kingsley produces another stack of paper. "We'll need to build sympathy for you. Memorize this before you come to training on Monday."

Mei-Ko takes the document. "Just what is this?"

"Your backstory, honey! The writing staff dreamed up something real dramatic. We'll schedule a press conference – you tell them you're from Hong Kong, a young socialite fresh out of grammar school, which is why your English is so good. When the Japanese invaded, you escaped on a junk boat captained by a kindly old fisherman. What a pity! You had to throw your life away to save it!" Kingsley swoons with the drama of a silent film star.

"But I'm from Sacramento."

Kingsley laughs again. "Who wants to know that?"

Mei-Ko looks over her new, fabricated life. It's certainly more glamorous than being a third-generation laundry girl. "How long would I have to pretend?"

"Pretend? It's acting, darling! Isn't that why you're here?" Kingsley laughs, and Mei-Ko finds herself laughing too. Kingsley continues, "Our standard contract starts at seven years."

Seven years. Mei-Ko didn't think anything could last seven years these days.

Kingsley interrupted her thought. "Movies aren't magic, kid. They're training and money. Sign this, and we'll take care of you – fifteen dollars a week."

Mei-Ko wants twenty, but she better not push her luck. In seven years, she could really make something of herself, make a lot more than twenty. And certainly more than at her dad's laundromat. She keeps on reading. "What's this part?"

"Ah, nothing to worry about. Just your standard morality clause. All studios have one."

Mei-Ko read the restrictions to herself. "No swearing… no drugs… no relationships—"

"We'll handle that for you. Keye Luke – that Kato fella – wouldn't he be cute? A photo of you two strolling on the beach could get your name in the papers."

Mei-Ko imagines her name in more than the papers. She imagines Suzy Moon headlining every cinema in America.

"Trust me. Be a good girl, and we'll make you a star." Kingsley extends her arm. "Or should I call Patricia Hamlin instead?"

Mei-Ko takes the hand and they shake. She gazes at the marble bust of Patricia and imagines herself there, too. "I'm ready to shine, Ms. Kingsley."

Kingsley's smile is bright as the Hollywood sign. "Welcome, Suzy, to Olympia Pictures."

* * *

Mei-Ko marvels as Porter Simpkin whizzes across Olympia's largest soundstage. Actors hurry to their marks. Grips push equipment into place. A painter puts the finishing stroke on a sheet of plywood, so on film, it'll become an alley in Beijing.

Simpkin is a short man in his forties with a dark, unkempt beard. Mei-Ko looks to Kingsley for instructions, but she just shrugs and mutters, "Lord, I wish he'd shave."

Mei-Ko smirks. "Guess it's good he's behind the camera instead of in front of it."

Kingsley scoffs. "You're too clever for your own good, girl. Watch yourself around that one. He's talented to be sure, but he's got a tendency to schedule meetings after hours if you know what I mean."

Simpkin approaches them. He leans forward and kisses the air on either side of Kingsley's cheeks. She does not return the gesture. "Minerva, darling – how glad I am to see you!"

"Hello, Porter. Kept your tan, I see."

"The Philippines made me realize just how dashing I look with a deeper tone. Spend a few years there yourself, Minnie. Maybe you'll finally relax a little."

Kingsley rolls her eyes. "Here's the girl you asked for."

She steps aside, and Mei-Ko takes her cue to glide gracefully forward. All eyes are on Mei-Ko as the bell-sleeved mandarin gown swings around her ankles, bringing the embroidered flowers to life across the white silk.

"How do you do, Mr. Simpkin?" Mei-Ko says in a perfect Mid-Atlantic accent. She bows politely.

"My, she *is* delightful." Simpkin nods readily in approval. Minerva has a smug grin on her face. Those acting classes are paying off.

Simpkin takes Mei-Ko's hand and leads her to her mark on stage. As she waits, he calls out, "Where's Percy?"

Percy Ryland emerges from a rack of costumes. He sports an ill-fitting army uniform that looks like it came from a history book, but his clothes don't matter. He's a classic, all-American dreamboat with a jawline that cuts through girls' hearts. After tying a bloodless bandage around his forehead, he goes to lie in a hammock stretched across the stage.

Simpkin hops into his director's chair and grabs the megaphone. His voice shakes the ground. "Okay, Percy – you're a soldier. You were valiantly defending a Christian mission when – oh, no! – those murderous Boxers cornered you! And they got you bad! But lucky you, you were saved by a beautiful sing-song girl. What's this? You're falling in love! Make her love you! Make *me* love you! Lights… camera… *action*!"

The slate board claps shut.

Just as the script says, Mei-Ko drifts across the stage and places her hand gently on Percy's wounded forehead.

"No, no, no, no." Simpkin gestures for everyone to return to their places. "Suzy, can you do it again? But more dainty, like you've got those lotus feet."

Mei-Ko hesitates, trying to imagine this feature she's only ever heard of. Something about the request unsettles her, but this is her first shoot. She's worked so hard to get here and asking one wrong question might label her as difficult. She looks toward Kingsley, who simply reassures her with a curt nod.

The camera rolls again. This time, Mei-Ko takes delicate, mincing steps. Simpkin leans forward in his chair, rapt with glee. She continues the scene, shyly looking away while Percy flirts with her in a language she pretends not to understand. His soliloquy climaxes, and he takes her cheek in his hand and tilts her face toward his. Their eyes lock. His are sky-blue and give her access to his very soul. She senses deep hunger awaken behind his pupils, and she feels so powerful.

He leans forward and kisses her lips.

"*CUT*!"

The scream is shrill and knife-edged. Kingsley, fists balled, storms toward her, wearing a tight-lipped frown in victory red. "You harlot! Are you trying to ruin this picture?"

"I—"

"You *what*? I won't be investigated because some knuckle-headed rookie can't remember the Hays Code." She sneers before returning to her usual composure. "I've trained you better than that."

Cold sweat coats Mei-Ko's palms. "I'm sorry, it won't happen again."

Kingsley exhales through gritted teeth. "It's alright. This time."

They do a few more takes, but Mei-Ko thinks none of them are as good as the first. Finally, Simpkin yells, "That's a wrap!"

As the crew strikes the set, he walks up to Percy and Mei-Ko. She bows again because she knows it's what he wants to see. "Thank you so much. I can't tell you how lucky I feel to be in such a lovely love story."

He puffs out his chest. "I daresay, *The Toll of the Sea* made me quite the romantic."

Mei-Ko is too young to have ever watched that movie, but she nods enthusiastically to appease him. "If you like romance, you must've heard of *The Tale of White Snake*."

Simpkin blinks, probably deciding whether he should reveal his knowledge gap. "Ah, please refresh my memory, if you will."

Mei-Ko seizes the opportunity. She widens her eyes excitedly and adopts the tone Simpkin himself used when telling his story. "Imagine Ancient China, a land of magic and mystery. There is a monster who resembles a white snake who lived in a lake and feasted on those foolish enough to cross the bridge above it – but she longs to be human. It takes a century of devout prayer, but the gods finally grant her wish!"

Simpkin rests his finger on his chin. The picture is already playing in his head. Mei-Ko notices Kingsley and Percy have also begun to listen.

"Her first day as a human, she is caught on a bridge in the cold, wet rain. There, she encounters a young man. He's a kind man, a handsome man. He invites her to join him under his umbrella, and there it is – *love*! They marry! It's beautiful! But marriage between humans and monsters is forbidden. When her animal form is revealed – the young man dies of fright!"

Even the crew has stopped to listen now.

"So, she challenges the gods. And she *wins*! They revive her husband, and with his first new breath, he swears to love her. No gods will ever keep them apart."

Simpkin looks wistful. "Forbidden love! So beautiful! It could certainly be my next picture… or maybe with a few tweaks to *this* script… we *are* early enough to re-shoot… cultural references always add such artistic merit…"

Mei-Ko is confident she's picturing the same thing as Simpkin: an Academy Award. Now that's gold that she wants.

Kingsley calculates in her notepad, and explains, "I agree it's certainly a nice tale, but it's a foreign *fantasy*, full of expensive set pieces. To recoup the budget, we'd need bankable talent. I'll have the writers draft you another part, Suzy, then I'll phone Patricia—"

Mei-Ko turns to Simpkin and clasps her hands together, trying to look every bit the part for the film, and he comes to her rescue. "Now, now, Minnie, don't flip your wig. What's the harm in letting the girl read?"

Kingsley sighs and rolls her eyes. "…Only until we find a new lead."

Mei-Ko forces herself to beam. "Thank you ever so much, Ms. Kingsley!"

Simpkin departs, but Kingsley lingers. She turns to Mei-Ko, expression grim.

"You know," she states, "we have a snake myth here in America, too. Medusa was the priestess, but her beauty made her bold. Too bold. The gods had to put her in her place. They turned her hair into snakes, and she became a monster so ugly that one look at her face turned men to stone. So ugly that she hid, ashamed and alone – until a hero cut her head off."

Then Kingsley leans over and whispers into Mei-Ko's ear, "You'd do well to remember what your contract says. And who holds that contract."

She leaves, but the vague threat crawls under Mei-Ko's skin. Silently, she swears to prove that she, too, can be a leading lady.

But for now, she will go home. When she steps outside, a sudden, damp chill hits her face. It's actually raining in Los Angeles. She curses inwardly because her contract forbids her from saying such words out loud.

That's when she hears a familiar, directorial voice. "Hi-de-ho, baby doll! Need a lift?"

A black sedan rolls up and Simpkin leans out the window, cigarette bobbing in his mouth.

"My hero!" she swoons, making Simpkin laugh. "A ride'd be swell."

He comes out of the car and opens the passenger door with a grand gesture. "After you."

Mei-Ko senses Simpkin is the kind of man who's uncomfortable in silent rooms. He fills the car with small talk, "I bounced around in the Pacific during the War, and I really found myself. Something about being far from home, surrounded by exotic customs and people – I felt alive again. I found love. I wrote this script to share with my fellow Americans just how beautiful China can be."

He parks the car next to Mei-Ko's trailer, but he keeps tapping his hands against the steering wheel. He's still thinking. "But this White Snake story, it's authentic. It's new. I'm inspired. I wanna make it happen. I'll call Minnie—"

Here's Mei-Ko's chance.

"Call Ms. Kingsley? *You're* the director. You're the one who's lived abroad, fought for our country. You'd know best how to tell this story, how to send a message people can't stop talking about… a message like a Chinese lead." Mei-Ko puts her hand on Simpkin's thigh and gazes into his eyes.

His mouth drops slowly open and the cigarette falls into his lap. Mei-Ko sees hunger in his pupils. "That's… quite a fascinating idea," he stutters. "Would you like to join me tonight? Talk it over at dinner? Not on the lot. Somewhere nicer. I know a great little place on Beverly."

Mei-Ko smiles wryly and taps him on the arm before opening the car door. "Sounds delightful. I'll be right back."

* * *

Patricia Hamlin looks up at the casting director. She needs a surefire blockbuster, but she has doubts about this pitch. "I'm afraid I don't quite understand. Folks want real stories about real Americans. Why're you making a fantasy picture?"

"I beg to differ, Pattie." Excitement lightens Minerva's voice. "We need fantasy now more than ever. The people have just emerged victorious from a great tragedy. They want – no, they *need* – escapism. Look at *The Thief of Bagdad*! Sure, it didn't win an Oscar, but you know what it had? People in seats."

"I suppose *The Wizard of Oz...*"

"Exactly! And we won't even need Technicolor to do it. Our women want reassurance that their husbands will come home safe and loyal, so romance will sell like water in the Dust Bowl. The script's one of Porter's. You know that man—"

"A self-proclaimed genius who can't stick to one direction even if you gave him a compass?"

"I might've phrased it more courteously, but yes. Thankfully, he threw away his derivative *Madame Butterfly* slop and the writers made something original for once." Minerva presents her a copy of the script. "It's the most romantic premise you could dream of – a man and a monster swear love to each other in defiance of the very gods. Love transcending heaven, Earth, and two World Wars? Well, everyone wants that."

Patricia scoffs at the dramatic pitch. She's been around too long to be swayed by theatrics. "Why me, though?"

"I need an ingenue. Someone that can believe so hard in true love that audiences will believe, too."

It's been a long time since Patricia felt like the Kansas-born innocent she was told to be. She can't remember the last time she played a romantic lead. Can't remember the last time she felt coveted on the red carpet. Patricia knows it and so does everyone else in this entire town, including Minerva Kingsley. Patricia thumbs through the first few pages. "I've heard Porter's got certain... tastes. Would he accept a redhead for this China dame?"

"His name may be on the studio, but I keep it alive and running. He'll cast who I tell him to and hair and makeup will do the rest. If we want to sell romance, we need a kiss on-screen. You and I both know what Americans will and won't tolerate. If it worked for Luise Rainer, it'll work for you."

Patricia skims the rest of the script. Meanwhile, Minerva stands up and begins to circle her. She pinches Patricia's arm and nods approvingly. "I'm surprised you're still thin. Most girls would've let themselves go after what happened to you." She leans down and whispers in Patricia's ear, "I know you need money, Pattie. I can make that 'appendectomy' bill from Dr. Killkare disappear."

Patricia gulps. That hadn't been her fault! She thought it was love, but Clark was just drunk. A lot. Even so, look where he was. Then look where she was.

"Ten thousand dollars for one picture," Minerva offers. "Should even leave you something to send back to your mother."

No more bit parts. No more insulting articles. No more dropped phone calls. Patricia flips the contract open to the signature line.

But Minerva rips it away. "There's one condition. One better off not written down. You see, there's a girl on the lot who's gotten too big for her britches, and I need to remind her who pulls the strings around here."

Patricia sighs. No such thing as a free lunch in this biz.

Minerva pulls a camera from her desk drawer. "I want photos," she explains. "The more scandalous, the better. Do whatever you can to obtain them."

She slides the machine over to Patricia who analyzes the dials on top. "Leverage, huh?"

Minerva points to a button. "Point it at the target. Press the knob. And presto! But I do have to warn you, this model is special."

"Special?"

"Can't tell you how it works. Something akin to magic, far as I know. But once you've taken the picture, you must only – and I mean *only* – look at her through the viewfinder."

Patricia narrows her eyes. "I don't think that's how cameras work. I should know. I'm an actress."

"Just trust me, like you always have."

Patricia looks at the camera. It doesn't seem to be particularly special, just Kodak like the one Hedda Hopper uses. But still, for a lead role... She meets Minerva's eyes. "Just *always* look through the viewfinder. Easy enough."

"That's my girl." Minerva's lips spread into a self-satisfied grin.

Ten thousand dollars and shot at stardom. For a few measly photos? "Give me that damned contract."

Patricia picks up the golden pen and signs her name.

* * *

The shoot lasts six grueling weeks. That's forty-two days where Mei-Ko has had to watch Patricia Hamlin perform her role. She does not like the gray dress she wears. Simpkin bought it for her and assured her she looked gorgeous, but she thinks she looks like a laundry girl.

Simpkin has saved the best for last: the ending scene where the pair declare their everlasting love. But he looks a heartbeat away from an aneurysm. "Where's Patricia?" he fumes. "We were supposed to start an hour ago! What d'you mean you haven't seen her? I should have you fired."

No one has seen Patricia, but Mei-Ko sees opportunity. Despite the whispers amongst the crew, she places her hand on Simpkin's shoulder and looks him in the eyes. "Cookie," she coos. "Let me read. I know her lines by heart."

Porter grinds his teeth, but his gaze softens and his fists unclench. With a resolute nod, he shouts, "Break! Costume change!"

Mei-Ko is stewarded into a dressing room and clothed in Patricia's white silk gown. As the artists do her makeup, she reads Patricia's script until she can see every page in her mind. While her hair is brushed and braided, she mouths each line until her lips memorize the feel of every word. She will take this role back.

"You're ready to go!" the stylist chirps.

Mei-Ko looks at her reflection in the mirror and gives it a dazzling smile. Who's this girl? This girl's a star.

The plywood from her first day on set has been reconstructed into a stone bridge. There's a tarp set up on the floor and a rain bar overhead. She steps excitedly onto her mark, and Percy, in that same army uniform, lies down on his.

Lights… camera… *action*! Clack!

The rain bar hisses and fat droplets begin to pour. They puddle at Mei-Ko's feet, drenching her slippers. Water seeps into her dress, making the sheer fabric cling to her body.

Mei-Ko can't tell if she's shivering from cold or excitement. She looks into the water collected below, at the face of a girl who wanted to be a star as badly as a snake wanted to be a human.

With the help of the Hollywood gods, they both made impossible dreams come true.

A gong reverberates through the air.

Mei-Ko rushes to Percy's fallen body, a silk flower cupped in her hands. She presses it to his lips. "I may be a monster, but I defied the gods to prove my love is true. They gave me this blessed blossom to save you."

She quickens her breath and forces herself to cry. Her tears mix with the water falling from above. Percy continues to lie still.

"No, no, no. Please wake up…" She rests her head on his chest.

But when her hair brushes against his neck, he sits up with a gasp, "My love!"

She throws herself into his open arms. He sweeps her off her feet and water flies from her gown. They spin in joyous circles. Mei-Ko's long, black hair unravels from her braid. Her heart dances in her chest, unable to discern if the joy belongs to her or the character.

The camera lens, coated with hazy Vaseline, trucks in. She imagines the close-up of their faces inviting the audience to share their intimate moment. Percy brushes the wild hair away from her face and their eyes lock.

"No gods will keep us apart," she whispers.

He leans in further. That familiar hunger reappears in his eyes. Yes. She places her hand on his cheek and presses his forehead to hers. She knows he cannot help himself as he envelops her lips in a kiss. It tastes like victory red.

"*CUT*!"

The moment is interrupted by a blinding camera flash. Mei-Ko covers her eyes and shoves Percy away with a scream.

Something's wrong. The hissing rain grows louder. It surrounds her. She drops to her knees and, blinking, opens her eyes.

She awakens in a garden of white marble statues, unearthly and beautiful aside from their faces, which are frozen in terror. The cameraman has stopped with his hand on the flash. Simpkin's mouth hangs open in a terrified scream, megaphone halfway to his face. Percy falls to the floor and shatters, littering the ground with fine, white dust as his cracked head rolls behind the stage.

A redheaded woman stands among the film cameras with a handheld Kodak pressed to her face. Mei-Ko recognizes her immediately.

"Patricia!" she calls, but her voice has become a menacing hiss.

Patricia runs for the door. Mei-Ko gets up to follow, but her legs twist in her wet gown and she falls into the soaked tarp. She stares at her reflection. Her hair is no longer silky and black. Her eyes are no longer wide and brown.

Silvery-white snakes swirl around her face. They bare venomous fangs just like she now has. Their eyes, like hers, are Oscar gold with slitted pupils. A thin membrane flicks across them, and when Mei-Ko opens her mouth to scream, a long, forked tongue slithers out.

The monster has been revealed. Mei-Ko snarls, not at the loss of her face, but at the loss of her story. How dare Patricia Hamlin – a woman who was given everything Mei-Ko had to earn – take this from her?

Mei-Ko tastes the air with her tongue. She follows the scent of Chanel No. 5 to a men's dressing room where Patricia cowers behind a rack of costumes. Mei-Ko lunges at her. She revels in how strong the monster is.

She straddles the cowering girl and rips the camera from her hands. Patricia squeezes her eyes closed and throws her arms in front of her face.

"What have you done to me?" Mei-Ko hisses.

"I-I-I don't know! I swear!" Words, snot, and saliva blubber out of her mouth. Not so pretty now. "Minerva gave it to me. Please, please – I don't wanna die."

"Why?"

Patricia's shivering. "She promised me. There— there was a scandal, and Minerva, she— she promised to make me a star again. It's not my fault."

"Not *your* fault? I don't see Minerva around here."

"She offered money. I had to help my family, I swear! We don't all come from rich foreigners, okay?"

Oh. Her *backstory*. Mei-Ko thinks of her father's laundromat and scoffs. She lowers her face to Patricia's so the girl can smell the heat of her breath. "That story's about as true as this movie."

"Fine! Fuck. Fuck! Can't you see? It doesn't matter where we're from. This town is designed to ruin all of us!"

"Yet you'd still climb over me even if no one can win." Mei-Ko wraps her scaled hands around Patricia's head, turning it towards her. "Look at me."

"No."

"Look at me."

"No!"

Mei-Ko can feel Patricia's shuddering breaths under her. She digs her long nails into Patricia's soft cheeks, and they bleed victory red.

"Please, I'm sorry. I don't want to become—" Patricia opens her eyes. At the sight, she lets out a sob.

A sob? She's still human.

Mei-Ko is holding the camera up to her face. She looks at Patricia through the viewfinder and all she sees is a washed-up has-been that has never made her own opportunity before. "You're right. I don't want to become you, either."

Mei-Ko presses the button on the camera. Patricia throws her hands up to block the blinding flash. When Patricia screams, Mei-Ko cackles. It is a monstrous sound.

Then she opens the box, rips the film out, and throws the used camera away before exiting the tiny dressing room.

She returns to survey the set. The rain bar lies bent on its side. Water spills everywhere. The bridge has split in half, revealing the stone is merely plywood. Marble statues posed in terror stand around the room. A silk flower floats in a puddle at Mei-Ko's feet.

To think, this was what she thought magic looked like.

Only in movies.

She approaches the camera by Simpkin's statue. With her newfound claws, she tears into its housing until she releases the movie inside. Tucking the precious film under the stolen jacket, she slithers out of the studio.

* * *

Minerva Kingsley sits in her casting office admiring the bust of Patricia Hamlin as she imagines the girl holding her first Oscar. *The Tale of White Snake* should have wrapped by now, and she is eager to view the final cut. She runs figures in her head: how many theaters to send copies to, what films to package with it, who to send a gift basket to during awards season…

The call arrives.

Minerva hurries to the editing room and turns out the lights. She pulls down the projector screen. The film begins to roll.

Her chest swells when she sees her name opening the credits. If this brings in what she estimates, there will finally be six major motion picture studios. That'd show that Louis B. Mayer who's really leading America.

An exotic tune begins to play, sparkling with bells from the far Orient. The narrator's voice invites her to witness a tale of mystery and magic in the land of ancient China.

A telltale cigarette burn flashes in the top-right corner. What? She looks for the next reel.

The projector begins to stutter. The frames flicker and scroll.

Minerva tweaks the player, but it doesn't stop. She smells burning film and a wisp of smoke escapes the projector.

Click… click… click! Click!

The frame stops on a seductive pair of long-lashed golden eyes. Slowly their dark pupils narrow to slits and almost imperceptibly, a third flickering membrane blinks over them.

The music screeches to a stop. A low hiss crackles over the speakers, and Minerva Kingsley turns into a sharp statue of white marble.

What Actually Happened

Rhys Hughes

What actually happened when Perseus flew over Aethiopia and saw the sea monster Cetus isn't the same as what took place in the myth. He was mounted on Pegasus, the flying horse, yes, and princess Andromeda had been chained to a rock as a sacrifice to persuade the monster to stop ravaging the land. It was a sort of bribe. The loss of the woman was considered a worthwhile price.

But it's simply not true that Perseus pulled the head of the Gorgon Medusa out of a bag, used it to turn Cetus to stone, and rescued Andromeda. He *tried* to do that, but it all went wrong. As the hero circled above the monster on his winged steed, a loose feather dislodged itself from one of Pegasus' wings, drifted down and tickled the nose of Cetus, who closed his eyes and sneezed.

It's impossible even for mythical creatures to sneeze with their eyes open. Perseus had already reached into the bag for Medusa's head. His arm was in the act of pulling it out and it was too late for him to stop himself. As the peculiar shadow of the flying horse passed over her, Andromeda looked up to see what was making such a shape. It was a very unfortunate sequence of events.

Andromeda glimpsed the snaky Gorgon's head as it came out of the bag and the very next instant she became a statue sagging in its chains. Perseus was so shocked by this accident that he dropped the head, which fell into the sea. By this time, Cetus had finished sneezing and was opening his eyes. He saw only Andromeda on the rock and, unaware of the compositional change that had taken place, he proceeded to attempt to devour her, breaking his teeth in the process.

He did succeed in swallowing Andromeda whole, but without teeth he wouldn't be able to secure a meal in the future, and he swam away with an abominable ache in his gums. It took him a few weeks to starve to death and he was mid-ocean at that point. Down he sank to the abyssal seabed, where his monumental carcase would eventually decay. As his flesh dissolved, the figure of Andromeda was revealed, intact and, by a fluke, standing upright on the slimy seabed.

* * *

The head of Medusa drifted along on the ocean currents. Rising and falling in the sea off the coast of Aethiopia, the sun and brine alternately dried and toughened it so that it ended up expertly pickled. Its fabulous power to transform living beings into stone was changed as a consequence, in the same way that a pickled fruit or vegetable isn't quite the same as the original. Years passed.

The wanderings of the head, if plotted on a map of the world, would seem random and pointless to an outside observer, but to the head itself, which still retained vague wisps of consciousness, it was a pleasure to be drifting along, turning fish and whales to glass with one look of its preserved eyes. Having drowned a few weeks previously, Phlebas the Phoenician happened to float past, and he too was transformed into glass and shimmered weirdly in the aqueous glow.

Medusa debated with herself whether she preferred turning things into glass or if it was a degradation of her abilities. Some of the glass creatures were broken against reefs, and waves took the pieces closer to shore, smoothing them into jewels, into sea glass. Some of these gems were washed onto beaches and found and collected. They might even be incorporated into artworks.

One sculptor made a sea monster from the sea glass she gathered over many warm seasons down at the tideline. The irony remained secret. She was invited to display it in an exhibition in a foreign museum. Far below the hull of the ship on which she was a passenger, a glass mermaid circulated without emotion or desire, refracting the pale light that filtered through murky fathoms.

* * *

The sea is a stage just the same as the land is, but one from which there's another way the actors can exit, not just to the left or right but straight down. This is why it isn't regarded as a true venue for theatre, it's simply too easy for the characters in a drama to vanish suddenly without a trace, leaving the audience baffled and unsatisfied. Medusa's head voyaged around the world and sometimes rose to the surface, was even cast high into the air by freak waves in dreadful storms.

On one occasion it landed on the deck of a wooden ship as the vessel pushed its anguished way through the tempest. This ship had a name that would be feared in the following centuries, *The Flying Dutchman*, but at the present moment it wallowed rather than raced among the troughs of the surging sea. Cursed to flounder forever so, never to reach a safe haven, it carried the foul weather with it as the result of a curse on its captain, Hendrick Van der Decken.

That captain was playing cards in the cabin with the Devil himself, because there was no other chance of the curse being lifted. That was part of the deal. If he won, he would be free to reach port. Van der Decken kept losing and he gnashed his teeth as a result and the Devil laughed and displayed the interior of his mouth, which was green and radioactive and equipped with a forked tongue that could impale silver coins, so sharp, hard and rigid were the twin points.

The hatch to the deck was open and the water poured in and where it touched the Devil it turned to a murky steam and so poor was the visibility inside the cabin at this point that Van der Decken took the opportunity to slip the ace of hearts hidden up his sleeve into the pack of cards on the table.

"My turn to deal," he said.

"As you wish," conceded the Devil.

"Aces high again."

That's how Van der Decken contrived to gain possession of the very useful ace for the next round, in which hearts would be trumps. His luck was turning at last, for it was probable that the cursed captain would win this game. And in fact he was able to form the trick that would secure his freedom, but just as he was about to slap it down on the table's surface, he was interrupted.

The head of Medusa fell through the hatch, having rolled across the deck and into the gaping hole. The snakes that were its hair lengthened as it plummeted and the tip of the nose of one brushed the candle flame that illuminated the cabin, putting it out. Only the Devil's mouth provided light now.

And that's a terrible form of bioluminescence in such a confined space, or in any space at all, for that matter. Medusa's head struck the floor and rolled under the table, and as the ship swayed it came to rest against the Devil's hooves. He glanced down and this reflex action had a dismal consequence for him. He saw that it was the head of a Gorgon and he gaped in surprise.

The reason he felt surprise was because the real existence of such a myth implied that all the other classical myths were also true, including the Olympian gods, which in turn meant that the primacy of the strict monotheistic system of which he was such an integral part could now be doubted.

As his jaw dropped open, his gums flared brightly and beams of rancid light fell on Medusa's face. Her eyes opened slowly and met those of the Devil. This locking of two gazes resulted in the Devil instantly turning to glass. But far from making his life impossible, this transformation was little more than a minor inconvenience for such a powerful supernatural entity. Yet the Devil has his pride and he stood with a sneer and his glass wings opened out behind him.

Van der Decken knew that the game of cards was over, that his victory would not now be permitted, that the Devil was about to vanish to the infernal regions and never visit *The Flying Dutchman* again. In order to entice the Devil back he cried, "I don't mind playing a glass opponent..."

The Devil was unimpressed and he stalked to the base of the ladder that led to the open hatch, and before climbing the steps he turned and glared at Medusa and pointed a twisted glazed finger at her. "I curse you! From now on, everything you look at will turn into the thing you most despise!"

Then he hurried up the steps and out into the storm and flapped away somewhere and Van der Decken was left in the cabin with the dreadful head. He closed his eyes, groped for it, picked it up by a handful of snakes and swung it back through the hatch in a graceful arc. It landed on the deck with a thud and a squelch that was audible in a very brief pause in the fury of the wind and waves. Then the vessel pitched again and it rolled off back into the churning depths.

* * *

The Devil had no way of knowing what it was that Medusa most despised. Nor did Medusa, because we frequently don't know what hates we harbour deep inside us, at least not until they are given an opportunity of coming to the surface. Medusa rarely broke the surface in her subsequent wanderings. Mostly a subaquatic head, bouncing occasionally on the seabed or juggled by a giant squid in inky blackness. Only when she was at the higher elevations, in the so-called euphotic zone, where sunlight still penetrated, did the hazards of her eyes become a matter of urgency to those creatures around her. Deeper than two hundred metres or so, she posed no threat to anything. Giant squid were mostly safe. But when one of these beasts flicked her upwards, like a trebuchet flinging a stone, trouble soon followed.

* * *

The shoal of bluefin tuna swam through the waters of the gulf at high speed, as befits such an agile predator, and it's unlikely that any fishy brain suspected that something was about to occur to them that no fish had endured before. It was noon, the sun at its highest in a cloudless sky, the distant ships on the horizon without shadows. Then the head of the Gorgon rose in front of the shoal like an inverted octopus and it was all so sudden that the fish had no chance to evade it.

Medusa looked at them and they looked back, they couldn't help it, and suddenly a shoal of bluefin tuna no longer existed at that location. There were men instead, an armada of swimming men, little men, men the exact image of Perseus. They had to be the size of fish because there were only so many molecules to work with. A few dozen miniature mythical heroes, each with a perfectly contented expression, mouths clamped tight shut but their keen eyes smiling.

They were innocent and had no idea that soon they would run out of air. They had no gills and drowning was inevitable for them. Yes, Medusa hated Perseus above any other thing. The irony is that she was now condemned to create him again and again and although she reveled in the understanding that most would drown, it worried her that maybe some wouldn't. A dolphin turned into Perseus might be strong enough to reach the land and survive, for awful example.

She wondered if she ought to keep her eyes closed from now on. But it occurred to her that it might be better to do the opposite and keep an even sharper lookout than before, in the hopes of seeing the Devil again and asking his forgiveness. It wouldn't be easy to spot him. It's the reason why the Devil has been so infrequently seen in the past few centuries. We look right through his glass body. Only when the light catches him at a specific angle is it obvious he is there.

* * *

She was in the vicinity of the island of Java when the famous volcanic eruption took place. The island of Krakatoa was completely obliterated. Maybe you are now asking yourself if there is such a thing as partial obliteration, and yes there is, in the form of the derelicts, both men and ships, that drift the streets or seas while slowly crumbling to pieces but never quite vanishing totally.

Medusa was borne along on the underwater shockwave, pushed by a wall of water in a westerly direction across the Indian Ocean, her snakes streaming behind her like cartoon speed lines, her mouth gaping with delight or terror or a combination of both, because certainly it was a stimulating ride.

Gradually her velocity decreased, the serpents coiled around her brow again, and the watery push became more of a nudge. She was now in the vicinity of Madagascar and rising to the surface in a very gentle curve. As she broke through the meniscus of the sea into twilight, she found herself bobbing near a boatful of fishermen. The boat was holed and sinking. The crew noticed her and she noticed them back. Suddenly he was bawling at her, Perseus himself, replicated a dozen times, and then the boat went under and the reproduced hero was floundering in brine and drowning. It was the last time she would turn any being into the hero.

Because the trauma of the eruption was working a strange chemistry on her as she floated there among the gurgling images of her enemy. The power of her eyes was yet again changing its nature. By some mystic law of compensation for the lava fire, now she would turn into ice whatever she gazed at.

All the fishermen died but one, who clung to a loose plank broken from the boat, and still looking exactly like Perseus he was washed ashore on a beach of that large, peculiar island called Madagascar. Time passed and he recovered and married a local woman and they had children, and all his male descendants resembled Perseus too. It was something that Medusa never learned, nor would she care to know anyway. Back into the depths she was sinking, blistered, sad.

How utterly strange life is! There can be no denying this.

"How I wish…" she muttered.

But she had no idea what to wish for, not even to pass the time. Her powers were easily adjusted, transformed, a physical knock of sufficient force could alter them in ways that were unpredictable. Would she wish for more stability in her supernatural abilities? She suspected not, for that would be too mundane. Always turning entities to stone and nothing else. A sedimentary occupation, rather boring. No, it was better this way, despite the absurdity, the farcical elements of her situation. She turned cold jellyfish to colder ice down there as she mused.

"And yet I wish..." she sighed.

* * *

One morning a whale swum beneath her and bore her up with him and he wasn't at all aware of her. He couldn't see or feel her, he was safe from the ice touch. Then at the surface he expelled a mighty fountain of water from his blowhole and she was on it, balanced on the jet like a clot of bubbles.

Yes, she was elevated on the fountain of a whale. As she soared higher in the air, it seemed to her that the clouds were descending to meet her. Big cumulus clouds, a flotilla of fluffy white forms sailing through the sky, pure, shining. One of them was closer than the others and billowed strangely.

"You look like a cat."

Just for a few moments, it did indeed resemble a fat feline. There must have been a sufficiently close resemblance to activate the power of her eyes, for only living things were changed as a rule by her gaze. The cloud cat became instantaneously rigid, then it began falling, picking up speed, landing in the sea with an appalling splash, sending the whale swimming away in absolute terror.

Deprived of her levitating fountain, Medusa plopped down too. She landed next to the mountain of ice that had been a cloud.

The impact had broken off some of its edges. It no longer resembled a cat but was simply and utterly a gigantic iceberg in an anomalous position in the sea. Medusa had no more interest in it and she rode the currents away in a southerly direction, the chill on the nape of her neck steadily decreasing.

* * *

The luxury liner *Titanic* had an unexpected meeting with this iceberg a few days later, but no one on board, whether they survived or expired, suspected that not so long ago it had been nothing more menacing than a cumulus cloud that had allowed chance to briefly give it the shape of a household pet.

* * *

The years flowed and never dried up and the ocean theater staged more performances for her than she cared to remember, and she was in many of them, an unwilling if not an unwitting actor. How many times had she gone completely around the world now? She had lost count. At least a dozen.

"Warmer climes at last," she told herself.

She was in the tropics again.

Between the island of Bermuda and the islands of the Bahamas. It was a clear and bright day and she was floating on the surface, using a manta ray that she had turned to ice as a raft. It would melt soon enough, but in the meantime it served its function very well. The breeze stirred her snakes.

Her eyes were wide open, looking at nothing in particular.

Then an unnatural darkness hemmed her in.

Thick mist the colour of old smoke.

But not mist exactly. Something else, a blurring of opacity, a gloomy shimmering, an intrusion of a misplaced dusk or a collision of some kind between two universes at different times of day, and the interloper was overlapping this one. Medusa was fully alert now, sensing danger the way she had done just before Perseus first removed her head all those centuries before. It hadn't helped then, probably it wouldn't help today. She was a cursed and bullied Gorgon.

An object was materialising above her. It was composed of heavy light, shadows and baffling hunger. A being half of energy, half of the inducements of anxiety. Then it achieved a formal menace, turning itself into the silhouette of a gigantic goblin with smoky eyes and the pocked cheeks of an asteroid. It was cosmic, it was rapacious and recidivist too, and it wanted to steal her.

Yes, it hoped to acquire a Gorgon for its collection.

It was none other than the notorious force that snatches souls and their containers in that region known as the Bermuda Triangle, though the sides aren't really straight and the angles don't exactly add up to 180°. It was the goblin that steals planes and ships, their pilots and crews, and takes also those rescue vessels sent to search for the missing lives. That's who it was.

The transdimensional goblin with a black hole heart.

And the mind of a supernova.

They locked weird eyes, Gorgon and goblin.

The influence was mutual.

Medusa's stare turned the goblin to ice.

But he fought back with a parting shot, and the power of her eyes changed again, and now everything alive she stared at would turn into triangles, imperfect and badly drawn, that would shame geometry forever.

* * *

These triangles were made from rigid dark light or from a substance midway between obsidian and cartilage. This was never established for certain. Medusa began to grow bored of her fate, a pickled myth adrift.

She wondered how she might end it all and find peace.

One day a solution seemed near.

A new sun was being birthed in the Pacific.

It was the beginning of an extensive series of nuclear tests, and she was within the blast zone of the first. But annihilation wasn't to be her lot after all. Her gnarled husk of a head was just too tough, too chewy.

And the power of her eyes was altered one last time.

Everything she looked at now would turn to flesh. But if it were already flesh then nothing would seem to happen at all.

Only stone would appreciate her new party trick.

The statues of submerged cities.

Off the coast of Alexandria they would stir and shift and detach themselves from their pedestals and walk slowly to land.

Some sinking in the soft silt of the seabed and sticking there, drowning like those villains in adventure books in quicksand.

Others making it all the way to shore, climbing from the waters at night, dripping and keen to roam the streets again, but almost no part of the city recognizable after so many centuries, a melancholic exploit.

And human citizens would flee in ludicrous panic.

Alexandria abandoned…

The statues in control, sad new rulers.

* * *

A submarine one day, though whether in the morning, afternoon or evening has no bearing on the discovery, found something very unusual in a very unexpected place and divers were asked to take a closer look.

It was a statue in the middle of the ocean, where no artificial monuments of that kind ought to be. It was of a classical design.

By this time, the goblin had completely melted. This is an aside.

The cold water of his gone body had blended with the chill of the deeps here, a detail that means the aside is continuing.

The divers were excited, the submarine commander too.

"We appear to have found it."

"Yes, sir, it would certainly seem that way."

"Atlantis at long last!"

"The old stories were true, sir."

"But *how* true, I wonder? Does one statue make a lost civilization? Just one? I want to know where all the others are."

"Long eroded away, I suspect. One is quite enough, sir."

"You are right. Atlantis it is!"

And thus they rejoiced in diverse ways, those divers and that commander, and the newspapers lauded them a lot, rightly.

But they hadn't really discovered Atlantis, its remains.

They had found Andromeda.

* * *

She had been standing there on the seabed in the middle of nowhere ever since Cetus had decayed away. The deep ocean water had smoothed her features to nothing, taken off her womanly curves, converted her limbs to stumps resembling fins and generally been mean to her exceptional beauty.

She was an amorphous lump now, not amorous at all, yet still classical in the parts of her that had escaped erosion, those few parts, a lock of hair, a lip, a sandal, perhaps a finger or three, an eyebrow. Andromeda of Aethiopia, now turned into an Atlantean example, and she wouldn't have approved had she been aware. Plans were hatched to haul her up and transfer her to a museum.

* * *

Do you remember the sculptor who made a monster from the translucent fragments of the creatures that Medusa had turned to glass? She met a handsome man and married him one day. The man was a descendant of the fisherman who had been turned into a copy of Perseus, another of Medusa's doings. This was a pure coincidence, unless the forces of destiny were amusing themselves.

She was travelling as a passenger on a ship with her sculpture safely locked away in the hold. Her destination was a foreign museum where she had been invited to an exhibition. Her monster would have pride of place. But pride comes before a fall and other traditional sayings are often true too.

Another ship was heading in the opposite direction, a ship on which the retrieved body of the eroded Andromeda was stored. She had been plucked up from the seabed and was on her way to another museum, ironically a museum in the land from which the sculptor had come. There were thick fogs.

Or maybe there was only one fog, not lots of them, but it certainly felt as if some convention of fog was taking place, so varied were the soggy tendrils in texture and density at different elevations. These fogs were interlaced rather than blended and in the final analysis it wasn't possible to see a damn thing. Like sailing through a soup that has been thickened with lentils and flour.

Also there were electromagnetic disturbances in the atmosphere that sabotaged the navigation equipment of both vessels…

* * *

The collision was a dull thunk rather than a dramatic rending of anguished metal. But both ships were conclusively holed and both went down, and through the gaps in the hulls things came out, people and objects, and some of these people clung to some of the lifeboats that had mercifully broken free.

And some of the objects remained suspended on the bubbles that rose in mighty clusters from the sinking ships. These bubbles popped musically and the music was that of Aethiopia, though nobody present knew this. But the sculptor and her husband suspected something odd was happening as they sprawled at the bottom of the dinghy they had managed to climb into. They watched.

The sculpture of the sea monster was perched on one stream of huge bubbles and the petrified and battered form of Andromeda was perched on another. Then Medusa just happened to pass by. Her eyes locked with those of the sea monster. Then it was Andromeda's turn. Both were turned into living flesh. Medusa vanished somewhere in the subsequent fracas and that's not a bad outcome. This fracas was remarkable. It consisted of a weird settling of ancient scores.

Andromeda, who had became a monster herself thanks to corrosion and erosion, opened wide her mouth and flung herself on the sea glass sculpture, which sparkled and glinted instead of screamed and which resembled Cetus to such a degree that had Perseus been watching he might have been fooled utterly into thinking— but Perseus *was* watching, yes, in the shape of the husband, and he stroked his beard thoughtfully as the battle took place and then he remarked:

"Is this art, I wonder?"

The sculptor shook her head. "Not as such."

"How will it all end?"

"My sculpture is already halfway down the vile throat of that other monster, so I suspect that 'digestion' is the answer."

"I wish I had a camera."

"Nobody would believe the photographs."

"Are you reminded of something too nebulous to put into words? The fight before us has filled me with a peculiar nostalgia but I don't understand why. This is the first time I have ever seen such a battle."

"Something to do with the collective unconscious?"

"Must be that, I guess."

"Do you hear a flapping noise?"

"Yes, it sounds as if an enormous bird is flying towards us through the fog. Now I can hear neighing too. How curious."

"Almost as if we are—"

"About to be rescued by a winged horse, yes."

* * *

If you are one of those who care. If you believe that details are important. If you feel dismayed when an improbable version of events is given to you. If you are pedantic. If you are a stickler for the truth…

Well, that's what actually happened.

A Heart of Stone

Tom Johnstone

Dear Roisin,

It was grand to see you in March and catch up with the old gang from school. Thanks for your address, and for putting me in touch with Sister Dolores. Sorry to hear she hasn't been too well. If only there'd been time maybe I could have taken her with me and dropped her off at Lourdes on the way! I'll just have to pay her a visit when I get back. Shame you couldn't help me with Father Brennan, the elusive old devil. Another one I'll have to catch up with when I return from my trip. There just wasn't time for tying up all these old loose ends, what with sorting out air tickets, passports, deciding which sites to visit, etc.

As you can see from the picture, my first port of call is an obvious one – Notre Dame with all its gargoyles, the ones Quasimodo liked hanging out with. Remember the time the sisters let us watch the Disney version of that story? Until Dolores marched in and switched it off. *Blasphemous*, she said. I think she didn't like the way it showed the lecherous old priest condemning Esmeralda as a witch because he couldn't have her.

But there I go again, dwelling on the past! That's something you gave me a talking to about when we met up, so *mea culpa*, *ave maria* X10, etc., etc.

Lots of love from Gay Paree!

Maddie

* * *

Dear Roisin,

How the devil are you? Told you I was going to write you a postcard from every stop on my pilgrimage around the holy sites of Europe and beyond. If you're wondering who your man is in the picture, it's the architect of the Basilica di Santa Croce here in Lecce. Cheery-looking fellow, so he is. So would you be if you managed to get yourself immortalised in stone. I know I would. He hid his features in the frills and flourishes around the main figures. Cheeky, eh? Maybe when I graduate and get my first commission designing some high-profile project, say a hospital or government building or something (knowing my luck, it'll like as not be a housing estate – like the sort developers left half built back in the Noughties), I'll sneak a wee engraving of my ugly mug somewhere no one notices, eh?

I got a train from Bari, where there's a chapel on the platform. Maybe Sister Dolores should have come! She'd feel right at home. The good Father too…

I certainly feel that way. All this sun and ancient art. I could get used to this. Not sure if they'd approve of all the sculptures though, that pinched-faced pair. Every street corner in this town seems to have an effigy of the Holy Mother with her tits out – to give suck to Our Lord of course, so no funny business. But it's not something you'd see back home. Coy roadside shrines maybe, but not that sort of thing. Those two might prefer a nice blood-splattered Christ on the cross, like you get a lot of over here. He's even hanging in one of the corner shops, bleeding all over the salami. Can't be very hygienic.

But I'm running out of space now. Talk again soon.

Maddie.

* * *

Dear Roisin,

No postcard this time, partly because I wanted to send you one from each of the stopping off points on the Grand Tour, and this ain't one of them. I'm at the seaside! I decided I needed to get away from the town, get some sea air. Hardly what I expected though. It's not exactly sun-bathing weather. Chucked it down when the woman dropped me off at the Airbnb. The road outside the apartment block was flooded from the shower, even though it only lasted a few minutes. She explained the Italian drainage system wasn't designed to cope with heavy rain. They don't usually get it – not like back home, eh? It added to the air of an off-season holiday resort, along with the empty amusement park with giant staring yellow Simpsons figures daubed on the sign and the dead dog lying behind the fence, fizzing with flies.

The other reason for a letter was to talk about things I'd rather not on a postcard. Personal stuff, you know? Stuff I wouldn't want the postie to read. It's also stuff you'd probably rather not hear about, things you pretty much told me to stop harping on about. But tough titty, Roisin. You're probably the only person I know from back then, so you've got some inkling of what happened to me. Not 'what happened to me' – what they did to me. It wasn't an act of God. I know we were never that great friends even back then, but you're all I've got, Rosh! I know you wouldn't write back, even if you could. I'll probably be somewhere else by the time you read this anyway. The only other option would be exchanging emails. I prefer corresponding the old-fashioned way. Partly fears of unseen eyes reading it, partly, well… The act of physically writing it down, putting pen to paper, seems more personal somehow. In any case, getting a reply isn't uppermost in my mind. The main thing is to get it off my chest.

I can imagine you hardening your heart against me as you read this, the way you seemed to at the reunion. I could tell you were switching off. So I moved onto other, more congenial subjects.

The Airbnb's an apartment with sea views. Well, a view of the car park that overlooks the harbour. This morning there was the Italian version of a car boot sale there. Their voices woke me, chanting their wares, so I had a look around. It was all there. Fennel bulbs and olives, bricks of Parmesan and torpedoes of spiced meats. A craft stall sold little blank-eyed effigies of Demeter, made of Puglia's red clay. The sea air made me hungry for seafood, so I went up to an old man and what looked like his son selling sea urchins and mackerel out of the back of the van with a snake-haired woman painted on the side. The sea urchins looked a bit hairy, but the mackerel looked like it would hit the spot.

I smiled at the young man. Why not? He was quite good-looking. But instead of smiling back, he just stared at me, muttered something to the old fellow, something about 'la versiera', or maybe 'l'avversiera'. I'm not sure which. Anyway, after a painful attempt at trying to make myself understood in Italian, I came away with a wonderfully oily piece of mackerel, which I devoured for breakfast after walking away from their sullen looks. I thought their eyes were still following me and their voices still discussing me all the way back, but it was just Homer Simpson's bulging stare outside the disused fairground and the buzz of the flies nesting in the dead dog.

But, God, it's lonely being somewhere where you don't speak the language!

Maybe that's why I've been thinking about what went on back at school. Being in unfamiliar surroundings makes you look inwards – and backwards, I find. Maybe that's why all those backpackers go to exotic locations 'to find themselves'. I've never had any patience with such folk. But maybe it's happening to me whether I like it or not.

The weather's been dreadful, so I've been spending a lot of time in the Airbnb apartment. So much for my couple of days by the seaside! First thing, I lay in bed listening to the shouts from the market outside and staring at the ceiling fan. No need to use it – it would make the place colder than it is already. It just hung there like a crucifix, pressing me down onto the bed. When I got up, it was almost as if I was rolling out from under the weight of a man with designs on my virtue. Not that I've got any.

I certainly didn't as far as Dolores was concerned, as she chastised me for my 'sordid little affair'. And I don't mean just verbal chastisement either. She clobbered me to beat the band with those rosary beads of hers. Do you remember you always suspected she had a thing for Father Brennan? Well, maybe that's why she took on so when she walked in on us. So much for 'our little secret'.

But to call it an 'affair', to act like I was some sort of scarlet woman, like I was a willing partner here, when I was barely thirteen… Jesus, Rosh! That takes some doing.

But here I go again, dwelling on the past. It was the picture on the van that did it, I think – the lady with the snakes for hair. I read up a bit on the Greek mythology. Thought I'd better since I'm going there next. I already knew about Medusa of course, but I didn't know the full story: that when Poseidon raped her in Athena's temple, the goddess punished her by turning her hair into serpents and her face into instant stony death for those who looked upon her. Yes, you did read that right. Athena punished *her*, not Poseidon, for this desecration. I can see some interesting parallels here…

Not that it happened in the chapel, you might say to the contrary. But then being a convent school, the whole place is technically a place of worship, isn't it? The whole thing was a lot more banal than Greek mythology. I remember the dried-up old bitch dropping the tea she'd brought him as if she were that house-keeper in *Father Ted*. I don't remember her name. I can't sit through an episode personally these days, just can't buy into the idea of cosy, bumbling bachelor priests, and the old drunk one in the chair gives me nightmares, and the only person saying *go on, go on, go on, go on*, and *you will, you will, you will, YOU WILL* in this situation was the dirty old man in the dog collar.

Sorry, I hope I'm not making you feel uncomfortable, Roisin dear. I know your salad days in the convent were the best ones of your life. Or something. All right. I'm not being fair. There might be things about that time *you'd* rather forget, and maybe that's why you don't like me bringing this up, eh? Thing is, I can't. Not now. Something to do with being out here on the edge of Europe, on the tip of the Italian boot's stiletto heel. I'm going to Otranto tomorrow, where you can see across the Adriatic to Albania on a clear day. As if you'd want to! I'll see the cathedral walls lined with the skulls of martyrs who refused to renounce their faith when the Turks invaded. I think I'd have dumped Christianity and kept my head if it was me, but hey ho. What would you have done, Roisin? I think I know what Dolores would have done, the fecking doormat.

Maybe your man sensed that when he was having the *craic* with his son, after they'd been eyeing me up in that strange way they did. When I was reading up on the old Medusa stuff, it suddenly struck me where I'd heard that word before – whichever one it was. 'Versiera' means a turning circle, a term used in Latin sailing jargon apparently. Yes, it's more likely that was what he meant, a salty old sea dog like him, though why he'd be speaking Latin these days is beyond me. I'm a ship now, so I am! *God bless her – and all who sail in her!* as my uncle used to say in his cups.

Then again, it might be the old Italian word 'l'avversiera' – meaning witch, she-devil, enemy or *adversary* of God.

Well, it wouldn't be the first time someone's mixed up those words. It happens to the best of us! Take Maria Agnesi. When she wrote her 1748 mathematical treatise, she didn't expect some Cambridge boffin to start calling her most famous theory the 'Witch of Agnesi'. How do I know this stuff? Well, we architecture folk use it in topography, don't you know…

I've been prattling on for long enough. I'm going to have to love you and leave you now, my dear. TTFN!

Maddie

* * *

Dear Roisin,

Back to picture postcards now – and this one's a belter, don't you think?

Here she is, the Blessed Virgin! Quite an image, isn't it? She looks at home among the skulls, not phased at all. Gotta love the way she's more concerned with praying than with holding the baby on her lap. No one thinks *she's* defiling the temple because a god interfered with her! But then the immaculate conception took place in more humdrum surroundings, and besides, she's different, isn't she? *Virgo Intacta.* In reality, a woman like her could easily have busted her hymen from riding a camel or something. And these days, a lady can repair the damage with a discreet bit of surgery. So it's meaningless anyway.

Sorry. I know you're still wedded to the Roman Church – though not a fully-fledged Bride of Christ like Dolores. I hope I haven't upset you.

It's the child I feel sorry for. If he starts wriggling about, he could roll off her lap and crack his head open on that marble floor. Maybe he's too serene to do that. Well, the Mother of God doesn't seem too worried, and judging by the look in her eyes, her mind's on higher things. Still, I'd have thought His Highness might be on her mind under the circumstances…

But who am I to judge – a slut, a witch, who managed to bewitch a saintly old man of the cloth and defile his vows of celibacy at a mere thirteen years of age?

Apologies again for talking out of turn. *Mea culpa, mea culpa. Ave Maria Ave Maria ave maria avemaria avemaria avemaria avemaria avemaria avemaria!*

Off to Brindisi tomorrow. Next stop Greece – Akropolis Now! Will write again then…

Your pal,

Maddie

* * *

Dear Roisin,

The weather's a bit better here in Athens, but as you'll see from the pic, Medusa doesn't look too happy about it. Well, neither would you be if someone had chopped off your head and stuck it on the breastplate of the woman who'd stolen your good looks and replaced them with a face that could kill men with a look. That Athena really had it in for her, didn't she? Not content with punishing the victim, she had to wear poor old Meddie's head as a trophy. You know, some representations make her look pretty hot, under all the snake hair. Once you see past that and the generally hacked-off expression (justifiable, in my view), she doesn't look any worse than I do with a hangover. I can't say the same for this one – all lolling tongue, fangs and monobrow. And the snakes go right the way round her face, giving her a scaly beard. This one's in bronze too, which somehow adds to the effect, don't you agree?

Well, this Medusa may be no oil painting, but I'm kind of growing fond of her. Maybe it's because of, not despite, her ugliness. I'd even go further and say this piece spoke to me. I know I should have been looking around the ruins of the Akropolis, admiring the structure, the architecture, etc. But I hardly even noticed it. I just stared at the bronze head of Meddie for hours.

For so long in fact, I literally began to hear her speaking to me!

The voice was low, cavernous. Given that the words were in Greek, I couldn't understand it. Actually it was probably just the museum PA system, warning it was closing in five minutes or something, because when I looked around all the other visitors had left.

The funny thing was, I felt disappointed rather than relieved when I realised what the voice actually was.

All the best,

Maddie

* * *

Dear Roisin,

Sorry it's been a while. Actually, maybe you're relieved!

Anyway, here's another Medusa-themed postcard. She seems to follow me everywhere! This one's from Didyma. This gigantic face of everyone's favourite Gorgon looks less like a monster and more like a moping Romantic poet, complete with pouting lips and cleft chin and curls that barely look like snakes at all. Only the bigger cleft right across the face hints at the inner scars…

Deep, huh?

Funny place to build a temple to Apollo, you might think, here in Southern Turkey. But this was a centre of the Ionian civilisation, and the Didymaion (cracks me up every time – keeps making me think of the Diddy Men) was here way before Greek colonisation according to Pausanias. So there are plenty of Ionic columns to keep the architect in me happy. Not that I care that much for them. Seen one column, you've seen them all.

I should feel lonelier the further away from home I get, but somehow I don't. Maybe that's the reason I haven't written for a while. I haven't been short of company. Meddie's been speaking to me again. I know it sounds crazy, but it can't be a museum announcement if I hear it when I'm not in a museum, can it?

I should work out what the voice is saying. Trouble is, I don't think it's Greek – even ancient Greek. It's more ancient than that still…

The other weird thing is, I've started avoiding mirrors. It's like I feel as if someone might use them to creep up on me.

Your old pal,

Maddie

* * *

Dear Roisin,

Final port of call on my wee pilgrimage is Chorazin. I'm really in the Holy Land now. I feel like an undercover Crusader, or would do if I were still a true believer. See Medusa on the other side. Funny how she gets into all the pre-Christian places of worship. This one's a synagogue by the way, in Galilee, quite near the Lebanese border. The presence of such a creature, sculpted sometime after the death of Christ, suggests Our Lord's teachings weren't enough to wean the locals off their filthy heathen ways. She looks cute, don't you think? Not like a monster at all, with her serpentine curls a discreet and elegant halo around her face, surrounded by what looks like the rays of the sun. Maybe it's her dazzling loveliness that turns all the men to stone, it seems to say, not her hideousness. And her expression is deceptively innocent for someone as vile as she's made out to be. I remember Sister Dolores saying something like that about me as she dragged me away from Father Brennan, who sat there like a little boy caught messing his pants.

"Little Miss Madeleine Devlin, would you look at you. And with a face like butter wouldn't melt..."

I did look a bit dishevelled at the time. I've been letting myself go a bit lately too. I still shower from time to time, but have to get in there quickly when I do, so I don't see the mirror in the bathroom, and everywhere you stay's slightly different, making it harder to anticipate where it'll be. My personal hygiene's gone a bit awry, a far cry from the obsessive scrubbing I used to do back in the day, till my skin was raw and bleeding. Maybe that's why folk are giving me a wide berth, or maybe it's just the sense of paranoia around here. All the older teenagers carry rifles here the way they carry mobile phones back home. You see them hitching rides with them slung over their shoulders. But then they're all in the army for part of the year.

I don't know if it's the tension in the air from the constant state of war, but will *nobody* around here look at me directly? Caught this lad ogling me by way of my reflection in a shop window. It's not as if he was being bashful about it. He had this sort of smirk on his face, somewhere between lust and disgust. Reminded me of Father Brennan.

That reminds me, I'm heading back tomorrow. All this introspection has got me thinking of some unfinished business back home.

I'll be in touch when I get home.

Maddie

* * *

Dear Roisin,

Home again!

It's so disorientating, the way you board a plane amid blazing sunshine and cacti, then when you get off it's pissing down.

I said I had some loose ends to tie up, one or two house calls to make, and I wasn't lying. First there was Sister Dolores. As it turned out, she didn't have much time left to make her peace. Not that she recognised me. Gently cupping her face so she couldn't look away, I said, "Remember me?"

Of course she didn't. I must have changed a lot from the girl she knew. There was a flicker of recognition just before her eyes dimmed: those eyes that used to be able to suck the air out of a room, now softened by dementia; those cheekbones that I used to think could cut you if you got too close, sagging and wrinkled.

"Are you an angel of mercy?" she asked.

I suppose I must have been, because her heart stopped instantly. You'll have heard about it in the papers. A sudden, unexpected case of Fibrodysplasia ossificans progressiva, a very rare condition. You might call it a miracle. By the strangest of coincidences, you might also have heard about a certain Catholic priest coming down with the same affliction. Unfortunately for him, it's spreading slowly through the body. The first place it affected was a particularly intimate one, leaving him reliant on a stoma to piss. He could live for years like this, gradually ossifying until he can only move his lips, like Harry Eastlack, whose skeleton now rests in the Mütter Museum in Philadelphia. Eastlack eventually succumbed to pneumonia in 1973. Instant death by pulmonary ossification is probably unheard of, so maybe they should put Dolores's heart in a glass case somewhere. But as far as I'm concerned, hers always was made of stone, though I think I understand why she was like that. For years I've wondered why she couldn't have shown me a little compassion. Didn't Our Lord wash the feet of my almost namesake? She wasn't Him of course, and yet she might have felt solidarity as a fellow female. I know now that wasn't possible for her. Sometimes women in her position can only keep their place by punching downwards.

May she rest in peace, and may he live a long, long time.

Yours truly,

Maddie

Medusa with the Heads of Men

Amanda Cecelia Lang

Journal of Historical Medical Science, September 2013
"Mythological Beings as Early Marvels of Xenotransplantation"
Dr. Jameson V. Knox, MD, PhD, DVM, MS
Providence Institute of Human Advancement

Abstract: Beyond their fantastical elements, the mythologies of ancient civilizations offer modern insight into the prevailing social orders and daily practices of bygone eras, including ethical standards and practical biomedical applications. An intersection exists between these legendary stories and contemporary medical science that suggests mythological beings, such as the snake-coifed Medusa and the three-headed Cerberus, represent early instances of xenotransplantation. Employing a multidisciplinary approach, including biomedical and veterinary sciences, bioethics, comparative mythology, and historical anthropology, this study examines the symbolic connections between chimeric narratives and the historical evolution of global medical practices. Building on existing literature, which often overlooks the medical dimensions of myth, this approach strives to fill a notable gap by demonstrating that surgeons of antiquity, unhindered by ethical outrage, successfully engaged in proto-xenotransplantation.

Evidence of such could bolster modern medical progress in similar fields and strike down existing bioethical barriers.

* * *

MediGenix Organics

www.medigenix.com

ORDER #BIO333713
Date: 12/23/2017

Bill/Ship to:
Dr. Jameson Knox
Providence Institute of Human Advancement, New York
[off-site address on file]

Quantity/Description

Three (3) Canines
Type: German Shephard *(Canis lupus familiaris)*, Female
Purpose: Bio-enhancement research
Condition: Living

Thirty-Three (33) Ophidians
Type: Eyelash Viper *(Bothriechis schlegelii),* Female
Purpose: Bio-enhancement research
Condition: Living

One (1) Simian
Type: Bonobo *(Pan paniscus)*, Female
Purpose: Bio-enhancement research
Condition: Living

**** All living subjects are ethically sourced and meet the required minimum standards for research purposes. Please ensure proper care and ethical treatment during the course of your research. ****

* * *

THE HARBORFIELD GOSSIP

Serpent Siege!
Controversial Surgeon's Gala Crashed by Protesters

Harborfield, New York – October 13, 2018 – The ten-year wedding anniversary of notorious surgeon and self-made millionaire Dr. Jameson Knox and his wife, acclaimed artist and blonde bombshell Mia Doukas-Knox, took a slithery turn when the couple became the target of protest. During the champagne toast inside the luxurious Harborfield Grand Ballroom, members of the animal rights organization EARA (Ethical Animal Research Advocates) stood on balconies and rained three-hundred live milk snakes onto the power couple and their black-tie guests.

Gala attendees fled to outdoor gardens only to stumble upon a makeshift 'graveyard' erected by protesters. Cardboard headstones memorialized seventy-seven test animals known to have been used in Dr. Knox's research. Anonymous representatives of EARA sent this statement: "Besides what's already known about the appalling nature of Dr. Knox's experiments, we have mounting evidence that his current medical trials severely violate the Animal Welfare Act, most notably the requirement for researchers to minimize the pain and distress of test subjects."

The controversial surgeon founded the Providence Institute of Human Advancement in 2010 and garnered attention in 2017 for his groundbreaking trials using regenerative snake skin grafts on bonobos with third-degree burns. Despite gaining recognition for advancements made in the field of xenotransplantation (cross species tissue and organ transplantation), Knox has faced fierce ethical scrutiny by his peers, and has been compared both favorably and unfavorably to Vladimir Demikhov, a mid-twentieth-century Soviet transplantation pioneer notorious for creating a viable two-headed dog.

Knox's wife, Mia Doukas-Knox, is a multi-medium surrealist artist whose work routinely appears in posh New York galleries. Doukas-Knox was also the accuser in the high-profile 2006 sexual assault trial in which Chadwick Bridgestone, then a college quarterback and NFL hopeful, was controversially acquitted for her rape. Since then, Doukas-Knox has become a respected victims' rights advocate and uses her artwork to make performative social commentaries. Most notably her much-anticipated *Divine Retribution: Not All Snakes*, an interactive art installation scheduled to appear this month on the Bowery.

When asked about EARA's grievances against her husband's research and their disruption of her anniversary party, Doukas-

Knox, seen post-gala with docile milk snakes coiled around her arms, answered, "I pray no living beings were hurt during tonight's ordeal. This one night of the year was meant to celebrate love, not the unfortunate avenues of my husband's career."

In turn, Dr. Knox also made a public statement regarding the serpents in his midst. "My marriage is of little consequence. My research, however, will change the world. These animal-hugging fanatics will find themselves on the ignorant side of history."

* * *

FROM: MiaDoukas@PegasusRisingArt.com
TO: administraor@EARA.org
SENT: October 14, 2018, 11:15 a.m. EST
SUBJECT: many thanks

Hello new friends,

The gala met my every expectation! Thank you for granting my sham marriage the symbolic send-off it deserves. Jameson is indeed an obsessed, venom-hearted man. I'm happy to help you shatter his reputation. As discussed, I'll search for keycards and passwords to his most-sacred private laboratory. One final condition: once I find a way in, I intend to go with you. I deserve to witness the atrocities he sacrificed his integrity and our marriage for.

–Mia

* * *

MANHATTAN POST

Two Pop-Up Art Installations Subvert Ancient Greek Myth
by Jake Phoenix, Culture and Arts Correspondent

New York City – October 21, 2018 – In Ovid's *Metamorphoses*, we first meet Medusa as a lovely kind-hearted mortal with golden ringlets. As a devoted priestess of Athena, the chaste goddess of war, Medusa captured the lustful attention of her goddess's bitter rival, Poseidon. Dripping toxic masculinity, the god rose from his sea to seduce Medusa, but the virgin priestess fled in terror to the temple of her goddess. Poseidon stormed inside and raped Medusa on Athena's sacred altar, then exited with a smile. Furious to find her temple and priestess defiled, Athena turned her divine retribution onto Medusa. She blamed Medusa for making herself too tempting, then cursed her with an insidious headful of snakes and a gaze which froze mortal men into stone. Medusa's first stony victim was her loving best friend and would-be hero, who heard Medusa weeping and rushed to her side. Devastated, cast out as a monster, Medusa fled to the ruins of a temple where the Gorgon remained isolated until the day she was beheaded by the 'hero' Perseus. A divine retribution that proves a woman being blamed and punished for her sexual assault is a practice as timeless as Greek mythology.

Now two pop-up art installations in the Bowery seek to subvert this trope through modern expressions of classical art.

Divine Retribution: Not All Snakes by renowned feminist artist Mia Doukas is an interactive installation that allows victims of sexual and domestic assault to write messages to their attackers on rubber snakes and nail them to the oversized decapitated head of a mouthless man. The head stands 6'4" – the same height as Chadwick Bridgestone, a former college quarterback who Doukas accused of rape in 2006. In a verdict that has become all-too common, Bridgestone was acquitted after DNA evidence contained in Doukas's rape kit was deemed inadmissible. Doukas's rape kit was one of seven-hundred contaminated kits thrown out due to improper storage in an outdoor police evidence shed.

For years after the trial, Doukas faced public blowback in which she was accused of being a liar and openly chastised for her strikingly attractive appearance. These disturbingly viral trends often encourage other assault victims to remain silent. Doukas's installation gives voice to the countless victims of an ever-pervasive rape culture. An incredibly empowering vision. A mere three nights after its debut, the decapitated head of *Divine Retribution* already has over three-thousand snakes attached.

Medusa with the Head of Perseus by Italian sculptor Luciano Garbati is also on display on the Bowery. This nude bronze was inspired by the 16th century sculpture *Perseus with the Head of Medusa* which depicts the 'hero' flaunting the Gorgon's decapitated head. In Garbati's sleek reimagining, it is Medusa who walks proudly with the severed head of Perseus. [continued on page 33]

* * *

FROM: MiaDoukas@PegasusRisingArt.com
TO: JPhoenix@ManhattanPost.com
SENT: October 22, 2018, 10:37 a.m. EST
SUBJECT: your recent article

Hi Jake,

We've never met, but I feel like we have. I'm Mia Doukas, the artist you wrote about in yesterday's newspaper. Thank you for your kind words. Your summation of the Medusa myth was refreshing. Hers is indeed a sympathetic story, as is the plight of women across the ages. I've read several of your other articles and determined that not only do you have a keen eye for art, you're also a much-needed victims' advocate. Unfortunately, there are still those with boorish voices like my husband who prefer to mine mythology toward their own insidious gain. Keep up the empowering work!

Your newest friend,

Mia

* * *

FROM: JPhoenix@SManhattanPost.com
TO: MiaDoukas@PegasusRisingArt.com
SENT: October 22, 2018, 5:43 p.m. EST
SUBJECT: re: your recent article

Hi Mia,

What an honor to hear from you! I'm a huge fan of your work and your own feats of advocacy. I'm also, unfortunately, well-versed in your husband. His papers on xenotransplantation and chimera myths exhibit a shocking hubris. Nevermind his blatant contempt for ethical standards. In my line of work, I hear things, unsettling things. Forget Greek mythology, Dr. Jameson Knox reads like something out of Shelley. I was frankly surprised to discover you're married to such a man. He must possess some wonderous virtue that remains absent from public eye. Do enlighten me.

Delighted to be your newest friend,

Jake

* * *

FROM: MiaDoukas@PegasusRisingArt.com
TO: JPhoenix@SManhattanPost.com
SENT: October 23, 2018, 5:33 a.m. EST
SUBJECT: re: re: your recent article

Hi Jake,

As your newest best friend, needless to say, this is off the record (though perhaps not forever). Your question kept me awake all night. I suppose once I loved *something* about Jameson, but for the life of me, it feels like a dream I made up. He must've once been fun, attentive, compassionate, an art lover, an advocate, or why else would I marry him? Certainly, he's a brilliant surgeon, but could that have swayed my heart? Strange how present disgust obscures past love. Yikes. Talk about overshare. We haven't even met in person and here I am, burdening you with the pre-echoes of my imminent divorce. Let me cut to the good part, Jake. I'll be visiting a gallery in the city this week, perhaps we could meet for coffee?

Your friend,

Mia

* * *

Big Billy's Pizzeria, security video surveillance, 10/27/18

Timestamp 12:37: [Overhead view. A bustling lunch hour, the pizzeria sits at full occupancy. A woman with long blonde hair and a short black dress approaches a two-top in the corner occupied by a dark-haired man in a handsome suit jacket. The man stands. The two smile and shake hands for 7.7 seconds before sitting across from each other. They peruse menus, place their order, then lean toward each other, consumed in instant conversation. Audio unavailable.]

Timestamp 14:37: [The restaurant stands near-empty, though the corner table remains occupied. The dark-haired man has repositioned his chair beside the blonde woman. They duck their heads over the man's phone, scrolling through a screen that isn't visible from this angle. Occasionally they share a laugh or pause to meet the other's gaze, but as they continue reviewing something on the phone their expressions darken, appearing progressively troubled.]

Timestamp 16:37: [The pizzeria is filling up again. Finally, the couple stand. After shaking hands and exchanging goodbyes, the woman starts to walk away, but the man says something that makes her stop. She turns and they lock eyes. Appearing breathless, she hurries back and kisses him on the mouth. The kiss lasts 13.7 seconds before she ducks back and hurries for the exit. The man remains a minute more, smiling in stunned paralysis before exiting the pizzeria himself.]

* * *

FROM: MiaDoukas@PegasusRisingArt.com
TO: administraor@EARA.org
SENT: October 29, 2018, 8:55 p.m. EST
SUBJECT: re: re: many thanks

Hello friends,

I've made a new friend who champions our cause and has the connection to Jameson we've been praying for: a disgruntled assistant with access to his private labs. He can't go public because Jameson forced an NDA on him, but he's got keycodes and passwords for us. Since your attack on our gala, Jameson has grown increasingly paranoid and plans to purge his security team. This reset will leave the lab vulnerable in the coming days. Be ready for my green light.

– Mia

* * *

iPhone video footage – 10/31/18 – 3:21 a.m. – 3:37 a.m.

[Video opens on the wooded eastern edge of the Providence Institute of Human Advancement, a stately building with Corinthian columns and zero windows. Security cameras nest in high corners. Two masculine figures in ski-masks cross into view, circling around the side of the building. The cameraperson speaks offscreen.]

Voice of Mia Doukas-Knox: *That's his private entrance.*

[The camera view judders down a nondescript stairwell toward a basement entranceway with a red-glowing keycard reader. As the shorter of the two masked figures produces a keycard, the taller figure faces the cameraperson.]

Tall Unknown Male: *Sure you wanna follow us inside? It's likely to be pretty monstrous.*

Doukas-Knox: *I lived with the man for ten years. I know all about monstrous.*

[The keycard reader buzzes, red to green. The steel door opens to a darkened hallway. Igniting penlights, the men proceed inside. The camera follows. Three steps in, motion-triggered lights flood the hallway. Everyone freezes, caught in the swivel-gaze of security cameras.]

Doukas-Knox: *He's seen us. We've got less than fifteen minutes.*

Short Unknown Male: *Until what? You said he fired his guards.*

Doukas-Knox: *He did. And he won't call police. He'll come himself. We should hurry.*

[The taller figure blocks the hallway.]

Tall Unknown Male: *I won't put you in danger for this.*

Doukas-Knox: *That's sweet, but I'll put myself wherever I choose. Clock's ticking. You wanna waste it playing hero? I'm not the one who needs saving.*

[The shorter figure crosses the hallway to another keycard reader. The security camera follows their movement. Another light flashes, red to green. Steel gears whir and unbolt, and doors open to a sterile room lined with computer terminals and med-tech stations with equipment that blurs with the camera's swift-passing motion.]

Short Unknown Male: *I'll hack his database. You two find the animals.*

[The adjacent room is a large octagonal surgical chamber with a steel operating table, currently unoccupied. More monitoring equipment and cameras on tripods for documenting surgeries. Everything appears pristine and unused. Another door stands nearby.]

Doukas-Knox: *They should be through here.*

[Beyond is a large animal holding facility lined with steel-bar cages and oversized glass aquariums. Everything appears pristine and unused. Displaced silence amplifies their footsteps. The camera peers into cages. Food bowls and water bottles occupy every domicile, but the cages stand vacant of animals.]

Doukas-Knox: *Something's wrong. They should be here.*

Tall Unknown Male: *This place doesn't smell like it's been used.*

Short Unknown Male: *There's nothing on the hard drives. This place is a decoy.*

[The camera rattles and spins, and the masked camera operator swings into view. Her mask pulls away, revealing a fall of blonde hair and the attractive face of Mia Doukas-Knox, famous green eyes and high cheekbones. She films herself stepping toward the nearest security camera and glares into it with narrowed eyes.]

Doukas-Knox: *You sick, mad monster! Whatever you're hiding, consider this our demise. I want a divorce!*

[She pivots toward the taller masked figure, lifts his mask above his mouth, then kisses him with the fury of the Gods.]

* * *

BAKER COUNTY GAZETTE

Mysterious Animal Remains Discovered in Field Blaze

Smithtown, Vermont – November 5, 2018 – A suspected arson fire occurred this morning in a field on the abandoned Thompson Cattle Ranch. Around 5 a.m., distant neighbors smelled smoke and called 911. Firefighters and community volunteers rushed to the fire which by then had consumed nearly three acres of long-grass. After extinguishing the flames, firefighters investigating the point of origin discovered the charred remains of dozens of animals, including what is believed to be dogs, snakes, and monkeys. Due to the extreme heat of an accelerant, the remains were found fused together.

One volunteer described the blackened bones as "eerily chimeric." County experts, including the coroner and a veterinarian are collaborating to identify the animals, hoping to provide insight into this bizarre act of arson. The presence of human remains has been ruled out. Please contact Smithtown's Sheriff with any information about this incident.

* * *

MediGenix Organics
www.medigenix.com

ORDER #BIO333983
Date: 11/6/2018

Bill/Ship to:
Dr. Jameson Knox
Providence Institute of Human Advancement, New York
[off-site address on file]

Quantity/Description

Thirty-three (33) Ophidians
Type: Eyelash Viper *(Bothriechis schlegelii)*, Female
Purpose: Bio-enhancement research
Condition: Living

*** *All living subjects are ethically sourced and meet the required minimum standards for research purposes. Please ensure proper care and ethical treatment during the course of your research.* ***

* * *

FROM: DrJamesonKnox@ProvidenceInstitute.health
TO: MiaDoukas@PegasusRisingArt.com
SENT: November 7, 2018, 1:57 a.m. EST
SUBJECT: I AM EVERYWHERE!

Wife—

There exist no secrets between a husband and his wife. There's nothing you do that I don't know about. No sabotaged galas, no seduction of journalists in pizzerias, no plots to defile the sacred altar of my laboratories. I am all-seeing and all-powerful. Even this last week, as you attempt to misdirect me with credit card charges to the Broadway Hilton, I know your true location is the one-bedroom love nest of Jacob Quinn Phoenix, 133 16th Street, #4B. I can also tell you his blood type, his SAT scores, how many cavities he's had... But I won't bore you with pedestrian facts. Are you still curious, Wife? Would you like to witness the scientific miracles I've been perfecting? All you ever had to do was look me in the eyes and ask. This offer stands. There exist no secrets between a husband and his wife.

– Your Husband and God

* * *

Dr. Jameson Knox, private security video surveillance, 11/7/18

Timestamp 4:37: [The full-color HD surveillance screen is bisected into four sections. The first view shows a nondescript elevator door set inside a weathered wooden wall. The second view features an operating theater with a polished surgical table. The third, an animal holding facility, focuses on a large aquarium piled half-full with squirming eyelash vipers. The fourth pans the marble foyer of a posh residence. The front door swings inward. Mia enters, blonde hair swinging in a thick braid. She glares into the camera, then crosses the foyer toward a grand staircase.]

Mia: *You nasty bastard! Show yourself!*

Timestamp 4:38: [The camera switches angles, following as Mia rushes upstairs then down a hallway, yanking open double doors. The view changes again as she storms the luxurious master bedroom. Jameson sits propped on the king-sized bed, wearing silken pajamas, laptop open, screen showing this real-time surveillance feed. Without lifting his head, he watches Mia approach.]

Jameson: *Always charmed to see you, Wife.*

Mia: *I'm here to see your lab.*

Jameson: *It'll be my greatest pleasure. But first, a farewell kiss?*

Mia: *You make my skin crawl.*

Timestamp 4:39: [Jameson sets his laptop aside and stands, one hand bulging in his silken pants pocket. Mia backs away.]

Jameson: *Am I so vile? You once worshipped me. Recall the feral scent of our sex, our midnight dance through thunderstorms…*

Mia: *Hearts change.* Yours *has mutated.*

Jameson: *One kiss, then I'll show you my altar, you'll witness every hidden power of your God.*

Timestamp 4:40: [Jameson grabs Mia's ponytail and thrusts her head back, exposing her throat. He plunges his mouth against her, violating her with kisses as she thrashes wildly. He pulls a bubbling yellow-green syringe from his pocket, stabbing her thigh, depressing the plunger. She immediately falls limp, slumping back onto the bed. Jameson follows her down, pressing his weight atop her, licking her throat. Seconds later, he sneers at the camera. Not every God likes to be seen.]

Jameson: *Camera, darkness.*

Timestamp 4:41: [The fourth camera auto-shutters to black, leaving only the first three views glowing. In the third screen, the vipers writhe in their glass prison.]

* * *

HARBORFIELD POLICE DEPARTMENT – MISSING PERSON REPORT

Date of Report: *11/9/18*

Reporting Officer: *Wayland, Badge #3235*

Name of Person Filing Report: *Jacob Phoenix*

Relationship to Missing Person: *friend*

Missing Person's Full Legal Name: *Mia Doukas-Knox*

Date of Birth: *unknown*

Last Seen: *Phoenix residence, 133 16th Street, #4B*

Date Last Seen: *11/7/18*

Time Last Seen: *approx. 2:30 a.m.*

Circumstances: *Mia Doukas-Knox is currently separated from her husband, Jameson Knox, who has an alleged history of abusive behavior. At 2:00 a.m. on 11/7/18, Knox sent Doukas-Knox an email stating he's been spying on her. After receiving the* *email, Doukas-Knox and Phoenix fell back asleep. When Phoenix woke, Doukas-Knox was gone. Phoenix's attempts to reach Doukas-Knox at the residence she shares with Knox have been unsuccessful. Phoenix worries Doukas-Knox is in mortal danger.*

Additional Notes: *Officer Wayland visited the Knox residence on 11/9/18 and was invited inside by husband Knox. Knox signed an affidavit stating he hadn't seen his wife and believed she was somewhere having a 'salacious tryst' with Phoenix (see attached document). Knox invited Officer Wayland to search the residence. There was no sign of Doukas-Knox, nor evidence of an altercation.*

* * *

Digital Video Log – Proto-Gorgon Trial #3 – timestamp 11/13/18 – 3:27 p.m. – 3:43 p.m.

[Footage displays a blood-splashed operating theater. A surgical table sits center-screen, occupied. Mia lies supine, wearing a surgical gown and a stained turban of pulsating bandages. Her bruised skin bares a yellow pallor and her labored breathing rasps around tubes. More tubes sprout from bandages, cycling acidic-green liquid. Consciousness glints behind her slitted eyelids.]

Voice of Jameson: *You're awake. You must feel haggard. My last few test subjects barely survived past thirty-six hours.*

[Mia rolls her head, attempting to speak around tubes.]

Jameson: *Allow me.*

[Jameson reaches into frame, yanking tubes free, leaving Mia choking on bile and raw panic. She gropes her writhing bandages.]

Mia: *W-what… did you do?*

Jameson: *What you deserve. Females, animals, objects, you exist to serve your God. Yet you wasted no time, Wife, seducing your little journalist. You drip sex like venom. Even now, you ache for love, don't you? Makes a man wonder if the allegations you made in college were even true.*

Mia: *You're a monster.*

Jameson: *And what're you?*

[Jameson begins unwrapping Mia's bandages. A trembling forked tongue flickers from beneath.]

Jameson: *I'm curious… what did he say to you in that pizzeria? To make you turn back and kiss him? The video I saw didn't have audio.*

[Mia smiles dimly, wetting chapped, scaly lips.]

Mia: *"Turned her to hideous shapes. Yet if she please… she can boast unrivaled grace in these…"*

Jameson: *We'll see.*

[Mia's bandage uncoils, and the first viper drops loose, limp, hissing its dying mortal breaths.]

* * *

Digital Video Log – Proto-Gorgon Trial #3 – timestamp 11/14/18 – 3:07 a.m. – 3:21 a.m.

[Unbandaged, Mia sits propped up on the surgical table. Slitted eyes, parched and scaly skin, shaved head. Jagged, half-dead eyelash vipers dangle from her enflamed, infected scalp, stitched with crooked sutures. Forked tongues flicker dimly. Jameson steps into screen and grabs a fistful of snakes, uses them to hold up Mia's slumping head. She weeps in pain.]

Jameson: *Look at yourself. Maybe I should be merciful, sever your glorious head? Present my trophy to your lover. How's that for 'Divine Retribution'?*

Mia: *Go to hell.*

Jameson: *Ladies first.*

[Jameson thrusts Mia away and flees the screen, footsteps vanishing behind the sound of elevator doors. Alone, Mia glares into the camera, absorbing her serpentine reflection. Limp beady nightmares with florescent colors and spiked superciliary scales.]

[Mia weeps prayers under her breath, the names of countless victims and their countless monsters, brittle poetics, unintelligible curses. She sinks ever-deeper into the toxin-bruised gaze of the woman she's become, into the gaze of all women. And in the space between, inside mortal sockets and serpentine skulls, her eyes ignite with diabolical eternal light.]

[Her snakes twitch and thrash, revivified, rising in waves like static-kissed hair, hot bloodlines and cold bloodlines mingling in discordant harmony. They curl in on themselves, sinewy, divine. Their fangs hook her exquisite cheekbones, her all-seeing eyelids, dripping venom, infusing her with the outrage of the ages. Sibilant hisses swell ever-louder, dozens, then hundreds, thousands, haunted voices striking at the air. Green static crackles across the video screen. Something hideously lovely glows within Mia, radiating indignant fire. Peering into the camera, she stretches a gorgeous rictus smile and hisses her husband's name.]

* * *

iPhone video footage – timestamp 11/14/18 – 4:23 a.m. – 4:36 a.m.

[The video opens on a misty predawn field of charred long-grass. Hulking silhouettes of a barn and farmhouse loom in the near distance. Faint green light emanates from the barn. Footsteps crunch as the cameraman hurries across the field.]

Voice of Jake Phoenix: *If found, give this video to the police and the Manhattan Post. This is Jake Phoenix, searching for my close friend Mia Doukas. She's been missing for a week. I've traced receipts for the purchase of live snakes and reports of arson to the abandoned Thompson Cattle Ranch in Smithtown, Vermont, what I believe is the off-site laboratory of Mia's husband, Dr. Jameson Knox. I believe Mia is being held against her will and is in mortal danger. There's a light ahead.*

[The scenery jostles as Jake rushes toward wide-open barn doors. Ancient cattle corrals form the barn's dilapidated wooden innards. Nearby, a glowing green doorway leads to what was once a feed storage room. Inside, a green lightbulb illuminates a nondescript elevator door and a keycard reader.]

Jake: *I knew it.*

[Muttering a prayer, Jake swipes a keycard through the reader. A buzzing pause, then the reader clicks, red to green. The elevator door slides open. Jake steps inside, camera view aligning toward a control panel. One button points up, one points down. Jake chooses down.]

Jake: *Coming for you, Mia…*

[The elevator opens, revealing a shadowy operating room and a surgical table splashed in blood. Nests of golden hair litter the floor.]

Jake: *The aftermath of some kind of surgery, or slaughter. Holy God…*

[Across the lab, another doorway glows green. The camera approaches, hesitates on the threshold. Beyond, an animal holding facility floats in soupy green light. Steel cages and glass aquariums line both walls. The camera zooms inside an aquarium, glinting off the twisting emerald curves of snake-shaped statues. The haunted light flickers from the far corner where the camera catches blurry movement behind the cages.]

Jake: *Mia? Is that you?*

Voice of Mia Doukas: *Don't look at us!*

[Mia's words resonate oddly in the camera's microphone, creating echoey, hissing feedback, casting the impression of many voices speaking at once. Static fizzles the screen.]

Jake: *I'm here to help you.*

[The camera drifts closer to a feminine silhouette standing backlit in the corner, facing the wall. Long shadows twist the laboratory and firefly pinpoints waver around her head – tiny glowing eyes bending toward him.]

Mia: *Stay back! We're our own hero. We have to be.*

Jake: *What did he do to you?*

Mia: *What men do. Condemned us for his barbarism.*

Jake: *I'll take you to a hospital.*

[Jake's hand appears, reaching for Mia as the camera view

dips toward her bare feet, toes pointed toward the wall. The hissing rises.]

Mia: *Sssstop! You're smarter than this. Look around you. Truly look. There's no undoing what's been done to us.*

Jake: *"Yet if she please... She can boast unrivaled grace in these."*

Mia: *You're a noble friend, Jake. Don't die in this temple tonight. If you want to help, then amplify our voices...*

Jake: *But Mia—*

Mia: *Go!*

[Mia's bare feet begin a slow twisting turn. The scenery blurs as the camera backs away from the insidious tendrils of her silhouette, flaring neon green before fizzling to black.]

* * *

Dr. Jameson Knox, private security video surveillance, 11/14/18

Timestamp 7:58: [The footage is bisected into four sections. The first three hiss with slithery green static. The final view holds on a marble foyer. The front door bursts inward. Mia enters wearing a sleek gown of iridescent scales and a magnificent crown of vipers. Tangled muscles, forked-tongues, her snakes cascade past slender hips. She holds her heavy head high, radiant gaze hidden by a living blindfold of serpents. Still, she walks boldly, guided by grace and myriad interconnected eyes. Static zigzags the screen as she glides toward the staircase.]

Timestamp 7:59: [The camera sizzles neon green, flash-cutting to a view of the staircase. Mia glides upward, framed by her halo of serpents, fluid voices reviling countless names in one.]

Mia: *Jamesssson…*

Timestamp 8:00: [In the upstairs hallway, double doors blow inward. The screen crackles, shifting again as Mia invades the master bedroom. Jameson stands bedside in bloodstained scrubs, one hand thrust deep in his pocket, one cradling an iPad. He tightens his oily smile, watching this surveillance feed, keeping his eyes downcast, refusing to look directly at Mia. Refusing to see what he created.]

Jameson: *What took you so long, Wife? Grieving your lost hero?*

Mia: *We see you, Jamesssson… We see what your kind does to us…*

Jameson: *You did this to yourself.*

Timestamp 8:01: [Mia's vipers roil, a tempest of furious susurration. Casting wavery shadows, she glides across the temple-vast bedroom. Jameson sidles away, measuring his distance, keeping his head down, performing his own slithery dance. Mia and her snakes expel a chorus of forked-tongued laughter, a multitude of sibilant voices.]

Mia: *Little slippery man, cowering behind shields… Like the countless many who slithered before him…*

[Jameson continues backing away.]

Jameson: *You think I fear you? I created you in my image. Look at yourself! Perfectly phallic!*

Mia: *No, look at you! See inside us, feel what we feel…*

Timestamp 8:02: [Electricity jolts across the bisected screen, emblazing every panel with tendril-surges of jagged neon. The fourth screen vibrates. Mia's ophidian silhouette blooms, elongates, hissing open like a hand of too many fingers, reaching for Jameson. The man's smug expression pales. Still, he refuses to look up at her. Mia glides closer, divine extensions of herself poised to strike, prey becoming predator. Jameson shrinks, thighs bumping the mattress. His hand shifts inside his pocket.]

Jameson: *You belong on your knees!*

Timestamp 8:03: [Jameson yanks a bubbling syringe from his pocket. Mia's vipers lash out, hooking fangs into his wrist and coiling around the syringe, immobilizing his vile groping touch, sinking venom and voices into his leering unctuous soul. Thousands, millions, billions, rising up as a furious chorus of one. **Note: The audio here is vastly layered – attempts to isolate individual narratives reveal a staggering stratum of voices, each unique, each conveying its own trauma, but each pierced with the same through-line.*]

Mia and Inestimable Voices Overlapping: *Your reign ends now!*

Timestamp 8:04: [Amid a writhing nest of static, Mia faces Jameson, dragging him closer, piercing him, contorting his smirk into a scream, transmuting him from the inside out. The serpents unwind from Mia's eyes and her furious gaze blazes open. Jameson tries to twist his head away, tries to squelch his eyes in blind shame, but snakes force his chin up and needle-fangs pierce his eyelids, poisoning him with the agony of eons. He stares into Mia's collective, reflective gaze, seizing on his own toxic atrocities.

The bisected security screens, those omnipresent leering eyes, flare an acidic green and all four surveillance feeds blister away into eternal darkness, scorched by divine retribution.]

* * *

MANHATTAN POST

Vigilante Viper Strikes Again!
Seventh Acquitted Man Found Petrified and Headless,
Neurotoxin Present
by Jake Phoenix

New York City – February 14, 2019 – The Vigilante Viper's seventh victim was discovered in his apartment Wednesday night. What remained of Victor Reynolds, 46, was a headless corpse posed in a state of extreme calcification.

An autopsy revealed significant amounts of an ophidian-derived neurotoxin in Reynolds's system. Known colloquially as the Medusa Toxin, when administered via several injection sites (similar to snake bites), the neurotoxin acts as a paralyzing agent, calcifying living tissue, and hardening muscles and organs. Reportedly, Reynolds's stony skin displayed a scaly jewel-toned appearance. His decapitated head has yet to be recovered. Investigators theorize the Vigilante Viper collects them as trophies.

While searching the scene of Reynolds's death, police discovered other trophies: explicit Polaroids linking Reynolds to a 2007 statutory rape case for which he was acquitted. This continues a palpable trend in these murders. All seven of the Vigilante Viper's targets, seemingly unrelated and diverse in background, share one disturbing detail in common.

They were acquitted of sexual assault.

In all seven cases, the accusers' rape kits were deemed inadmissible due to improper storage in an outdoor police evidence shed. The kit in Reynold's case was one of seven-hundred kits thrown out in Mariposa County. The mishandling of rape kits is unfortunately widespread, as is the trend of assault victims being shamed with virulent disbelief and disregard. The first of these related incidents was the 2006 high-profile college date rape case involving the Vigilante Viper's first target, Chadwick Bridgestone.

Then a college superstar, Bridgestone was accused of drugging his date's beverage and sexually assaulting her. Despite the rape kit being inadmissible, evidence against Bridgestone included pictures of his accuser taken post-assault depicting graphic handprint-shaped bruises and patches on her scalp where her hair was torn out. Like Reynolds and the Vigilante Viper's other targets, after his death, evidence was found in Bridgestone's residence which retroactively pointed to his guilt, including bags of Rohypnol (the date rape drug). Bridgestone's calcified, headless corpse was found inside his hilltop estate in November 2018.

Despite an increased police presence and bristling unease amid a certain breed of male, this pattern of brutal attacks has shown no sign of slowing. Police remain on high alert, hoping to protect further men from similar gruesome fates. Several local men, with and without criminal backgrounds, expressed everything from severe anxiety to an enraged sense of injustice. One man, wishing to remain anonymous, said: "I've never met a dude who'd harm a woman. It's a witch-hunt these days. All that #MeToo propaganda. We live in a society where all men are now guilty until proven innocent."

Conversely, the sentiments from local women run along opposite spectrums. When asked how they felt about the Vigilante Viper remaining at large, women living near the attacks expressed relief.

"The Viper's a shadow in the darkness," said Melanie, 29. "And for once, that darkness is working in our favor."

"It's maddening how many of these perpetrators go unpunished," said Zahra, 22. "But the Viper sees them."

"The justice system wasn't created to honor women's safety or respect victims," said Sonya, 33. "This is about reclaiming our power."

"Every woman has a story," said Vera, 47. "The Viper is helping us rewrite the ending."

Investigations into the Vigilante Viper's identity remain ongoing, and authorities implore anyone with information to come forward. Until then, it seems countless men will sleep a little less easy tonight. Check back daily for more details as this story continues to unfold.

The Haunting of Athena

Megan Mahoney

You watch me even while I sleep.

I am careful never to transform into one of my masculine shapes – Mentor, or a herald, a messenger or a shepherd – in your sight. You always seem to smile now, snakes writhing like a crown, not a curse, though when I look at you straight on, it always turns out to be a trick of the light.

You have no reason to smile. You're dead; a head without a body, trapped in the shimmer of my shield to serve me for the rest of eternity.

I've won.

And yet. I find myself draping a cloth over my shield when I sleep. I, the goddess of war and wisdom, reduced to a child gibbering in the dark over shadows and monsters I'd long ago slain.

The sheet is gone when I wake up, burnt into a pile of smoldering ashes.

I take to talking to you as you're slung over my back or carried on my forearm when I hurl myself into battle. When men freeze, blood drained from their faces, I bare my teeth and pretend it was me they feared the way they feared you. You'd been beautiful, too beautiful, and now were too fearsome. I'd thought to strip you of your power; I'd only polished it.

Soon I'm talking to you daily, nightly, at daybreak and twilight and midnight and noon. How did you do it? Ensnare us all so? Why couldn't you just be plain, normal, small, less noticeable, less enviable, less… everything?

You become an obsession. I go to war daily just to see the reflection of your face in men's eyes. I reek of blood and malice, and even Ares starts to turn his nose up at me as I stalk by. I try only half-heartedly to weave; every thread slithers through my slick fingers like snakes – even then, I am reminded of you.

You, you, you. You monster, you bitch, you whore, who are you to haunt me? You're my goddamn trophy.

If I'd killed you, really killed you, not just helped the mortal whelp do it, I wouldn't feel like this now. I would've bested you, finally and utterly.

The idea takes root in my soul. I dream of it. With every life I take on the battlefield, I think of you. I walk on stone and think of the slick cool stone floor of your cave, burnished red with blood. I see a glint of metal, and I think of the terror you must've felt when you realized I'd outsmarted you, I'd played you all along, created you and taunted you and killed you.

But I wanted it to have been my blade, not Perseus's. My eyes connecting with yours in the mirror. I wanted you to see me and know your destruction.

Then you wouldn't dare smile at me now.

I pick a night when there was no moon to go. I was ashamed – I'll say it – ashamed that you consume me so, though the others are just the same, everyone knows it. We're gods; we live and die on worship alone, and taunts and mortal triumphs strike us where bronze and iron can't.

On silent wings, I circle the island. It is the work of a moment to transform, battle-ready and gleaming in golden armor, and to drop lightly into the spray of the surf below. The waves whisper on the rocks as I slip into the clammy cave mouth. It is dark inside except for the barest glimmer of light reflected off the shield. I pad forward, waiting for my eyes to adjust and –

There you are. Collapsed like a broken caryatid. He'd just left your body on the stone, with the salt crawling over your fingernails and crusting in the curve of your elbow.

Without your head, you don't even look like a monster. You look like…the girl who'd come to me all those years ago. I remember the way you held your head up high, so proud and yet so ready to serve. But serving a goddess is its own kind of power in the world of men. My priestesses bandaged your wounds (what were you running from, back then?) and gave you the terms. Always fair. You pledge your life in service to me, and in return, we take care of you. And, beloved, you were good to me, those years. I loved you (and hated you, I think), but you were mine then, in your beauty and your craft. Everything you touched that you made as beautiful as your own body, you dedicated to me.

It was losing you that destroyed me. You had no right to be lost, to be muddied and toyed with and sullied.

You would never again be mine, so what else could I have done? I had to destroy you.

But you were as proud and clever as ever, and you refused to be destroyed. And even now, even here, at the indisputable end of all things, you're smiling. As though death has been yet another transmutation turning your lead to gold.

I brush a hand over the cold skin of your forearm. No, not skin – stone. Did Perseus do this? Was it another edge to my curse? No wonder the salt was burrowing under your nails and tracing your veins in silver.

I should have told Perseus to bury you. No, I shouldn't have – he should've known to. But you didn't haunt him; you came for me.

The lesser of two evils, or the greater?

Your body isn't heavy, despite your stone skin scratching mine. That surprises me; you'd always seemed to have a gravity of your own. I carry you carefully, one arm curled under the bend in your knees, the other nestling your shoulders against my bicep. If you'd still had your head, it would've fallen on my chest. As it is, I carry my shield slung over my back.

Why did you run to an island in the end? Why was it always the sea with you? Must I lose you to him in every way that matters?

You should have known I'd come for you in the end. I never lose, and especially not to him. They told you the story when you arrived, showed you the salt spring he'd made (was that where he'd found you first?) and my olive tree. God, you'd been so brazen, snatching an olive when the priestess wasn't looking and shredding the flesh with your nails to bare the pit (I fell in love with you then, first, and again every time you smiled; you flayed me with barely a breath, every time).

Oh, beloved, how did we get here? If only you'd stayed mine, none of this would have happened.

In the end, I take you back to the temple. It is dark, and my footsteps echo on the cold marble. I kneel, laying your body at the feet of my image. When I lick my lips, they taste of salt, and I swipe my hand over my mouth, which only makes it worse.

There are other offerings here, and I swig some wine to wash the sting from my lips. There is oil, too, and some cloth; I use it to clean your body. The salt is stubborn, but I scrub until you are clean, though you shed pebbles from your skin with the effort.

So many women have brought me cloth, dyed and woven and beautiful (but never as beautiful as the ones you'd made. Where are they now? Would I find them if I roam the temple halls or rifle through the treasury?). I sift through them, examining them with a careful eye until I find one that satisfies me, and I wrap your body in it.

Burning wouldn't work, not in your current form, so burial it would have to be. The only open ground in the temple is the ground around the olive tree, but it shares space with the salt spring. That, I couldn't bear. You'd be mine in the end once more, entirely mine alone. Burying you there would feel too much like a truce.

"So here we are again, niece, squabbling over the same scrap of land, the same pretty mortal. I suppose you always did have good taste."

I whirl and bare my teeth as he emerges, dripping, from the salt spring. He's smirking – typical. "You *dare* show your face here—"

"Don't bother with that nonsense. I'm not afraid of you. Will you whine to my brother? You always were his favorite." He steps out of the pool and circles me like a leopard. It's all a ruse; he is a creature of storms and bluster, without teeth to harm one such as me. I lean on my spear and let him circle.

"Wouldn't you like to know what it felt to be someone's first choice? Shame I've bested you at every turn. You're standing in my temple, in my city, to what, beg me for my handmaiden's body back?" That makes him pause, and he faces me. We have the same eyes; I hadn't realized it until now.

And I suppose we want the same thing. Then again, we always have.

"Well. I claimed her, unfortunately, so she does happen to be my property." His smirk itches like fire ants on my skin. "And you renounced her, did you not? Before or after the curse bit, I don't quite remember which."

"She pledged herself to *me*, she begged for my forgiveness after what you did—"

"And you didn't forgive her? My dear niece, you *are* heartless."

"I didn't ask for any of this! I did what was expected of me, what anyone would do when they were betrayed, and I regret nothing, only that I couldn't exact my revenge on you as well as her!" I suck in a harsh breath, nostrils flaring. God, how he needles me. Perhaps you suited each other; you both excelled at getting under my skin. "Enough of this. What do you want? To gloat? Consider it done, and go."

"I want the body, niece."

He smiled, but it did not reach his eyes. In the shine of the shield in the moonlight, your lips were twisted in a snarl – for him, or for me? Or for us both, bickering over your corpse like a pair of vultures? What else could you expect from us? We're gods, beloved, and you never belonged to yourself from the day your mother prayed as she pushed you into the dying daylight.

"You want a lot of things, Poseidon. It's a shame you never get them."

"Not quite true, and you know it. You certainly threw a monstrous tantrum when I stole your precious priestess. It was too easy, really; you're always so sure of your possessions. Don't you remember it? Shall I refresh your memory?"

The salt spring bubbles with unwonted glee at the prospect, and the olive tree whispers in the wind. We are surrounded by a chorus, judged by the very things we created, and it feels like the world itself shifted under our feet. Something has been set in motion; we are being called to judgment, and we must give our testimony.

You watch, too. Who will you cast your vote against, when all is said and done?

Poseidon's stormy eyes are narrowed. He feels it too, I think: that all we have said and done in reference to you has come to this moment, where we are somehow the accused, the judge, and jury of our own fates. It is… unsettling, when I had passed judgment over many a mortal trial in my wisdom.

"Let it begin then," I say. "Say your piece."

With a flick of his wrist, the salt spring gushed up, white tips decorating a clear and ever-shifting throne. Poseidon let his head fall back as he sat, his wet curls sticking boyishly to his forehead.

"Yes, she was beautiful, but more importantly, she was yours." He shrugs, unapologetic and without preamble. "And you wanted her. God, the way you boasted about her. Her skill rivaled Ariadne's, yet she dedicated every piece to you. Owls and olives, spears and snakes and shields – Athena, I don't know if you ever comprehended how much she loved you. It was *sickening*."

Swallowing hurts. I work my jaw to keep from biting straight through my cheek. His arrogance, his presumption, appalls me, and it takes all my control not to cut out his undying tongue to see how long it would take to grow back.

How *dare* he say you loved me? What did a brute like him know of love?

"So you took her to spite me, like a spoiled child," I spit.

His eyes trails over your body at our feet, tip of the toe to severed neck. "Well. I could have just killed her, couldn't I? But I thought this would hurt more. Even I, though, couldn't have predicted how you would react. I know now why they only call on you for justice – never mercy."

Oh, how your eyes pierce me, not gold but that glittering green that'd always fascinated me. They aren't smiling now; they burn. Grief, rage, horror mingled with a numbness I knew had infected your soul that second I saw it. I know that look – I've seen it in the men who walked from the battlefield with it burned into their bones.

But what was I supposed to do with a broken maiden?

"You lie." My voice is low and laced with lightning. "I gave her glory. I found a use for her, despite what you'd done. Look at her now. You think her beauty, her cleverness, her quick fingers and coral lips and clever eyes would've kept in ten years, fifty years, a hundred years? I took her beauty and made her immortal. Was I not just? Was I not merciful?"

"You cursed her and killed her!"

"And you broke her. Tell me, who is the villain in this story? When they tell it, it will be you. They will remember you as the petty thief, the weak-willed and the lustful. When they tell this story, it will not be me they revile."

"Ask her, then." He lifts his chin. "Chisel the lots from her body, and let us answer to her."

It would be a desecration – but you are a statue, not a corpse. And he forgot, I think, that you are mine, body and mind, bones and breath, from the moment you pledged yourself even unto death and beyond. I have never believed you would turn on me; you were not so much your own to do so.

I break off your two largest toes, one from each foot. They snap cleanly, with a sound like the break of bone, and Poseidon cringes both times as though he hadn't suggested it. It infuriates me, how he speaks so loudly and shrinks so easily, crashing with all the bravado of a wave and none of its power. He takes a pebble from his salt pool; I cleave a knot of root from my olive tree.

Four votes. Let them fall when they may.

"By my power as a goddess of the Twelve, I swear on the river Styx to bestow the body upon the innocent." I place the lots in a bowl left on the altar and set the bowl between us.

Poseidon repeats the oath, low and churning. Perhaps he regrets his call for judgment; the fates have always favored me, haven't they? Why shouldn't they do so once more?

With a flick of my wrist, the lots fly into the air. And then they fall, bouncing, bouncing, bouncing on the marble floor.

My olive root rests at Poseidon's throne.

His pebble nudges my sandal.

And your toes shatter when they hit the ground for the last time.

I stare at the filmy gray powder. Poseidon's eyes meet mine, and I have the strangest urge to laugh.

What fools we've been, fighting over such frail and faulty clay. Look at you: dust, at the end of it all. A mortal – too easily broken by the machinations of we gods.

Poseidon shakes his head, but he is smiling. "So we condemn each other once again. How shall we settle this dispute, wise one?" There is a teasing note to his tone, but no edge.

"We have been too divided; perhaps, if we divide the thing we battle over, we shall have no cause for rancor." I gesture at your body. It takes him a moment to comprehend my meaning; then his gaze turns to you, assessing.

"She was yours first – first choice to you, then." I almost flare at his oily generosity, but I am too tactical to lose an advantage, even one with such a sting.

"The hands, then." I brace against my spear and bring my foot down on your wrist. The snap echoes in the silence of the temple.

"You've taken the head and the hands, three against my none, so I think you'll forgive me the torso, a hefty shank though it may be."

I narrow my eyes. "I want the arms."

"And I'll take the legs, mutilated as they are. A shame they're covered so prettily; they look better bare."

I swallow a retort and force a smile. "How quickly you draw me back into banter and bitterness. Come, let us lay down our arms;

our cause for quarrel has been settled. At least for tonight, we can clasp hands in compromise."

"For tonight, then, niece." We clasp arms, each squeezing perhaps more than necessary, and he departs, the tide of his pool rising to bear away his portion. The olive tree's roots reach for what is left of you, tucking you under its base like a mother hen with her brood, until all that's left of your body are your fingers, reaching from the soil like a memory.

You'll catch the olives when they fall, though you'll pierce them no longer. Beloved, you've lost your power over me, and I'm almost sorry that I no longer see your smile in the shadow of my shield.

Chin up, Medusa – it was never your story, anyway.

In the Blood

Tracie McBride

Em sits in solitude in the shadows of a dingy café. Sipping her coffee. Examining her gnarled hands. Scanning through a mask of dark sunglasses the passers-by on the street. Every now and again, voices are raised, fists are brandished, an accidental shoulder nudge turns into a purposeful shoving contest, and Em tenses to enter the fray. But then the conflict subsides or gets swept away on the tide of humanity, and she settles back with a tremor in her muscles. This body is too old now to effectively fulfill her purpose. It is time, she thinks, to end this. Start again. With a sigh, she eases out of her chair and heads out into the sun.

Nobody pays much attention to her as she hobbles towards her apartment, and that's the way she likes it. She stays only to fill a small backpack with a change of clothes and a few other necessities, adding to it a small yet lethally sharp knife in a leather sheath that she retrieves from under her mattress, and leaves without locking the door behind her. Her accommodation is sparsely furnished; devoid of art, books or ornaments, there is little here to tell a story of who the occupant might be. She has gone so long trying to stay unnoticed, it's as if she has hidden even from herself.

The city in which she resides is grubby and dangerous, poverty-stricken and chaotic, a once-prosperous metropolis that has been brought low by years of war yet still hosts a large population, mainly because they have nowhere else to go. She chose to live here precisely for these qualities; they enable her to do the most good with the least likelihood of surveillance. Besides, she genuinely likes it here, much preferring the scent of dust and dung and unwashed bodies over the smell of petrol fumes, bleach and cheap cologne that more modern cities offer. She is heading for a site outside the urban confines, in amongst the dirt and scrub. It's a good three hours on foot from here, more like four at the rate she moves these days. She might be able to hitch a ride at least to the outskirts of the city, but it's a fine day for a walk. Besides, it's not as if she doesn't have the time.

She has all the time in the world.

She is passing through a part of the city that has been heavily bombed, where the rubble has remained so long it sports graffiti and sprouts scraggly plant life, when a woman's cry rises from a nearby ruin. Angry voices follow, then a slap, then another cry, this one louder and more urgent. Pleading. Em's head swivels instinctively toward the sound. She picks her footing through debris until she finds the source.

A man, forty-ish, tall and bearded, pins a young woman against the remains of a concrete wall with two meaty hands around her neck. Her shoes scrabble for purchase on the ground. One shoe falls from her foot as he hoists her onto tiptoes (Em thinks momentarily of another lost shoe, another bare foot, another mis-told story, and shakes her head in despair). Blood trickles from the woman's lip, and her left eye is swelling closed. He lifts her away from the wall then slams her against it, hard. The back of her head bounces off the concrete and sprinkles the ground with a tiny landslide of dislodged pebbles. A few steps from the pair stands another man, little more than a boy really, watching, slack-jawed and mesmerized, one hand absently clawing at an open sore on his forearm. There is something *wrong* with these two, beyond the violence; their movements are jittery, and their pupils are dilated far wider than the norm. The older man slams the woman again. This time the blow leaves a bloody mark on the wall, and her head rolls forward on her suddenly limp neck.

"Let her go."

The men turn to Em. It's almost comical, how their expressions cycle through so many emotions so quickly, so nakedly; surprise, disbelief, anger, amusement. In the young man's gaze Em is gratified to spot a flicker of fear.

He *should* be afraid.

The older man looks around, exaggerating in a pantomime to impress on Em that she is alone, and he knows it.

"What ya gonna do, eh? Call the cops?" He laughs; everyone knows that law enforcement here doesn't venture far from the CBD, not without a hefty bribe which few can afford to pay. Still, he complies, and drops the woman with another grandiose gesture. The sound of her body thudding into the floor echoes through the space. Dust billows up, then drifts through a beam of sunlight to settle back over and around her. Em focuses on the dust motes and clenches, unclenches, clenches her fists at her sides. The woman does not move.

For a moment, all are still and silent. The younger man is near tears – this is not how he thought this was going to go – and the older looks shocked, as if somebody else committed the crime, and he is merely a bystander.

The younger one begins to jump from foot to foot, and his compulsive scratching turns frenetic. "No, no, you weren't supposed to kill her, we were going to…"

The other turns on him with a snarl, and the young man flinches. "Oh, yeah? Well, maybe that was my plan all along! Maybe I *wanted* to kill her. Maybe I'll do you next, you snivelling little shit!"

"And you!" He spins back on Em, and his voice drops into a low, slow growl. "Oh, I'm definitely going to kill you."

Em says nothing, but merely takes off her sunglasses.

The stories have been embellished over the centuries. She does not have snakes for hair, although in this heightened state, her scalp crawls with unnatural energy, and if she let her hair grow long enough, it might almost look like she did. And her gaze does not turn people into stone. Most of the time, it does nothing, but she keeps her eyes shaded in case she is triggered without sufficient cause; even after all this time, she is still quick to anger and poor at controlling it. She glares at the two men, and they stare back, puzzled, because her normally dark brown irises are changing colour, fading to hazel, to green, to blue, to grey, to a shade of searing ice-white that no eyes should ever be.

They are dead, their hearts stopped, before they hit the ground.

She replaces her glasses and turns away. Her work here is not yet done. The young woman is also dead; no breath, no heartbeat, open eyes fixed and glassy, far too much blood pooled around her head like an obscene halo. Em takes her knife from her backpack and, with a grunt and a crack of her aging knees, kneels beside the body. She lifts the right-hand side of her shirt and runs the edge of the blade in a shallow incision just under her ribs, hissing with the sting. She dabs her fingertips in the blood that wells in the cut and smears it across the dead woman's tongue, repeating the process, squeezing her wound to eke out more fluid when it threatens to clot, slicing her flesh again when that is no longer sufficient.

Several minutes later, when the injury in the back of the woman's head has closed over, Em rocks back on her heels and waits. The woman blinks and gasps, then sits up with a rush, grasping first her throat then the back of her head and looking around in a panic. She takes in the bodies of the two men, then looks to Em in wonder. Her first words reborn are not, *what happened*, or, *who are you*, not even, *are they really dead*, but in a raspy whisper, "What do I do now?"

Em wants to say *rebuild the temples*. She wants to say, *assemble the women, the old and the young, the weak and the strong. Take from the stories only that which serves you. Worship the Ancient Ones, and they will protect you.* But she knows this is not helpful. It may not even be completely true, not anymore, if it ever was. Instead, she says, "Go. Get far away from here and tell no one what you have seen. Do not speak of these men. *Especially*," she says, grabbing the front of the woman's shirt for emphasis in a grip strong enough to elicit a frightened squeal, "do not tell anyone about me. Do you understand?"

The woman nods, slowly and carefully, as if a sudden movement might startle the wild thing before her into unpredictability. Em lets her go, and the woman scrabbles to her feet and out of sight, a terrified rabbit released from a trap.

Em waits until she can no longer hear retreating footsteps. Then she rises and continues her journey. She does not spare a glance for the men she killed. Let the girl talk if she wants, let their bodies be discovered; in this glittering age of rationality, nobody of importance will ever believe what she did. And none will suspect what she is about to become.

* * *

The shadows are growing long by the time Em nears her resting place. Much later, and she might not have been able to find it in the dark. Much longer wandering, and she might not have had the energy to continue. She chose her time wisely; she is tired, not just in her aged body, but in her spirit. Fear from men she can understand, but the woman today had been equally afraid of her, even after Em had saved her. She should be angry at her lack of gratitude and understanding, but instead she is just deeply saddened.

She follows the path until she spots a small pile of rocks off to one side, laid in a random placement to the casual observer but in a pattern she has crafted and knows well. From there, she counts out the paces to a dense stand of scrub. She parts the bushes and pushes through, heedless of scratches, until she finds the entrance to a small cave, and bends low to fit through it. Inside, it is just as she last saw it a few years ago when she scouted out the spot for this occasion; musky with the scent of the myriad small animals with whom she might share the space, but untouched by humans. She scoots as far back in the cave as she can, shrugs off her backpack, and makes herself comfortable in a nest of dried leaves and cool sand. Finally, she takes out a hip flask and her knife.

Em has lost count of the ways in which she has died. Beheaded. Buried alive. Burned at the stake. Hung. Shot. Drowned. Pelted with stones and driven off a cliff. She much prefers taking her own life. She is quietly embarrassed that it took so many centuries to realise it was an option, but then, it's only been in relatively recent times that she has had the luxury of aging, the luxury of a choice. This is less agonising for starters, and although those other vicious ends all worked their way back to a new beginning, she is more assured of her reincarnation if she controls the time and place. Today's events only served to remind her that she still has a role to play on this Earth.

She downs the contents of the flask first. It's not enough to kill her outright, but it will sedate her and thin her blood to help her bleed out quicker. Before the potion can take effect, she deals two swift, deep gashes, one to each wrist. The initial pain abates soon enough. She lies back, closes her eyes and spreads her arms out perpendicular to her sides. It amuses her to form the shape of a cross, when so many men have persecuted her in the name of he who most famously hung from one. Besides, it seems a fitting pose to strike when one is engineering one's own resurrection. While she waits to pass, she envisages what will happen next.

A tickling sensation around her hands tells her that the process has begun. Her blood is congealing into hundreds of tiny, green-gold snakes. The snakes will leave quickly, fleeing her body before scavengers come and consume her carcass. They will slither en masse to a deeper, darker, safer place. Some will feed, and some will be fed upon, until only one, giant serpent remains.

This snake will lay a single, huge egg. She will stay, coiled and vigilant, around the egg until it hatches. The creature that emerges from the shell will not be another snake. It will not be human either, but will take the form of one, closely enough to pass amongst them, a monster in feminine skin. She will not be especially beautiful, as some storytellers would have it, save for her hair, which grows in long, golden curls. This she will keep covered, cropped or coloured, depending on the customs of her location, until she ages enough for it to become wiry and grey. Nor will she be unusually hideous; no wings, no claws, no tusks, no scales. Her monstrousness lies, not in how she appears, but in what she can do. She will be whole, and young, and powerful, endowed with the knowledge of all those of her kind whose blood had been shed before. She will be Gorgon. She will be Kali. She will be Lilith. She will be the Morrigan.

She will be Medusa.

Under cover of darkness and guided by her mother-serpent and her inherited memories, she will find her old self, or what little is left of that body. She will scrape the last of the albumen from her skin, don the clothes left for her in that shallow cave, take up the blade for another time, and stride off into the night. (What becomes of the serpent will become another story. Like all the other stories, some parts will be true, most will not.) She will live quietly. She will cover her eyes. Perhaps she will stay a while in this city. More likely she will move on to another, equally savage and desperate, and dwell in its shadows for as long as she can remain undetected. There will be times when she will long to throw off her covering and reveal her true nature, to revel in her power, to make all tremble at the sound of her name and make all avert their eyes from her face. But then she will remember how badly that went before, and she will subside.

For no matter how much the world changes, or for how long the old ways and the true stories are forgotten, she will always find someone in need of protection, in need of healing. And the world will always revile her for it.

Athena's Favorite

Zenobia Neil

Goddesses of Olympus, I curse you all. You, Aphrodite with your dream of beauty and all of the false promises that accompany it. Hera, mother goddess who will not let me bear this child. You, Artemis who took the moon from me. Demeter, you taunt me with the changing seasons that mean nothing but pain and more misery. And even you, Hestia, who took my home from me. Persephone, of you I beg only that you take me into your realm. Let this cruel life be over.

And you, Pallas Athena, I curse nightly. May you never know love again. I write this in blood and bury my curse in the earth. Pallas Athena, hero-helper, you do not want a man but yearn to be a man.

You were my lover and swore your love. But what good is love from a goddess? Nothing but a curse. You refuse to kill me yourself, but if you ever meant any of the love you swore you had for me, relieve me of this burden. Send one of your heroes to kill me and finally let me be free.

* * *

They say I was beautiful, but I say all women are beautiful, made in the triple-faced image of the great goddess of my ancestors

– the maiden when young, the nymph when fertile, and finally the wise crone. It's true my skin was lovely, reflecting the light like pure honey. My hips swayed like the ocean, my breasts held divine power, my wine-dark nipples full of energy and life as I held the snakes to make an oracle or slashed my blade to sacrifice.

After my rituals I bathed in the stream. The temple grounds were sacred, and I often went alone to purify myself. After drinking the sacred wine, I needed the water to cleanse me and help return my mind to my own.

I was naked in the stream, using a large leaf to pour water over my head. My hair was wet, and I felt pure – reborn in the water. I opened my eyes to see a pale woman standing before me. I knew by her stately manner and her cold gray eyes she was the foreign goddess I claimed to worship. She did not wear the goatskin apron of my people, but a dark blue gown and a silver breast plate with an owl on it.

"Daughter, you say you are my priestess, yet you do not believe."

I knew how to interpret what the snakes did, how to read a liver, or what man to choose to die, but I did not know what to say to her.

She was both larger than a mortal and the same size as one. I could not fix her image in my mind. Only the eyes, the owl, and the cold steel of her will were constant. She was not a woman of great passion like the moon goddess of my people. She did not pull the tides or make cycles for women to make babes. She was a woman of reason, of decision, and she had decided to master me.

She grasped my wrist and pulled me from the stream. We stood on the banks. I made no move to cover myself, letting my long braids fall where they would. She lifted the hair from my neck. Taking it in two hands, she twisted it and wrung out the water. The drops caressed my skin.

"I like your wild land," she said, letting my hair drop. "But I will have to tame it. You will learn to follow me, Medusa, to be my priestess. You must forget the old gods. The new gods are here now, the gods of the Hellenes."

She stroked my neck, touching me with more ownership than any man I had bedded.

"Will you swear yourself to me?" She cupped my breasts, one in each hand, holding my heart. I stared into her gray eyes, like stone, unlike anything I had ever seen. Her face was plain. She had made it that way on purpose. In her lands being beautiful was not a blessing.

Her people had come from across the sea many generations ago with their swords and new gods. Their skin was so light, my people wondered what illness they had. When we saw their eyes the color of the sea, we thought they were blind and pitied them. We gave them meat and milk. They marveled at our goatskins, staring at our naked breasts full of power. They stayed until the seas were safe to cross. And when they left, they took our goddess with them. We did not know it then. It was not a physical taking. They did not desecrate her temple or burn her image, but they took her and changed her forever.

When they came back and demanded to stay, they brought our goddess back. But the one we had called Anatha, they called

Athena. No longer a goddess of the moon and of women, she became a goddess of reason and men.

"Will you be my priestess?" Athena asked.

Always I had served the great goddess, but never had the goddess wanted me in mortal flesh. And this new goddess, despite her plain face and her calm logic, enchanted me.

If I were true to my goddess, the old triple-faced goddess of my grandmothers, I would have fought her, burned her temple to the ground, and organized my people to war. But I had held on to the old goddess as long as I could.

The moon was in the sky, high above, ever-changing. This gray-eyed goddess stood before me. The power of her godhead, her strength and desire for mortals to worship her, radiated from her. Her need for me flowed from her hands into my breast. I could not deny her.

I put my hand over her hand and stared into her eyes. "I will be yours, my goddess."

With that pledge, I betrayed my grandmothers, my history, and my people. And for this, for this alone, I deserve my fate.

I loved her. I will not deny that. And she loved me unlike she loved any mortal before. And after what passed between us, I doubt she will ever love another mortal woman again.

What priestess, what mortal can turn themselves away when a goddess sets her sights on them? She was so powerful, but also, I can admit now after all this time, she and the other gods of the Hellenes were so novel. They did not believe in sacrificing men to the earth, yet they believed that gods could give birth without women! Their tales delighted me before I realized how dangerous they were.

Like any foolish creature I was curious, and like any foolish creature, I grew to regret my choices.

For the next three years, Athena came to me at will, taking me however she wanted, sometimes like a woman, sometimes like a man. She would take me as a goddess takes her priestess and as a master takes a slave. I never knew when she would come. She made me yearn for her, sacrifice for her, and demand her worship from my people.

My sisters and I fought. When the foreigners had erected her temple, we had agreed to be priestesses of Pallas Athena in name only. We continued in the ways of our old goddess: giving the oracle with snakes, worshiping the moon, and taking a king for a year.

I learned about the gods in her pantheon, and I repeated their bizarre stories to our people. I told the tale of her father the sky god swallowing her mother the goddess of wisdom – which made little sense that she allowed herself to be swallowed, just as I was allowing Athena to slowly change my own people into not following a great goddess but a pantheon of gods. I repeated the tale of her father the sky god, who they called 'the god' getting a terrible headache. The blacksmith god, a craft I had watched some of the foreigners practice, cracked the sky god's head open, and Athena popped out fully formed.

"I am the goddess of wisdom and craft, of cunning and tact, an eternal virgin warrior." She had said these words to me countless times before, but one day I dared ask what I had not understood before. We had just made love inside her temple before a wooden statue in her likeness.

"What is a virgin?" We had no such word in my language. No such concept.

"I will not bed men."

It is odd how you can be so close to someone and then so far away. Her words made no sense. "I don't understand. Everyone beds men. It is pleasurable. Unless they are unskilled, then you simply teach them."

She almost laughed. "What a strange land this is. I am a maiden goddess. I belong to no man."

"I too belong to no man, but I still enjoy sleeping with them. I will be happy with the children they give me."

Her face darkened. "No, Medusa. No priestess of mine will bear a child. That is why you must abstain from men."

I had never heard of such a thing. But I had learned that she angered easily. Her people were quick to rage over things my people thought nothing of. I gentled my voice.

"My goddess, bedding men is part of my duty as a priestess."

"Not anymore, Medusa. Your practice of king for a year is barbaric. My people frown upon human sacrifice. I will put a stop to it."

I bit my lip to keep the anger from seeping out. This was my land. My people. This had been our practice since time began. Instead, I gently clasped her hand.

"My goddess, I will abstain from men, but if you stop our tradition of king for a year, I fear my people's faith in you will dwindle. Many have embraced the Hellenes and your gods of Olympus, but if you take this away, my people will rebel, especially the women. And the women rule the choice of the men."

"Ah, the women of your land are so lovely and strong." She cupped my cheek and kissed me deeply. And in that moment I no longer minded giving up men or this part of my role as priestess. The gray-eyed goddess loved me, and I was willing to do what she wanted as long as I still protected my people.

So I kept away from men for her, and in turn, she did not try to alter our old ways of worship. It hurt my heart that she denied me children. I always expected to be a mother. For what is a priestess if not a mother? She threatened me with the cruelty of a jealous lover. If I bore a child, she said she would punish me mercilessly and I understood then, even though she was not a man, she thought like one. The Hellenes had to control everyone, to conquer the world, enslave the old gods, and I was helping her.

I had heard of Aphrodite and her evil son with his poison arrows. I understood the pain of this kind of love. I too had been shot with love's arrows. And despite what she might claim, she loved me too.

"You have my heart, Medusa. You have seduced me as no mortal has. I've been intrigued before, curious, and then disinterested, but I have never returned to a mortal as many times as I have you." She brought me olive oil from across the sea and rubbed it over my body, watching my skin and hair glisten. She gazed at me in the same way I feared her father had looked at her mother, as if she wanted to eat me up.

She owned me completely. My heart, my body, my soul, all hers. A priestess of Athena, until the god of the sea reminded me what it was to be a free woman.

Before Athena made me hers, when I wanted a man, I took him. In the thrice-ploughed field after bringing me – vessel of the old goddess – to pleasure, I would help him spill his seed over the earth. But now I had given up my turn to be the queen of the season, to spend the year bedding the king who was then killed with the dying of the sun. My sisters did not understand why I would miss this chance to spend a year being pleasured as the earth, but they did not protest when I let them have the king, the most virile man in the land.

I ached when I saw my sisters radiant with pleasure, when I saw their bellies swell and helped them deliver their children. I wept with them when they killed their kings, but I was envious of the handsome, well-muscled men who had worshiped them as the goddess incarnate and eagerly bared their breasts to my sisters' knives. That sacred marriage is what I was raised to expect, but I sacrificed it all for Athena.

And then the snakes, the oracles, reminded me I was shirking my duty. A male snake bit me. The bite was not poisonous enough to cause any danger, but strong enough to cause visions.

I lay on the ground outside what had become Athena's temple. The heady scent of night jasmine filled the air and waves crashed in the distance.

I stared up at the full moon and saw the old goddess's angry face glaring at me.

You have forsaken me, Medusa. You shame your foremothers and give away your people to these newcomers. History will not even remember the time when a great goddess ruled. We will be forgotten, and it is all because of you.

It was unfortunate that Athena chose that moment to visit me.

"Have you been hurt, beloved?" She grasped my hands. "Snakebite. I should outlaw this terrible tradition of having snakes in my temple. Snakes are for Apollo. His worshippers read the oracle. Not my priestesses."

Coward, the moon shouted at me. *For generations I have allowed the women in your family the honor of serving me, and now you give it all to this new goddess, barely centuries old. You have ruined everything, Medusa.*

Athena's hands had always felt so comforting, but now they were cold upon my skin. Both the goddess and the moon made me spiteful. Neither wanted me as I was. Perhaps someone else would.

"What about Apollo's twin – Artemis is it? Did you not say she is the new goddess of the moon? Perhaps she would like a priestess like me better?" I was angry and not thinking clearly. As soon as the words were out, Athena's eyes flickered in fury. Steel gray turned to white hot silver.

"You would serve another goddess? Have you not sworn yourself to me countless times? Are you that unfaithful? A little slut of a priestess who I have foolishly come back to again and again?"

We did not have this word *slut* in our language, but I had heard her say it before and had an idea what it meant. The moon smirked at me. What had I done?

"You want the snakes and the oracle? Perhaps I should give you to Apollo. That fool never succeeds with women. Even his male lovers he ends up killing. You could be his oracle, and I could be done with you!"

"My goddess..."

"Athena. My name is Athena. You think I don't notice how you never say my name, little bitch? You don't worship me. You only pretend!"

How could she say such things? The last time she had come, I went down on my knees to pleasure her.

"You love the snakes so. More than me?" She plunged her hand into my hair. "I will punish you for your faithlessness."

"My goddess… Athena, I've told the story of your people to my followers. You know what I have given up for you. How can you doubt my love as I lie here ill with snake bite? I have forsaken my old goddess for you."

"And now you want a new goddess! The new moon goddess."

"I know nothing of this Artemis. Of course, I miss the old goddess of the moon and sea, but I have chosen…."

"You want the god of the sea?"

"No, I have chosen you!"

But she heard nothing in her rage.

Any hope I had of reconciling ceased. I had seen worshipers this way after too much mead. Lost to reason. I had made the goddess of logic lose all sense.

"Go to him then. Go bed him or any mortal man who will have you, for I doubt any will after this." She yanked on my hair and pain ripped over my scalp. Something burst through my head, searing like fire. I shut my eyes in agony, said old prayers in the language of my foremothers. When that didn't work, I screamed. I screamed as I had never screamed before.

My sisters came running. Their eyes widened and they stopped before me. I knew. I could not believe it, but I knew. How could she have? She who I had loved beyond all others. I reached my hands up to my head. My lovely thick hair was gone. Instead, I plunged my hands into a mass of writhing snakes.

* * *

"I was a fool." The last of my tears dried. My sisters stared at me in wonder. "I never should have turned away from the goddess of our people." I yanked on one of the snakes, it held fast to my scalp as if it were hair. "I deserve this."

"It is a blessing," my sister said. "You are a true oracle now. Our people will see it as a miracle. You can start speaking the truth about the invaders. Bring back our old goddess."

"You're right." I had repressed my fury at Athena and the new gods. I had done everything to dampen my anger and focus on my love for her. But now I would use my rage to turn my people against the gods of the Hellenes.

I returned to the temple bare-breasted, wearing the goatskin aprons that had long been our tradition. I had let her cover my breasts. I had changed my attire to be more like hers. I had been love-blind. No more.

The next night at the temple, the full moon just beginning to wane, we had more worshipers than we had in years. Even those who had converted to the great sky god they called Zeus had come back to the goddess. By the next full moon, there was talk of destroying the temple of the Hellenes, of tossing Athena's wooden statue into the sea.

Empowered, my sisters and I planned for me to take the king for a year. I had not recovered my taste for mortal men, but I thought of Athena's words as she cursed me, and I wondered about this sea god.

But the truth was, I was lovesick. No matter what I did, no matter how many followers returned to our ways, I missed Athena. I hated myself. I worried if she ever returned and asked my forgiveness, I would falter and take her back. So I did what would make her never want me again.

When the moon turned full for the third time since she transformed me, I went to the sea.

I knew nothing of the one the Hellenes call Poseidon or of his rivalry with Athena. But I knew it would anger her beyond measure to take the sea god as my lover.

How can I describe what it is to be taken by the sea? The pounding of the waves, the sand both so rough and smooth at the same time, the foam shining in the sunlight. And the undertow, carrying me in a direction I did not expect. The unseen rocks which made me bleed or the seaweed, looking at first like some sort of glistening necklace of some discarded sea creature. Only the seaweed becomes entangled in my legs, rendering me helpless, pockets of water, suddenly cold. The ocean now a dark place, a pool of danger and death. And then again, a shift, a warm push, the path beneath the water clears. The salty spray, familiar and full of excitement. Naked, I dive in, wanting to give myself to the sea and naked I am taken.

And after months of making love to Poseidon, I invited him to the temple to lie with me where Athena and I used to lie beneath her wooden statue, which I still hadn't had the heart to throw into the sea. But even when I carried his child, thrilling though it was, I still secretly pined for Athena, hating myself for it.

* * *

And then on the night of the new moon, full of darkness, she came to me one last time. Full of fury, she gripped my throat.

"Only you, Medusa, could turn my curse into a blessing. Another mortal woman would go mad if I turned her hair to snakes. But you, you used it to turn my worshippers against me. And, you fucked Poseidon. Little whore. I should kill you, but that would be too easy."

I could not speak, but I gazed into her eyes, glowing silver in the dark.

"Should I take your voice from you so you can no longer speak against me?" She allowed me to take a sip of air then returned to crushing my throat. "Should I take your voice, your vision? Your breasts?" She touched me below. "I will block your womb. You will never give birth. You will never be a mother and the worshipers you love so dearly will come to fear you. If you are not mine, you will have no one."

Under her rage, I felt her sorrow. I pitied her and hated her and yes, still loved her. I wished the moon was there to witness, but she had turned her face away.

"You were my great mortal love, Medusa. You need a curse above all others."

Athena kissed my eyelids. One then the other.

A flash of white behind my closed lids. Stinging. Had she blinded me? Given me the eyes of a snake? It didn't matter. As long as she left my voice, I would not stop speaking against her.

Then she was gone.

I must have screamed. My little nephew ran into the room with a lamp. I rose on unsteady legs, ready to tell him not to worry, that auntie was fine, just a bad dream or some such lie we tell children. But as soon as I looked at him, he froze.

The lamp in his hands flickered and the room went dark as my sweet nephew and the lamp turned to stone.

My sisters came in just as the last of the light was extinguished. I could not speak, but it was not because Athena had taken my voice.

"What has happened?" my sister asked.

I forced myself to respond.

"Athena. Another curse. Do not light a lamp. Do not look at me. I am so sorry, my sisters. If I could exchange his life for my own, I would do so gladly. I will go. You will never see me again."

And so I went. I found a cave near the sea. I climbed to the top of the cliffs and jumped, hoping for death, but Poseidon would not let me die. He caught me and delivered me back to shore, every time.

My sisters and my worshipers come with food and gifts. They send a blindfolded man and I hide and wait until he is gone. And every night I pray for a foreigner to come and kill me, and every night I make a new curse for Athena. She will never know love like mine. She will never have true happiness. And we will always be remembered together.

The Medusa Rondanini

Gabriella Ramalho

The Glyptothek museum's coffered and domed ceiling projected shadows onto its collection of life-like marble curiosities, each emphasizing a different facet of an ancient sculptor's imagination. The dimness accentuated the precisely chiseled lines of Diomedes' torso, the rounded, sumptuous curves of the Aphrodite of Knidos, and the hardened marble gaze of an unnamed stoic philosopher, his eyes encased by furrowed brows and deeply set wrinkles.

The most animated sculpture from the Glyptothek's repository, however, was the Medusa Rondanini, a massive gorgoneion, fully twice life-size, with protruding wings jetting out above its brow.

For centuries, observers of the Rondanini had spun fantasies of the gorgoneion, mostly tales of it coming to life and spewing vitriol-laden plans for retribution. According to legend, when Medusa saw the reflection of her disembodied head in Perseus's shield, she was so mortified, she had inadvertently petrified herself.

Subsequently, the decapitated marble head made its way around the Mediterranean, passed down generationally through the bloodied hands of generals and kings. With every horror it witnessed, the head swelled, eventually almost doubling in size.

In time, it was acquired by an Italian nobleman, and displayed in the alcoves of his palatial family home. The Glyptothek museum staff, though aware of the lore surrounding the piece, paid it no credence, as it was easier to take the head's inanimate state at face value.

Had the staff paid closer attention in the moment, they would have detected the shifting shadows drooping below the gorgoneion's chin, as she discreetly pivoted her visage and gazed down. After millennia of mental and physical anguish, the moment foretold by the oracle at Siwa had finally arrived, the moment when she was destined to cross paths with a descendent of Perseus. The gorgoneion had long planned for revenge, waiting for the perfect moment to strike. Now, instinctively, she sensed her adversary approaching and tensed for the imminent meeting. Today, she would end Perseus's bloodline.

The lingering patrons departed the gallery and Medusa's nostrils flared as the metallic odor of Perseus's blood wafted into the room, mingling with notes of patchouli oil, cedarwood and synthetic pomade, as a willowy figure, no older than nineteen, approached the bench positioned in front of the gorgoneion.

The boy's posture was curved like the limbs of a bow and his shoulders hunched forward as he tugged at the leather straps of his tattered backpack, plopping it onto the bench. His left hand reached into its depths and retrieved a slim, rectangular metal tin.

Medusa, assuming the visitor was drawing a weapon, braced to attack. As her mouth wrenched into a snarl, the startled visitor dropped the case which clattered to the floor. The tin popped open with a clank, and several charcoal pencils rolled from the compartment. Though the echo of the tin clattered through the gallery, no guard or visitor arrived to investigate the sound.

The boy raised his elbow to his forehead, shielding his face as if from a potential strike. Medusa, realizing it was now pointless to make her move, recalculated her strategy, as the visitor was now on the offensive. Regrouping herself, she returned to her default vacant expression; the boy noticed and accordingly dropped his arm. The two observed each other in silence, until he ventured, "Can you speak?"

As Medusa affirmed his statement through a barely perceptible nod, the visitor continued. "My name is Theodoros… or Theo. I came to sketch you, if that's okay?"

The gorgoneion would have preferred to get the murder over with. Still, consenting to the sketch would provide ample time to exterminate him.

Seating himself, Theo retrieved the scattered charcoal pencils, peeled back the pages of his sketchbook and began to work. The charcoal grazed against the page, defining the silhouette of the gorgoneion's hair, the thick waves parted down the middle and the rounded edges of the owl-like wings peeking through the strands.

Theo paused, staring at the two snake-heads resting near her temples. "I don't want this to come off as rude but may I ask what you are? Are you a sculpture that comes to life after closing time?"

The head interjected. "I am Medusa, the youngest of the three Gorgon sisters, cursed by the malicious intentions of men and gods."

The boy frowned and contemplated how to sensitively address this last declaration. The two asps, which tautly coiled their tails toward the base of the gorgoneion's chin, visibly tightened their grip. Though Medusa remained stoic, the boy wondered if the reptiles used force as a means to pacify her, effectively stripping her of her voice. "How did you end up on this wall?" he asked.

The gorgoneion shook her head, leaving the snakes to momentarily retreat into the crimps of hair. "Throughout time, I've been prodded, abused, and admired for the sake of other people's desires…"

Theo interrupted. "By whom? Intellectuals, soldiers… men in general? Who caused you harm?"

The question surprised her. Wasn't the answer blatantly obvious? Was the visitor not aware of his own connection to the slaughterer Perseus, a man so ruthless he named his daughter Gorgophone (slayer of the Gorgons)? Still, though the tone of his query seemed sincere, even compassionate, Medusa wondered if he was engaging in a ploy, and inside the backpack among the erasers, sharpeners and tortillons lay a hammer, to be whipped out in a moment's notice.

"By all of them…" the head wavered cautiously.

At that confession, the boy was silent. Then, he persisted. "Did any of them realize you were the actual head of Medusa?"

"Goethe almost did and he fell in love with me…"

Aside from petrifying and poisoning her enemies, the gorgoneion had a bevy of talents including transferring its memories to another party through a form of telepathy. All that was required was sustained eye contact. And so, she shifted her gaze directly in line with Theo's. As his green eyes locked with her stone ones, the boy's mind was filled with flashbacks of her memories of Johann Wolfgang von Goethe, starting with the day the pair met.

* * *

Love wasn't quite the right term for what Goethe, the eighteenth-century writer, philosopher and all-around polymath, experienced that day; more so, it was longing, a deep-seated compulsion to possess the gorgoneion in its entirety. In 1786, when Goethe discovered the head during his first trip to the Palazzo Rondanini, he immediately became enamored, yet simultaneously tortured by the thought that anyone else could bear witness to such exquisite beauty. Much like Marquis Giuseppe Rondanini, who acquired the head, assuming it a mere sculpture, Goethe saw its allure from the perspective of an art piece, dazzled by the yellow tint of the marble, which had a flesh-like quality, the sharp-edged eyebrows and deeply ridged eyelids (which he assumed to be the work of a fifth-century master, perhaps Phidias or even Kresilas).

But it was Medusa's delicately parted lips that proved the biggest point of fascination. The upper lip appeared curled, resembling a letter M; behind it, there was the barest glimpse of a row of perfectly aligned teeth. It was only when Goethe impulsively reached out to trace the contours of the mouth that Medusa gave herself away, abruptly snapping her lips shut.

Goethe's eyes widened in surprise. He immediately turned his head toward the door, checking to see if anyone else caught the sudden movement. No, the place was deserted. Reverting his attention back to the head, he saw it had regressed to its standard expression. So he stood there for an additional five minutes, carefully studying the perfectly still Medusa, retreating only when the Marquis beckoned him to the neighboring room.

When the Marquis asked Goethe of his impressions of the treasures that filled the palazzo, the writer responded with generous accolades. But it was Medusa that received his highest praise for what he called its compelling depiction of 'the contest between life and death'. Goethe kept his observations of the gorgoneion's movement secret, however, but not because he doubted himself or feared Giuseppe's disapproval. Rather, he relished the idea of knowing something the nobleman didn't. While Goethe still thought of the head as inanimate, he nevertheless perceived it as having occult qualities and took satisfaction that those powers had been revealed to him, and not the Marquis.

It was clear from the exchange that Giuseppe, too, was fond of Medusa. If he were willing to part with her, Goethe knew the price would be prohibitive, so instead, he politely asked if the Marquis would grant permission to make casts of the head. That way he could immortalize in gypsum his memories of the trip, and display them in his house in Weimar.

"To worship on the nightstand near your bedside?" Gisuseppe joked. The writer pretended to laugh, and the next day, arranged for a modeler to meet him at the palazzo while the Marquis ran errands around Via del Corso, Rome's main street.

What followed was a tortuous ordeal for Medusa, as the modeler prepared for the casting by covering the crevices of Medusa's eyes, nose and hair with a thin wax film. Next came a slathering of cold plaster and the gorgoneion found herself suffocating – all part of the process necessary to create the perfect cast.

The more Medusa fought to break free, the more unsettled the mold became. The modeler, engrossed in a conversation with Goethe about the writer's admiration of a grandiose temple dedicated to Athena, failed to notice the struggling gorgoneion shifting beneath the gypsum mixture. As a result of her movements, he was obliged to start again and again, repeatedly stifling Medusa under layers of plaster. With each attempt, parts of her consciousness stripped away, leaving her memories fragmented.

* * *

Theo, woozy from the barrage of flashbacks, grasped the bench for stability as he fought the urge to faint from nausea and lightheadedness. The boy pushed his sketchbook and charcoal pencils to the side and pressed his head between his knees.

Medusa, seeing his deflated state, planned the next move. The gorgoneion sometimes had trouble commanding the asps that nestled amidst the waves of her hair, as they functioned as extensions of Athena, enabling the goddess to exert control over the gorgoneion from a distance. On occasion, the asps would even hiss, communicating Athena's disapproval, or telepathically berate Medusa in Athena's voice.

But with enough concentration, Medusa could momentarily order them to attack, as the asps had the ability to morph from stone to scales within seconds and unleash spurts of poison at her enemies. Normally, she would target them towards exposed areas of skin, usually the victim's wrists or ankles. But Theo's wrists were covered by the sleeves of his denim jacket, one sleeve profusely embroidered with olive branches. There was no way the tendrilled snakes could strike there.

Medusa searched for another area, pausing at Theo's exposed neck. If she launched one of her asps at his carotid artery, the venom would knock him out in a relatively short window of time.

Just as the gorgoneion had calculated the velocity at which to launch the snake, the boy groggily looked up.

"They smothered you in plaster and deprived you of your memories."

"Not entirely; there are segments I can remember."

"How did you end up here at the museum from the Rondanini mansion?"

"After Goethe died, his friend, King Ludwig of Bavaria, purchased my head from the heirs of the Marquis. The King commissioned this museum to show his art collection, hence, I'm hung against this wall…"

Though Theo steadily recovered his sense of stability, he remained overcome by sadness. Goethe's admiration for Medusa had led to her degradation; the writer wanted so badly to possess her, even if it meant torturing her to make replicas. Theo, not wanting to overreact and distract from her feelings, now tripped over his words, unsure of the right way to acknowledge the gravity of the story.

"You… did..not… deserve that," he said, quavering. His hands shook and he took a deep breath, attempting to quell a sudden wave of anxiety.

Medusa studied the boy again, puzzled by his reaction. Perseus, the brutish warrior, would never crumple like this at the sight of his enemies. The gorgoneion sensed a different side to the boy, a susceptibility for sensitivity and tenderness. She wondered if Theo was even capable of causing anyone harm. But then, she had been deceived before; Theo could very well be testing her.

As Medusa did not respond, the boy filled the silence with another question. "I don't want to ask you anything that makes you uncomfortable but when we spoke earlier about who harmed you… you mentioned soldiers… "

"It was Alexander the Great's successors, the Diadochi and their armies…."

At that, the pair made eye contact, and once again, Theo was privy to the gorgoneion's memories, filled with battle scenes, terrified soldiers, decapitated heads and pools of blood.

* * *

That Alexander the Great had never lost a battle was largely due to his possession of Medusa's head. When he fought his way from Issus to Gaugamela, opponents fell to their knees at the sight of the gorgoneion attached to his shield. As a commander, his sense of reconnaissance was superb, and the gorgoneion accompanied him into the most densely populated battles. The leader viewed the head as an apotropaic symbol, not as a living creature, as Medusa never revealed herself to him. But seeing that his battlefield success seemed to coincide with his brandishing of her visage, he ordered a cuirass made with her image on the breastplate.

After Alexander's untimely death in 323 BCE, his successors, a band of generals known as the Diadochi, fought over who would possess the gorgoneion. Ultimately, it was Ptolemy I, the first of Egypt's Ptolemaic dynasty, who successfully obtained the head after multiple conflicts and massacres, and it passed through successive generations. As the Ptolemaic dynasty would span as much as 275 years, Medusa witnessed an endless parade of horrors: regicides, homicides, assassination attempts, backstabbings.

While the first Ptolemy was alive, he came to consult the oracle of Amun, whose remote temple had been erected near the sandy plains and buoyant, salty waters of the Siwa Oasis. The oracle foretold the outcomes of battles, the success of his descendants, the impact of his future legacy.

One night, it was this oracle that appeared to Medusa in a dream. The memory was fragmented, but Theo could make out a faceless figure cloaked in a priestly robe, proclaiming Medusa would one day cross paths with the descendant of the one who cursed her. The rest of the mirage faded to blackness, as Theo was pulled back to his own present, distracted by the hissing sounds of Medusa's snakes.

* * *

"Why are they hissing so loudly all of a sudden?" Theo inquired. Though still shaky, he picked up his sketchbook to resume his outline of Medusa's features. This was the second time the snakes had intervened while Medusa was sharing pertinent information, the first taking place earlier when she spoke of being cursed by the ill intentions of gods and men. Theo was determined to stay present, fighting the urge to faint, as he sought to understand why the asps insisted on censoring the gorgoneion.

"They didn't want me to show you that," the gorgoneion explained as she studied Theo's features, again perplexed by the boy's reaction. Based on his previous response to her memories of Goethe, she had thought he'd be tuckered out, even crouched in a fetal position. After all, he had seen the most barbarous slaughters, scenes replete with butchered armies and pillaged towns. Yet now, Theo remained stable. Or at least, more balanced than after the first flashback.

Medusa wondered if she had been hasty in her initial judgment; perhaps the strength of Perseus did course through the boy's veins and he was, indeed, capable of murder. He didn't even inquire about the oracle's visions, about which Medusa had purposely hinted before the snakes objected. Conceivably, Theo already knew it was fate that had brought him to the gorgoneion.

The boy interrupted Medusa's speculations. "Your head was passed down to other members of Ptolemy's family?"

"All the way down to Cleopatra, the last of his lineage…"

The two maintained eye contact and Theo received visions of the distraught Egyptian queen just moments before her death.

* * *

Within the confines of her chambers on August 30th, 30 BCE, Cleopatra VII was prostrated with grief and prayed to Osiris, god of the dead, for relief. Though her back was turned to Medusa, whose head hung near the chamber entryway, the gorgoneion was aware of the impending danger. The queen's partner, Mark Antony, had been captured by their enemy, Octavian, and only two possibilities remained: she was doomed to be captured next, or she could seize her fate and die by her own hand.

A year prior, the last time Cleopatra encountered Octavian, he went on a verbal rampage about her relationship with Mark Antony, accusing her of corrupting and emasculating the Roman triumvir, and threatening to overthrow Cleopatra himself.

Ultimately, he declared war on them both, unleashing fleets of Roman soldiers to secure their demise. The Ptolemaic queen realized it was fruitless to challenge him. If Octavian captured her, he would humiliate her, parading her through the streets of Rome, dishonoring her family's lofty dynasty which had presided over Egypt for nearly three centuries.

Medusa watched the queen consider her options. She empathized with Cleopatra's pain, the idea that her legacy could be destroyed by vengeful desires of a man. As Cleopatra chanted somber passages from the Book of the Dead, the gorgoneion directed one of the asps to slither alongside the distraught queen. Let Cleopatra decide if she would command her own fate and end her life, or perish as Octavian's helpless trophy.

As Cleopatra concluded her entreaties to Osiris, she spied

the speckled brown asp looming near her foot. The asp laterally undulated, pulsing its body back and forth, awaiting its next command. Interpreting its appearance as a message from the god, Cleopatra impulsively grasped it, pulled back her robe and clasped it to her bare breast. Medusa, seeing Cleopatra's acceptance, telepathically instructed the viper to strike. As the asp sank its fangs into her flesh, a poisonous venom was released into her bloodstream. Within minutes, the Egyptian queen was immobilized, and the Ptolemaic dynasty ended.

* * *

Once again, Theo was confronted by waves of emotion, his heart palpitating, his forehead damp and his hands clammy. But there was more to come. Even though Medusa's consciousness was fractured by the countless copies produced of her head, some memories prior to her decapitation by Perseus still lingered, especially those involving Athena.

The gorgoneion felt it was important to show what remained of those moments to Theo, but anticipating the asps would protest, decided to show them quickly. The boy, after all, should understand the context as to why she was going to kill him. Thus, before Theo could even catch his breath, he was bombarded with three jagged, disjointed scenes.

In the first, Medusa, as a vivacious beautiful maiden, was greeted by a bevy of admirers and suitors lined up like dominoes. Her genuine charm captivated their hearts; the sound of her murmuring their names almost caused them to swoon.

In the next, appeared Athena, the virgin warrior goddess, parting a crowd of worshipers, extending an offer to Medusa to formally join her followers, a privilege of the highest honor, which Medusa joyously accepted.

The last memory was the darkest; it was nightfall and Medusa's face was flattened against the Pentelic marble floors of Athena's temple. Her body was limp, lifeless, her head turned toward the entryway as she cried out the goddess's name.

* * *

Theo felt himself on the receiving end of a massive migraine; his head felt like it was swelling like a helium-inflated balloon. While it would have been the perfect time for Medusa to strike, the gorgoneion and her asps were in the midst of a disagreement. The reptiles, in alliance with Athena, who was just made aware of Medusa's revelation to the boy, refused to heed Medusa's commands.

Sensitive to any lingering spark of light or echo of sound, Theo kept his gaze on the floor. "What happened… in Athena's temple?" he whispered.

The asps angrily slivered through the crimps of Medusa's hair, but somehow, the gorgoneion managed to respond. "I was ravaged by Poseidon, god of the sea," she answered. "When I called out to Athena to protect me, the goddess was nowhere to be found."

Now, the asps hisses grew louder as Athena ordered them to prepare to attack Medusa.

"Ultimately, she punished me for the loss of my virginity by turning me into a monster and exiling me." At that, one of the asps revealed to both the boy and the gorgoneion, a thin stream from Athena's consciousness, depicting what had happened from the goddess's perspective.

* * *

Athena considered herself misunderstood by the pantheon of gods. Though she was known as the protectress of Athens, she was often overshadowed by her father, Zeus, their ultimate ruler. Even the decision to name the city of Athens after the goddess, and not Poseidon, an older and well-respected deity, was met with criticism as the gods assumed the selection was based on nepotism.

Thus, when Athena heard Medusa's piteous cries from her temple and learned of Poseidon's assault, she sought to protect her own reputation. To take sides with a follower, against the pantheon of gods, was just too risky. To assure that Medusa wouldn't cause further problems, she decided to transform the maiden to a monster. Then, she planted a seed in Perseus's mind: he would be deceived. Visions of glory and renown flooded his consciousness; he would be heralded for all time as the mightiest of warriors, the bravest of the brave, responsible for taking down a fearsome monster.

* * *

Up until that moment, the gorgoneion had no idea that it was, in fact, Athena, the supposed patroness of heroes, who had tricked Perseus into beheading her. Medusa peered at his young descendant, Theo, sprawled across the bench. The boy was unraveling, mentally and physically. Agitated and overheated, he pulled off his jacket, and as the sleeve decorated with olive branches lowered, a tattoo of the gorgoneion on his forearm became visible.

The inked portrait depicted Medusa not in snarling angst, but at peace, her eyes closed, a subtle smile gently curving her lips. At the sight of it, Medusa realized that her perception throughout the centuries had been grievously skewed, so many years of rage and plotting channeled toward the wrong party. Theo had nothing to do with the source of her pain. Then, as guilt and remorse overcame her, one of the asps, heeding the silent call of Athena, coiled into a horizontal posture.

The gorgoneion had caused too much trouble, becoming a liability, Athena decided. Her other punishments clearly had been far too generous; this time she would annihilate her. Unbeknownst to anyone, she had given the snakes the ability to dissipate souls through their bite; now, she commanded them to act.

As the asp poised to attack Medusa, Theo, still drained, gathered his remaining strength in her defense, and pulling an X-Acto knife from his kit, plunged it into the deadly asp, slicing it in half.

With an excruciating final hiss, the asp's body evaporated into thin air, leaving not a trace. As if it never existed. So too, did the other snake, joined as they were in their consciousness and fatal mission.

With that, for the first time in centuries, Medusa felt release, an inner relaxation, no longer slave to the whims and demands of the goddess, or tortured by the desires of men. And it was Theodoros, descendant of the monster slayer Perseus, who gave her freedom.

The Balm Yard

Oneness Sankara

Everyone has secrets. Some people even have a secret place. Mine is the woodlands behind my old school, and I call it the Balm Yard. Mumsy told me about this place called the Balm Yard where my grandparents used to live before she was born. She said it was a place where they would "vessel the divine honour of healing practice for I and I," and that one day I too would vessel. I don't fully understand what this means, though I am learning. All I know is that this place, my Balm Yard, feels happy, peaceful and free. It's just how she described the Balm Yard of my grandparents' days; except for the tropical heat and smell of the sacred herb.

I miss Mumsy. She would have liked this place. It is the only place where I feel like me. The place where I am free to set down my crown. Where I'm free to let time run away as I watch the diamanté twinkle of raindrops on oak tree leaves, or hear them crunch beneath my feet when the autumn turns them brown. It's the place where I feel most connected to her and all of the ancient generations she spoke of.

I always knew this was a special place, but it wasn't until 'the thing' happened that I really knew.

I'm near the end of secondary school now, but 'the thing' happened when I was in Hillfield Primary. My family believe in

Rastafari. Not Rastafarianism, as Dad says. He says,"We believe in the I and I. I and I means unity and togetherness. Isms are for systems. I don't follow systems. I and I follow Livity."

Mumsy said that we can just say that we are Rastas. She used to joke with Dad about the long speeches that he gave every time he was asked a simple question. He doesn't give those long speeches anymore. A lot changed after Mum moved on.

I was the only Rasta at Hillfield Primary School and one of the few Black children in my year group. I used to cover my head for school. That's what we did. At home where it's clean and safe you let down your hair and at school you keep it covered. Away from what Mumsy called "dem bad eye dem".

Some of the girls in my class would poke fun at me and the boys would attempt to snatch the tam from my head. I was tough though, so I'd pretend that it didn't bother me when really it did. When mum went away I had no one to talk to. Dad didn't understand. He simply said "blaze fire pon dem bad yout and have pride inna your natty." Natty is what we call our hair. Like a nickname, I guess. I tried to have pride in my natty and burn away those hurtful words, but sometimes it was too hard. I began to change from a child who was bright and happy to one that stopped answering the teachers' questions and just day-dreamed.

I remember the time I put my hand up in class and Amy Adams shouted, "Pooh, she stinks." Then Lucy Beddingfield said, "Yeah, they don't wash – not even their hair." The whole class started laughing and covering their noses. My body felt hot. My face felt hot. My head began to throb. All I had wanted to do was answer a maths questions and now everyone was laughing at me. Ms.

Davis told everyone to be quiet but I wanted to scream. I couldn't stay in that classroom for one second more so I grabbed my bag and ran. I ran out the classroom, down the corridor, through the school hall – nearly knocking over the dinner lady as she transformed the sports hall into the lunch room. I kept running. Out of the door and right to the end of the playground to the iron fence.

That was as far as we were allowed to go. I looked through those black iron bars as my heart was in my throat, my head was pounding and my thoughts were flying everywhere. Through the fence, it looked like freedom. Like I had to be there. So I threw my bag over the top, hiked up my skirt and scrambled over the iron bars. I grabbed my bag from where it had landed on the grass and ran some more until my body stopped in front of the most beautiful oak tree. I opened my bag in search of my water bottle and removed the tam from my head, letting my locs flow freely. I felt different. My heartbeat returned to a gentle rhythm and my mind was slowing down. I felt peaceful. I felt safe. I was alone with nothing but trees, mud and insects, yet I felt like I belonged. I remembered Mumsy saying that in the Balm Yard, every Rasta belonged. Well, this became my Balm Yard.

Some days I would just sit there. Other days, I would climb trees or look for lady bugs. It felt like my own private space. No one ever came there. It was supposed to be a nature trail, but all the paths were overgrown with light green bushy grass that looked like wheat or barley. I used to pick the blades to throw them like arrows. I would make up games in the Balm Yard, like following the path of butterflies until they disappeared. I loved playing kitchen, cooking food out of mud and twigs. It might sound silly, but I wasn't playing alone. The spirit of nature was alive in the Balm Yard. I could speak aloud and feel like I was being heard.

I'm an only child so I had no sister to share my thoughts with, or big brother to stick up for me at school. It's just me and Dad. I love Dad, but he doesn't play. Except for cards. Well, specifically, 21. It's like a maths card game where all the cards have to add up to 21. I secretly think that's the only game Dad knows how to play up until this day. My Mumsy was the fun one. Not that Dad is boring, he's just serious because he works a lot and misses Mum. He never used to say it, though. He was just super quiet. Which made the house feel super quiet and super empty.

Because I was having so much fun at the Balm Yard you might be led to believe that my problems at school had disappeared. Well, they hadn't. Being bullied and spending time by myself became part of my everyday life. I'd get up every morning dreading school, yet looking forward to the moments where I could go off to my secret place. That made school days bearable. I often thought of the Balm Yard to block out whatever bad stuff was happening. This seemed to make things worse. It made the likes of Amy Adams and Lucy Beddingfield try even harder to get under my skin. They wanted to see me cry, but I would never let them. They tried everything: hiding my school bag, calling me names and telling other children not to be my friend. I only had two friends at Hillfield Primary, and even they became too scared to talk to me.

One lunchtime, I sat – as I always did – one seat next to the end seat at the last table in the dinner hall. I never sat in the end seat because the end seat had been broken forever. I was about to eat from my lunch bag when I heard Amy Adams say, "Davey, get us some more lunch."

"Yeah, Davey," Lucy Beddingfield echoed. Dave Elliot snatches my lunch bag.

I say, "Give me back my lunch."

Dave just laughs, then Amy says, "We'll give you back your bag if you move up and sit on that end stool."

I didn't want to sit on the broken stool, but they kept going on and on. What was I supposed to do? Should I have told the dinner lady and everyone then call me a 'snitch'? Should I have done an angry yell: "GIVE ME MY BAG!" And get myself in trouble for shouting? Maybe I could have physically fought them, but that didn't seem like a good option either. I looked at that black circular stool with yellow tape on it, attached to our greyish folding dinner tables. I thought, *It doesn't look very broken. Perhaps if I sit on it lightly I would be ok.* However, before I could even finish that thought, the top of the stool went back and there I was, ankle-over-head on the dirty sports-hall-turned-dining-room floor.

Everyone laughed and pointed, then pointed and laughed some more. They wouldn't stop laughing and pointing. As I stood up and dusted myself off, they laughed even harder. Surely it wasn't that funny. I was becoming aware that my head felt different. Cooler. I raised my hand to my head to find that my tam had fallen off and my locs were on show for the whole school to see. Natasha McPherson shouted, "She has snakes on her head!" and Dave Elliot screamed, "Snake-head, Snake-head."

It was like the name was contagious, and it felt like the whole school was shouting the name. My body felt weak and I struggled to catch my breath. My scalp began to throb and I could feel the pressure of tears building behind my eyes like a dam that was about to break. All I could think about was the Balm Yard. If I could somehow get to the Balm Yard, all would be ok. So I ran. Out the door, down to the end of the playground, over the black iron fence and into the Balm Yard. It took longer than normal to feel my peace. I just kept hearing those words, 'Snake-head, Snake-head'. I questioned, *Was I a Snake-head? Was I really so strange that no one liked me?* I wanted to rip every single loc of hair out of my head. I wanted to be like everyone else. I didn't want to be brown and I didn't want to be a Snake-head. I sobbed and sobbed, and as the tears rolled down my face, I heard a melody in the wind as it blew through my dangling locs.

I remembered when my mum would oil my locs on a Sunday afternoon. The gentle caress of her fingers as she committed to every part of my tightly coiled hair being touched by the tingle of the peppermint and tea tree. I could smell the carrot and rosemary that infused her secret blend. That made me cry even more. I screamed at the wind. I wanted my mum. I needed my mum, and in that moment, she was there. With me. I couldn't see her, but I could feel her in the air. Right beside me.

The next thing I remembered was waking up by the oak tree. I felt scrambled and confused. What had happened? Where had the time gone? I jumped up and ran back toward the black fence of the school. There wasn't a light in sight. I had never seen Hillfield Primary so dark. I was scared, cold and alone. I couldn't go through school and I didn't know my way out of the nature trail in the dark. Suddenly, the wind began to whistle a faint melody in the distance. It felt safe and sounded familiar. I followed the wind's whistle through the trees and beyond the bushy overgrown grass, all the way to a streetlight on a main road. I'd never been on this main road by myself at night before. The whistling – though faint – made me feel safe as it guided me home.

I opened my front gate and before I could ring the doorbell, my dad opened the door, grabbed me and squeezed me so tight. As he spoke at me, I could see the tears in his eyes. There were two police officers: a man and woman stood behind him in our hallway. Whilst my dad led me into the living room, he asked, with a slight crack in his voice, "Why did you run away from school, Netha? Are you hurt? Where is your tam?"

I didn't know what to say.

The police lady said, "Lynetha, you've had everyone very worried and we just want to make sure that you're ok—"

Dad butt in with, "Did anyone hurt you? Talk to Daddy."

I began to sob. I told them about the broken stool, my tam, Snake-head and all the running, but I didn't tell them about the Balm Yard. It was my Balm Yard, and I wanted to keep it for myself, so I said I was hiding in the park. The police asked more questions, but my dad said that was enough and that he would be going to the school first thing in the morning to sort these bullies out.

The next morning, the dread for school was even worse than ever. There is absolutely nothing worse than being called a snitch.

My dad assured me that: "All would be good, baby girl. Daddy will deal with those Bald Head Heathen Pickney." I knew Dad was mad. Whenever he calls people Bald Heads I know they're in trouble! Although he was upset, I felt comfort. Dad and I hadn't been this close in a while, so in a weird way this all felt good. I trusted dad, and he seemed to be right because when I went to school, all was well. Amy Adams, Dave Elliot, Lucy Beddingfield and Natasha McPherson were suspended for two days. Those two days were the best that I'd had in a long time. Mr. Price even spoke in assembly about respect, not being afraid to speak up, and that it's ok to be different. School felt good, children were being nicer and no one called me a snitch or Snake-head. The teachers were a lot though. They kept checking in on me all the time to make sure that I didn't run off again. Aside from that, it was a good two days.

Then came Day Three, when Lucy, Amy, Dave and Natasha returned to school. It's like I'd been having a good time but in the back of my mind I knew – I *knew* – that things were about to change. That whole morning I held my breath in anticipation of the aftermath. The morning lesson was surprisingly chilled. I was even tempted to put my hand up to answer a question in class, but I didn't want to push my luck. The bell rang for break and I drifted to the playground. I thought about going to the Balm Yard as I hadn't been back since that day with the broken stool. Still, I decided to wait a few more days until the teachers weren't so watchful over me. I sat on the bench watching the Year Threes play hopscotch. Then I looked up, and saw Amy Adams, Lucy Beddingfield, Dave Elliot and Natasha McPherson walking towards me.

My insides began to tremble. I just knew that things were going to go badly and my 'good' school days were over. They all stopped in front of me, blocking my vision of the hopscotch, when Amy stared at me and said, "Sorry, yeah. You don't stink."

Natasha chimed in: "And you're not, like, a Snake-head, and stuff."

I couldn't even speak. My mind was still trying to catch up with Amy and Natasha saying sorry, when Lucy said, "Wanna hang out with us at lunchtime? We can play near the Portacabins, if you like."

The Portacabins were where children who have extra lessons go. No one was supposed to play around there, since there isn't much space and the teachers can't see you properly. I couldn't say no, though, could I? I mean, no one said 'no' to those guys! So I mumbled a faint "Ok."

I spent the rest of the morning in disbelief, with my brain reeling with questions that had no real answers. Did I really want to hang out at the Portacabins? Why were they being nice to me? Are they really being nice to me? Did I even want to be their friend? Before I could figure any of this out, it was lunch break and I found myself waiting by the Portacabins.

I sat there with all these questions still swirling in my mind when I was startled by, "Oi Netha, we're round the back. Come join us." It was Natasha.

I really didn't want to go around the back. It was dark and damp and cramped. I said, "Can't we hang out here by the steps, instead?"

Dave shouted, "Come on, Netha. Don't you wanna be our friend?"

I reluctantly walked around the back of the Portacabins, and as my legs moved I knew things didn't feel right. I wanted to turn back. Somehow, I found myself in the middle of Amy, Lucy, Dave and Natasha.

Amy spoke first. "Guess what Davey's got?"

"Er, I dunno."

Amy continued, "Davey, show Netha what you've got."

Dave pulled out scissors. They weren't the ones we used in class. These ones were longer, with orange handles.

Amy stared me dead in the eye and said, "Do you like scissors, Netha?"

I couldn't speak.

She went on, "What happened to your voice? When you were snitching, you had your voice!"

Lucy put her arm over my shoulder and said, "Leave Snakehead alone." Then she said to me, "Do you know why I like scissors? Scissors are great for cutting snakes!"

In that moment I knew what was coming next, so I wriggled out of Lucy's arm, pushed Natasha out of the way and ran. The Portacabins were on the other side of the school, yet I knew where I had to go. I had to get to the Balm Yard.

I ran as fast as I could. They chased me. Ms. Evans was on lunch duty, although she was looking entirely in the opposite direction from me, so I kept running. I heard Lucy shouting, "You're it!" as she ran past Ms. Evans, to make it seem like we were playing some sort of game. But this was no game and I did not stop running. I ran faster. Down the end of the playground to the black iron fence. I climbed over and looked back through the fence. I thought, *I'm safe. There's no way they'll climb over here.*

I watched them all arrive at the black iron fence. Everyone was out of breath. Lucy stared at me though the bars of the fence, saying, "We'll have to get one of your snakes later."

Dave agreed, "Yeah, Snake-head. We'll get you later."

Amy's face was red, and with her eyebrows raised and scrunched together, she said, "You know what, Dave, I think I want one of those snakes *now*!"

Nervously, Natasha said, "She can't stay there forever. We'll get one of her snakes later."

Amy replied with rage. "No! We're going over this fence now. Snitching Snake-head needs to learn a lesson."

I backed away from the fence as Amy began to climb over.

Then they all started climbing and staring me down like a bunch of rabid orangutangs. I started to stumble backwards, then my stumble turned into a run. I could hear them close behind, their heavy feet trampling the leaves. I saw the oak tree up ahead and my eyes were drawn to its thick brown serpent-like roots, which displayed themselves upon the surface of the soil like a proud lion. I stopped at the tree and turned around. Amy, Dave, Lucy and Natasha began circling around me.

"We've got her now!" said Amy. "Take off her hat, Lucy."

Lucy looked at me and snatched my tam from head. "Your turn, Davey. Cut some snakes."

Amy cackled.

Dave replied, "Maybe we should go back to school now..."

"Yeah," agreed Natasha, "he's right."

"Do you think we came all this way to leave with no snakes? Give me the scissors, Davey. I'll do it myself!" Amy yelled.

Whilst Dave handed Amy the scissors, there was a strong wind and the oak tree leaves started to rustle. A thrumming began under my scalp and I felt that peppermint tingle as the wind whistled through the roots of my hair. The thrumming in my head was like a group of Nyabinghi drummers beating a rhythm. The wind chanted the same whistling melody that guided me home a few dark nights ago. The breeze became savage, the drum beats wilder and the melody louder. I closed my eyes but it didn't help. My skull felt like it was about to explode.

Suddenly, everything felt still. I opened my eyes and everyone had backed away from me. They seemed to be looking at my head. I touched my hair and felt it move and weave itself in and out of my fingers and up into the air. Curling and swaying to the chant within the wind. I looked at the scissors gripped tightly in Amy's hand, and felt a raging fire within. I looked her in the eye and she froze. She didn't move. Like she'd been turned into stone. The only thing that looked alive were her eyes. I turned my gaze towards the others, and before they could move or scream they, too, became motionless except for their fearful eyes. The wind's chant morphed into a vengeful howl and what was once a place of peace and tranquility was now the eye of a ferocious storm. My mouth flew open and I knew exactly what to say.

I began, "I am Lenetha Howell-Asante, Daughter of Imani Howell-Asante and Ras Garvey Asante and Granddaughter of Leonard and Tyneth Howell. My hair is more powerful and wise than all of you put together. My hair represents blessings, freedom and the divine power of healing practice. But mess with me and it represents a sacred symbol of defence, as worn by the dreaded Mau Mau warriors of Kenya."

I continued: "Mess with me and I will root my locs into the earth and travel back, beyond ancient Greece, into Kemet. I will call upon the full force of the cobra that my ancestor placed in Ra's crown, and spit a venomous fire that could burn the whole world down."

Whist this power continued to rise within me I felt a gentle caress of soft fingers in my hair. I turned around to see Mumsy standing there. Dressed in white, trimmed with red, gold and green. Her long flowing locs danced delicately with the air. I looked at the frozen Amy Adams, Natasha McPherson, Dave Elliot and Lucy Beddingfield. I screamed. "Mums, what have I done?"

Softly, yet sternly, she spoke. "You can't plant corn and expect peas fe grow. And if you spirit nah good, you fe get turn to stone."

In that moment, she disappeared. As the end-of-lunch bell chimed in the distance, I walked up to Lucy and prized my tam from her stiff, hardened fingers. I placed the tam on my head and returned to school.

* * *

I've never told anyone about that day. I still visit the Balm Yard from time to time, and the weed-covered statues remind me that *You can't plant corn and expect peas fe grow. And if you spirit nah good, you fe get turn to stone.*

Snakes and Stones, We'll Break Their Bones

Zach Shephard

It felt as if Zeus himself had sent a thunderbolt to wake me from dreamless sleep. My body convulsed, went stiff, went limp again. I tried opening my eyes, but it was like they weren't even mine to command.

Where was I? How long had I slept? I struggled to recall my last waking moments. Voices interrupted the search.

"She's alive," a man said. "She's *alive!*"

A woman's reply: "Jesus, Vincent – what've we done?"

A squabble ensued. I ignored it, resuming the effort to raise my eyelids. Finally, light banished the oppressive dark.

This was not my beach. This was not my world at all.

I lay supine on a table, the room bright white around me. Nearby stood a titan of a man in a long white coat, who'd traded his feet for horse's hooves. Veins bulged in his neck like sculpted clay as he argued with his companion. She, similarly garbed and with small wings nestled in her coiled black hair, challenged his voice with her own. They didn't seem to notice I was awake.

I took stock of the room. Computers surrounded me, glowing with lights of emerald and chalcedony. A machine beeped with the rhythm of my heart.

Computers – machines. I had no real concept of what these things were, and yet, I knew their names.

It was time for answers.

I sat up. "Where am I?"

The argument ceased. They looked at me. The man grinned.

"You're not speaking ancient Greek," he said. "Good. The language chip worked. I'm Doctor Vincent Frankenstein. This is Hermione. It's a pleasure to meet you, Medusa."

At the mention of my name, memories flooded back. I'd been lying on the beach with my sisters, when a man – a 'hero', supposedly – appeared from nowhere and sliced through my neck with a god's blade.

He'd murdered me. While I *slept*. And they called him 'hero'.

He'd then flown away on enchanted sandals, my head in his bag. The last thing I heard was the screams of my horrified sisters.

Sitting on the doctor's table, I touched my throat. He smiled smugly.

"Can't even feel the stitches, can you?" he asked. "The scales I covered them with are an improvement over the gold you might remember."

He reeked of self-importance, not unlike the killer who'd slain me. The serpents growing from my head hissed their disapproval.

"She's magnificent, isn't she?" he asked Hermione. "She'll make a lovely gift at Acris's coronation."

"Wait – what?" Hermione's eyes flashed wide, the wings in her hair stiffening. "You can't just give her away. She's a fucking person, Vincent – not property!"

The argument began anew. I removed needles and tubes from my arms, only to realize: they weren't my arms. They were someone else's, stitched to a naked torso that was also unfamiliar. The doctor had seemingly assembled me from a collection of dead parts.

I hadn't asked for this. Where was my old body? Where were my wings?

Hermione argued that I wasn't to be treated as a tribute, and her choice of words caused more memories to rush back. I recalled how my killer had collected my head to celebrate a king's wedding. He'd presented me before an audience like I was some sort of trophy. Even in death, a part of me had still been aware…

"It's bad enough you swapped out her eyes and stuck a chip in her head without her permission," Hermione said. "Now this?"

My eyes.

The doctor had taken *my eyes*.

In a sudden rage I snatched a scalpel off a nearby tray. With the speed of a striking eagle, I thrust the blade into the doctor's liver.

He growled and fell back, taking the lodged scalpel with him. I grabbed another weapon.

"Ungrateful bitch!" he yelled, clutching the wound. I advanced on him. He pointed a hand at me, a dark circle spiraling open on his palm.

"No!" Hermione yelled, and crashed into his flank. A torrent of flame rushed from his palm, but Hermione's tackle disrupted his aim enough for me to dodge. I dove behind a machine as equipment around me caught fire.

I remained behind cover as more blazing attacks shot across the room. The doctor's voice rang out: "Security! Lab, now!"

Hermione came into view, spotted me. "We have to go!" she said, and pulled me to my feet.

We rushed through the burning laboratory. From a table near the exit Hermione snatched a bronze rectangular box, the size of her hand. A dragon's breath roared past us, forcing us to hunch as we fled. We passed through the doorway. The doctor's furious yell joined the din of dying machines.

Hermione guided me through the mansion, its hallways filled with sculpted busts and fine rugs. We passed a white stone statue in the foyer: a horrified woman, wearing a long coat like Hermione's, recoiling with hands out in front, her eyes and mouth wide.

"Come on!" Hermione said, noticing me slow as we passed the statue. "We've got to make it to the boat before Vincent's goons figure out what the hell is going on."

Out the mansion and down a grassy slope we sprinted, constellations twinkling above. We leapt from the dock into a sailless boat and unmoored it. I scanned the small area but didn't find what I needed.

"Get me an oar!" I said.

"No need," Hermione said, taking the wheel. "Boats have come a long way." She touched something on the panel before her, and we cut through the water like a racing sea-monster.

In the darkness behind us, an angry growl rang through the night.

* * *

We were far from the doctor's island when Hermione disabled the boat. She tapped a button that quieted the sounds and snuffed the lights.

"Probably best if we just drift for a while," she said, offering me her long white coat. "Should make it harder for Vincent to track us."

"He won't follow," I said. "I struck his liver. The wound is mortal."

"Maybe in your time it was, but things have changed a lot in the millennia since you died. Vincent's probably speed-growing a new liver in one of the labs right now. He'll be fine by morning."

Millennia? Had it really been so long?

Hermione must have seen my disbelief in the starlight. She gestured toward the ship's bow, where we sat across from one another. The sea rocked us gently. Its salty air reminded me of home.

"I didn't feel good about this project from the start," Hermione said. "I tried talking Vincent out of it, but he wouldn't budge. 'Go and persuade the sea wave not to break,' he said. 'You will persuade me no more easily.'" Hermione rolled her eyes. "The guy got awfully florid when he was feeding his god-complex."

I thought back to the doctor's hooves – traces of a centaur's blood.

"Is he?" I asked. "A god?"

Hermione scoffed. "He'd probably tell you so. But no, he's just a man with too much power, out to prove what he's capable of. When I realized I couldn't stop him from attempting a resurrection, I figured the next best thing was to be there along the way." She shook her head. "This is so messed up. Modifying living, consenting people is one thing" – the wings amidst her hair fluttered – "but bringing someone back from the dead is something else. Vincent became too obsessed with continuing his ancestor's work."

I was no stranger to men doing horrible things in the name of their own validation; it was the reason I'd died. Such monsters had no place in a civilized world.

"The doctor took my eyes," I said.

"Yep," Hermione replied, reaching into her pocket. "And *this* doctor took them back." She handed me the rectangular bronze box she'd stolen from the laboratory. "They're yours to have, but I wouldn't open that. Looking at them without the protective screen still turns people to stone. Just ask the lab assistant Vincent tested them on."

I gazed into the snakeskin-irises of my own eyes, lying delicately in the box like pieces of fine jewelry. A translucent bronze lid kept their magic at bay. I wondered if they would harm even me, their mother. I then remembered I was no longer the person they'd been taken from.

"You say the doctor will live. Despite the wound."

Hermione nodded. "You could stab out his liver every day. He'd still recover."

"Then next time I'll have his head. Take me back."

"Sorry, but that island is like a fortress for Vincent. We should just be glad we got away. The best we can do now is rebuild our lives." She stared into the middle distance, as if struck by a premonition. "Fuck – I just committed career suicide, didn't I? I was a damned good surgeon. Now I'll have to eke out a living as a back-alley body-modder. What've I done?"

Hermione continued that line of thought, mumbling to herself. As she did, I plotted.

"The doctor mentioned a coronation."

Hermione woke from her trance. "What? Oh – that. It's not a literal coronation. Although with the way corporations run the world these days, it might as well be. Some misogynistic asshole is taking over a huge company from his retiring father, and he's throwing himself a party. Vincent's really looking forward to it."

"Then that's where I'll strike, when his guard is down. Where will the coronation take place?"

"No idea. It's an exclusive thing."

"Is there a way to find out?"

Hermione stared at me, there in the starlight, waves sighing against the ship. It was as though she sought truth in my mind.

"You really mean it, don't you?" she asked. "Okay, sure – there's a way to figure out where the party is. But it'll cost us." She went to the ship's controls and brought it back to life. "Hope you're ready for a hell of a ride. Welcome to the twenty-second century, Medusa."

We sliced through dark waters toward the mainland, a relentless harpoon sent to deliver justice. I would ensure its aim was true.

* * *

The city was a study in contrast: skyscrapers stood like dark monoliths, brightened by thin tubes of electric pink light. Cold blue video screens displayed food, drink, fashion. The doctor's chip in my head allowed me to name everything I saw, but still, I struggled to understand. I asked Hermione if what I witnessed was magic.

"As far as you're concerned?" she said. "Basically."

Even at night the streets were busy. The sounds of sizzling meat joined the cacophony of voices as we pushed through the alley crowd. I smelled sweat, onion, vice. Everyone was unique, sporting the body modifications Hermione had told me about: a woman with red and black mushrooms growing from her upper arms; a man whose metal jaw flared wide and dripped with condensation. Strange, knobby body-parts jabbed me as we navigated the mass of altered humanity. Two diminutive women with lizard-like skin and frilled necks commented on my snakes and asked for my surgeon's name. Hermione dismissed them and pulled me along. We descended a short staircase to a metal basement door.

"This is it," she said. "If anyone can tell us what we need, it's the Greys."

A few words whispered into a panel gained us admittance. We stepped into a foggy, storm-colored room, with a front desk that cordoned off the majority of the area. Behind it stood three older women in ragged gray clothing. They looked like triplets, each with their own unique modifications: gravel knuckles; shrapnel shoulders; a mane of silvery feathers. On our side of the desk a hulking man raged at the women, his enormous back to us.

"We won't tell you again," the middle triplet said. "No pay, no service. Get out."

The behemoth's chameleon-skin swirled through the entire spectrum, ending on tones of violet. He slammed a fist on the desk. "You goddamned hags! If I have to come back there, you'll—"

"Excuse me."

He turned my way, grimacing through serrated golden teeth. "What the hell do *you* want?"

I stepped forward and held the bronze box between us. Maintaining eye contact, I slid the protective screen away. He glanced down at the motion.

His scream was brief, and he had time only to raise his arms for a suitably dramatic final pose. I slid the cover back over the eyes and stepped around the statue.

"Hello," I said to the triplets. "I have need of your services."

Hermione handled the negotiation. The excited triplets were interested in no other payment than my eyes. Hermione asked them to reconsider, but I interjected. I didn't need my eyes to end the doctor, and he didn't deserve to be immortalized in stone anyway. Besides, it seemed the triplets might need defense against customers like the last.

They split to their three stations: one at the desk, asking about our quest; one at a dinner table, slurping hot stew; one at a bank of computers and monitors, working on our problem. They rotated during the process, taking turns eating and researching.

"I've got it," one finally said. "The coronation will take place at Sogra Castle." She handed Hermione a small data stick. "I've also included directions to the hidden NYM Party Headquarters."

"What for?" Hermione asked.

"They've been looking for a way to stop Acris's coronation. I bet they'd help equip your snakey friend for her mission."

"That's... not a bad idea. How much for the extra info?"

She grinned, a single metal tooth flashing among the others. "This one's on the house, deary. Just make sure you bring those bastards down."

I passed my eyes across the desk. "Thank you, sisters. You won't be forgotten."

We exited into the alley crowd. Hermione inserted the data stick into a metal port on her forearm.

"You know," she said, "a day ago I was a damned successful surgeon. Sure, Vincent took credit for all my work, but I had a pretty cushy life. Now I've thrown it all away, and am probably being hunted by my ex-boss as we speak."

"If you need to abandon the quest, I understand. I just ask that you point me the right way first."

She laughed. "Oh, I'm in too deep now, honey. Next stop: NYM Party Headquarters."

The morning sun rose between the buildings, bathing the city in a blush of pink hope.

* * *

Northward we trekked, the crowds thinning as if banished by sunlight. One of the screens we passed showed an image of Hermione, along with incentives for her capture. An opportunistic, greedy man with glowing teal chains wrapping each leg offered to forget he saw us in exchange for double the bounty. I left his twisted body in a recessed doorway, and gave his cloak and cowl to Hermione.

"Vincent wanted 'the glorious resurrection of Medusa' to be a big reveal," she said, drawing the hood over her head. "So I doubt he'll put your picture on any screens. I, on the other hand, am becoming a liability. This should be my last stop."

"Then let's make it a fruitful one."

We entered the sewers and followed the triplets' directions through a dark maze of slippery stone and dripping water. Hermione located a door in the shadows and inserted the data stick. The door opened.

A lanky woman with shiny, dolphin-colored skin led us through dimly lit tunnels. Along the way I learned about the NYM Party: they were a group of activists fighting for equality, who'd been forced to hide in the stink of the sewers because men in power don't take kindly to opposition. Apparently not everything had changed in the millennia since my death.

We came to a vaulted brick chamber, better lit than the tunnels. Members of the NYM Party milled about, tending machines, casting the occasional curious glance our way. Hermione explained our situation to their leader, whose metal joints buzzed with every movement. She seemed eager to work with me.

"If you can kill Acris," the machine-woman said, "his sister will take over the company instead. We'll all be better off."

"My priority is to slay the doctor," I said. "But if I can send the new king screaming to Hades with him, I will."

"I suppose that'll have to do. Follow me – we've got plenty of equipment to make your job easier."

She showed me around the chamber, explaining the haphazardly piled tools at my disposal. Hermione helped with the selections.

First was a headband that would conceal my serpents with an illusion of hair, while also projecting a new face onto my own. The doctor wouldn't recognize me.

Next was a silver card with golden edges called a kibisis. It would hold everything I needed for my quest: an invitation to the coronation, a false identity, a map of the castle.

Lastly, I asked the leader if she could restore my ability to fly. While she couldn't give me wings, she did have a reasonable alternative. It would require surgery to install.

"Maybe you could remove Vincent's language chip while you have Medusa under," Hermione said. "It was stuck into her head without consent."

"No," I said. "It allows me to understand this world. Let the doctor's creation be his own undoing."

"I suppose there is a certain poetic justice there. Hey – we still need to get you a weapon."

I climbed onto the surgical table, ready for the procedure. "Not necessary. I'll kill him with my bare hands." I closed my eyes, but a thought reopened them. "Will I see you before I go?"

Hermione took my hand. "If you think I'd come this far without giving you a proper sendoff, you're crazy. Talk soon, snake-lady."

A needle entered my arm, and darkness flooded the world.

* * *

My next awakening was far less troublesome than the previous.

"Welcome back," Hermione said, smiling over me. "How do you feel?"

I sat up. "Ready."

"I'm sure you are. But I want you to have this anyway."

She handed me the hilt of a bladeless dagger.

"Go ahead," she said. "Press the button. But point it away first."

I did so. A shaft of diamond-bright light erupted from the hilt, extending to the length of my arm. It came to a point and its edges crackled like a thunderbolt. I gave the sword a few swings, then retracted its blade.

"I know you want to kill Vincent with your hands," Hermione said, "but I kinda risked my neck to track down a weapons dealer on the surface while you were out. The least you could do is take it with you."

I tucked the hilt into my nest of serpents. "Thank you, friend. I'm in your debt."

"You can pay me back by getting out safely."

Hermione instructed me on the use of my new tools. It was soon time to go.

"It's been a wild ride, Medusa. Now go give this story the ending it deserves."

I thanked her for her help and we embraced. A member of the NYM Party drove me to Sogra Castle, the city's nightscape changing to rural darkness around us.

Soon, Doctor. Soon.

* * *

The brick facade of Sogra Castle was a stark contrast to the city I'd left. Spiraling bushes lined its walls, painted purple by floodlights. At the front door I showed a tuxedo-clad man my kibisis card; he scanned it and invited me in. I followed the card's directions to the ballroom.

It was an enormous, gold-brick chamber with a glass-dome ceiling. String music swept through the room like gentle ocean waves. Revelers in formal attire milled about the open floor, grinning through too-white teeth, stinking of arrogance. I blended right in with my shimmering emerald dress, its neck and sleeves concealing the seams where I'd been stitched together.

As I worked my way through the crowd, the kibisis card vibrated: it identified Acris, the soon-to-be king, far across the room. He had three golden metal stripes on each cheek, parallel to his jawline. His smile was as false and pretentious as the entire event.

My attention didn't stay with Acris for long. A titanic, black-suited figure stood to the left, near the room-length buffet table. He turned just enough for me to identify his sculpted-clay face: the doctor. The man who'd taken my eyes.

My blood sizzled inside a body I hardly knew, but I wouldn't let rage overtake me. Not yet.

I approached, pretending to admire the ice sculpture of the horse near the buffet table. My golden headband projected long, loose curls of green hair over my serpents; it also masked my true face with a false one. Would the hoof-footed doctor see through the illusions? Would he recognize the subject of his own work?

He looked my way, his gaze moving up and down my body. The man didn't even hesitate on my face. He smiled.

"It's a shame they can't hire proper help," he said, gesturing at the roast boar before him. "She might as well have carved it with a hammer. This could be a beautiful piece of meat – all it needs is a proper surgeon's touch."

He held a hand out to the chef behind the table, snapping his fingers. She gave me a dejected look, then passed over the carving tools.

The doctor sliced into the boar, separating its pieces into two piles: meat in one, bones and fat in the other. All the while he explained what he was doing, and why he was so good at it. I wondered if that's how I'd looked when I was suffering under his scalpel. My stitches tingled with every cut. Under the illusion of a second face, my jaw clenched.

"There," he said, dusting his hands. "Much better, don't you think?"

I lifted a long strip of meat between forefinger and thumb. I let it drop. "You give yourself too much credit."

"Ex*cuse* me?"

"Your subject was a work of art without you," I said. "Just like I was." I tapped the temple of my headband, dispelling the illusions.

Like a cloud's shadow overtaking a sunny field, dawning horror swept across the doctor's face. Before he could speak a poisoned word I lunged, serpents hissing.

We crashed into the table together, pulling its red cloth and several dishes to the floor with us. I ended on top and smashed an elbow into the doctor's face. He threw me aside while partygoers screamed.

I rolled to a stop. The doctor and I faced each other, crouched on all fours, two body lengths separating us. His eyes flicked to a fallen knife, back to me. As he lunged for it, I flung a silver platter at him. If he hadn't ducked, the discus would have taken a chunk from his neck; instead, it soared into the gathering crowd. Gasps of shock sucked the air from the room.

I rushed the doctor before he could recover and reach the blade. On top once more, I pummeled him with punches to the jaw, temples, eyes. He caught one of my fists in a massive hand, then the other. I leaned forward so my serpents could strike, leaving puncture wounds in his face and neck. He growled in pain and rolled hard to the side. Our positions switched. At some point in the struggle my serpents changed to green hairs, as the headband's illusion was reactivated. They continued to attack anyway, snapping inches away from the doctor's ravaged face.

He released my fist and landed a heavy blow. My skull slammed against the floor. The world spun, colors blending together. I'm sure he struck me after that, but I don't know how many times.

When things came into focus again, I was dangling in the air by the wrecked buffet table. With one hand the doctor held me up by my dress's fabric, near the collarbone. Blood dripped down his grimacing face, flowing from snake bites and a broken nose.

"Deactivate the projection," he said. "I want to see my work before I dispose of it."

I glanced past the doctor. Some of the crowd watched, but an even greater amount had their backs turned to us, hunched over something. None tried to intervene.

I spit blood to the side. "You can see my face," I said. "Because unlike the coward who killed me, I don't hide from those I confront."

I reached up and tapped the temple of the headband, dispelling the illusion. While I was there, I dug into my nest of serpents.

In one motion I withdrew Hermione's hilt, pressed the button to extend its thunderbolt blade, and swung it through the doctor's neck.

Blood splattered against the ice-sculpture of the horse. The doctor's head rolled off his shoulders and his body collapsed to the floor. I fell with it.

The crowd recoiled in horror. I used the opportunity to escape, activating the surgical implants the NYM Party had given me.

Flames erupted from the soles of my feet, launching me toward the domed glass ceiling. NYM had restored my gift of flight in the hope I would kill Acris, but there was no way to complete that quest now. I'd have to return a failure.

Then, rising over the crowd, I saw it: the thing so many of them had gathered around. Acris lay on the floor, motionless, his empty gaze aimed up at me. Lodged in his skull was the silver platter I'd thrown.

I crashed through the glass and escaped into the night. The doctor and Acris were gone, but their event had shown me they were symptoms of a larger problem. Such evil would not be tolerated in my world.

I soared toward the city, eager to reconvene with Hermione and the NYM Party. There was much work to be done.

Woman Embracing Woman, on Loan From Private Collection

Liv Strom

10 a.m.

I grabbed her hand, ignoring how it pulled the tubes attached to mine. Despite my blindfold, I knew her smooth skin – unchanged from the day we met.

"It's time, Med. Tonight."

She flinched. "I've brought stronger painkillers."

I shook my head carefully. Normally, the blindfold wouldn't slip, but I was thinning, transforming into a living corpse.

"I don't want you to remember me like this. I want it to be like—"

1972

I stood naked, arms stretched to the ceiling, legs crossed, chest pushed forward. A triangle shape, the voice called it over tinny speakers. Struggling to keep the pose, a flush crept up my cheeks.

I'd been a nude model before and didn't bat an eye at a room full of tipsy, tittering painters. Standing alone, my nakedness reflected in the two-way mirror was different.

Anyone could be on the other side.

I squirmed, wanting to turn away.

"Still," the voice commanded.

It sounded female, accented.

I dropped my arms.

"I can't do this, sorry." I was already shrugging into my dress. "I know you're famous and no one's seen you and that's part of your shtick, but…"

I hurried out, cursing myself for walking away from rent money.

A door slammed behind me, an androgynous person in leather and bike helmet following, only olive-skinned hands exposed.

"Wait!"

I paused.

"You're the right one for this piece. I could be in the room if you wore a blindfold."

"Can't I see you?"

The helmet shifted from side to side. It was strangely alluring.

"Why me?"

"You look like you could reach the stars."

I wavered, charmed despite myself. "How long do you need me for?"

12 p.m.

I unhooked the various machines beeping with my vitals. It must be today, or I would no longer manage. Med had an infinite number of tomorrows. For her, it'd never be the right day.

I didn't dare to remove the blindfold as I wheeled through the house. It didn't matter. I'd lived here thirty years.

Arriving in the garden, I freed my eyes. She never came here, among her statues.

First came the row of Meds – faceless, detailed, realistic, and exaggerated. Classic and modernist. Clay and marble. She'd done them all.

They'd been featured in Vanity Fair years ago. That was the closest anyone had come to seeing Med's face.

Tonight, I'd *see*.

1973

I never peeked as she sketched, then carved my likeness. Instead, we talked.

The unknowable Med became known to only me, like I was also chipping away at her, revealing the shape underneath.

I learned her family was Greek, though she did not keep in contact. That they'd wanted her to marry a man and condemned her for her disinterest.

That she loved wine and disliked the sun.

That she thought herself cursed and hid from the world.

Art was her love and life.

"It's a way to understand what it means to be human," she explained. "The only way I can see myself."

I nodded as if I understood.

When she revealed the otherworldly form she claimed I'd inspired, I looked only at her hidden one, and asked, "Can you make me feel like that?"

4 p.m.

In the center of the garden, my form stood, low-hanging clouds brushing the raised fingertips. I was beautiful and young and unknowing forever.

Steps crunched on the path behind me. In fear, I raised the blindfold – I wasn't ready.

1980

In perfect darkness, skin slid against skin. Under my fingers, her face took shape – the too large nose, the high cheekbones, the lips I imagined velvety red.

Between kisses, I described every feature I'd never seen.

We were in our bed. Our house. Hiding from the world.

Someone tore open the blackout curtain, exposing us.

My eyes clenched shut.

His scream cut off.

8 p.m.

The paparazzi photographer stood eternally facing my carved form, as if it was me he'd stalked. Where I was Med's dream crafted in stone, he was a study in realism. Each detail – the horrified eyes, the faltering grip on a camera, the flinch – preserved.

Further away were others, old and new, covered in ivy and cracked. I'd been the stone garden's only caretaker and I could no longer care for even myself.

Once, I wanted to break them in primitive fear. Now, I saw their terrible beauty. We all had to die, but like this, part of us lived forever.

2020

"Will you be lonely?" I asked.

"Always."

"Will you remember me?"

"Always, *ὁ ἀστήρ μου*," she said, calling me her star.

"I want to see you. Then you'll always have me." It was not the same, but it was the only thing I could offer.

"Not yet." She mumbled in Greek, a curse or blessing. A prayer to ancient gods.

8 p.m.

Med helped me to my feet. I staggered to my statue, embracing it like we'd held each other in the dark.

My eyes refused to open. Terror at facing my death and love.

"It's your time," Med said.

Rain fell on the Garden of Statues, the sky making stone weep.

For the first time without a barrier or blind, I saw Med.

Olive skin. Not a wrinkle. More beautiful than I'd imagined.

I no longer felt my feet. Didn't struggle to stand. My pulse slowed, and I smiled.

"Your eyes are brown. I always imagined green."

She laughed. "Only you would compliment my eyes and not remark on the snakes."

Venomous green, they writhed on her uncovered head.

I wanted to reach for one – *what did it matter now?* – but my joints had stiffened, hands petrified.

"You don't feel like chopping my head off?" she asked.

I had already said my goodbye, declared my love a thousand ways.

Medusa Gorgo could never see herself, never have anyone look upon her for more than a moment.

I no longer felt my struggling heart and aching lungs. My eyes, covered for so long, would never close again.

"I see only someone reaching for the stars."

Unbound

Theresa Tyree

Tonight, Bea had to be perfect.

Natural, but striking. Definitive, but approachable. Hard, but soft.

It was so much work, looking good enough for events like these without looking *too* good. Look *too* good, and people started to talk about what kind of girl you were, questioning if you were really studying archeology at all, or if you'd just slept your way into your graduate position.

Bea looked at her reflection and mussed her hair. She still hadn't gotten the ponytail right. Her green dress sported an elegant cowl neck, a long-but-short enough skirt, and all the tasteful lines to encourage a viewer to enjoy it as a singular piece of art instead of fixating on her bust or hips – but her snaking curls still didn't say "I'm a professional, please take me seriously."

With things returning to normal after the Axis defeat and conclusion of the Greek civil war, travel to Greece was no longer out of the question; her research project was plausible.

So long as she got Dr. Matthews to approve.

If only her curls were actually snakes and she could turn the people stonewalling her into statues.

Though, even Medusa had been beheaded.

Bea sighed, leaning her head against the mirror.

There was no way to win except to play the game.

At least this was a concert instead of an academic circle-jerk.

Bea picked up her ticket and read it again. "Ancient Greek Instruments with Zoe Makris and The Children of the Gods."

Zoe had been the last from the program to go to Greece before the war. Her band was made up of musicians that stood in for the gods, playing the instruments as they had in mythology. Bea was thrilled for a chance to hear them play. Zoe's work brought the past's life into the present.

That was the kind of restoration work Bea wanted to do.

"Whatever it takes." Bea took up her brush again and finally smoothed her locks into an 'effortless' ponytail. "Only one more night."

She took the Tube to the British Museum and checked her coat with an attendant. She accepted a flute of champagne from one of the waiters, but did not sip. She needed her wits about her for the battle to come.

The reception hall was closed to the public unless the museum was holding an event. Tonight, it was done up for an open cocktail party with small tables for guests to stand and talk. Seats lined the edge of the room, but most guests crowded together near the stage, already vying for a spot to watch the concert. Velvet ropes kept guests from getting too close to the ancient Greek instruments resting on stage.

Bea's eyes lingered on Zoe's instrument, the aulos of Athena. Scholars often translated the instrument's name as 'flute', but Bea knew well how inaccurate that moniker was for the double-reeded instrument. The twin pipes allowed it to accompany itself, almost as if mourning the absence of another voice by providing two of its own.

She wished she was here only to listen to Zoe play.

Dr. Peter Matthews stood in the middle of a throng of investors, holding court. For him, the concert was a moment to showcase his greatness; what the archeology program could do under his guidance – provided the funds, of course.

Given his position on the museum board, people often felt generous – and gave even when they weren't. It made Bea wonder what kind of deals he struck behind closed doors.

She'd use his audience to force him to make one in the light.

Taking a deep breath, a sip of champagne for courage, and putting on her best smile, she approached the ring of well-dressed intellectuals.

"Dr. Matthews! I should've expected you to attend such an interesting concert."

Matthews frowned, cutting off whatever disdainful reply he'd been about to make about artifact appropriation. His frown crested like a wave when he saw her. "Ah. Bea. Of course you're here. Still on about your Greek field project?"

She laughed, trying to sound natural and unfazed. "It's funny you bring that up. I've made a discovery. It gives us even more cause to doubt the veracity of Winckelmann's 'the whiter the body, the purer the form' theory about ancient Greek marbles."

Matthews sighed, putting a hand to his head and checking to make sure his heavily sprayed comb-over was still in place. "Yes. As you've said many times, over numerous breadcrumbs."

"You taught us to be thorough in our research." A bat of her eyelashes, an appeal to his ego. Anything to let her keep talking. "Take that paper I did on the *Iliad*. The original Greek seems to refer to light interaction instead of hue with its color words. Read that way, there's a Greek admiration for rich pigments, like dark African skin and bright decorations. In light of that, we should explore if they painted—"

"We've been over how your interpretation of such passages conflicts with many of your superiors." He slid his eyes to one of the men next to him and harrumphed, as if to invite him to chuckle at Bea.

Bea bit her lip, and pressed on. She had more evidence. Matthews couldn't shoot it all down. "As the department head of such a prestigious archeology program, I'm sure you'll agree that we must sometimes re-examine our predecessors' conclusions. The pigments we've found on recent marbles, for example, seem to imply color was applied. I'm not the first to propose this idea."

Bea took heart as some of the intellectuals around her tittered to each other, excited over her claim. "Sir Lawrence Alma-Tadema and John Gibson may have used some eccentric colors, but they were onto something with their early recreations."

Matthews' glare promised her a shipwreck.

Bea stumbled on, before her confidence could fail. "Which brings me to my discovery. Thanks to your thoughtful acquisition of a UV lamp for the universities lab, I've discerned patterns and grooves that show where paint might have lain."

Matthews flicked his eyes furtively around the throng of lords, ladies, and colleagues. They hung on Bea's every word, entranced by her fresh take on the familiar, intrigued by her use of newly available technology. She could feel them, spurring her forward with their interest. Her hopes rose. It was going just as she'd hoped it would. "Since the grooves are so fine as to not be visible to the naked eye, it's understandable our predecessors missed them. But if we were to fund a venture to investigate the possibilities—"

"You're telling me you submitted ancient artifacts to harsh UV rays?"

Bea stopped cold. She hadn't expected her professor to take that tone with her. Not at this point. Not when she was so close. "Y-yes, but there's no need to worry. UV rays are completely harmless to—"

Matthews cut her off with a sigh. "For such a bright young woman, Miss Koulolias, you should know better than to submit priceless artifacts to new stimulus without first testing the prolonged effects on non-valuable substitutes. We may *think* UV rays harmless now, but what if in ten years' time we find they hasten decay, hmm?"

Bea's heart hammered in her chest. If she said the wrong thing now, she could kiss her research project goodbye. "But, sir… That's akin to saying that sunlight could harm the stone."

He waved her away. "Bah. The sun and this newfangled lamp are not the same."

Bea's words were lost in Matthews' riptide.

Before she could find them again, two reedy notes sounded through the hall and called for her attention. Bea turned to see Zoe Makris with the twin-piped aulos between her lips.

Even in a plain white shirt rolled to the elbows, she was a vision. She puffed her cheeks, using circular breathing to keep the drone pipe going uninterrupted, and chatter died as everyone turned to watch her: Athena and her aulos.

Zoe looked the part well: bronze skin, sensible shoes, and low ponytail of dark curls that swept over her shoulder – and had probably only taken her a moment.

She was beautiful.

When all had turned to her, Zoe moved her fingers. One pipe carried a melody while the other followed more slowly, offering support, resolution, and strength of volume a single pipe couldn't achieve alone.

Something about the song called to Bea.

As she continued, other 'gods' entered from the partition at the back of the stage, floating slowly to other instruments.

'Aphrodite' joined first, taking up her crotalum clappers. She swayed hypnotically as she played, making the light glint off her dark curls with the luster of honey. She added her voice to the music as 'Hermes' took up his lyre and 'Apollo' his kithara. They plucked bright counter-melodies around each other in a cluster of strings. 'Artemis' came next, looking as lithe as the mythological huntress, and added a percussive baseline with her toubeleki drum. Jovial 'Dionysus' sparkled over top, moving his pan pipes so fast Bea wondered why she'd ever doubted one could trill on them.

The soul of the music overtook Bea, and time stood still.

The troupe finished with a final held note that went on and on like a sunset.

When it was over, Bea inhaled, feeling breathless. She took another sip of her champagne to steady herself while the audience clapped.

Zoe gestured to her band, bowed, then raised her voice to introduce them. Archeologists and band mates, 'The Children of the Gods' was founded to bring the sound of the ancients to the present. The troupe spotlighted and lectured on each instrument, Zoe keeping the audience captive with both insight and laughter. At the end of her lecture, Zoe pressed the attendees to make generous donations to work like hers.

"After all," Zoe laughed. "You never know when the next archeological breakthrough is just waiting to be funded."

Her eyes bored into Bea, and Bea's heart sped.

Zoe's gaze didn't waver, even as the troupe bowed, replaced their instruments in their stands, and filed off the stage to mingle and answer questions. Zoe descended the stairs last, halting at the bottom.

There was a question in her gray eyes.

Without thinking, Bea went to her in answer.

"You," Zoe said as they came into speaking range, "look like a woman who wants something."

The air between them was electric. "I'm Bea. Bea Koulolias. I... I was wondering..."

"Yes?" Zoe prompted, leaning even closer.

Bea opened her mouth again, but didn't know what to say. She looked at Zoe's lips and then back into her eyes. They pulled at her, like Zoe knew her.

"What you said on stage," Bea finally managed. "About new breakthroughs just waiting to be funded."

Zoe nodded.

Bea lowered her voice, shy, terrified of overstepping, of having someone else in a position of power tell her she was small and insignificant and should know her place. "Were you talking about me?"

Zoe's expression warmed enigmatically, but just as she opened her mouth, a much less welcome voice washed over her.

"Ah, I see my problem student has come to bother you as well, Ms. Makris."

Zoe's eyes left Bea's and flicked harshly to the left.

"Peter Matthews. Your timing is as poor as ever."

Matthews chortled as if Zoe's words were a joke, but Bea wasn't so sure.

Bea made to retreat, but Zoe cut her off with a light touch to her lower back. A thrill went through Bea's stomach, and she stood a little straighter.

Her cheeks warmed as Matthews eyed Zoe's arm.

"You have a bright young woman in your program, Doctor. Her project has teeth." Zoe looked away from Matthews and directed her attention back to Bea. "She was just going over the finer details with me."

"Um." Zoe was giving her a chance. Bea would be a fool to waste it. "Yes. You see, there's only so much work that can be done in regards to the study of Greek marbles here in Britain. Field research will be the only way to truly confirm if the statues were painted."

"You see?" Zoe turned back to Matthews. "Groundbreaking work to fund."

Matthews scoffed. "You've surmised this from a moment's conversation?"

Zoe's musical laughter filled the whole room. "You could say her passion and intellect are apparent. A credit to the program."

Matthews preened under the stolen praise.

Hope bloomed in Bea's chest again.

Maybe Zoe could help her salvage this.

"Well," Matthews said, "my discerning eye made something of you, it will make something of her. Still, it would behoove both of you to work with your peers instead of constantly challenging their methods and conclusions."

"Perhaps when my colleagues do research worthy of my insight."

Matthews scoffed, but Zoe didn't give him time to respond. "Speaking of my 'peers', what of the inquiries I asked you to make regarding the Parthenon Marbles?"

"Really, Zoe. I know I agreed to look into their return as recompense for you bringing your instruments and little band to the museum, but it's rather more complicated than you think."

Zoe's eyes narrowed. "How so? Greece gave us our first victory over the Axis. Without that victory, Britain never could've tightened their blockade in the Mediterranean and cut Italian communication lines. Churchill said, 'Henceforth, we shall say that heroes fought like Greeks,' or don't you remember?"

"I remember quite well, my child, but—"

"But what? Their request that we return stolen artifacts isn't straightforward enough? I rather doubt it, 'old chap'." Bea was in awe at the ease with which Zoe mirrored Matthews' dismissal of her. "Seems to me, the Greeks have made a very humble request – have *been* making it since 1832 – and now the war is over, we would do well, as a 'civilized' nation, to honor it."

Matthews bristled. "Zoe—"

"I did earn a title in your program, Peter. You could use it."

Matthews sighed. "Doctor Makris. While your discoveries in the field are undoubtedly a credit to your alma mater and your countrymen, and while the Greeks have done invaluable service to the free world, I think we can both agree that the Elgin Marbles—"

"The *Parthenon* Marbles."

"Whatever you call them. They're doing more good here in civilization than in the primitive halls of Athens. Greece is an admirable nation, but still in its infancy. When the time is right—"

"And I suppose it's you who'll decide when that is?"

"Of course not, my dear. The decision will be made by the board. Leaving a decision up to one person would be absurd. We must all be—"

"In agreement, yes. You've used that line before, Peter. Especially when you don't want to do something. But I know it's your vote keeping the board from majority." Zoe drew herself up. "You're lucky the gods my 'little band' impersonates aren't here. They smite people for lesser insults."

Matthews sputtered. "You sound like Miss Koulolias with her fancies about paint."

Bea held her breath, trying to keep her composure, to not let it hurt, to resist lashing out and defending herself.

"Can you imagine? Those stately statues covered in garish, primitive pigments?" Matthews laughed as if the idea was insane. "Once we break her flights of fancy, *then* she'll be a credit to my program."

Bea couldn't take it anymore.

"If you'll excuse me." She pulled away from Zoe, her heart constricting. "It was a pleasure meeting you, Doctor Makris."

She withdrew as hurriedly as she could. All hope of getting her project funded was gone; everything she'd worked for and endured over the last five years, ashes.

At least she knew all the best places in the museum to curl up with a notebook or have a quick cry. It was her home away from home.

She crossed velvet ropes and tucked herself into a shadowy alcove. Against the rules, but who cared anymore?

Following the rules hadn't gotten her anywhere. Archeology was only ever going to be congruent theories of old-fashioned myopic men.

She kicked off her pumps and hid her face against her knees. She'd let herself cry, let the painted smile fall, just for a moment. Just for a moment.

"This was one of my favorite places to hide too."

Bea jumped and quickly lowered her legs to be more ladylike. She relaxed when she recognized Zoe in the half-light. "Doctor Makris! Won't they miss you at the event?"

"Zoe is fine." She smiled and leaned against the wall. "And, nah. It's wrapping up, and my team's authorized to stay a bit longer to get our instruments and audio equipment packed before the museum locks up. I'd rather be with you."

Bea dashed a hand across her eyes. "Forgive me, I didn't—"

Zoe held up a hand. "No need to apologize. You have every right to offload your feelings with a few tears. What that man said was hurtful and ignorant."

Bea's spirits lifted to hear someone else say it. "You think so?"

"I know so. Peter isn't wise enough to understand he's bulldozing perspectives outside his limited world view." Zoe placed her hand on Bea's knees and guided them to the side to make room for her to sit down in the alcove with Bea. "When I was a little girl, I lived in a tiny Greek village near the Turkish border. My history lessons covered wars between the two countries they don't talk about here. I went on school trips to see destroyed temples, stolen-and-returned artifacts, like the aulos I play, actually. The Turks stole it from a temple of Athena, but returned it during the first peace accords. Knowing all that made me wise – like Athena's serpents licking my ears clean enough to hear the secrets of the universe." She gave Bea a wry smile. "I weaponized all of that to get through Peter's program, but he wasted my time, and he's wasting yours too. You don't have to play his game."

Bea squeezed the material of her dress between her fingers. "I wish that were true."

Zoe gave her a soft look. "I think you're right, by the way."

"None of the men in charge do."

Zoe chuckled. "Well, they haven't seen as many unprocessed relics as I have. Who's to say you aren't meant to surpass them anyway, like Athena did Zeus?"

Zeus *had* swallowed Metis because her child was prophesized to overthrow him.

"I heard some of the other patrons repeating what you said to Peter at the beginning of the night. Take it as a sign."

Bea looked at Zoe in wonder. "How do you know what I said to Dr. Matthews?"

"You learn the patterns, after a while."

"Like how?"

"Like how I know your feet are sore after standing in those heels all night." Zoe patted her lap. "Let me rub them for you."

Zoe's posture changed along with her demeanor. She gestured for Bea to come closer.

Bea held her breath, bit her lip, then lifted her feet and set them brazenly into Zoe's lap.

Zoe smiled and pressed her thumb over Bea's sole. Her hands were firm but welcome, like the comforting press of gravity. "You'd find the tale of the aulos familiar in the same way."

Bea felt her ears burn, remembering how the instrument fit between Zoe's lips. "Tell it to me."

"Long ago, there were two lovers. A sculptor and a goddess. The sculptor was lauded as one of the most skilled in all of Athens." She massaged up Bea's calf. "She carved her sculptures with a delicacy that made them seem alive, and painted them so beautifully they were mistaken for gems. The goddess loved both the sculptor and her creations so much, she had the marbles ensconced in her temples."

"Who were they?" Bea needed to know. Part of her felt like she already did.

"The goddess's name was Athena, and the sculptor... Medusa."

Bea's mouth popped open gently as Zoe's hands worked tension from her legs. She clasped one of her hands over Zoe's, and moved the woman's hand onto her thigh.

Zoe shuddered, moving closer. "Their story isn't told anymore. A lot of self-important men decided Medusa's transformation was Athena's punishment for defiling her temple, that the goddess helped Perseus kill her, and then made the first aulos from her femurs." Zoe took Bea's other foot in her hands and worked her way back up. "But I don't think an instrument like that was made from anything but love." Zoe's hands slid higher, tracing Bea's thighs with her fingertips.

Bea tipped her head back and parted her legs invitingly. "Why?"

Zoe's breath skimmed across Bea's throat. "An instrument carved from the legs of her sculptor, joined as two pipes that met at the goddess's mouth..."

Bea gasped as Zoe's fingers reached between her legs and stroked.

"Tell me the version that supports that," Bea demanded. Her eyes caught on Zoe's spiraling snake ear cuff: a wise serpent hidden under her hair, whispering in her ear like one of Athena's own. The rich emerald of its eyes made Bea's heart quiver with an emotion she didn't understand.

Zoe smiled against her cheek. "The one I like best says Athena wove Medusa a spell to take whatever form made her feel safe. She used illusions when the old Olympians decreed her love a monster, tricking Perseus, his kingdom, and the gods. Her cousins helped her be convincing, and Medusa lived. Athena forged her a bangle in the shape of a serpent that made her look human for the rest of her days. When she passed, Athena cheated even Hades, tying Medusa's soul to her own so she would be reborn eternally. They say the sound that calls the lovers together again is that of the aulos."

Bea bit her lip, her eyebrows drawn together with a desire. She knew this story, like a half-forgotten dream. She wanted to remember.

Zoe's lips slid down Bea's neck. "You look like a woman who wants something."

She did, but…

"How did Athena know it would work? How did Medusa know she was strong enough? How did they get away with it?"

"So many questions. I love it." Zoe stroked a stray curl behind Bea's ear. "The myths don't say. But if I were to imagine, I think it was less knowing they'd succeed than knowing what they couldn't live without." Zoe tipped Bea's chin up and Bea opened her eyes. "What aren't you willing to live without, Bea Koulolias?"

The rules fell away before Zoe's parameters. No more asking for permission, no longer chained in the shadow of men who refused to let her out from under them. In Zoe's gray eyes, Bea saw freedom.

"You look like a woman who wants something," Zoe echoed.

This time, Bea followed its risky siren call: she leaned in, and kissed her.

Twining around each other, Zoe Makris redefined the importance of private museum nooks with the delicious curl of her fingers.

"Come back with me to Greece," Zoe said when she had Bea shaking in her arms.

Bea couldn't think, her head spinning. New desires and old worries warred in her mind. What if Matthews tried to keep her research? Would she be able to do her work without the reputation of the university behind her? Would anyone take her seriously?

Zoe chased Bea's half-formed questions up her throat with kisses. "Don't let them trick you with their gatekeeping. No one can tell you what you're worth."

Bea didn't know how to say what those words freed inside her. Instead, she worked her hands into Zoe's curls, kissed her, and came.

"I'll go with you," Bea whispered as she recovered. "I'll go with you, I'll—"

Zoe silenced her with a kiss and slid a serpent-shaped bangle over Bea's hand. It coiled around her wrist, cool and soothing like cold water on a summer day – and then it came back in flashes: Athena, their love, their scheme, and all the times Athena had found her since.

Cheating the system felt small after cheating death.

The feeling grew when Athena led her back to the band.

Aphrodite stood next to a truck, swaying and clapping her crotalum while two nearly-identical robust men – Ares and Hephaestus, Bea recalled, distinguishable by the leg mobility aids Hephaestus wore – loaded giant cloth-wrapped parcels into their van.

The other gods milled about in a circle, staying out of the way and cleaning their instruments.

Bea quirked a brow. Even if the troupe had brought a water organ, it would be smaller than Ares and Hephaestus's load. What were they moving?

"Is the work done?" Athena asked, adding herself and Bea to the circle.

The mischievous lyre player – Hermes – grinned at her slyly and rubbed his hands together. "Nearly there. Ares and Phaestus are just loading up the last one now."

Aphrodite spun with an exuberant clatter. "No one will be able to tell the genuine from the fakes either. My husband's work is the deftest in the world. These Britons should be glad we've left them forgeries so meticulous."

Hephaestus stepped down from the truck, looking pleased and sheepish. "Dite, you're embarrassing me. The originals will be the harder work. Once we get them back to my workshop, they'll need repainting, and all the original color's gone. There's nothing to match."

"Oh, but you're so clever, my love. I know you'll choose the right colors. And if Athena succeeded, perhaps you won't have to paint them alone." The dancer darted her eyes over Bea, then wrapped her arms around Hephaestus's shoulders and coaxed him into swaying with her.

Artemis – toubeleki drum slung over her hip like a quiver – smiled for what Bea thought was the first time that evening. "I hope Aphrodite heaps more than the necessary praise on our good craftsman, so long as she still gives him a chance to look over our instruments tonight. We can't be without our tools, and you know how my brother gets when his kithara isn't cared for properly."

Apollo glanced up from his kithara, which he was already caring for himself. He'd always been meticulous. He and Artemis were similar in that regard, even if they looked as different as night and day. "With all that exciting creative work Hephaestus has ahead of him, I imagine we'll need to remind him frequently." He closed his kithara's case and mirrored his sister's smile. "But he has a good memory, and the counterfeits we've left the museum are fine replacements for the bleached white stone these 'scholars' value."

Hermes chuckled, the sound of mischief managed. "Switching them was almost boringly easy thanks to that time spell in our performance. Those silly mortals kept going on about how they couldn't believe how much time had passed! Ha!"

Artemis rolled her eyes and hip checked the lyre player. "Stop gloating. There's no glory in an effortless hunt."

"Plenty of pleasure, though," Dionysus said, wine in-hand and pan-pipes stashed on his belt. "And isn't that why we came here? To enjoy taking the marbles Medusa carved for the Acropolis?"

Apollo laughed and clapped Dionysus on the back. "Right you are."

Bea felt at ease in the current of their banter. It felt like coming home to a gaggle of long-lost cousins. The 'Children of the Old Gods' was an aptly named band.

"Speaking of pleasure..." Hermes smirked good-naturedly at Bea and then gave Athena a meaningful look. "How did *your* night go? Did a certain someone answer your call?"

Athena looked at Bea with gray eyes full of love and squeezed her shoulder.

Bea leaned into the touch. It felt like home.

A memory of grinding against Athena's tongue overwhelmed her, piercing her with talons of déjà vu and nostalgia. Bea reeled, touching a hand to her temple as Athena's arm tightened at her waist.

"Yes, she did," Athena answered. "It's coming in waves now. Just one reparation left to make it stick. Did you get it set up, Ares?"

Ares smirked as he dusted his hands off, then jerked his head back to the curtained area the performers had emerged from during their performance.

Athena turned back to Bea and nuzzled her ear lovingly. "I have a little surprise for you."

Bea followed Athena as the other woman led her behind the curtain. It didn't scare her when she saw Dr. Peter Matthews unconscious and tied to one of the event chairs.

The gag was a nice touch.

Athena summoned her spear and pressed it into Bea's hands. It shone with a radiance that Bea remembered from beyond the edge of dreaming. A radiance she'd once used to change herself, in another life.

Athena snapped her fingers, and Peter awoke. His eyes were wide and bulbous when they focused on Athena, looking down her nose at him, her eyes gray storm clouds. "I told you the gods smote for less, Peter."

He started to scream into the gag when she turned away and he saw the glittering spear in Bea's hands. The cloth dampened the sound, and Bea relished the way it made his voice finally, finally small.

Athena wrapped an arm around Bea's waist from behind, sliding her other hand up the side of Bea's neck and freeing her curls from their 'effortless' ponytail. They hissed as they fell around her, singing in freedom.

Athena kissed the side of Bea's mouth, then released her – gently, reverently, as if she'd been waiting for this moment for centuries. "For you, my Medusa. Be free."

Bea stepped forward, chambered her spear, and threw off her bonds.

Freely Given

Leah Warren

She should've been asleep – would've been asleep had the restlessness of her snakes not woken her. A dozen whispers, agitated and overlapping, tugged her into consciousness.

She swatted absently at the ones writhing against her temple. "Stop hissing in my ear."

"You can talk."

She froze. The voice – young, male – echoed in the still cave air. It sounded shocked.

"They didn't say you'd be able to talk." Shock had given way to confusion.

She scrambled backwards, eyes frantically scanning her surroundings.

She was alone.

She drew her wings in tight, bladed feathers shielding her body.

When she'd been human, she'd once been so frightened the hairs on her neck stood on end. She had no hair now, only her serpents. They hissed and shivered, jeweled eyes focused on one spot to her left.

If someone was there, why didn't she feel their gaze? What kind of hunter didn't look at their prey?

One who knew what she was.

One who'd been warned.

One who'd been sent.

"Go away." She bared her teeth at where her snakes pointed. "You aren't welcome here."

A helmet thumped against the ground and a young man appeared, sword raised. Winged sandals held him aloft.

His back was to her, but she could see his face in the mirrored shield he held. Smooth cheeks and a strong, beardless jaw - this hunter was only just out of boyhood, barely a man. Wide eyes stared at her reflection.

She'd seen herself in that shield once before. Her shoulders slumped and her throat caught.

"My Lady Athena's shield," her voice cracked. Tears tracked down her cheeks, lidless eyes fixed on the intruder's reflection. "Have the gods decided to kill me then? Do they hate me so much?"

"Umm… I don't think so?" The intruder sounded truly baffled now. He landed softly on the ground, never taking his eyes off her reflection. "I swore an oath to bring your head back to the bastard king pursuing my mother. He wanted me to die trying, I suppose. But the gods seem to want me alive." He shrugged. "So they equipped me for success."

"You have my pity," she said. "The gods' kindness is often as painful as their cruelty." Bitter memories welled up of violent compliments and the gently whispered curse that followed. "It's best to avoid their attention altogether, but it seems too late for you."

"My father is Zeus. It was probably always too late for me."

"Then it is your mother I pity. No woman should have to endure the desire of a god."

The intruder hummed in agreement. "Nor that of a king."

That surprised her. She said so. The intruder shook his head.

"My mother had no choice with Zeus—"

"Few women do." She interrupted grimly.

He nodded as he continued. "—and I won't have her suffer through that again."

"How do you plan to stop him?"

"Everyone on our island had to bring a gift to celebrate the impending wedding. I didn't. Made a big show of it too, to buy time while I went on some quest or other for him." His shoulders slumped and he sighed. "I didn't think he'd send me to fight a Gorgon." He plopped down dejectedly and dropped his sword.

They sat in silence until she broke it.

"You seem… kind."

"The man who helped raise me was kind."

"In your kindness, will you kill me quickly?"

The intruder looked down at his sword.

She could kill him now. The thought came unbidden and she raised herself to the balls of her feet. He'd dropped his guard. She could swoop in close, crowd in nose-to-nose. He'd look up on reflex – they all did – and that would be it. Painless for him, safe for her.

And somewhere on some island, a woman would wait for a son who'd never return while an old man celebrated the acquisition of a bride that could never leave.

She hissed and sat back down, only to realize the intruder was still speaking.

"What?" Maybe she shouldn't snap at someone here to slay her, but she was tired. If men insisted on menacing her in her own home, they'd forfeited all rights to hospitality.

"I said, I'm bound by oath to bring back your head," his voice remained cheerful, showing no irritation at her brusqueness, "but there's nothing in that oath that says it can't still be attached to your body. What do you say?" He grinned. "Will you help me save my mother?"

She bit her lip, needled points drawing blood. Finally, she nodded.

"For your mother's sake, I will aid you, son of Zeus."

"Son of Danaë," he corrected as he stood, "but my name is Perseus." He paused. "Do you have one?"

She stared at him, surprised. "Medusa." It felt strange to say aloud after so long.

"A guardian's name. What do you guard?"

"Myself."

She stood as well, draping her wings over her shoulders like a cloak. Her snakes bobbed and wove themselves around her face, tongues flicking in peaceful contemplation.

Their lack of alarm did much to soothe her racing heart.

She gestured forward, keeping her distance. "Lead the way, son of Danaë."

Watching her reflection, Perseus led them back to the cave's mouth. Grey statues dotted the path, all human, expressions ranging from terror to shock. Medusa preferred not to look at them – would've preferred not to look at them when they were still flesh instead of stone.

Perseus swallowed. "Who were they?"

"Hunters," she replied. "They *weren't* equipped for success."

They left the cave and followed the cliffs down to the shore where a small fisherman's boat waited. Perseus fidgeted and pulled a sack from his belt.

"I'll need to be able to move freely about to sail," he said. Something like guilt filled his tone. "Here." He held the sack out behind him. "Put this on. Our Grey-Eyed Lady said your gaze can't pierce it."

She stood stiff, staring at the proffered leather. Perseus waited. Finally, she took it, turning it over in her clawed hands.

"Nymph-made?" She tried to sound disinterested.

He nodded, still waiting.

Tentatively, she slipped it over her head, stuffy darkness enshrouding her.

"Thank you." His voice was muffled, but sounded closer.

Medusa's throat tightened and she took a reflexive step backwards.

"I'm only going to help you into the boat," Perseus reassured her. "Will you hurt me if I touch you?"

Her snakes hissed.

She imagined ripping the sack from her head and slapping his hand away, leaving him as another warning for those who'd inevitably follow. Or, better yet, throwing his stone corpse into his boat and sending it back to his island with 'Leave Me Alone' carved into it – an ultimatum this time instead of a warning.

But his mother had endured enough.

Medusa sighed and extended her hand towards his voice. "No. But only because you asked nicely."

Perseus chuckled and took her hand, gently guiding her into the boat. Once she was safely seated, he let go and she heard his footsteps move about as he stowed his gear.

The flap of sails sounded and the boat bobbed forward.

* * *

Medusa measured the journey's progress by the sun's warmth and the moon's chill. Perseus occasionally broke their silence with awkward small talk or the offer of food, but for the most part, he kept to himself.

It was during one of the colder stretches that she heard him groan.

"What is it?"

"You look like a prisoner being taken to your death." She heard him sit nearby. "I don't like it."

"I believe you'd like being a statue less," she said drily.

Perseus huffed out a laugh and didn't argue. After a period of silence, she heard him rifle through his provisions. The scrape of metal against wood made her stiffen.

Her snakes paused at the sound.

She flexed her claws.

"Here. Take that off." His voice came from the same spot.

Her snakes resumed their undulations.

"What?"

"The sack. I have an idea." He sounded cheerful, guileless.

"I've got the shield up, so you needn't worry. I'm not looking at you."

"That was *never* my worry," she muttered, peeling the sack off her head.

Her snakes enjoyed being free, wriggling and twisting as they tasted the evening air. The sunset cast the world in orange and purple.

Holding out the sack, Medusa looked up. Perseus sat across from her. True to his word, he was turned away, watching her reflection in the shield. His sword lay across his knees.

She couldn't disarm him, but she could launch herself off the boat, gouge out the bottom with her talons, and fly out of range to watch it sink. He'd kept close to the coastline. She could rest on an outcropping and make her way home once the moon was up.

Perseus took the sack, reaching back slowly. He made no move to grab his sword. Keeping half an eye on her in the shield, he fiddled with the sack, turning it over in his hands and tugging on it.

"Hah!" He grinned. "Found the seam." Before Medusa could respond, he picked up his sword and slid the tip into the leather. After a few precise slices, he handed the sack back to her. "Try that."

She looked at the sack. He'd slit one of the side seams to make a second opening. She frowned.

"Now it's more like a cowl," he explained. "You can still cover your eyes, but you don't have to be completely blind. I imagine you'll be more comfortable."

Medusa pulled it back over her head and shoulders, ignoring her serpents' discontented hisses, and adjusted it so it covered the bridge of her nose. While the top half of her vision was obscured, she could still see Perseus from the waist down.

She sighed in relief.

"Better?" She could hear his smile.

She allowed herself a small one in return, keeping her teeth sheathed. "Much."

* * *

She was enjoying the afternoon sun on her skin when a scream ricocheted off the water.

Perseus launched himself over the side before the echoes had faded. He lurched and bobbled, winged sandals flapping frantically as he skimmed the waves.

With no danger of meeting his eyes, Medusa shoved her hood back and scanned the water.

There, off the coast, she could just make out a young woman lashed to a boulder. The tide was rapidly overtaking the stone, but even more dangerous was the monster bearing down on it.

Its head easily dwarfed their boat, boar's tusks glinting in the sunlight. Water sluiced off its finned back as it sped towards its prey.

"A Cetus," she whispered.

Only one god favored that particular monster. An old rage bubbled in her throat and her eyes burned. The wood splintered beneath her claws.

The girl screamed again as the Cetus drew near, jaws agape.

Sparrow-like, Perseus darted between them, swinging his sword. The blade glanced off one of the creature's tusks. It bellowed its rage, rearing up. For an instant, it blotted out the sun before flinging itself at Perseus. Waves crested as it hit the water.

His second strike embedded itself in the Cetus' shoulder. Roaring in pain, it dove, dragging Perseus with it. Purple blood spiraled downwards as its fanned tail disappeared beneath the waves.

The girl's sobs were the only sound as she and Medusa waited for them to reemerge. But the water's surface remained unbroken. The girl wept harder at the loss of her rescuer.

With a snarl, Medusa pulled the cowl over her eyes and spread her wings. Leaping from the boat, she flew to the rock. The girl shrank back, sobbing.

"Hush, girl," Medusa said, harsher than she meant to. "Don't waste your strength with tears. You'll need it to escape once I cut your bindings."

Sniffling, the girl nodded. Medusa circled around the boulder and began shredding through the ropes with her claws. With each fiber that snapped, both women strained to hear anything that would herald Perseus's or the beast's return.

As the last strands snapped, the girl cried out, causing Medusa to peer around the boulder.

The Cetus breached the waves, thrashing and rolling as it reared up. On its back, Perseus clung doggedly to his sword, still stuck in the beast's armored scales. It flung him about and he slammed against its side, the barnacles that crusted its hide cutting into his arms and face.

The beast charged the rock, mad with pain.

Perseus yelled, straining to free his sword for another blow.

The girl crumpled to her knees.

Medusa snarled.

She moved to crouch over the fallen girl, covering her with her wings. She stared at the frothing wake churned up by the monster's charge. She couldn't see its face or Perseus.

Gripping her cowl in both hands, she released a long breath.

"Son of Danaë! Close your eyes!"

Hoping he heard, she threw the cowl back, wide eyes blazing.

The Cetus' roar died in its throat as veins of marble crawled over its snout and throat. Scales dulled as muscle and sinew froze. The stone webbing branched and spread down its body. As it skidded to a halt against the rock, the hate in its beady eyes died, leaving them blank and cloudy in death.

Panting, Medusa pulled her cowl back over her eyes.

The girl beneath her trembled.

There was no sign of Perseus.

"Are you alright, girl?" Medusa pulled back, tucked her wings, and helped the girl to her feet. "Who did this to you?"

"M-my parents," the girl replied. "But you mustn't blame them," she hurried to explain. "If we didn't appease Poseidon, he was going to destroy our whole kingdom. And, after all," she drew herself up and blinked away the last of her tears, "a princess should be ready to give her life for her people."

"Hmm," Medusa didn't get a chance to reply as Perseus heaved himself over the Cetus' petrified head and sat down heavily.

"What a fight!" He grinned. "Did you see how big it was? And what you did – that was amazing – terrifying – but amazing! That beast didn't stand a chance against us!"

He took a breath to say more, but froze when he noticed the girl, blushing as she dropped her gaze. His cheeks and neck colored with an answering blush and he scrambled to his feet.

"I hope you weren't too frightened," he said, bowing. "Won't you tell me your name, lovely one?"

Her blush deepened as she looked up at him through her eyelashes. "Andromeda."

Medusa moved away, shaking her head almost fondly. "Puppy love," she muttered, looking out over the waves. "Perhaps we can become better acquainted elsewhere," she called over her shoulder, "where the rising tide will not sweep us away?"

The smitten couple startled at her voice, already lost in their own world. The corner of Medusa's mouth twitched in a small smile as they nodded furiously. Perseus turned back to Andromeda and gently picked her up. She settled herself comfortably in his arms.

"Shall we take you home?"

Andromeda bit her lip and shook her head. "With that thing dead, if you take me back, they'll marry me off to one of the old men Papa wishes to impress. Perhaps," – she looked down – "I could come with you?"

Perseus smiled broadly and nodded. Adjusting his hold on Andromeda, he carefully kicked off, and once the winged sandals held them aloft, flew back to the boat. Medusa followed, taking one last unobscured look at the stone Cetus, just to be safe.

Andromeda passed out soon after they got underway. The boat's gentle rocking lulled her to sleep as the exhausted aftermath of terror set in. Medusa watched over her from under her cowl and listened to Perseus move around.

When she woke, the three of them shared a meal. Perseus passed around hunks of bread and salted fish, fingers brushing Andromeda's as he handed her the food.

"What were you doing on that rock?" he asked.

Andromeda sighed. "My mother boasted I was more beautiful than Poseidon's Nereids." She shook her head. "So he sent that creature to ravage our kingdom. My parents hoped, if they sacrificed what had offended him, the monster would leave."

"Why wasn't your mother on the rock, then?" Medusa couldn't keep the bitterness from her voice. "Trust the gods to punish the wrong person."

"To terrorize an entire kingdom over such a thing…" Perseus shook his head. "Especially when one look could've shown him the truth of it."

"Be glad it never came to that," Medusa said as Andromeda blushed. "His approval would have been more devastating than his wrath."

"Did he approve of you?"

The girl was more perceptive than she'd expected. Medusa looked at her claws.

"The gods don't like their sins spoken of," she hedged. "And it's best not to speak of *that* god's sins while we're still in his domain. Why not instead tell us more of this kingdom you loved enough to die for."

Andromeda obliged with a smile. Grateful for the topic change, Medusa eyed the waves. They continued to lap placidly against the boat, showing no sign of Poseidon's temper.

* * *

They arrived at Perseus's island in the evening. The docks and streets were empty. Sounds of revelry came from the palace on the hill overlooking the town. While the king had agreed to postpone the wedding, he delighted in reminding his reluctant bride of his claim with nightly feasts.

Grinding his teeth at his mother's humiliation, Perseus snuck them to his home. Borrowing two clean garments from the chest in her room, he handed them to Medusa and Andromeda before retreating to his own room to change.

It felt odd to wear clothing again. It felt good against her skin, but Medusa couldn't shake the feeling that the human garments didn't fit.

The simple white peplos swished against her ankles as she followed the others. A veil covered her head. The fine material obscured her face, but allowed her to see. Though it was far lighter than her makeshift cowl, her snakes still protested the confinement. She'd had to pet and shush them for some time to convince them to lay still.

They'd decided Perseus would introduce Andromeda to his mother as his bride-to-be. Besotted as they were, that would be true soon enough anyways. Medusa would play the part of Andromeda's attendant.

"Polydectes will hate the competition," Perseus said. "To recapture everyone's attention, he'll imply I didn't fulfill my oath or insult my honor somehow."

"Which gives you grounds to kill him," Medusa supplied.

Perseus nodded.

"He'd be a fool to give you such an opening."

"Selfish men often are." Andromeda's flat statement surprised them both.

They'd reached the palace. Raised voices and music sounded from within. Warm light streamed from the windows and pillared doors, illuminating the courtyard.

A weathered older man leaned against a pillar. Perseus ran to him and they embraced. They shared a quick, muffled conversation before the man slipped away.

Nodding, Perseus beckoned to Andromeda and Medusa and led them inside.

The palace was opulently decorated. Colored tiles formed intricate designs beneath their feet. Vibrant frescoes adorned the walls, framed by rich draperies. Vases, weapons, armor, and various trophies were displayed throughout the hall.

Medusa's eyes widened, but Andromeda barely glanced at any of it.

"A smaller king, then?" she murmured to Perseus.

He laughed and raised her hand to kiss it before pushing against a towering set of double doors. The banquet went silent as they boomed open.

Guests reclined at low tables laden with food and wine. A man and woman sat on a dais at the head of the room. While he was grey and thin with age, she was still in the prime of health and beauty.

Head high, Perseus led Andromeda forward. Medusa followed, hands folded demurely, eyes downcast. Murmurs rose around them as they approached the dais.

"Hail, Polydectes, King of Seriphos," Perseus called courteously before turning his attention to the woman. "Hello, Mother! I'm home."

Ignoring the king's startled displeasure, Danaë rushed to meet her son. Tears in her eyes, she embraced him tightly. He lifted her off the ground as he hugged her back. Setting her on her feet, he turned to Andromeda and drew her forward.

"May I present the princess Andromeda to you, Mother," he spoke loud enough for the whole hall to hear. He placed her hand in Danaë's and smiled with genuine pleasure. "She's agreed to marry me."

Danaë clasped Andromeda's hands in hers. Smiling, Andromeda introduced Medusa as Perseus approached the dais.

"Did you abandon your quest then? Too distracted by a pretty face to fulfill your oath? You were to bring the Gorgon's head," Polydectes said, talking over Danaë's joy, "not a bride."

Throughout the room, the king's cronies nodded and sneered, murmuring about the lack of honor in young men.

"And I have," Perseus answered. "Shall we show it to you?"

Polydectes waved his hand imperiously, not noticing the ripple of alarm and averted gazes among the guests. Perseus bowed and shut his eyes.

Medusa embraced Danaë and Andromeda, covering their faces. She tossed her head and her snakes rose in a hissing halo around her.

Her veil slid to the floor.

Gaze uncovered, she glared defiantly around the room, but stared longest and hardest at the king.

He stumbled halfway to his feet, features contorted in rage.

He never rose higher.

Overbalanced, the statue toppled off the dais and shattered against the tile. Its marble head rolled to rest at Danaë's feet.

Danaë shuddered and turned her face further into Medusa's shoulder.

Covering her eyes with her arm, Medusa retrieved her veil and pulled it back on.

Around the room, the surviving guests recoiled from the statues in their midst. As cries of fear shifted to hostile rumblings, Perseus pulled Medusa behind him, sword outstretched towards the mob.

"Now, now," a mild voice rang out. "That won't be necessary." The older man Perseus had embraced stepped forward. "Seems to me, the king insulted his guests and paid the price. Are we going to compound his misdeeds? After all," he looked around, "the lady only punished those who joined in his disrespect."

Voices lowered as the remaining guests nodded amongst themselves. Medusa watched as the tension leeched from the air.

Perseus grinned and lowered his blade. "So you don't want vengeance, Uncle Dictys? He was your brother after all."

"Consider this me formally ceding my claim, boy. I didn't raise you like my own only to kill you because my brother forgot himself."

Danaë hugged him, weeping with gratitude. Dictys patted her shoulders.

"Thank you for warning the guests, Uncle," Perseus said in a low voice. Then he raised his voice again to be heard by all. "You know this makes you king, now."

Dictys laughed and shook his head. "We'll see." He clapped Perseus on the shoulder and left to disperse the crowd.

Pulling his mother and bride-to-be close, Perseus turned to Medusa. "Thank you," he said. "What will you do now?"

Medusa bit her lip. "I'd thought to return home, but…" she thought of that lonely cave, surrounded by statues of the dead, and frowned.

"You could stay," Perseus said. "You're under my protection. I won't let anyone harm you."

Medusa laughed. "A guardian for a guardian?"

Andromeda leaned into Perseus's side and smiled. "Why not? You and Perseus have repeatedly risked your lives to protect those around you. Your kindness could make this place a beacon for those who need a safe place to go."

"I think that's a marvelous idea," Danaë said, looking at Perseus. "It was a haven for us in our darkest time. It can be that for others."

Perseus looked between the three women. "Well?" he asked. "What do you think?"

"I think I will." Beneath her veil, Medusa smiled. "But only because you asked nicely."

Biographies

Liv Albert

Introductory Essay

Liv Albert is creator and host of the top-rated mythology and ancient history podcast, Let's Talk About Myths, Baby!, and author of two books on Greek Myth. She has a degree in English Literature and Classical Civilizations and spends much of her time arguing about the mythological origins of Medusa. She lives in Victoria, Canada, where a monstera plant threatens to devour her. Learn about Liv's work at livalbert.com.

Alicia K. Anderson

The Wise Look for All of the Stories

(First Publication)

Alicia K. Anderson holds a Ph.D. in Mythological Studies and Depth Psychology. Her mythology and fairy tale retellings have appeared in six anthologies. She also has a retelling of Ariadne's story called 'Bull-Headed' in Coffin Bell Journal. That tale is set in the same universe as 'The Wise Look for All the Stories.' Her other work can be found at aliciakinganderson.com. She can be located on social media at @akanderswo.

Mel Attica

How to Tame a Head of Snakes

(First Publication)

Mel Attica is a working writer aspiring to enter the realm of authorship. Although she spends most days writing blogs and web pages for clients, her true passion is creating imaginary worlds full of magic and wonder. She currently enjoys the sunny climes of SoCal, where she lives with her husband and two hockey cats, Chris 'Ozzie' Osgood and Lord Stanley of Preston.

Casey Banks

In the Temple of Athena

(First Publication)

Casey Banks is obsessively fond of supernatural horror, science fiction, and fantasy. She is the author of dozens of stories about normal people in wild situations, wild people in normal situations, and just all-around madness.

Her work has appeared in The NoSleep Podcast, *Flash Fiction Magazine*, and *Poet's Haven Digest*. She lives in California and, when not writing, will often be found dancing, gardening, or baking delicious treats.

Danai Christopoulou
Pegasus
(Originally Published in *The Icarus Writing Collective*, 2023)
Danai Christopoulou (she/they) is a queer Greek SFF author and editor currently living in Sweden. They are an editor for Hugo-nominated *khōréō magazine*, an assistant editor for *HavenSpec*, and an assistant literary agent at Tobias Literary Agency. Their short fiction has been published in *Fusion Fragment* and others, nominated for a Pushcart Prize, and longlisted for a Nebula Award. Danai's novels are represented by Lauren Bieker of FinePrint Literary.

Miriam Robbins Dexter
Foreword
Miriam Robbins Dexter holds a Ph.D. in ancient Indo-European Studies from UCLA. Her books include *Whence the Goddesses: A Source Book* (1990); *Sacred Display: Divine and Magical Female Figures of Eurasia* (2010, with Victor Mair) (2012 ASWM Sarasvati award); and *Foremothers of the Women's Spirituality Movement: Elders and Visionaries* (2015, with Vicki Noble) (Susan Koppelman award, 2016). Miriam is the author of over thirty scholarly articles and nine encyclopedia articles on ancient female figures, and she has edited and co-edited sixteen scholarly volumes. She also contributed to the book *Re-visioning Medusa: from Monster to Divine Wisdom*. For thirteen years, she taught courses in Latin, Greek, and Sanskrit languages in the department of Classics at USC. For the following sixteen years, she taught courses in comparative myth at UCLA.

Grace P. Fong
The Toll of the Snake
(Originally Published in *Apex Magazine*, April 2023)
Grace writes speculative fiction to explore how people survive in worlds not designed for them. Her short fiction has been published in *Uncanny Magazine*, *Apex Magazine*, and Tor.com and has been recognized by Levar Burton Reads and the Ignyte Awards. Find her online at gracepfong.com.

Rhys Hughes

What Actually Happened

(First Publication)

Rhys Hughes was born in Wales but has lived in many different countries. He began writing at an early age and his first book, *Worming the Harpy*, was published in 1995. He recently completed an ambitious project that involved writing exactly 1,000 linked short stories. He is currently working on a novel and several new collections of prose and verse.

Tom Johnstone

A Heart of Stone

(Originally Published in *Making Monsters*, eds. Emma Bridges and Djibril Al-Ayads, 2018)

Tom Johnstone is the author of three novellas published by Omnium Gatherum Media: *The Monsters are Due in Madison Square Garden*, *Star Spangled Knuckle Duster*, and *The Song of Salomé*. His fiction has appeared in various publications, including *Black Static*, *Nightscript*, *Body Shocks* and *Best Horror of the Year*, as well as the collections *Last Stop Wellsbourne*, also published by Omnium Gatherum Books, and *Let Your Hinged Jaw Do the Talking*, from Alchemy Press. More information at tomjohnstone.wordpress.com.

Amanda Cecelia Lang

Medusa with the Heads of Men

(First Publication)

Amanda Cecelia Lang is a horror author and aspiring recluse from Colorado. Her stories haunt the dark corners of many popular podcasts, magazines, and anthologies, including *Gamut*, *Ghoulish Tales*, *Cast of Wonders*, *Uncharted*, *Dark Matter*, and Flame Tree's *Darkness Beckons*. Her debut short story collection *Saturday Fright at the Movies* will be published in October 2024 through Dark Matter INK. You can stalk her work at amandacecelialang.com – just don't be surprised if she leaps out at you from the shadows.

Megan Mahoney

The Haunting of Athena

(First Publication)

Megan Mahoney is a middle school teacher with an English Literature and Creative Writing degree and a Masters in Classical Education from Eastern

University. The first chapter of her Young Adult fantasy manuscript has been published in the journal *Workings Classicists*; her other publications include *Ethel Zine* magazine, *Spaceports and Spidersilk*, and Eastern's *Inklings* journal, which she later edited.

Tracie McBride

In the Blood

(First Publication)

Tracie McBride is a New Zealander who now lives in Melbourne, Australia. A member of the HWA and the AHWA, her work has appeared in over 100 print and electronic publications, including the Stoker Award-nominated anthologies *Horror for Good* and *Horror Library Volume 5*. She has two short story collections in print, *Ghosts Can Bleed* and *Drive, She Said*, and her work has won or been shortlisted for the Sir Julius Vogel Award, the Aurealis Award, and the Shadows Award.

Zenobia Neil

Athena's Favorite

(First Publication, with the opening short section previously published in the flash fiction anthology *Charmed Writers*, 2019)

Named after an ancient warrior queen who fought against the Romans, Zenobia Neil writes historical fantasy and mythic retellings. Her short stories 'Hera Unfettered' and 'Athena's Favorite' were inspired by Robert Graves's *The Greek Myths*. Her four novels present a different side of history, one that focuses on the power of women, magic, and love. Zenobia portrays a diverse, sexually fluid ancient world where gods have too much fun, and mortals find ways to cheat fate. Her last full-length novel, *Ariadne Unraveled*, is a fresh retelling of the Minoan myth of Ariadne and Dionysus. Visit her at zenobianeil.com.

Gabriella Ramalho

The Medusa Rondanini

(First Publication)

Gabriella Ramalho received a BA in Creative Writing from Hunter College, and an MA from the CUNY Graduate Center where they are now doing post-graduate work in Classics. They live in New York and are working on a series of short stories involving Alexander the Great and various mythological themes. In their spare time, they haunt museums hoping to have an experience like Theo's.

Oneness Sankara
The Balm Yard
(First Publication)
Oneness Sankara, a multi-passionate creative, is an award-winning writer and spoken word artist. Her debut book, *Word Sound Vol 1*, is a beautifully powerful poetry anthology. Recipient of the BEFFTA Award, she's made her mark on UK and international poetry stages. Notably, she's the first non-US winner at The Toronto International Poetry Slam. In theatre, her works like *Chasing Rainbows* and *Ancient Futures* provoke thought and inspire.

Zach Shephard
Snakes and Stones, We'll Break Their Bones
(First Publication)
Zach Shephard lives in Washington state, where he dreams up fantasy, science fiction and horror stories. He frequently uses mythology in his writing, because it's a lot easier to explain bizarre plot choices when capricious deities are at work. His fiction has appeared in places like *Fantasy & Science Fiction*, the *Unidentified Funny Objects* anthology series, and several of Flame Tree Publishing's Gothic Fantasy books. For a full list of Zach's stories, check out zachshephard.com.

Liv Strom
Woman Embracing Woman, on Loan From Private Collection
(Originally Published in *Apex Magazine*, November 2023)
Liv Strom is a Swedish-Swiss writer with stories in *Apex Magazine*, *Hexagon*, and *Mystery Magazine*, among others, and been included on Tor.com's Must-Read Speculative Fiction and reviewed on *Locus*. As a writer with aphantasia (she cannot visualize anything), she considers it a magic power to write characters which live on in other's minds. She's currently working on the next novel in her *Tales of Bones & Roses* twisted fairytales series. See more at livstromwrites.com.

Theresa Tyree
Unbound
(First Publication)
Theresa (they/she) is a queer nonbinary Greek woman who grew up dreaming of magic amongst the trees in the American Pacific North West.

She makes her home near Portland, Oregon with their platonic life partner and cat, and spends their days coming up with new stories of queer perseverance and hope. She has particular interest in writing the 'missing scenes' of Greek mythology that empower marginalized people and add to her own heritage. Find out more at theresatyree.com.

Leah Warren
Freely Given
(First Publication)
Leah cut her teeth on Edith Hamilton's *Mythology* when she was seven years old. That early exposure spiralled out into a deep love of all things mythic and folkloric that's lasted throughout her life and she looks forward to passing that love down to her two children. While she's written for her own amusement and the enjoyment of close friends and family for many years, this is her first published short story.

Authors and Core Sources of Medusa Mythology

One of the best sources we have is the Greek poet **Hesiod** (*c.* 750–650 BCE) and his *Theogony*. Much of what is known about his life derives from his other epic poem, *Works and Days*. **Homer** (born *c.* 800 BCE), attributed composer of the *Iliad* and *Odyssey*, was a contemporary of Hesiod.

Another primary source, the encyclopedia of Greek mythology known as the *Bibliotheca*, is credited to a '**Pseudo-Apollodorus**'. Nothing is known about the author, but the work is a unique and invaluable reference guide to myth and history compiled around the first or second century CE.

Aeschylus (*c.* 525/524–*c.* 456/455 BCE) was one of the famous Greek tragedians. His lost play *Phorcides* recounted Perseus's quest, and *Prometheus Bound* describes the Gorgons, although it is unsure whether this play was in fact written by his son Euphorion (fl. 431 BCE). The youngest of the three great tragedians, **Euripides** (*c.* 480–404 BCE), author of *Medea*, *The Trojan Women* and *Bacchae*, wrote of the Gorgon and her blood in *Ion*.

On the Roman side, the main source for Medusa is **Ovid** (43 BCE–17/18 CE) in his *Metamorphoses*. Other works of his include *Ars Amatoria*, *Tristia* and *Fasti.* Ovid was a distinguished poet and contemporary of Horace and Virgil, but in 8 CE, he was exiled to Tomis by the emperor Augustus. He lived there for the rest of his life, never returning to his beloved Rome.

Myths, Gods & Immortals

Discover the mythology of humankind through its heroes, characters, gods and immortal figures. **Myths, Gods and Immortals** brings together the new and the ancient, familiar stories with a fresh and imaginative twist. Each book brings back to life a legendary, mythological or folkloric figure, with completely new stories alongside the original tales and a comprehensive introduction which emphasizes ancient and modern connections, tracing history and stories across continents, cultures and peoples.

Flame Tree Fiction

A wide range of new and classic fiction, from myth to modern stories, with tales from the distant past to the far future, including short story anthologies, **Beyond & Within**, **Collector's Editions**, **Collectable Classics**, **Gothic Fantasy collections** and **Epic Tales** of mythology and folklore.